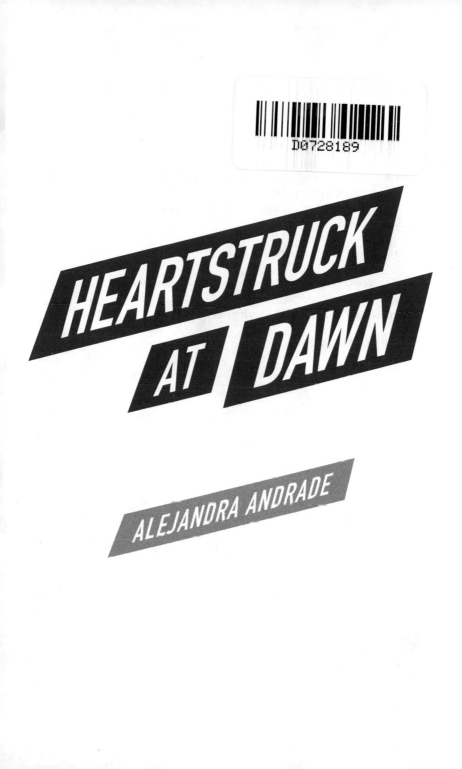

HEARTSTRUCK AT DAWN

ALEJANDRA ANDRADE

FIRST EDITION

Book Cover and Interior Design by David Provolo
Cover Art by Sulamit Elizondo

ISBN (hardcover): 978-607-29-2878-7
ISBN (paperback): 978-607-29-2879-4
ISBN (ebook): 978-607-29-2934-0

www.alejandra-andrade.com

Follow the author on Instagram: @alejandra__andrade to learn more about the upcoming books in the Moonstruck Series.

Read a sneak peek of Book Three of the Moonstruck Series: *Awestruck at Dusk.*

Go to: https://cutt.ly/AwestruckatDusk Or Scan:

For those who look at the sky and wonder,
dream while awake, stare at the moon and marvel,
and the wild souls that wish for love, truth, and freedom.

TABLE OF CONTENTS

CHAPTER 1

Shards

August 20, 2009

THOMAS CALLED ME *every* single day at 6:00 p.m. sharp, but I never took the call because I didn't care to listen to another of his empty apologies. I'd already broken up with him. We weren't dating anymore. Aaron and Caleb threw him out of my apartment the last time I saw him. Couldn't he take a hint?

My head still felt like it wanted to explode. I was *furious* about his behavior, the things he said, and most of all, for kissing me.

I know. I kissed him back.

But the familiarity of him, of his lips, mixed up with that stupidly relaxing pill ... It didn't matter anymore. I *was* an idiot.

Caleb convinced me to meet up with Thomas. Yes, *Caleb*. He thought if I talked to Thomas one last time, he would back off. And he was right. Thomas needed real closure—for me to tell him it was over *for good*. I didn't want things to end on such a sour note either.

Caleb's encouragement on the matter was helpful and made me feel more at ease and prepared to handle the whole situation going on with Thomas. I wasn't alone. Sometimes I kept forgetting that I had a solid support system behind me.

The flower arrangement Thomas sent me that week had to be moved from the living room's coffee table to the foyer table because you couldn't even watch TV or see the face of the person seated in front of you in the living room. It was *that* big.

Thomas's portrait used to be the first thing you saw when you came into my apartment. I took it down. I knew he wouldn't like it once he saw the empty wall, but I needed to be firm with him. And I honestly couldn't stand to look at it anymore.

I needed one less thing to worry about.

Caleb and I had talked a little more about *us* during the week. I never knew I needed him that much until he mentioned the possibility of leaving. I had taken him for granted. But his job was like any other—another could quickly replace it in a heartbeat.

It'd been scary to realize that.

The important part was that he decided to stay. I mean, I'd been crushing on this guy for *years*. However, I did worry about what all the kissing really meant and what his expectations of me were. Too much happened recently. And my biggest fear was getting hurt, hurting him, hurting our relationship, or worse—all of the above.

Proceed with caution.

I told him I needed time to process everything, and he was very understanding of the situation that I'd just gone through. He didn't care about that. He was mostly glad that Thomas was a thing of the past.

But an unfamiliar feeling of uncertainty lay dormant in the back of my mind—a sleeping lion in its den. I wanted to be ready for him, but I couldn't stop thinking about William. It became an infatuation. One I needed to start detaching from immediately. I was determined to *claw* him out of my mind if necessary.

I *had* to.

Wasn't Caleb all I ever wanted?

When I saw him, I was so happy. He made me smile. But every night before going to sleep, my chest would riot against me. I couldn't go to bed feeling okay. But why? I was trying, like *really* trying.

Things had to get better.

My chest needed to stop complaining, and I needed to focus on the great things I had in front of me. That was my new mantra.

And there were lots of great things that I had going on with Caleb. Like the way he made me feel so wanted, his perfectly delicious lips, and the way he kissed me.

He knew me. I was safe with him. That had to be enough.

Thomas said he'd drop by the apartment by the end of the day to talk, and I was nervous but hopeful too. I went for a morning run with Caleb and David, hoping it would help ease the nerves.

I came back from our run and showered. The doorbell rang as I poured myself a cup of coffee, but I hadn't been informed about Thomas arriving.

Could it be William?

Of course not. An obvious example of the importance of clawing him out of my mind. *He doesn't care anymore, silly.* Or did he even care at some point?

He was never around anyway. Filming, he'd told me in his last text.

I dismissed the idea altogether, but another part of me, the one that enjoyed playing tricks on me, quickly got up, hoping it would be *him*, making me rush to the front door and open it with giddy anticipation.

Wrong brother.

"Hey, Billie," Tobias said with that big, sincere smile of his. He glanced over my shoulder at the massive flower arrangement behind me and raised a brow. Some flowers were dying—symbolic.

"Hey, what's up?" I replied, forcing back a smile while my last shred of hope shattered on the inside.

"I just wanted to check up on you and see how you were doing. I haven't seen you at the gym."

I hadn't resumed my training with Grant precisely because I

wanted to avoid Tobias or any other Sjöberg family member. I tried getting in touch with Grant. However, his phone was disconnected.

The elevator chimed behind us, and Aaron came walking out of it.

"Miss Murphy, sorry to interrupt. You were not answering your phone, but Mr. Hill is downstairs."

I turned to look at Tobias and puckered my lips to the side. Tobias would probably report back to William, making him think that there was still something going on with Thomas, but I needed to stop fretting about what William thought or not. I tried to explain everything many times, but he made it perfectly clear that he didn't care to listen.

"Send him up."

I need to stop caring.

Aaron replied with a nod and left.

"Well, it's ah—good to hear you're doing fine, Billie. If there's anything you need, you know where to find me."

Tobias had proved to be a good friend but looking at him was difficult because it inevitably reminded me how things went south with William. He helped a lot the day of the fire, and I wanted to let my bitterness aside to tell him how thankful I was that he'd been there for me and for having stayed in touch to check on me afterward.

"I'm sorry," I said to him with a sigh. "The past few weeks have been difficult—too many changes. I haven't got the chance to talk to Grant, but I'm so grateful for what you both did for me. You didn't have to but—"

"Please, don't mention it," he said with a frown, shaking his head a few times.

"Did Grant change his number?" I asked. "I haven't been able to reach him. I want to thank him directly and be able to let him know once I'm ready to resume our sessions."

"He did. I'll ask Will—" He broke off. "Um, I don't have your number, and I didn't bring my phone. But I'll make sure you get it. I'll text you later."

Frustrating.

He couldn't even say *William* in front of me.

The elevator doors opened in the distance. Thomas, Aaron, and David walked out in our direction. Caleb preferred not to interact with Thomas, especially after everything that happened. He couldn't stand him.

"I think I better get going, Billie," Tobias said, looking back at the three of them.

"Hey, man." Thomas clutched Tobias's shoulder and offered his hand to him. So unlike him. "I'm sorry about the other day. I was so worried about Billie. I acted like a real asshole with everyone, including your brother. I can't thank you enough for all your help."

Tobias's lips parted slightly; shock drowned his eyes. I don't think he expected that sort of reaction from Thomas. He nodded and told him there was nothing to be thankful for and excused himself to leave.

"Hey, babe," he said, kissing my cheek. "Can I come in?"

Babe. I was starting to hate that word.

"Sure."

Thomas caught me off guard too. I wasn't expecting him to act like this after being thrown out of my place, although I did appreciate him behaving accordingly.

Aaron glanced at me behind Thomas, waiting for confirmation that I was comfortable with the situation. I replied with a simple nod and looked away.

"We'll wait out here," he said firmly. Aaron wasn't buying Thomas's goody-two-shoes act.

We walked inside, and Thomas immediately saw the flowers. "I hope you liked them. I meant that," he said, tapping the card where he'd asked for forgiveness.

"They're beautiful. Thank you." Every word that came out of my mouth felt like walking on broken glass. I was being mindful about what to say and how to say it.

Thomas stopped to stare at the empty gallery wall for a second with a deep crease in between his brows. He bobbed his head a few times and made his way to the living room with an air of defeat. You could tell he wasn't happy that I'd taken his portrait down.

We sat, and I waited for Thomas to do the talking. He held his hands together, rested his elbows over his knees, and anxiously shook his feet.

"I'm so sorry, Billie," he said as a creative opening statement. "I feel like that's all I've been doing as of late. And I want to change that. I really do. I want to stop asking for your forgiveness. But to do that, I need you to give me another chance." He let out a breath through his mouth and looked me in the eye. "I lost it the other day, and I admit that. But please, just let me fix this."

I didn't know if forgiving Thomas was the solution. The real problem that I saw was that he had shown his true colors more than a few times. He was controlling, manipulative, and jealous beyond reasonable measure. But I had already told him that when we broke up on the phone—sort of.

Just looking at him was exhausting.

Most of all, I was angry about how he ruined my bet with William. It was much more than a game. It was William's way of letting me know who he was, in his own way. But Thomas took that away from us, and he made William feel like shit. And, ultimately, Thomas drove William away from me.

"I don't know if I can go back to where we were before all of this," I said, my brows bunching up. "I'm sorry."

"Why?" He grimaced. "Please, just tell me why? I'm willing to change and be better for you. Please believe me."

He moved closer to me, and I flinched away almost imperceptibly.

"We're caught up in a vicious cycle. Something bad happens, you're sorry, I forgive you, on repeat," I explained. "But you're not doing anything different to make things better—to break that cycle." I was so fed up with the toxic stimulation Thomas had going on. "I can't change who you are. That's not how it works. I'm honestly finding it hard to keep up with"—I waved a lazy hand back and forth between us—"all of this."

He looked pissed now. Not that I would stop because of it.

"Not to mention how extremely disrespectful you were the other night. I know you're sorry about it, but I haven't been able to brush the feeling off. And we didn't even talk about what I saw under your bed."

Thomas readjusted himself on his seat and leaned in to say in a low almost creepy voice, "Those condoms were *not* mine. I would *never* cheat on you—you know that." His jaw clenched, and his nostrils flared for a couple of loud, heavy breaths. I don't know if he wanted to intimidate me into believing him, but I wasn't planning on playing along.

And did I know that he would *never* cheat on me? With Thomas, I didn't know what to expect anymore. And I honestly didn't care. I was done with him.

"Look, it doesn't matter. You don't have to explain yourself to me. I'm not your girlfriend anymore, and you don't owe me anything."

"Please, don't say that." It was a plea, but his voice was getting rougher. What was I to say? It was the truth, and I needed him to understand that we were *not* dating anymore. I tried pulling the plug nicely, and it didn't work before. It wasn't easy, but I needed to be firm.

"The empty condom packages you saw under my bed belong to Nicholas," he finally revealed.

"Nicholas?" Thomas's go-to scapegoat.

It was an interesting turn of events, and I wasn't sure if I would eat that up. Not that it would make any difference.

"He uses the apartment from time to time. That's why we keep a spare key in the safety box outside. You can imagine my reaction when I came back and saw them after you told me about it. I guess that's why I've never felt comfortable taking you there, knowing I don't have the place to myself."

He seemed genuine. Still, I couldn't help but think about his love-hate relationship with Nicholas. Why did Thomas allow his behavior? Did Nicholas have something on Thomas? It felt that way because seeing Thomas interact with Nicholas didn't match up with his personality. Thomas wasn't the pushover type of guy. And it seemed to me like Thomas had given Nicholas one too many chances.

Fortunately, it wasn't my problem anymore.

"Okay," I said with a shrug.

"So, that's it?" he asked with irritation. "That's all you have to say? Do you believe me?"

"I do."

I wasn't sure if I did or not, but there was no point in arguing or getting into any further details. There was nothing he could say or do that would convince me to get back together with him. And he needed to know that.

"Thomas, there's no easy way to say it, but I'm sure of this." I took a deep breath. "I *don't* want to get back together. I'm done. I'm sorry things had to end this way, but I can't move forward after all that's happened."

I swallowed the huge lump in my throat after telling him that. It was hard to say it, but I knew it was for the best. "I'm sorry," I repeated as he stared at me in silence.

"It's because of him, isn't it?"

If he only knew …

He meant William, of course, unaware of my current situation with Caleb. Thomas could ask anything he wanted, as he always did, but I was done explaining myself. I kept quiet. *Let him think whatever he wants to think.*

"He's going to chew you up and spit you out. You know that, right?" He lowered his chin and stared into my eyes.

Wow. Okay.

My eyebrows flew up with shock. Thomas didn't know that I wasn't even getting the chance to get to the *chewing* part with William, so to speak. But he didn't need to know anything else about me.

"Will he?" I taunted him. Probably not the best thing to do, but that right there was what I meant about Thomas letting his true colors shine brightly. His B-side.

"I'll never give up on you, Billie. You need to understand that." He reached out for my hand, but I recoiled away from his touch. It was dangerous. I knew that much. His touch, his lips, his words. The situation was proving to be more challenging than I thought.

"I wish you didn't have to make this any more difficult," I said to him.

He stood up with a huff and marched toward the front door. I followed Thomas, careful not to catch up with him but close enough to make sure he would leave.

As he passed through the foyer, he kicked the Matisse he bought for me at the MoMA. It was leaning against the wall. He then stuck a hand out and dramatically pushed the flowers off the table, making the vase crash on the floor into a million pieces.

There he goes.

I was sure he would be *sorry* by the end of the day, but I wouldn't be there to hear his apology anymore.

He opened the door and let it bang against the door's bumper, leaving it wide open as he stepped out of the apartment. Glass shards surrounded my bare feet. It was best not to move an inch. Aaron reached out for Thomas's arm, but he violently shoved it away.

"Don't fucking touch me, Aaron," he snapped back at him and stormed out through the emergency exit. An excellent choice. It would've been too awkward for him to wait for the elevator to come up after the little scene he'd just made.

David walked inside my apartment, picked me up, and carried me to the living room. He then asked me to stay put.

I swear that if anyone had told me that the actor was Thomas and not William, I'd believed them in a heartbeat. He was dramatic as fuck.

CHAPTER 2

Blind

August 28, 2009

BEING OFFICIALLY FREE from my toxic relationship with Thomas was liberating. It was as if I'd just arrived from Paris—hopeful again. Suddenly I had time for my friends. I was in a better mood, eating better, and overall feeling happier.

The fall term at Parsons was starting soon, and Nolan and I had signed up for all our classes together. School had proven to help keep my mind off things, and I definitely enjoyed it. Having done so well on our final presentation with the Sagaponack photoshoot was encouraging too. Lily was stunning in every photograph we took. Some of our classmates were really impressed when they saw it was actually her.

Lily loved the copies I printed out of the best photos we shot at Sagaponack. I gave them to her before she went away for work. She told me it gets hectic for her right after the summer with Fashion Week. She was gone most of the time—constantly traveling and working like crazy.

We remained close friends and texted often but never talked about William, of course. She kept asking me how I was doing all the time, but my answer was always the same: *I'm doing great!*

It was the truth. I was feeling ... pretty good.

CJ and Nina were glad to see me doing better without Thomas but knew nothing of what had gone down with William. I'd also kept the Caleb situation all to myself.

They were both expecting me for lunch, and Caleb came up to my apartment to check up on me. I was getting ready and listening to a playlist my father asked me to put together for him when he knocked on my door.

"Mr. Cohen," I said as a joke, pulling my head out the door, looking over his shoulders to check if he was alone. Since apartment 9B was not occupied, there wasn't much movement on my floor to worry about. So I grabbed his hand and pulled him inside. "I'm almost ready, okay? I'll be right back."

Caleb waltzed into the foyer, and I knew it was hard for him to do so as a guest. The awkwardness was plastered on his face. I could tell that the dynamic we had of blurring the lines was still challenging for him. Even though we weren't dating or in a formal relationship, he had opened himself to me about his feelings.

Every time we tried to find a space to talk or meet in private, it felt like sneaking around. As if we were doing something that we weren't supposed to be doing. And I didn't like the feeling.

We weren't too crazy to feel that way because if my father found out about Caleb's intentions with me (and mine too), I'm sure he'd sent him back to Tel Aviv in a jiffy. We didn't want that. *Nope.*

I walked out of my room and saw Caleb standing stiff as a starched collar, my music playing in the background. He hadn't dared walk any further into my apartment. He didn't know how to make himself comfortable here.

I stood in front of the foyer table, making sure I had everything I needed in my purse. It was funny to see Caleb fidgeting with his hands. He didn't seem to know what to do with them. He kept placing them inside his pants pockets, pulling them out again, rubbing his forehead, then his neck, and then they inevitably went into a loose fist in front of him—his bodyguard stance.

He couldn't help it.

"Caleb, relax. We're all alone. Mimi's gone for the day, too." I reassured him.

"I know. It's just weird, you know, trying to be casual when I've been accustomed for years to behave in the exact opposite way."

Caleb had been following me around for over four years. That's a lot of time. I was sixteen when my father hired him, and Caleb was twenty-two. The first day I met him, I couldn't believe my eyes or keep myself from staring into *his* whenever he talked to me. I was captivated by his beauty. And I'm almost sure he quickly realized that.

Caleb was a gift from the Universe. I felt empty, lost, and he came in like, *hey, I got you*. And he really, really did.

He saved me.

Things had to be even more formal in Paris. There were more protocols to abide by. That's why he struggled with loosening up, even though I insisted on him to relax around me when we were alone.

"You look beautiful." He swept me with his gaze and shook his head a few times with a smile.

"What Difference Does It Make" from The Smiths started playing in the background.

"I love that song. I didn't know you liked them," Caleb said, offering his hand to me. There was this tender side to him I thought was endearing. One I hadn't had the opportunity to know this much before. But he was opening up to me more and more each day. And so was I.

"I do. My father introduced me to them, and now, I can't stop listening," I said with a laugh, taking his warm, somewhat calloused hand with mine. He pulled me closer to him and ran a hand around my waist.

"I wish I could take you out sometime," he confessed, looking down at me. "Although I know that would be tricky—wait ..."

Caleb started singing the song with his adorable accent. He arched my back and kissed my cheek, which caught flames quickly after that. I loved how he finally allowed himself to let go and relax.

"We should get breakfast someday after one of our runs. That's casual enough, don't you think?" I suggested, looking up into his lovely eyes, his arms still firmly placed around my waist. "I don't think it would raise any suspicions with Aaron or David."

"Ah, yeah. Aaron knows," he said with a snort.

"Knows—what?"

"How I feel about you. He's known for a while. And he would never say anything to your father, so don't make that face."

For a while.

"Since when?" I wondered how much time *a while* meant. I had to ask.

"He figured it out quickly after the Noelle incident." He laughed. "I went *nuts* that night after you came back from the bar. I wanted to destroy and burn shit up. And Aaron was there to see it. He calmed me down and suggested I go out for a run instead. So, I did and came back somewhere around three in the morning."

"Caleb! Why wouldn't you just—talk to me about it?" I broke away from the embrace but held his hand with mine, my gaze still fixed on his.

"You saw me with Noelle that same day. What did you want me to say? Oh hey, I kissed this girl you went to school with a few hours ago, but you can't talk to the guy? Besides, I told you on your birthday how much I hated the day you met Thomas. Sometimes I think it's my fault you ended up with him. If you hadn't seen me with Noelle, you probably wouldn't have wanted to go to that bar. Am I right?"

He was right. But the odds of meeting Thomas that day were

in our favor. If I hadn't gone to the bar, I would've returned to the Residence, and my father would've wanted me to say hi to his guests like he usually did. I don't know. Things that are meant to happen will always find a way to do so.

"I think what you're trying to say is: If you *hadn't* kissed Noelle that day … right?" I laughed. He chuckled a little bit. "Me meeting Thomas wasn't your fault. Maybe we wouldn't be standing here today, like this, if I hadn't met him."

Caleb nodded once, but I could see he would forever blame himself for that. And he was too stubborn for me to convince him otherwise.

"Let's do it then." I encouraged the idea of us going out for breakfast someday. "No suit and tie, and definitely no curly earpiece." I flicked the earpiece, and Caleb grabbed my wrist when I drew my hand away. He pulled me closer to him again, and my heart immediately doubled its beats per minute—pounding hard and fast against my chest.

He looked so ridiculously handsome, and his lips were so tempting, but we hadn't kissed since that night on the rooftop. I'd been careful to avoid it to keep myself from making things more confusing for both of us. But that didn't mean I didn't want to, and by the hungry look of his fiery hazel eyes, I knew he was craving to kiss me too.

I harnessed my impulses and achieved self-control. But there was a motive behind my prowess that lingered at not a very subconscious level.

William.

I missed him!

I missed the way he made me laugh and angry at the same time. And how he always found a way to keep me entertained, intrigued, and curious. I never knew what to expect with him, and I enjoyed that—a lot.

But most of all, I missed talking to him, his lips, and the way he kissed me. Like he knew what he wanted and *how* he wanted it, which were the same things *I wanted.*

But William claimed he didn't want any of those things anymore, and I didn't want to think about what I wanted right now.

The hardest part of breaking up with Thomas was, ironically, forgetting all about William. I hadn't run into him since the day he saw me kissing Thomas. I still couldn't get over that stupid kiss I didn't even want to begin with.

Why did he have to kiss me? And why did I have to kiss him back?

Anyway … back to Caleb.

His face was drawing nearer, but I turned to the side and tried smiling sweetly. Caleb kissed my cheek as I squeezed his hand a little harder, trying to make up for the kiss I'd just turned down. I really wanted to kiss him, but I wasn't ready to do it again. Not when my mind was elsewhere.

"Let's go," he said. "You're going to be late." He offered me a heartfelt smile and released my hand. We wandered out of my apartment as two people who weren't about to kiss a few seconds ago.

David drove hastily to the sushi place where I was meeting Nina and CJ for lunch. Once we arrived, Caleb walked me to my table. *It's your father's orders,* he insisted. My father felt more apprehensive than usual after my breakup with Thomas.

My phone buzzed as I looked around the restaurant for my friends.

"Don't be mad," CJ said over the phone when I took the call.

"Are you somewhere else? I can still make it."

"No. We're not showing up."

"What do you mean? Is everything okay?" I was genuinely concerned.

"We set you up on a blind date. I'm sorry, please don't hate me. His name is Charles, and he's super yummy. You'll thank me later.

Ciao ciao!" He ended the call with a cheerful tone. I gawked at my phone's screen with indignation.

A date? A *blind* date? *Hell no.*

"What's wrong?" Caleb asked reactively.

I intended to leave when I heard someone calling my name. I turned around toward the voice, and a classically handsome guy walked up to me. Tall, perfectly combed dirty blond hair, big white smile, five o'clock shadow, and gray-blue eyes. I could say, *totally my type,* but that sort of guy is easily anyone's type. Unfortunately, I wasn't interested in staying.

"You're Billie, right?" he asked, closing the distance between us. "A pretty redhead. I'd say you're a match for the description Nina gave me."

I spotted Caleb glaring at me from the corner of my eye, probably wanting to know what the heck was happening. Since I was in shock and didn't know what else to say, Charles introduced himself and offered me his hand. I shook it and said it was a pleasure to meet him.

"Could you—excuse me for two seconds?" I asked Charles. He shot a grin at me and said he'd wait for me at the table. I managed to smile and walked away to give me the two seconds I'd requested of him.

"What *the hell* is going on?" Caleb whispered through his teeth. His jaw popped. There was nothing he hated more than surprises and a sudden change of plans.

"Nina and CJ set me up on a blind date," I whispered back. "They don't know anything about … well, anything. They just know that I broke up with Thomas a little more than a month ago, and for whatever reason, they believe I'm ready to start dating again."

"You're not honestly thinking of going through with this, are you?" Caleb seemed exasperated. "Your father won't approve. He instructed us to run a background check on anyone who wants to … date you." He lifted a brow and glanced at Charles.

Jesus.

"Background checks? And what am I supposed to do? He's sitting there, waiting for me," I replied, looking over my shoulder. Charles waved two fingers my way when he saw me looking at him. "He seems harmless. I'll sit with him for a while, and I'll SOS you once it feels right. Come on. It'll be fun." Caleb agreed with hesitation, seemingly annoyed, but I just wanted to be done with this and leave.

"I have to see his ID, though."

"Caleb! No, you ..." He ignored me and darted toward the table ahead of me.

"Excuse me, sir. I'm going to need to see some ID," Caleb said to Charles with a deep voice and a thick accent. Charles stood up with haste, pulled out his wallet, and handed his ID over to Caleb, who took a picture of it from both sides.

"Here you go, Mr. Donnelly. Sorry about the inconvenience, but it's protocol."

Caleb turned around and stood on a wall nearby as he did on my first date with Thomas. I honestly didn't care if he wanted to linger nearby. I just thought it was unnecessary.

"Nina didn't tell me that you had security," he said as an opening statement. "I think that's pretty badass."

You're kidding me.

The conversation mainly consisted of questions about my security detail and quickly shifted to Charles's family vacation home on the Amalfi Coast. And oh, that other vacation home in Barcelona. Yawn.

What he lacked in good conversation, he made up with his good looks.

"So, do you want to order?" he asked, picking up the menu.

"I'm on a rigorous diet," I replied. I wasn't going to order a big meal when I planned on leaving soon. But I was freaking starving! I could've ordered an entire tuna. "I'll just have the edamame."

Charles signaled the server to approach the table with a wave of his hand and placed our order, unimpressed by my lack of appetite.

Charles talked about cars, but it wasn't the fun type of car conversation. More like the bragging type. But as he told me about the many sports cars his family owned and allowed him to drive at his will, I drifted away into thought.

I couldn't stop thinking about the Porsche conversation I had with William on our way back from the cottage and how much fun I had when we texted that day.

"So, Nina said you're a photographer," Charles said out of the blue, grazing my forearm with his index finger. "If you ever need a model, I can make a space for it in my schedule." He shot a smug little smirk my way.

He did have a pretty face, but I wasn't very fond of him touching me like that. "Ah—yes." I tried smiling as I pulled my arm away from his reach. Caleb glared at us or, better said ... at Charles.

Enough. I texted Caleb directly.

Me: SOS. 5 minutes.
Caleb: 5 min OR if the guy lays a finger on you again. Whatever happens first.

Damn it.

Using the SOS beacon always made me feel terrible, but there was no way I could stay any longer on this date. The conversation was annoying, and I hadn't agreed to it. The arm grazing situation wasn't ideal either.

It bothered me that Nina and CJ had set it up without my consent. I knew they didn't mean any harm by doing so, but I would've appreciated it if they'd asked me first. I guess they thought I would say no, and that's why they tricked me into it.

Caleb and David approached my table. Charles seemed excited about that—interested. "Miss Murphy, sorry to interrupt," Caleb said, looking at Charles. "I'm afraid we're going to have to cut your—lunch short."

"Why? What's wrong?" I asked with concern, fully immersed in the roles we were playing. I can't say it wasn't fun.

"I cannot discuss any further details at this moment, but if you could, please follow me. We'll take you back to your apartment where we can explain the situation," Caleb added as part of the charade.

"It's too bad you have to leave, Billie. Can I at least get your number?" Charles asked. He looked disappointed, and I did feel bad about leaving suddenly, but I wasn't in the mood for any of this, and Caleb watching everything was even more grueling.

I was about to give Charles my number because I'm a wuss and didn't have the heart to say: *No, you can't have my number because I'm trying to figure things out with my bodyguard*, when Caleb interrupted, "You'll have to clear the standard security check first, Mr. Connelly."

That, too.

"It's Donnelly," Charles replied with a frown, tossing his napkin on the table, looking at Caleb.

"Of course"—Caleb cleared his throat—"once you're authorized, we'll get in touch with you and provide you with Miss Murphy's contact information."

Right.

"I'm so sorry," I said to Charles as I stood up to leave. He seemed entertained by the theatrics Caleb pulled off on him.

"Don't worry about it, Billie. I hope we can reschedule some other time." He smiled a genuine-looking smile.

"Sure thing," I lied with a grin, feeling terrible on the inside.

We finally left. David was driving me back to my apartment, but I asked him if he could stop somewhere to get a slice of pizza. I was starving, and I wanted to make it up to Caleb. It must've been awkward for him. I know it was for me.

David parked on the curbside of what he swore were the best pizzas in Manhattan. I didn't even know which ones were the best anymore. The three of them argued about it all the time. And don't get me started on kebabs. I was afraid even to utter that word in front of Aaron and Caleb.

Caleb opened the door for me. "Are you hungry?" I asked casually. He nodded once with a smile and tugged his earpiece off, letting it hang over his shoulder.

"I know I'm wearing my suit, but at least I can take this thing off," he replied, following me inside. David seemed like he was pretending not to listen to our conversation and stayed behind, standing beside the SUV. He must've known something was happening between us. But I trusted him.

We sat at a small high table with our ridiculously huge slices of pizza sitting on our plates in front of us. I grabbed my slice and took it to Caleb's lips. "First bite's the best one." He looked at me and took a bite. "You deserve mine."

He grabbed his slice and offered it to me as he chewed. His Adam's apple rose and fell as he swallowed; his eyes trained on my face. "You do too."

I looked away, unable to hold his gaze any longer, and parted my lips to take a bite. But he pulled the pizza away from my reach and said, "Don't you *dare* look away."

"You're making me nervous," I said, glancing at him.

"Well, that's the idea." He brought the pizza to my lips again. "Now, bite." I smiled and did as I was told, looking straight into his eyes. He immediately took a bite after I did.

Who knew eating pizza could be this … entertaining?

We continued eating as regular people do and talked non-stop. Our conversation was easygoing. We mostly laughed as I told him about how my blind date had gone. He'd heard some of my conversation with Charles, of course.

"I don't think Mr. Connelly's going to get clearance."

"It's *Donnelly!*" I laughed and moved on to tease him as we remembered anecdotes from our time in Paris and how the girls at school went crazy for him all the time.

"There was only one girl I wanted, though," Caleb said, dropping his pizza crust on his plate.

"Noelle?" I joked. "For a second there, I almost forgot you're into blondes."

"Oh, come on," he whispered, placing his forearms on the table, his face drawing closer to mine. "You know my favorite color is red." I swallowed my pizza and felt my cheeks getting warm. "And this right here is my favorite shade." He grazed my cheek with his thumb.

Okay. He finally convinced me. I approached his face, my sight fixed on his lips, when my phone buzzed on the table, making Caleb recoil. I silenced the buzz but let the call go organically to voicemail.

"Does he call you often?" Caleb asked, looking at my phone's screen.

It was Thomas.

"Just every day." I sighed.

"Why don't you just block him?" Caleb suggested, tapping his lips with a napkin.

I don't know why I hadn't thought of that before.

"Done." I smiled back at him, wondering if we could pick up where we'd left off. But the moment was gone, and people were crowding up inside the restaurant. The right thing to do was to give up our table to other diners. Besides, pizza was the last thing on my mind right now.

He kissed my cheek before standing up and placed his earpiece back on.

Nothing happened here.

CHAPTER 3

Two Birds, One Kiss

A FEW HOURS after we came back from eating our pizza, Caleb, David, and I went out for a run. I didn't have time to run in the morning since I was busy organizing my school schedule with Nolan. Classes started in three days.

When we returned from the park, I invited Caleb to join me on the rooftop. It was almost seven, and the sun was setting.

I couldn't stop thinking about that kiss he almost gave me earlier. He'd been so patient with me, and I wanted to show him how much I cared about him even if I was taking my time—that I was willing to explore things with him.

The fact that he wasn't wearing his suit was even better. It made things feel more authentic. But the muscles in his arms showing off from his t-shirt seemed *unreal*, as per usual.

Caleb was always covered up to the neck in those suits they wore all day. That's why my favorite part of our runs was seeing him in his sportswear. It made the idea of us feel more likely and less forbidden.

We lingered at the far end of the rooftop railing, the same place where we stood a couple of weeks before. We were both so sweaty, but I didn't mind because we were enjoying ourselves talking and laughing without a care in the world—just the two of us. Caleb was Caleb, and I wasn't his job.

The rooftop access door closed with a thump, and I prayed to Odin that he wouldn't send William my way before I even dared to turn around to see who it was. But I wasn't in the Norse God's good favor because there he was, and he wasn't alone.

William walked in with Tobias, and not one or two, but *five* other girls. Freaking five against two because *that's not greedy.*

They all looked ready for a party; it was Friday, after all. The girls were all dressed up in high heels and short, elegant dresses. William's cologne ruined my state of mind altogether.

Needless to say, he looked utterly handsome. His broad, muscular, but not bulky back and chest were beautifully showcased against the perfectly ironed fabric of his white button-down shirt, which he neatly tucked inside his gray slacks. A fancy belt surrounded his waist.

Butterflies flooded my chest, and I tried to squash them but failed miserably. As much as I tried to overlook the attraction, it was stronger than me.

Chemical.

Unavoidable.

Inescapable.

The door opened once again, and Erin waltzed in, looking all … pretty. *What the hell is she doing here?* She was so self-absorbed that she didn't even see me standing here with Caleb. Not yet at least.

I couldn't *stand* her. I couldn't stop staring, either.

Erin wore her dark brown hair up in a low bun and a sparkly golden dress that accentuated her artificially tanned skin, which somehow, she pulled off nicely.

Didn't William hate her guts?

He placed his arm around Erin with a too-uncomfortable-to-watch familiarity. But our eyes never met. The angle in which I stood was directly facing their way. And I wasn't going to move an inch. Not for them.

Tobias waved his hand in my direction with a big, heartfelt smile. But not William.

Oh, come on!

He knew I was standing right there behind him! But he kept true to his mission, which consisted of giving his back to me. He acted like he didn't even know me. And I, like none of that was bothering me.

We'll wait and see how much longer you can go without looking this way.

Caleb noticed the change in my mood after they arrived and asked me if I was okay, but I nodded and persuaded myself to draw a smile on my face. He then asked me if I wanted to leave, but I wasn't running away because William had stepped on the rooftop.

Hell no.

I got there first. If anything, he should've been the one to leave. But they didn't seem like they were going anywhere.

To William, I was a ghost—a spectrum. I was nonexistent.

Gone.

On the other hand, Erin was a walking, living, and breathing miracle in four-inch designer heels. She had resurfaced from the dead, sporting a bleach-white smile with an agenda to torture my soul.

I could see how William's acting skills came in handy for him in situations like these because his attitude made me doubt myself about having even met him before. Maybe it had all been a figment of my imagination—a dream.

Yeah, I don't think so. I would never forget the sweet taste of cinnamon in his mouth when we kissed. You can't make that up.

Caleb and I talked and pretended as if they weren't there. From the corner of my eye, I observed how William never even *once* dared to look in our direction.

I wanted to provoke a reaction out of him and refused to believe he wanted to stay away from me. But back with Erin? Really? He'd made it clear he wanted nothing to do with her—that he couldn't stand her.

Just looking at her made my stomach churn. I'd rather see any of the other random girls clinging to him instead of Erin.

Ah, the simpler days.

William was furious about the ruined bet, disappointed about Thomas's kiss, and God knows what else. But the things I felt with him I'd never felt before. And something told me he was right there with me.

That night at the cottage, he allowed me to see *him*. And I opened up myself to him too as I've never had before—he saw me.

But I fucked up.

And somehow, William believed that going back to Erin was the reasonable choice to make. He deserved better, and I thought at some point that I could be that for him, but I was wrong.

Caleb's phone buzzed. It was Aaron calling him. He excused himself to take it, walking a few steps away from where we stood. I ventured to peek in William's direction for the millionth time, only to watch him place an awkward kiss on Erin's lips.

It was an absurdly quick and sober kiss but maddening to watch.

I bit the corner of my bottom lip and looked away, pretending my body temperature wasn't rising to a disturbingly unhealthy level. I was tempted to throw a tennis shoe at him for his own good because my sudden degree in Psychology informed me that he needed to stop sabotaging himself like that.

"Hey." Caleb walked up to me again with a smile. I extended my hand to him and pulled him near me. He looked in William's direction and said, "I hated seeing him kiss you that day on our way back from the Hamptons. I was a second away from losing it."

It must've been hard for Caleb to endure it, but it'd been impossible for me to refuse William. He had me hypnotized.

"I know. I'm sorry." I pulled his earpiece off.

I thought about how easy it would be to kill two birds with one … kiss. But it was useless to stand there pretending not to care. I didn't want to use Caleb to make William jealous. He didn't deserve that. And I *did* want to kiss Caleb, but this moment wasn't ideal.

"I think we should go," I said instead.

You win, William. You can have the rooftop.

"Wait," Caleb whispered. "No suit, no tie, no earpiece. Just as you requested, Miss Murphy." He grabbed my waist, pulling me closer to him, and leaned in to kiss me without warning.

It was a lengthy and unmistakably affectionate kiss. Caleb's lips felt insanely good. His tongue brushed softly against mine, and for a second there, I forgot about William standing there.

For a second.

But I remembered at some point and found the strength to pull away from Caleb's delicious lips. I had to.

"Let's go," I muttered, his lips a quarter of an inch away from mine. Caleb nipped his lower lip, and a proud smile drew on his face when we turned around and saw William blasting a thousand-degree Fahrenheit glare our way. Erin was still oblivious to her surroundings—laughing and talking to her friends.

Good.

The smile on Caleb's face told me he was thrilled about getting even. Now William got to see *him* kissing me this time.

We both gave excellent use to this kiss. Caleb got the opportunity to flaunt it to William, while I hoped it would make him snap out of his self-induced trance.

I didn't care if he was pissed! I just wanted him to show me something. I couldn't handle the silence, the indifference. I knew he would never be happy with Erin. It was all for a good cause.

"Off-duty?" William asked Caleb as we inevitably walked past them to leave. Unfortunately, Erin saw me, recognized me, and tugged at William's arm, trying to stop his interaction with us.

"You bet," Caleb replied with a smug expression on his face, intertwining fingers with mine. I peeked over my shoulder one last time and saw William's eyes scorching with ... something. I don't know what, but something brewed deep down in the wells of them.

Mic drop.

That's all I wanted to see.

But I said it before. I needed to claw him out of my mind. And I didn't even know how to do it. It didn't seem to me like I was doing a great job at it.

Caleb walked me to my apartment, and once I opened the door, his hormones found the courage to step inside, shut the door behind us and *really* kiss me.

"I know—it's risky—doing this here—at your place," he said in between kisses as we made our way into the living room, running his hands up and down my back.

"Yes," I replied with a soft laugh. "A terrible idea."

He quickly removed my tank top, leaving me in my sports bra, and slid his hands to my waist. "Just this once, okay?" He searched for my gaze, awaiting confirmation. I replied with a nod, and his lips found my neck.

Once. *Right.*

He sat on the couch and pulled me on top of him. "I'll send Aaron away next time"—he pulled his t-shirt over his head—"and I'll take you to my place." *Damn, those abs.* "It's cozy"—he tossed it on the floor with a smile—"and you'll love it there."

Caleb glanced at my lips and met them with his. He was *kissing* me as if we would die in a few minutes. It was so raw and intense that I had to break away from the kiss for a second and take a good look at him. I cupped his face with my hands. This was really Caleb. I couldn't believe it. So many times, I fantasized about having him kiss me like this.

Caleb laughed under his breath, probably at the shock that must've been so obviously drawn on my face and said, "It's just me." He kissed my neck with a delicious groan, *slowly* moving down to my collarbone. I closed my eyes and gasped. His lips felt *so* good on my skin. He pulled my waist closer to him, and then … my doorbell rang.

"Kiddo!" My father shouted from the other side of the door.

Shit shit shit!

I immediately grabbed my tank top, threw it over my head, and pulled it down. When I turned around two beats later, Caleb was standing up beside me with his t-shirt back on.

I looked at him, begging with my eyes for an answer. *What do we do now?* I was in shock—unable to think of a solution. He whispered he would leave through the service entrance once he heard my father coming in. I nodded, shooing him away. Yes, that was perfect.

"Coming!"

I walked hastily to the foyer, and Caleb disappeared into the kitchen. I took a quick look at myself in the mirror before opening the door just to make sure everything looked good and that my I-just-made-out face wasn't showing in front of my father.

My cheeks were pink. But heck, they always were for one reason or another. There was nothing else I could do but open the damn door.

"Hey, Dad!"

At that moment, I understood Caleb's fear of having my father find out about us and why he thought making out in my living room was the worst idea ever.

It'd been nerve-wracking to imagine what would've happened if he walked in on us because he *did* have a key.

The situation was going to be more challenging than I thought. And I hate to say this once again, but Caleb's always right because *just this once* couldn't have been more accurate.

CHAPTER 4

Blinder

September 10, 2009

GRANT'S CLASSES HELPED channel the hurricane of emotions in my chest, and I couldn't go any longer without them. He was expecting me at the gym at seven, as usual.

The gym inevitably reminded me of William.

We had many *interesting* encounters there. Some were more awkward and annoying than others, but it was impossible not to think of him there. And after all, Grant was William's trainer, and it was thanks to him that I met Grant. So how could I *not* think of him?

Even if I knew he must've been miserable with Erin, the reality was that they were back together, and I was still trying to figure things out with Caleb behind everyone's backs.

Well, behind almost everyone's backs.

William and Tobias had seen me kissing Caleb on the rooftop, which meant Joel, Lily, and Eric probably knew about it too. Those Sjöberg brothers were gossipy and then some. But it wasn't too hard to figure out that something was going on between Caleb and me after what they saw.

William was running on the treadmill when I arrived at the gym ten minutes before my class started. He wasn't supposed to be here. Grant stood beside him, chatting, but fell silent immediately after he saw me approaching the entrance.

William glanced at me next and went from running at full speed to making the treadmill stop abruptly. He stepped off and rushed to get his things, walking right beside me without even acknowledging me. Grant was taken aback by William's explosive reaction.

"William, you need to cool off, man! You can't just stop like that! You're gonna give yourself a heart attack!" Grant shouted, but William didn't seem to care about his cardiovascular health and stormed out of the gym without replying to Grant.

My breathing became shaky and shallow after seeing William's reaction. I wasn't even expecting him to be there, yet he *knew* I usually trained with Grant at seven.

If seeing me was such a nightmare, then he shouldn't have come down to the gym. I was *not* going to hide in my apartment to avoid making him uncomfortable. He could find himself another place to workout.

"I swear something's off. He's been in such a bad mood these past few weeks," Grant told me. I shrugged and lifted my right arm in front of me so he could bandage it. Dating Erin wasn't an easy task, I supposed.

A few minutes before my class ended, Tobias walked in with his usual cheery smile. He was always in a good mood for a change.

"Hey, Billie!" He took a seat on the bench. I turned to look at him and greeted him with a jerk of my chin. My focus went back to punching the pads Grant held out for me. That right there was my therapy.

The class ended, and my phone buzzed on the bench. I sat down to catch my breath and took the call. Grant always left me undone after training.

"Hey, CJ! ... Yeah, I'm a little out of breath, just finished boxing

with Grant ... Hmm, nothing much. It's Thursday. I have an early class tomorrow at nine ... No, no, no, stop right there ... CJ, come on, we've talked about this. I don't like blind dates ... What do you mean you've confirmed? ... You have to cancel it ... STOP laughing. This isn't funny ... Well, call him and tell him I can't make it ... No ... I'm not going ... Yes, but ... No!"

CJ rambled on about how great this guy was, intelligent, and not at all like Charles. He swore he couldn't cancel on him on such short notice.

"Ugh! Okay ... But this is the last time I'm doing it. I swear I won't show up on any other dates, especially if it's at the last minute ... Yeah, we'll see about that ... Okay, bye."

My phone buzzed again in my hand a few seconds after ending the call.

CJ: Oh, I forgot to tell you.
CJ: David has your date's ID info.
CJ: You know, for the background check ;)
Me: Where did you get David's number?
CJ: I have my ways. Now get your redhead ass ready and make me proud.

I shook my head at the screen.

Caleb wasn't going to be happy about it, but I planned on doing the same thing as the last time. I needed to talk to CJ and Nina about these blind dates. Letting them know about Caleb and me was necessary to stop them from setting me up with other people, even if I didn't know what we were or where we were headed.

"Blind date?" Tobias casually asked as if we were having tea and biscuits. I thought I'd whispered when talking to CJ on the phone, but Tobias's hearing abilities were right up there on the busybody expert level.

"My friends are setting me up on these—dates," I said, standing up to leave. "This is the last one, though."

"I thought you and your bodyguard—"

"No! Um ... well i-it's not—" I stammered, trying to explain the nature of my relationship with Caleb to William's freaking brother.

"Hey, it's cool. I get it. You're single and having fun, right?"

I wouldn't say *fun* was the right word to describe my situation. Maybe complicated? But I didn't want to get into that topic with Tobias.

"I need to go, Tobias. I'm sorry. I'm going to be late. I'll see you around," I replied as I gathered my things. "Grant, thanks again!"

I texted the guys to let them know I had dinner plans at 8:30 p.m. I assumed David had informed Caleb about the date, and that was making me breathe a little faster. I didn't want him to get the wrong impression that somehow I wanted to date other people.

I got ready as fast as I could and hurried to meet Aaron and Caleb in the lobby. I tried dressing in nothing too fancy: jeans, flats, and a nice blouse with a brown leather jacket with my hair down parted in the middle.

"Can you ride in the back with me?" I asked Caleb as he opened the door.

"Sure," he replied, unwilling to meet my gaze. He pressed his lips together and sat beside me. He looked pissed and then some. "What's up?" *Oh, yeah, he's pissed.*

"It's another blind date," I said, twisting my fingers on my lap.

"I know. He's clean as a whistle. Breezed through the background check." He seemed annoyed by that too.

"CJ cornered me into it. He confirmed on my behalf. I told him to cancel several times, but he refused." I took his left hand with both of mine. "I assured him I wouldn't show up on any more dates after this one. They're only doing it because they don't know about our … situation."

"Sure, don't worry about it," he replied calmly. He knew how I hated Thomas's jealous fits, and he even experienced them firsthand on more than a few occasions. He tried his best to seem casual about the blind date, but I knew Caleb well, and he wasn't happy about it.

His facial expressions weren't matching up to his words, nor the carefree tone he was using. Trying to figure him out felt like attempting to put a puzzle together made of all-black pieces.

The restaurant was near my place, so the ride was relatively short. I didn't have enough time to sort things out with Caleb.

But I had to do something. I didn't want to go on this date, knowing Caleb was angry and uncomfortable.

A second before we stepped out of the car, I grazed his chin with my fingers and leaned in for a slow and deep kiss. I wanted to reassure him and let him know I didn't care about the blind date. I cared about *him*.

He grabbed my neck and pulled himself in, giving in to the kiss completely.

"You're so sexy when you're angry," I said with a laugh.

"I'm furious."

"I know." I kissed him again, knowing I needed to stop myself at some point and get out of the car, but that accent of his was irresistible. "I'd rather have dinner with you instead," I whispered in his ear, kissing it afterward. "It won't take long. I swear there won't be others. Tomorrow, I'll talk to Nina and CJ and tell them everything. I promise. Besides, I know you love the SOS beacon, so start thinking about what you're going to say this time."

He finally yielded a smile and gave me one last peck on my lips before I checked myself in the mirror for my overall appearance. Caleb knocked twice on the window, and Aaron opened the door for us. We stepped out of the car and walked inside the restaurant.

The guy I was meeting saw me coming in and stood up to greet me.

"Hi, nice to meet you. I'm Ren. Ren Mori. You must be Billie," he said with a grin.

"Yes, I am. Nice to meet you, Ren." He was cute and looked decent for a change. Ren had jet black hair, dark brown eyes, and a friendly face. He wore jeans too, and a navy-blue, short-sleeved Lacoste shirt.

Caleb helped me to my seat and walked out of the small French restaurant. Ren eyed Caleb with curiosity but didn't ask or comment a thing about it.

The place was cozy and dimly lit. Caleb surely hated the romantic atmosphere. I thought he would stand beside us, but it would've been too awkward if he did because there was nowhere for him to stand without obstructing the small restaurant's circulation.

Ren's two years older than me and very polite. He told me his father is Japanese, and her mother is Spanish. He explained how he grew up in Spain but came to New York for college in Columbia.

I mentioned how my mother was from Madrid, and we switched to speaking Spanish for the rest of the night just for fun. It'd been a while since I spoke Spanish with anyone, and I enjoyed it.

We talked about my time living in Paris and how the restaurant reminded me of it. The conversation kept flowing naturally, and the server took our order as we ate bread with butter.

We ate our meal and talked about art, photography, and books. I was so relaxed and enjoying myself that I completely forgot about the SOS beacon.

Ren excused himself to go to the bathroom. I took my phone out of my purse and saw several texts from Caleb.

Caleb: Ready when you are.
Caleb: I'm really going to change it up this time with SOS.
You'll love the excuse I'm using to take you away.
Caleb: Everything ok?

I didn't know what to do! I didn't want to use the beacon on Ren because I didn't think he deserved it. He was so nice, friendly, and interesting to talk to. He was distracting me and helping me forget all about the drama surrounding my life.

And even though Ren was cute, I didn't feel instant romantic chemistry with him on the date, but I did like him a lot. I thought Ren and I could be good friends.

The beacon would have to wait.

Me: Everything's ok. Almost done with dinner. I'll hold off on the beacon, ok? It's not what you think it is.

He didn't reply for the rest of our date. I knew that might've thrown him off, but I knew I could explain.

The server brought the check, and I offered to split it, but Ren insisted on paying.

We stood up and climbed the short flight of stairs back to the street. Caleb was right outside the door, smoking with a sour face. He wasn't even talking to Aaron. He watched his feet as he paced slowly on the sidewalk.

He flicked his cigarette away once he saw us coming out and opened the door for me, huffing the smoke over his shoulder.

Ren told me he had a great time and asked for my number. We kept speaking in Spanish at that point, which I guess was even more annoying for Caleb.

I gave Ren my number out of courtesy, and you didn't have to speak Spanish to figure out I was dictating my number to him. But what was I to do? I could always tell him I was dating someone else if he ever called or texted me. I didn't see any harm. Ren asking for my number didn't mean he intended to contact me or that we had to go on another date.

"Let's do this some other time," Ren said in English, tucking his phone back in his pocket. "Soon."

Soon. Okay. Well, maybe he *was* planning on calling me.

Shit.

I thanked Ren for dinner, said goodbye, and stepped into the car. Caleb rode in the passenger seat next to Aaron.

He. Was. Furious.

I thought he would sit with me again on the way back. Since Aaron knew about us, it was the perfect moment to spend time together without having to hide. But he didn't want to sit with me, and I didn't blame him. He probably thought I liked Ren. And I did, but not in the way he was thinking.

Caleb didn't say a word to Aaron or me on the short ride home, but I knew I could explain. I just needed him to give me the chance to do it.

As we approached the building's entrance, Caleb jumped out of the moving car. This time the car was *really* moving and not about to stop like when he usually performed that move. He closed the door as he walked away without looking behind.

I guess he was *very* eager to get as far away from me as possible.

Aaron hit the brakes roughly and told me to remain inside the vehicle as he stepped out to join Caleb, locking me inside the car.

What the hell *is going on?*

Aaron didn't park right in front of the apartment building's entrance but a few feet back. I looked in their direction and saw them arguing with a tall guy wearing jeans and a dark red hoodie. I could recognize that silhouette if he were standing in a crowd.

Thomas.

I wanted to step out and see what the problem was for myself, but I was locked in. I couldn't open the doors from the inside. That's when Thomas turned around, somehow sensing I was inside the SUV.

He seemed flustered. Upset. I didn't understand why they wouldn't let me handle it.

Thomas made a run for it and stepped outside my window, banging it a few times with his fist. "Billie? I know you're in there. Please, I just want to talk."

As much as I tried pulling the handle, the door wouldn't budge because I was a child that needed child-lock protection enabled on the SUV's doors.

Aaron removed Thomas from beside my window and tossed the car keys to Caleb, who stepped in the driver's seat and sped away.

I didn't enjoy seeing Thomas in that condition. It made me anxious and sad. He was clearly hurt, and I knew I could probably fix things if they just let me talk to him.

"Caleb, what's going on? Let me talk to Thomas. I know how to handle him."

"I'm sure you do," he replied with a stiff bordering on a sarcastic tone.

"What's that supposed to mean? Tell me what's going on," I demanded. I was a second away from losing it. I knew Caleb was pissed off and sulking about the blind date, and I knew he was quick-tempered, but I didn't understand what was going on with Thomas. I was expecting him to explain.

"Let me concentrate on getting you safe from that *psycho* first, and then we'll talk."

CHAPTER 5

Single

SAFE FROM THOMAS? They reacted as if he were a convicted felon. I knew Thomas had a hard time with the breakup, but that didn't make him a *psycho*. Caleb was exaggerating, as he always did. And the blind date had only made things worse, making his tolerance level drop to the floor.

Caleb parked a few blocks away and sat silently behind the wheel, staring out the window with a tense jaw. I crawled to the front and sat next to him on the passenger seat.

"Caleb?" I placed my hand on his arm. "Please talk to me. You know I hate being left in the dark. What's going on?"

He wouldn't reply, so I reached out for his hand and held it in between both of mine because I knew I needed to address the blind date situation first if I wanted to get any answers out of him.

"Look, Caleb, I had fun tonight. I'm not going to lie about it. Ren turned out to be a really nice guy, and I found it distracting to talk to him. I completely forgot about the SOS beacon," I explained, tugging on his hand to have him look at me.

He finally did, and I continued. "I don't feel attracted to him. I'm sure we can become good friends, but that's it. It just—didn't feel right to leave him."

"You gave him your number, and hey, you're only twenty years old, you're single, and living in New York City, for crying out loud … You should be allowed to have some fun."

There were more than a few maddening concepts in that statement. But, single? I released his hand from my grasp.

I knew we hadn't formalized anything yet between us, but I didn't consider myself *available*. Even if nobody knew about us, it's not like I was open to dating anyone else at the moment. That's why I thought it was weird for him to want to catalog me as such.

But it was enlightening, at least, to know he probably still went around town announcing he was single.

"What's *only twenty* got to do with you and me?" I asked, somewhat offended. "So, I'm just this—girl who needs to go out and date a bunch of random guys and ignore my feelings because I'm *just twenty*, and that's what I'm supposed to be doing?" He kept silent and refused to look at me. His gaze was set on the windshield.

I hoped that meant I had his attention.

"When have I *ever* done shit my age? You've known me since I was sixteen, Caleb. You used to make fun of me, of how lame my weekends were and how cute you thought that was. So now you want me to go crazy in New York so I can live a little? When we're *finally* trying to figure things out between us?"

"Exactly." *Oh no, he didn't.*

I huffed once, sharp with exasperation because he knew me. He knew that's not what I enjoyed doing. And it's not like I was *ever* going to be allowed to *go crazy*. "So? You don't want to give us a try? Is that what you're saying? Because I need to *live more*?"

Is he dumping me? It kind of felt like it.

"I'm scared, okay!" He finally snapped. *That's it.* I needed him to explode, to allow me a glimpse inside his mind. I couldn't deal with the frowns, the lip-pressing, and the eye-rolling anymore. I needed *words*, and I needed him to throw them at me.

Right now.

"I've been waiting for this to happen for a while, but it doesn't feel right. Something's ..." Caleb clutched the steering wheel and rested his forehead on it for a few seconds. "It doesn't feel like what I thought it would be, what it *should* feel like. I think I know the answer, but it freaks me out that you can't see it.

"And I don't give a shit about getting hurt. I can deal with myself. But I *don't* want to lose you. And I certainly don't want you to end up hurt from this because I know you don't want to lose me either."

"And you think this is not scary for me too? I'm terrified! I know we're gambling with our friendship to explore something beyond it. But I'm *here*, and I'm willing to give it a try. So why aren't you? Because I went on a blind date?"

"You're *not*"—he laughed a low, sad laugh—"willing to give this a try. Not really. That's the whole point of this conversation. I don't feel like you're onboard. And yes. All this—blind date nonsense is getting on my nerves. It's annoying as fuck, and I wonder if you would've risked your *whatever it was you had going on* with William when you came back from your lovey-dovey weekend at the Hamptons by going on a couple of blind dates because 'you couldn't get out of them.'"

What?

"What does William have to do with *any* of this?"

He laughed again, but it was scaring on exasperation this time. "I'm trying to make you see—" Caleb looked away again, taking a deep breath. He fixed his gaze on mine and carried on with a more collected tone. "I'm trying to make you see how you don't *know* what you want. And unfortunately, that kinda makes me doubt what I want too."

Ouch.

The SUV's cabin became a vacuum—an insatiable black hole sucking in all thoughts, words, and sounds. And I wanted to tell the black hole: *let go of me; you're hurting me* because I still had thoughts to put into words, but it didn't budge. It sucked us both right in.

And after a few minutes that lasted a lifetime of me finding myself unable to comprehend, to fathom, what was happening right now, the void scattered. My breathing became audible, and then Caleb's. And his eyes popped up again, warm brown and faded green whipped up into irises.

And with that, I gained clarity.

Caleb's breaking up with me.

We weren't dating, but it still felt like a breakup, but now I was standing on the other side, getting a real taste of what rejection feels like.

And I don't know if I found my voice or my voice found me, but I was back to articulating. "So, to recap ... I'm not old enough to know what I want?" I was still making these stupid questions because I refused for the conversation to be over. Done. Like us.

"Well, do you? Know what you want?" he asked, directing his questioning gaze at me. "I don't think it's got anything to do with age, though."

He was making a solid point. And I didn't think *knowing* mattered. What about feeling? Why couldn't that count? Be enough ...

And it wasn't. I knew it wasn't.

My ex was standing outside my apartment, demanding to talk to me. Wounds raw and open on both sides, even if at some point, I learned it was best to avoid looking at them.

And by mentioning William, my deepest, darkest secret, he made it feel like I had his name written on my forehead. He made it so unsettlingly obvious that it stung because ... *yes.* I couldn't stop thinking about him, even if I didn't want to. Even if it led nowhere.

A dead end.

And the answer to his last question was no. I wouldn't have

risked my *whatever I had going on with William* by going on the blind dates. And that was possibly Caleb's most painfully accurate observation of the night.

We both knew it, but we wouldn't speak of it because it's as if he'd stumbled upon my diary and ended up reading a page or two of William's perpetual chapter. And I caught him, and I don't want to know what he knows, and he doesn't want to tell me either.

That's what it felt like.

Caleb knew me too well, and I kept forgetting.

My curiosity had launched us on a delicately menacing process that set our friendship at risk—again, just as he said. He'd already said it all, and I was just picking up the pieces from the floor of my mind, lagging, trying to reformulate the truth into a more digestible resolution.

A part of me, though, believed that the risk might be worth the hassle. That something incredible could result from this. And my stubbornness refused to let go because it's hard being on the other side, thinking something must be wrong with you.

Something.

I needed more— an answer that would put me at ease.

My hand searched for his, just to make sure he wouldn't slip away because I *needed* him. I always did. But I knew that wasn't something to throw lightly in someone's face. Not again, at least. Once had been enough. Or was it twice already?

"I know I want to at least try," I finally chose as a reply. He looked at me, stunned. He probably thought I would remain in a state of silent continuum until it got late enough that he would have to take me back home, thus signaling the end of the conversation.

And then we would each go to bed, him being right and me being wrong ... as usual. And we would wake up the next day dissolving back into whatever was left of our friendship.

I refused to believe we couldn't try without making a mess!

But he didn't.

"I don't want to try. I'm sorry, Red. I really don't. Not anymore. We're gonna burn our relationship to a crisp if we keep going at it like this."

A numbingly warm sensation jetted back and forth from my stomach to my chest, meandering with pure and unadulterated rejection.

"All this time. All these *years*. The way you looked at me—the things you said and did, and how I reacted to them. You were aware of it all," I said to him, wondering if he'd forgotten what his life had been like before this moment—if his memories had evaporated into nothing. "I know you have feelings for me, Caleb. Why would you push me away like this? Why won't you at least try? It feels like you're giving up."

I kept fighting, but I couldn't see that it was the rejection I was fighting off. It took me a while to understand that.

"It's definitely easier to give in and just ... wreak havoc," he muttered. "I would probably get fired for this in a heartbeat, and you know it. And I won't lie to you and say that I'm not tempted not to give a shit. But I love my job."

His job. A job. *Hi, I'm the job.*

"So, you'd rather keep your job than try?"

"*You* are my job. And I'm telling you I *love* my job. Don't you fucking get it?"

"I really don't." This is what denial looks like and how it communicates. I don't know how many *yous* are inside one's mind. But sometimes one *you* gets it, but another doesn't, and conflict erupts.

So, *you* listen, and *you* know, and *you* understand, and *you* freaking agree to all of it. But there's a stray *you* making a fuss out of things, and it needs time and convincing. A single word or phrase that will make sense of things. To allow for release and integration.

Caleb was kind enough to give me that.

"Look, it used to be just you and me before, right? In Paris. And now—now everything's changed. You've changed. I guess I have too, I—I *can't* lose you"—he grabbed both of my hands and stared into my eyes—"and this is the *only way* I get to keep you. Please don't make me say shit you already know."

Shit you already know.

We were getting there.

But the horrible anxiety inside my chest was demanding, and it whispered that he was packing his bags to leave. To leave me. And I couldn't handle it.

But that's what he meant. He *knew* I needed him, and if we went down this path, the possibilities of things going to shit were higher because my father wasn't going to make it easy on us. He knew that too. We both did, even if he avoided the subject altogether—a terrifying subject.

When he told me about that job in Tel Aviv, my mind went into survival mode, and I thought that trying to make *us* work would be the only way to get him to stay.

And it hurt like hell to hear him tell me all these things because they were the truth. And the truth stings and burns and bites back at you until you acknowledge it.

I could feel the struggle, the eagerness to fight against the facts: I wanted Caleb to stay, I wasn't ready to risk him leaving, and I didn't know what I wanted.

It's just that I couldn't brush off the feeling of rejection. It was harder having Caleb be the one to say these things to me. Even though he was right about everything, it still hurt.

He was doing the talking for me. I needed to understand that.

I took a deep breath and let it out with a sigh. My mind felt like a unit now. A solid-state drive. "Just ... you're not leaving me for some job in Tel Aviv, or some shit like that, right?"

"I promised to stay. And that's what I'm aiming at."

I knew it was the right thing to do. The safe thing to do, but I was heartbroken.

"Okay," I muttered, giving in to full integration.

"Come here." Caleb extended his arms, and I moved over the bulky central console and threw myself at him, holding him tight. My face flush against his chest. "I *adore* you," he whispered in my ear. "I'd do anything for you. You know that, Red. *We* are forever."

I knew that.

"And you're sure there's nothing wrong with me? You're not making all this up to—"

"Stop. Okay? Just—stop. I'm *not* going anywhere. You're stuck with me. For good."

CHAPTER 6

A Kiss Goodbye

WE WERE STILL WAITING inside the SUV a few blocks away from the apartment building, and Caleb's phone finally buzzed. Aaron informed him that *the situation* had been handled, and Caleb drove me back home. I didn't even dare ask how they *handled* Thomas. It was best not to know. I trusted them to manage things in the best way possible. And I knew they wouldn't hurt him.

I concentrated on breathing slowly and evenly to keep the tears in check as Caleb drove me back home. I knew this was the right way to go, and I kept reminding myself I would still see Caleb every day, but my stomach was upset, and my eyes felt heavy from the quake of emotions I'd just gone through with Caleb.

I instinctively searched for his hand and held it during the short ride back home. He held mine back without objection. I couldn't remember the last time I sat in the front seat of a car. It was kind of cool.

"I'll walk her," Caleb said, tossing the car keys to Aaron, who was waiting for us outside the building.

It made me feel at ease that Caleb was walking me up to my apartment. I wasn't afraid of Thomas. I knew he wouldn't hurt me, but it startled me to see him in such a bad condition. It was a shame that things had to end like this.

"Can we talk about Thomas?" I asked Caleb as we walked toward the elevators. "What's going on?"

"Yeah, well, he's ah—been making appearances outside your apartment, trying to get a hold of you." Caleb looked away and summoned the elevator.

"What? Since when?"

"Ever since you blocked him two weeks ago. I guess he figured out you did, and well, he didn't take it so well. Your father's upset about this, as you can imagine." The elevator doors opened for us, and Caleb gestured for me to go inside. I just hoped this wouldn't augment my father's already heightened apprehensiveness.

But Thomas's behavior *was* getting out of hand.

"What do you think I should do?" I was concerned. "Should I talk to him or—"

"Nothing—no. *No.* Let us handle it. There's nothing to worry about. You let me do the worrying for you." I understood why Caleb had been following me inside the restaurants and standing right outside my classroom's door. They were amping up the security without me noticing it altogether.

I unlocked my apartment door and turned around to hug Caleb.

It was an important hug. It meant things were going back to normal with us. I don't think either of us was thrilled, but *it is what it is.*

"Can I have one last kiss?" he asked. "I swear I won't—"

I shut him up by giving him the kiss he'd asked for. I really wanted it too. A single goodbye kiss couldn't harm anyone.

I hoped.

He ran his fingers through my hair and down my neck. His other hand found the small of my back and pulled me even closer to him. I stood on my tiptoes and reached out for his neck with my arms. Caleb was making it hard for me to accept we were going back to being friends with that kiss.

Those freaking lips …

Caleb took a few steps, our lips still locked, until he had me gently pinned against my door. His kiss intensified by the second, and it didn't seem like we were saying goodbye.

"You have to," Caleb said in between all the kissing, "make me stop at some point—you're—God, please."

I didn't know how to stop either! I could've been there all night kissing him against my door if he didn't break away from me. It seemed to me like we would go at it for a while, so I searched for my door handle and opened the door. "Do you want to come in?"

Caleb removed his lips brusquely away from mine. Took a step back. Stared at my lips.

"What's wrong?"

"No, um"—he closed his eyes, tightened his mouth, ran a hand along the length of his face—"I should—it's best if we stop. If I don't—"

"It's okay," I said in a breath, still panting, heart racing, lips eager to carry on. But he was right. It was best to stop. We wouldn't want to complicate things. I summoned a smile but deficiently accomplished drawing it on my face.

"You're not expecting your father, are you?" He peeked over his shoulder.

Ohhhhhh.

Caleb told me before that he had a hard time pretending like sneaking around wasn't awkward. And my father arriving when we were making out in my living room the other day had been unsettlingly scary. I could tell he was still affected. It'd been *unforgettable* on the hair-rising spectrum.

But I got carried away and completely forgot about that ever happening, but no. I wasn't expecting my father, and he never barged in unannounced. Not that it wasn't a possibility. The last time I'd forgotten I was expecting him for dinner. That was totally on me—my fault.

"I'm not"—I took a step forward, but he took half a step back—"expecting him." I was baffled because he kept staring at my lips like he wanted more, but his body kept shying away from me. *What's it gonna be?*

He finally closed the distance between us but totally curveballed me with a hug as his last display of affection. And then a kiss, yes, a tender kiss on my cheek that lingered on for a few seconds.

"That was one hell of a last kiss." He placed the words gently on my ear. I felt the heat rising to my cheeks, and I swore to myself it'd be the last time I'd blush for Caleb and probably anyone else for a while.

He caressed my cheek with his thumb, and I twitched my mouth into a smile. "I ... agree."

He took a few steps back and said, "I'll see you tomorrow morning. I'm on duty. I'll drive you to school, okay?"

I nodded.

Listening to Caleb say that was so meaningful to me. So helpful and necessary because I *was* still going to see him every day.

I couldn't help but feel like I would wake up to find that he was gone.

He shot one last smile at me and turned around to leave. I rushed inside my apartment and shut the door, pressing my back against it with a sigh. That's when I realized my face was dripping wet with tears that'd come out involuntarily the moment I stepped into my apartment.

I brushed them off my cheeks with the back of my hand and dragged myself to my bedroom.

My phone buzzed inside my purse. I swore it'd be Caleb sending me a text just to seal our entire interaction.

W.S: Do you ever think of me?
W.S: When he kisses you?

What? I didn't have the energy to deal with this shit right now. I'd tried contacting William for days. Weeks! He blocked me, and now he was texting me? Asking me ... that? He was dating Erin, so why did he care about my thoughts?

I looked behind my shoulder, feeling observed because the timing of his text was pristine. As if he'd seen me kiss Caleb a few minutes ago.

Too exact—precise.

My hands shook. I didn't know if I should reply or not. It was like a wave of overwhelming emotions crashing against me. I could feel the outrage seething up from my subconscious, waking up and making a scene inside my head. I was still stunned. Still hurt.

Still ... curious.

Me: Never.
W.S.: Great. I know what that means.
Me: It means on no occasion.
W.S.: That too, smart ass.

And there it was again, that chemical cocktail of dopamine, endorphins, and adrenaline William could *fix* for me in an instant, triggered by both excitement and exasperation. And I chugged it down without a second thought. Every single drop of it. Every damn time.

He got me hooked on it, but I didn't know it.

I needed to sandblast the surface of my too transparent demeanor and make it less sheer, less obvious for people to read right through me. Caleb could, and William obviously did somehow. But I would *never* concede to it.

Me: Go to hell.

CHAPTER 7

A Weird Night

October 20, 2009

ALMOST A MONTH and a half had gone by since Caleb and I decided to go back to our regular, day-to-day dynamic. But it was understood we couldn't go back to exactly where we stood before he opened up to me about his feelings.

We didn't feel pressured anymore. The kissing had stopped, but there was still some inevitable flirting here and there. We had fun with it and didn't think there was anything wrong with doing it. We couldn't help it, either.

I'd found peace in my decisions. All I wanted was to keep Caleb close to me, and once I understood that he wasn't going anywhere, everything fell into its right place.

William's presence was somehow gone from the building. I hadn't seen or heard from him after telling him to go to hell. Maybe he did as he was told. But damn, I couldn't seem to get him out of my head. Knowing he slept two floors above mine made him feel so close yet out of grasp.

I needed to get myself programmed for a lobotomy because not only was thinking about him pointless, but he was also in a relationship with someone else. I couldn't allow these thoughts to mess with my new zen mode, so I just pushed them back down into a dusty corner of my mind.

God knows I tried to kick them out, but it was useless. The thoughts refused to leave my brain. They were somehow ingrained now. It was better to take a step back and let them do their thing because they got territorial and liked to flash their pointy teeth at me.

So back to the dusty corner it is.

Nolan and I worked on a midterm project together after school. It was a little past five in the afternoon, and he had to leave to get to work on time. I walked him down.

We were going over our to-do list for the project on my phone's notepad. Nolan seemed suddenly distracted and grinned at my screen.

"What?" His smile was contagious and made me curious about what was triggering it.

"I met someone," he finally revealed. "Her name's Emily."

"Oh, my God!" I squealed. "Tell me all about her!" I hugged him with excitement, but he went stiff as soon as I held him.

I pulled back with my brows in a bunch, hoping I hadn't done anything wrong, and saw him looking over my shoulder. I inevitably peeked that way and saw William, Joel, Lily, and Tobias walking our way. My reaction was to grab Nolan's arm because I could already feel how my knees threatened to buckle on me.

They were all dressed up and probably attending some kind of fancy event. Lily was *breathtaking*, and William *had* gone to hell and back because he looked irritatingly hot.

He wore a dark blue suit, white shirt, no tie, a few buttons undone, and I wasn't prepared for it. But I guess no warning would have sufficed.

Lily walked up to us and hugged me. I hadn't seen her in a while. She remembered Nolan and greeted him by his name. He seemed excited about that.

William's golden buttery hair was perfectly done, and not a single strand was out of place. His face was clean-shaven, and his skin a bit tanned. It all made his absurdly blue eyes stand out even more.

Couldn't he just stay in hell? Or maybe I had joined him.

Tobias and Joel said hi to me as they walked by. William took a quick glimpse at Nolan, then turned his gaze at me as he walked beside us.

He nodded once and said, "Guille," with that deep voice of his.

Just before William walked out the door, he stopped for a second, as if he'd forgotten something, but he crossed the threshold and left. Two black cars waited for them outside. William followed Tobias toward the first car and out of my range of vision. Joel waited for Lily by the second car parked right beside the apartment building's green sunshade.

"You look beautiful, Lily. That dress is gorgeous," I told her as I looked at her up and down with awe.

"Thank you, Billie. I missed you!" She hugged me again. "I just arrived a couple of days ago, but I was *exhausted*. Let's hang out soon, okay?"

"Sure thing. Um, so—where are you guys going?"

"Movie premiere. One of Billy's." She smiled a tight smile.

"*Sötnos!*" Joel shouted. "We have to go!"

Lily apologized for having to leave so abruptly and told me she would be in New York for the rest of the month. "I'll text you!" she promised, walking away.

"You okay?" Nolan asked, brushing his dark waves off his face.

I had previously opened up to him about the Thomas-William situation that went down on the day of the fire. He knew my interactions with William were almost null.

So to answer Nolan's question: I was okay. But having him look *that* good was a slap in the face—unfair.

"Oh, psh, of course. You're running late." I herded him to the exit. I didn't want to analyze my feelings right now. And he was going to be late. "Tell me all about Emily tomorrow, okay? See you at school."

He left, and I rushed to my apartment to get changed for my training with Grant.

☾

Grant's class was grueling. I couldn't even lift my arms to wash my hair while I showered. I was exhausted but I needed to get dressed to meet CJ and Nina for dinner. Once ready, I realized I still had ten minutes left before having to go, and curiosity got the best of me. I'd abstained from googling William, even though he suggested I did, until now. But I'd learned plenty about myself in the past months, like the fact that I was undoubtedly masochistic.

I *needed* to know everything about the event he was attending. I wasn't sure about how premieres worked, but surely there'd be many photographers there. There had to be at least a few pictures online for me to look at by now.

All I wanted was to see him wearing that perfectly tailored suit without having to pretend to look the other way.

I'm only human. And he looked anything but.

William Sjöberg premiere October 20, 2009.
Search.

Okay.

I took a deep breath and pushed my hair over my shoulder. A bunch of pictures of him came up from the red carpet. I kept scrolling until I clicked on one, which took me to a website with a heavily stocked photo gallery from the premiere.

I'm officially a stalker.

There were plenty of shots of William posing on the red carpet, some with the three brothers together, others with just Lily and Joel, and more of Lily alone. It was so surreal to see them in that kind of scene. I still couldn't grasp it.

I skipped through the photographs of other celebrities and guests I didn't care to see and browsed for more until I saw her.

Erin *fucking* Powell. She looked beautiful.

Click. Erin and William smiling at the camera.

Click. Erin and William staring at each other, smiling.

Click. Erin staring at William while he smiled for the camera.

Click. William grabbing Erin by the waist, whispering to her ear while she laughed.

Click. Click. Click. Click—more of the same.

I shut my laptop with a violent thrust, hoping it would shatter into pieces.

Careful what you do with your spare time. Talk about trying to be super productive gone wrong.

If only I'd taken a longer shower.

C

An unexpected whirlwind of irritation enveloped me in the worst mood ever as I got in the car to leave for dinner. I couldn't get those images out of my head, but what bothered me the most was that seeing them had affected me.

It's like when you're feeling sick, or something hurts, and you google the symptoms only to find out you're going to die a painful death.

Moral of the story: don't google shit.

Caleb's eyes seemed to notice the gloomy atmosphere surrounding me, but he withheld from commenting about it. Not only was he perceptive, but he was smart too.

We arrived at the restaurant, and I couldn't hide my frustration. I'd been able to do it many times before, but not today. I was caught up in a vicious cycle. I was frustrated, and then I was frustrated about being frustrated because I didn't want to be!

I shouldn't have come to dinner.

"You okay?" Caleb asked gently in barely a whisper as I stepped out of the car.

"I'm fine," I replied without looking at him.

He walked me to my table and greeted my friends.

"Hey, Caleb," Nina said with a too-cute-for-my-current-mood kind-of-smile. He smiled back at her because *why the hell not* and excused himself.

Breathe.

I fidgeted with my bottom lip and stared at an invisible point across the restaurant, waiting for someone to do the talking.

I couldn't stop thinking about William looking so happy with Erin. Their body language in the photographs made them seem like the happiest couple in the world.

When he talked about her in the past, I got that he didn't care to see her again. She *cheated* on him, for Christ's sake! I really didn't get it.

I supposed he was a great actor because he either lied to me about his true feelings for Erin in a very believable way or faked his interactions with her at the event.

But who cares, right? So he's a liar. That's Erin's problem.

"Billie?" CJ snapped his fingers in front of my face, trying to catch my attention. I apologized and brought my attention back to the table.

"Your costume? For my party next week?" *Oh, the party.* CJ had previously told me how he celebrated his birthday every year with a Halloween-themed party and how his costumes were always over the top.

It would be my first time attending, and I was excited about it, but I couldn't focus on that while my mind kept going round and round in circles about the premiere.

"I'm still thinking about it. How about you?"

"It's a surprise," he replied. "But it's going to be grand." I had to smile. CJ's positive and enthusiastic energy was always infectious. Nina mentioned how she would go costume shopping on the weekend with Juan Pablo.

"And would David happen to have a shift on the 30th?" CJ asked. He had a silly crush on David, and every time he was on duty, CJ found a way to end up talking to him and entertain him for a while.

Aaron thought CJ was too distracting for David, or so Caleb told me once in confidence. "Don't you like, text with him often?" I asked CJ.

"Why?" He peeked over my shoulder toward the window. "Did he mention something about it?"

"I—no. I don't talk about that sort of thing with David. I don't think he knows I know you guys talk," I explained. "So, when's the wedding?"

CJ grabbed the straw's paper wrapping, made it into a tiny ball, and threw it at me. Nina and I laughed. "Have some mercy. Tell me if he's gonna be there. I don't want to ask him directly."

"I'll know by next Sunday when they send me the week's schedule, but I'm sure I can work something out," I replied with a wink. CJ bit his bottom lip with a smile. His chin resting on his fist. His head slightly tilted to the side.

"So, who are you taking as a date?" Nina asked me. "You know I could always fix you up with someone."

Date? I wasn't aware I had to ask someone to come with me, and I didn't want to know anything about guys, dates, or anything on that semantic field. "Can't I just go by myself?"

"Of course not, silly." CJ intervened with a grimace, almost insulted by the question. "It's a couples party. It always has been that way. I thought I'd explained this to you." He seemed frustrated. But he hadn't mentioned any of it to me. "Don't worry. You still have time."

No effing way! I felt like I wanted to cry from the anxiety of thinking about who to take to the party. Nolan would've been the perfect choice. But he was already dating Emily. And from what I could tell, he liked her a lot.

"And who are you taking, huh?" I asked him. He was hoping for David to go, but it's not like he counted as his plus one.

"Some guy. You don't know him, but he's just a friend. Wouldn't want to make David feel too jealous." He glanced out the window again. "Maybe a little."

I wondered what David thought of CJ; if he liked him as much as CJ liked him.

CJ stared at me as we ate. I was unusually quiet. He played with my hair, twirling it in between his fingers. He finally asked me if there was something wrong. "You seem, I don't know, off—dull," he observed.

Dull, indeed.

Nina agreed with CJ. I told them I was just tired because of school, homework, and exercise. My answers were cryptic. I wished I could just tell them everything, but I was weird about sharing deep personal stuff with anyone.

Besides, I didn't want to go around announcing how I couldn't stop thinking about *William Sjöberg*, who had a girlfriend, by the way. Probably me and ten million fans too. It felt pathetic.

Why couldn't he be, I don't know, an architect or anything else but *that*? I liked it better when I thought he was a chef.

But he wasn't, and my answers didn't seem to convince Nina and CJ about everything being fine with me.

We paid the check, and I excused myself to the restroom. CJ ran outside to talk to David, and Nina followed him. When I stepped out of the restroom, a couple of text messages dropped in from Ren.

Ren M: Hi, Billie!
Ren M: What are you up to?

I planned on replying on my way home. Ren and I would casually text but hadn't gone on any other dates. I told him I wasn't ready to date, and he was super cool about it. We were chat buddies. Our conversations were always interesting, and I needed practice with my written Spanish, which wasn't the best.

Ren's name went down on my mental list of possible guys to take to the party. He was right up there on top of the list with no one else below him.

And then the night got weird.

I stepped out of the restaurant to find myself turning into an uncomfortable fifth wheel on someone else's double date.

I felt sick to my stomach. Possibly heartburn or indigestion.

No ... more like tangling, scorching knots assaulting my entrails.

CJ was making David laugh, as usual. And Nina's body language *screamed* to get Caleb's attention at all costs.

Caleb leaned his back against the SUV. Arms crossed at the chest. Nina stood beside him, her shoulder flush against him. She had the whole shameless flirting starter pack going on: the squinty eyes with the side-smile, the nodding with raised eyebrows, the headshaking with the eye-rolling combo, and the light shoulder shove. Caleb didn't seem bothered by any of it.

I never thought I'd miss Juan Pablo.

Maybe that's what Caleb wanted—to enjoy New York City and

the pleasures that came with it—making it seem like *I* was the one that needed to be doing that instead.

And there he was, back at it, flirting with my friends. *We'll always have Paris*, I guess.

Caleb could join William in hell.

Was I losing my mind? How can someone be so moved by two different people at the same time? Ugh, but they were two *very sexy*, charming, hot, interesting guys. And seeing Caleb's interactions with Nina was driving me nuts. But not as much as William and Erin's did.

It didn't help, though, that I'd bumped into *this image* of such an unadulterated display of flirtation, having had an internal tantrum about seeing the premiere photographs just before arriving for dinner.

The soggy feeling of jealousy merged into a two-headed monster, and it was staring back at me, whispering about its plans to stick around.

A swarm of seconds elapsed while I took in and analyzed the scene before me. I could've been mugged right in front of them, and no one would've noticed. They were fully immersed in their interactions.

I cleared my throat. "Sorry to interrupt."

Caleb and David immediately straightened themselves up. Caleb opened the door for me, and I offered my friends a ride as I always did, to which they usually declined.

"That would be great, Billie. Thanks!" Nina said, her reply too fast for my liking. I said they *usually declined*. She was already sitting in the car beside me before I could even sigh from the restrained exasperation.

CJ jumped in the front seat with David, which resulted in Caleb and me making a sandwich out of Nina, who sat between us.

Suddenly I learned about the paranoid tendencies within me

because it all seemed too planned. As if they were hoping I'd offer a ride to keep the conversation going as long as possible. And that's what they did. Talk.

I distracted myself by replying to Ren's texts instead of blocking out Nina and Caleb's conversation by counting stop signs. I lost count fairly quickly.

Nina glanced at me for a second. I felt her gaze prying into my phone's screen. "Are you talking to Ren?" she asked loudly. She then whispered, "Is he hot or what? You never told me how the date went."

Nina! But having knowledge of Caleb's pristine eardrum calibration, I knew he'd heard her.

This is the part where I wished she would turn around and resume her chit-chat with Caleb, who now seemed very interested in our conversation, by the way.

"We're just friends," I replied. Fast. And kept typing.

"Why don't you invite him to the party? I'm sure he'd love to come," she suggested.

"Could work," I said, still focused on my screen.

Nina was getting on my nerrrrrves.

I love her, but my sullen mood got the best of me. CJ and Nina didn't know a thing about my prior *situation* with Caleb. And Nina was still in a relationship with Juan Pablo, but she couldn't help herself around Caleb, and I didn't blame her.

No one could.

It's not like I didn't understand where she was coming from, but that didn't mean I enjoyed looking at how comfortable they seemed talking to each other.

Nina was so outgoing and—*touchy*. She even ran a hand through Caleb's shorn, dark brown hair, and that's when I started counting stop signs again.

We arrived at their apartment, and Nina and CJ stepped out of the SUV.

"Thanks, Billie!" CJ yelled. "I hope to see you *both* at my party next week." He swayed his finger from side to side between David and Caleb. They laughed. I didn't know who would be on duty that night, but something told me they were both going to be there.

"Say hello to Juan Pablo for me, will ya?" I said to Nina with a wry smile. Maybe she'd forgotten that she had a boyfriend. It didn't do Caleb any harm to remember that either.

"Oh. Ah—of course, Billie! I will," she replied, noticeably taken aback, increasing her pace to catch up with CJ.

Acting this way was so unlike me. I was out of control. And honestly, I felt like a world-class bitch.

I went back to texting with Ren, trying to get my mind off things. We discussed a book he was reading, and I promised to add it to my to-be-read list.

And I wouldn't say I was *angry* at Caleb. I think. It wasn't his fault that girls found him irresistible. But I was having a shitty day, and I didn't want to see him flirting with Nina, of all things. I'd prefer it if he did that in his free time. It wasn't easy for me not to feel jealous, and I didn't think it would ever be.

Caleb walked me up to my apartment and asked me again if I was okay.

"I'm okay."

Can everyone please stop asking me if I'm okay?

"You don't seem okay."

"I'm just having a bad day. But I don't feel like talking about it, okay?"

I'm allowed to, aren't I?

"Okay." He sighed.

Okay … "Good night."

He turned around and shuffled away. I unlocked my door, and instead of biting my tongue and walking into my apartment, as I should have, I opened my big mouth and said, "If you're going to flirt with my friends, at least have the decency to do it while I'm not there to see it. You know, like in the good old days in Paris."

Caleb stopped and turned around slowly.

Shit.

"I wasn't flirting, I—she kept making conversation, and I was just trying to be friendly," he explained.

He didn't owe me any explanation, and I shouldn't have said anything, but I couldn't stand it. I couldn't stand myself. Another floating me was watching me, judging me—fully aware of my irrationality.

"Thanks. You seemed friendly enough," I returned, tying my hair into a pony.

Will somebody please *shut me up?*

My phone buzzed once in my hand. I inevitably turned to see the notification—another message from Ren.

Caleb snorted and shook his head with a crooked smile. "Say hi to your blind date who's *just a friend* for me, will you?" Caleb bolted toward the emergency exit and left through the stairs.

I wouldn't have stayed any longer, either, if I were him.

CHAPTER 8

Proof

WHAT A MESS!

I don't think I've ever been in a fouler mood in my entire life. I tried focusing on my breathing as my therapist in Norway used to suggest all the time. I could hear her voice saying, *breathe*. It was usually soothing.

Not tonight.

Warm water running down my back had to do the trick. I took my time in the shower and immediately crawled into bed afterward, trying not to scare the serenity away. It was best to call it a night and let the day simmer down and fade to black.

Sleep wouldn't take over me, so I grabbed a book. But the words made no sense to me. I tried staring at the roof, hoping to get bored and inevitably succumb to slumber, but my mind wouldn't stop fidgeting. Speculating.

I forced my eyes shut, but it was useless.

After rotating these activities for a couple of hours, my restlessness dragged me out of bed. I changed into jeans and a loose t-shirt and filled my water bottle wishing I could turn it into wine and went up to the rooftop to clear my head.

A little fresh air was probably all I needed to chill out.

Notifying the guys about going up wasn't something I was interested in doing. They insisted I should always inform them of my whereabouts when moving inside the building, and I usually did. But not tonight.

The door was heavy as I pulled it to step on the rooftop. I let it drop back with an intentional thump, expecting the tall silhouette leaning against the railing to turn around and reveal its identity. But I didn't need the person wearing a perfectly tailored blue suit to turn around to know that it was *him*.

Hell. No.

William saw me because I made him look my way when I almost sealed the door coming in.

"Guille!"

Shit. I couldn't catch a break.

I fled the rooftop and made my way down the stairs, but I heard the door pounding from afar, followed by the sound of fast-clicking shoes that rushed down to the fourteenth floor. I pushed the down button more than a few times.

Come on, come on, come on.

The elevator arrived, but those *door close* buttons never actually close the doors any faster.

William caught the closing doors, prompting them to open up again.

"Hi," he said plainly, extending his hand to me as if I were trapped on the elevator, and he was there to save me. "I'm back from hell. Come. I'll tell you all about it." He offered me a tight-lip smile. *Asshole.*

"I'm a regular," I replied, leaning back and sipping on my alcohol-free water. "So there's nothing much you can tell me about it."

William snorted.

The last time I had anything to drink was at William's house in the Hamptons. At least I was reasonable on that end. Having sharp senses around him was always helpful. I knew how sneaky he could be.

"Weren't you headed for the rooftop? I'm sure we can share it." He threw one of those annoying smirks of his at me.

William was still holding his hand out, offering it to me. His fingers swiveled back and forth, urging me to step out.

The idleness triggered the elevator's long alarm, and the doors started closing at a painfully slow rate. William grabbed my hand and pulled me out, making me gasp.

"I'm out, now what?" I sipped on my water again and raised a bored eyebrow at him.

"Now we go to the rooftop." He wanted to start ordering me around already.

"No."

"No?" He made it sound like he'd just arrived from Mars instead and was getting familiarized with words.

"You don't want to be anywhere near me right now, *trust me*." I summoned the elevator once again. But it didn't open up immediately. It must've gone down to pick up someone else.

"And—why would that be?" he asked, his head tilting.

"Because I can't even stand myself right now."

"Let's work on getting that fixed then." He walked up the stairs, and I followed him because I'm a half-human half-magnet type of person. And the only logical explanation was that William had to be made of iron.

We walked to the far end of the rooftop, and William looked up at the sky and laughed a brief, leveled laugh. "That moon," he said, pointing up.

Waxing crescent. I'd become a moon expert.

You could barely see it, but it was there.

That moon, indeed.

"Nothing beats the full moon," I chirped, hoping to irritate him.

Lies. The crescent moon was now my favorite moon, of course.

"You'll come around."

We stood in silence for a while, but it wasn't uncomfortable. I'd missed him. And having William standing beside me was doing wonders for my state of mind. I could feel myself relaxing. Although I still hated him for ghosting me a couple of months ago and getting back together with Erin.

His hand played with mine while I held onto the railing, but I flinched away from his touch. He had a girlfriend, and I wasn't going to participate in this type of dynamic. I was only here to talk.

"Will *this* ..." he whispered, attempting to touch my hand again, "make anyone angry?"

"Probably Erin," I replied bluntly, pulling away again.

"I meant your boyfriend."

"The only person who's in a relationship right now is you."

"But I saw you today with him, in the lobby." He grimaced, confused.

"Nolan? He's a good friend from school," I clarified. "You, on the other hand, shouldn't be trying to reach out for another girl's hand."

"We're *not* dating," he said roughly, a hint of annoyance coming out of those three words.

Yeah, right.

"William, stop lying. I saw you today."

"Did you, now? Where exactly?" He raised his left brow. I had just admitted to having stalked him online.

"Ah! Well, that's not important. The point is that I saw you, and you looked—happy." I stammered, trying to divert the attention from googling him earlier.

"Is that why you're in such a bad mood?" He laughed weakly.

"Of course not, don't be so self-absorbed." I rolled my eyes, feigning irritation. "Not everything's about you." Except it was.

How could he *not* be self-absorbed when he looked so painfully handsome and smelled like a delightful fall breeze, Italian oranges, and other manly spices? I had to concentrate on my breathing so my eyes wouldn't wander. I wanted nothing but to stare at him freely until I memorized every inch of that perfectly tailored suit and how it fitted his heavenly body.

"Tell me," he insisted with a charming smile, trying to ruin my bad mood.

"About … ?" I hesitated, faking incapacity to follow up with a conversation.

"Where did you see me with Erin? Did you—*google* me, Guille?" He laughed, but that wasn't funny! I saw him kiss Erin on the rooftop a couple of months before, and the premiere photographs were enough confirmation that not only were they dating, but they were going strong. I wasn't going to fall victim to his charms. Right?

"I did." I pulled my chin up. I had to embrace it.

"Well, if you googled the event, then you *must've* seen that Erin's my co-star, so it was only natural, and expected, for us to attend the event together, pretending to like each other, of course. For the optics," he explained.

"Erin's an actress?" I asked, and he cracked a full-on belly laugh.

I didn't get the joke, but that's a movie I would never want to see. Erin and William going at it on the big screen? Nah-ah. I hoped they were brother and sister in it. Although I was convinced that wasn't the case.

"Oh, I wish Erin could've been here for this. It would've helped to mitigate her insufferable ego," he said in between laughs that were fading out into the bustle of the city below us.

"You must be one hell of an actor then," I said, allowing the sarcasm to drip from each word.

How was I to believe that what I saw in the pictures was all an act? It looked real enough to me. Real enough to ruin my day.

"I am." He grinned and searched for my hand again.

"William, I saw you kissing her on the rooftop the other day. Why deny it?"

"It's not what you think it is."

I shook my head with disappointment because I'd heard that line before, and it felt wrong to allow him to grab my hand and get close to me if I wasn't sure if he was in a relationship with someone else or not.

A part of me was dying to reach out for his hand, to pull him close to me, to have his lips meet mine—to end the agony. But the small yet smart part of me cautioned me to think twice before giving in.

Concentrate, Goddammit.

"It's hard for me to believe you're not in a relationship with her after all I've seen," I admitted. "Besides, I thought you weren't speaking to me."

"Well, I—I've been having a hard time with that," he whispered. He took a deep breath. "I did get back with Erin. I don't really know why. She kept— insisting. Apologizing. I thought I could give her a second chance."

There you go. I knew I wasn't crazy.

"How merciful of you." He couldn't reply to any of my texts where I said I was sorry and wanted to explain? But give the cheating ex-girlfriend a chance, while you're at it.

He chuckled, seemingly amused by my annoyance and pulled me closer to him. His warm, sweet breath collided against the coldness of my cheeks while the brisk night breeze steadily swirled between us. I remembered that delicious cinnamon scent from the last time he kissed me.

He gently tugged my hair tie, and my hair fell over my shoulders, on my back, around my face. "I like your hair down." *You've told me.* He teased my hair to blend out the crease from the tie. His fingertips on my scalp gave off tiny sparks of electricity. *Please stop, continue.*

"Erin and I are done. For good. I couldn't do it. I don't trust her, I don't—love her."

"And I—don't believe you," I whispered back. He tucked a strand of hair behind my ear, grazing my jaw with his knuckles when he pulled his hand away from my face. "Prove it."

"Challenge accepted." He leaned in to kiss me, but I pulled back before his eager, mouth-watering lips could meet mine.

"Not like that."

I knew he loved games, but I needed to make sure he was telling me the truth before I gave in. It was the hardest thing I had to do.

"So, *he* can kiss you, but not me?" he asked with indignation, unwilling to pull away from me. "Is it Caleb, then?"

Seeing me kiss Caleb had affected him, and I was so glad it did.

"He didn't leave at the first chance he got." I took a step back. "And he listens to me when I have something to say."

I still had some deep bottled feelings regarding our conversation following the fire incident. Or lack thereof. William shut me out, but *now* he wanted the opportunity he didn't give *me* to explain himself regarding Erin. And I had to agree to it and believe everything? That was unfair and totally not happening.

"You were kissing Thomas, and I thought that—"

"You didn't let me explain! And now you want me to listen? You told me that I was just like every other girl that's hurt you before. Do you still believe that? Because if you do, there's really no point in even pretending to have a civilized conversation right now."

William needed to know he wasn't the only one who felt like shit that night. "You pushed me away," I reminded him, "and I was trying to let you know what *I* wanted. And then you—disappeared. But it doesn't matter anymore."

My mercilessly ill mood was proving its resilience.

"It *does* matter to me. But I was furious—offended. I don't really believe any of the things I said. I admit to having a fragile ego, okay?" He tried holding my hand again, but I wasn't ready. "And what do you mean by *wanted*? Do you no longer want the same things you did?" He tucked another wind-dancing strand behind my ear.

"Honestly, I don't know what I want anymore." I took another step back just to be safe. "I thought I did." What I wanted was to be sure it hadn't all been just an infatuation on both sides, mostly his, or maybe a game he liked to play. If he wanted me, I needed him to make me *feel* it. I was done with pretty words and empty promises. And looking at those premiere photographs didn't help either.

He was used to things being easy, handed to him at a snap of his fingers. And it's not that I wanted to make things unnecessarily hard for him, but maybe that way, he would know for sure if what he wanted was me or not.

"I'm going to be away for a few days. I'll be promoting the film in Europe, and Erin's going to be coming along. But you have to know that whatever you see is not real."

I bit the corner of my lip, trying not to imagine them on a publicity tour together, pretending like they were still a couple.

That just made me want to puke.

My phone buzzed with an incoming call; it was my father "I need to take this," I told him, walking backward toward the exit.

"Is that one of your blind dates?" William yelled, leaning against the far end of the railing. "You've been keeping yourself busy!"

Tobias, you snitch!

"One of many!" I exclaimed, opening the rooftop door. If he had to pretend to date Erin, then I could pretend to have a bunch of blind dates waiting in line for me.

"I know what you want, Guille! And I'm going to refresh your memory!"

I closed the door shut and took my father's call, hoping William was a man of his word.

CHAPTER 9

Hope

October 21, 2009

TALKING TO WILLIAM last night was the leading cause of my renewed state of mind when I woke up this morning. Even though I wasn't sure if I believed him, I wanted to. My mind and my gut were still arguing about it.

My father wanted to have dinner with me. We usually had takeout at my place, but he was going to leave for a few days. He insisted on taking me somewhere nice.

I went to my 7:00 p.m. class with Grant, hoping to run into Tobias. I had some unfinished business to attend to with him.

"Hey, Billie!" Tobias said as he waltzed into the gym, looking cheerful like he always did.

"You betraying—tattletale-snitch-informant!" I said to him as a joke (but not really) as Grant took my gloves off.

"Whoa, Billie!" He lifted his hands and approached me. "Grant, why don't you hurry up and take those gloves off her hands."

"Whatchu do, man?" Grant asked with a grin as he kept to my bandages. "You know I'll be on her side either way."

I high-fived Grant and said, "Yes, why don't you tell him."

Tobias made a face that led me to believe he was about to say he didn't know what I was talking about.

"I don't know what she's talking about!" he exclaimed with a nervous laugh.

Ugh!

"Does the word *blind* ring any bells?" I clued him in.

"Ohhh! That!" He rubbed his hands. "Um, well, it's not like I ran up to tell him about it, you know? Billy's curious like that and asks a lot of questions, and ... shit! Okay, I shouldn't have said that either, but you know how he is. I'm sorry, Billie. I-I didn't mean to cause any trouble," he said in between stammers. I couldn't help but laugh.

I kind of liked the fact that William was asking around, wanting to know about me. Thanking Tobias was what I should've been doing instead because William knowing about the blind dates probably gave him the extra encouragement he needed to wake up from his daze.

"Don't worry. I know how he is. But I don't get why he's so curious, though, if he's back with Erin." I threw the hook in the water and hoped Tobias would take it. We couldn't pretend like Tobias didn't *know* what had happened before with William and me.

"I don't know. It's complicated, I guess. Billy doesn't talk much about his relationship status with her," he replied. That's not exactly what I wanted to hear. The words *complicated* and *relationship* don't go well together. Why hadn't William shared what he told me with his brother? Was he lying to me?

"Anyway, I have dinner plans to get to," I replied, trying to sound casual.

"Another blind date?" Tobias asked, raising his brows. He wanted to sound playful while expecting an honest answer from me. I shrugged and told him I'd see him around. Let them join the speculation club for a while.

☾

Someone knocked on my door. I assumed it was Caleb because he knew how much I hated my doorbell. I grabbed my shoes and purse and rushed to open the door. He probably wanted to walk me down to the car to meet my father.

"Hi!" I said with a smile.

"Hey, Red," he said, looking a little gray. "You seem to be in a better mood today."

Oh.

I'd forgotten all about the discussion we had last night. My little chat with William had brightened my mood, but Caleb still looked troubled. It was best if we sorted things out before leaving.

"Caleb, I'm sorry about yesterday. I swear I didn't even recognize myself. You're free to … well, do whatever you want and talk to whoever you wish. I shouldn't have said anything about it. I'm really sorry."

It stung to say it, but it was the truth. However, I preferred it if Caleb did the flirting around in his free time rather than in front of me. The unfair part was there was no way for *him* to escape witnessing who I saw, talked to, dated, and even kissed—at times.

"I'm sorry too. You were having a bad day, and you expressed that to me. I should've been more receptive to it, and I wasn't." He shook his head with embarrassment. "Ren's your friend, and I shouldn't be meddling in your affairs like that, even if he wasn't just a friend."

"Caleb, you know how much I care about you. I want us to always be okay, no matter what." I walked up to him and gave him a tight and affectionate hug. I settled my cheek on his chest and stayed there for more than a few seconds. I liked it there. So warm and safe.

Our relationship was tricky, but we needed to make it work. His hugs were always so cozy—easy.

The elevator doors opened behind us, and my father stepped

---

out of it. Caleb and I quickly broke away from the embrace, but it was too late.

"Hey, Dad!" I said enthusiastically, trying to create a diversion from the fact that he had just seen me and Caleb hugging. *Damn it.*

"Good evening, Mr. Murphy," Caleb said, taking a few steps back and holding his hands in a tight fist in front of him. The lines of his face were cold as stone.

"Good evening, Caleb," my father replied with an equally leveled tone. *Shit!* "You look lovely tonight." He kissed my cheek. "Don't you agree, Caleb?"

Dad! What the hell!

Caleb cleared his throat, noticeably uncomfortable. My father *was* expecting an answer because he wasn't looking away from him.

"Ah—" Caleb hesitated, unable to find the correct answer to my father's trick question.

"Dad, we're going to be late. We should go," I suggested instead, grabbing his arm. My father gave Caleb one last look and asked him to lock my apartment after grabbing my purse. Caleb had a key, and I'm sure my father regretted that decision.

If this is how my father reacted to a simple hug, imagine if he knew about all the *other stuff* that happened.

But there wasn't going to be any *stuff* happening with Caleb anymore. I understood now why he'd been so uncomfortable with the situation. My father could be a little exaggerated when it came to his *little girl*, and Caleb was aware of it.

As the three of us uncomfortably made our way to the lobby, my father's phone rang. He excused himself to take the call outside. Senad held the door for us. Caleb was waiting for me to walk out of the building, but I pulled his arm.

"Hey," I whispered. "Don't worry about it. I'm sure he didn't take it the wrong way." Caleb stood stiff as a board with his bodyguard stance, looking everywhere except my way.

"Miss Murphy, I suggest we start moving out," he said with a flat and grave tone, nodding once at the door.

"It's going to be okay. It's my fault. I was the one who hugged you." I kept whispering, looking over my shoulder a few times.

He seemed significantly affected. I wanted to reassure him that there wasn't going to be any trouble because of it. I knew how to handle my father. He would ask a few questions, and I would answer them in a way that would make him feel at ease.

Caleb's gaze traveled from the distant horizon to where my hand now rested on his arm.

"Caleb, look at me!" He kept a straight face and refused to make eye contact. I was done begging. I turned around and huffed my way out of the building. He followed me, of course, because he had to.

David was already sitting behind the wheel, and my father had just ended his call. A huge, bulky man in a black suit stood beside him. He looked somewhere around 6'5" and sported a completely shaved head—by far the scariest man I'd ever seen. But his brown eyes seemed friendly enough once he directed his gaze at me. I hoped.

"Mike, this is my daughter Billie," my father said to him.

"Nice to meet you, Miss Murphy," he said with a deep voice, extending his hand out to me. I shook it and said it was nice meeting him too.

After the quick introduction, my father instructed Mike to take his car to the restaurant and that we would meet him there. He wanted to ride with me.

My phone buzzed when I took a seat inside the SUV.

W.S: Hej, älskling.
W.S: What are you up to? Any exciting blind dates tonight?

My father glanced at my phone and cocked his head with a

creasing brow. "I hadn't realized you were using an iPhone now. When did you get it?"

"Well, my Blackberry fell into a pool during the summer when I was at William's house in the Hamptons for the photoshoot. So, I ... bought this one as a replacement," I lied. I wasn't going to tell him that William had bought it for me.

Caleb must've heard my phony explanation, but I didn't care. He surely preferred it if I didn't start talking about William.

I put my phone away and decided to reply to William after dinner. It wasn't going to do him any harm to wait for my response.

My father took my hand in between his and said, "I've been getting reports about you going on blind dates, sweetheart." I didn't understand why he brought it up in the car where Caleb's bionic hearing abilities could listen in without obstruction. "Caleb, I'm interested in your opinion about this topic. Do you think it's safe for Billie to go on these dates?" That's why.

Caleb sat still as a pond in winter. He turned around and replied firmly, "Mr. Murphy, I don't think that's for me to decide. It's our responsibility to keep her safe no matter what, as we always do."

"But according to the standard protocols in place, what would you advise?" My father insisted.

"Dad," I whispered. "I don't think I'll be going on any more blind dates. My friends set me up on both without my consent, but I talked to them, and it's not something that will be happening again," I assured him, but he wasn't backing down.

He wanted Caleb to participate on the subject because he asked for his opinion once again. He didn't have a choice but to keep expanding.

"A blind date puts us as security agents in a position where we cannot investigate much about the person prior to the meeting. And asking for the person's information upon arrival might be—invasive and uncomfortable for both the person in question and for Miss

Murphy, as well," Caleb explained. He didn't want to oppose the idea altogether but instead hinted it *could* complicate the logistics.

"I don't want my daughter dating anyone who doesn't go through a thorough background check. And Caleb, I want you to attend to this specific matter if such a situation should arise in the near future. If you deem the person inappropriate, I want you to inform me immediately. And I expect you to comply, kiddo," he said, looking at me.

"But Dad—"

"I'm not taking any chances. Not after what happened with Thomas."

This was extreme. So now Caleb got to decide who was fit to date me or not? Ridiculous!

Luckily, I wasn't looking to date anyone soon. I was probably going to CJ's party on my own. I wasn't in the mood to invite someone as my plus one. And William was dating Erin for all I knew. I still didn't know if he was lying to me about everything.

Luckily, we arrived at the restaurant, and the blind date conversation came to a halt. My father's face looked stern as we got out of the car. Seeing me hug Caleb had made him feel more uncomfortable than I thought. But I felt like there was something else bothering him.

Mike and David stayed outside while Caleb walked us both to our table. He helped me to my chair and excused himself afterward. As soon as Caleb left, I asked my father if there was something wrong and insisted on how I could tell he was upset about something.

The server approached us before my father could answer. We ordered our drinks, and my father finally started talking.

"Is there something going on between you and Caleb?" he asked bluntly. My hands felt sweaty and began to slightly shake under the table. There wasn't anything going on with Caleb, but something *did* happen. And it made me feel so guilty that it did, although I didn't regret it one bit.

"Of course not. You know we've been good friends for years."

"Why was he hugging you?" He was dead serious. But I couldn't let this affect Caleb in any way.

"Actually ... *I* hugged him. I was in a terrible mood yesterday, and I wasn't very polite to him. I apologized and hugged him afterward. But that was it," I assured him. He didn't look too convinced.

I'd never felt cornered by my father like this before. I saw a raw concern on his face. He seemed disappointed too. I didn't know if he was disappointed in Caleb, in me, or both of us.

"Did Caleb give you that iPhone? You know I allow you to use your credit card freely, but I always check the statements, and I haven't seen any charges for an iPhone."

I immediately denied it but lying about how I got it felt wrong. Besides, it would be absurd to say I was carrying that amount of cash with me because I never did, and he knew that.

"It was a gift," I confessed. "I couldn't get my old phone to work. And, um—William bought the iPhone for me. He wanted to help and wouldn't let me pay him back for it either."

"So, are you and William ... ?"

I took a deep breath. This was a full-on interrogation.

I explained how we were just friends and apologized for having him worry about everything. His features were softening back.

"No, no, I'm the one who should apologize, kiddo. I'm sorry. I've been so worried ever since you broke up with Thomas," he explained with a furrowed brow. "I'm considering having you move back with me for a while, at least until we can get things with him under control."

No!

Moving back with my father was the last thing I wanted to do. I had to convince him. But did he say *getting things with Thomas under control?* I didn't know things were *out* of control. He was probably trying to be extra careful with the situation.

"I don't think that's necessary. I haven't talked to Thomas in a while. The last time I saw him was more than a month ago when he showed up at the apartment building, but Caleb told me they were handling it."

I wondered if there was something they were trying to hide from me. It wouldn't be the first time. I knew my father had done that before, plenty of times, in his attempt to keep me inside a pink sparkling glass bubble.

"Is there something I need to know?" I asked, hoping to maintain the practice of keeping me in the dark in the past.

His face went grim again for a heartbeat, but I saw how he persuaded himself to draw a smile on his worried face. "No, you're right, kiddo. I'm probably just exaggerating. When I travel, I get anxious about not being here, but I know Aaron, Caleb, and David are doing an excellent job in taking care of you."

I rode the wave of interrogation and tried making a few questions myself. "Any news on mother? On the investigation, I mean."

"Oh, kiddo. You shouldn't be worrying about such things. All you need to know is that you're safe and that things are being properly handled."

"Is that why you're so anxious when you leave town for work?" He seemed uncomfortable with my questions. As he always did whenever I brought up the subject. He liked asking the questions but not answering any of mine. "I feel like I'm old enough to know. How could you still not know what happened that day?"

"Kiddo," he said firmly but smiled afterward. "With patience and time, all shall be explained." *That freaking quote again.* He stabbed a vegetable with his fork and took it to his mouth. "You have to try the tzatziki with the grilled eggplant."

He quickly changed the subject and asked about school and my boring midterms.

The check arrived, but I wanted to make sure my father felt at ease about the whole *Caleb hug situation* before we left. "Dad, I'm sure Caleb's feeling worried about what your thoughts were regarding the hug. Could it be possible for you to talk to him about it? Maybe tell him I've already cleared the air?" I feared Caleb would behave differently around me if my father didn't talk to him.

"Oh, of course. Don't worry about that either. I'll talk to Caleb."

My father left with Mike in his car, and I rode back home with David and Caleb, who still maintained a solemn and expressionless face on the entire way back. I tried making small talk, but he kept his answers short and evasive.

I remembered I had a few texts from William I had to get to, so I focused on that instead. Analyzing Caleb's attitude wasn't a task I wanted to get sucked into.

Me: I'm sorry. I was having dinner with an older man.

A couple of minutes later, William replied. I wondered if he had his phone attached to him because he always responded fairly quickly. When I wasn't being ghosted, of course.

W.S: How much older? Here I was, thinking I was too old for you.
Me: He turned 54 a few months ago.
W.S: You're shitting me, right?

I laughed out loud, imagining William's face. How I wished I could've seen it. Caleb snorted and readjusted himself on his seat, easing back into statue mode. David smiled, and I apologized for startling them.

Me: 100% not shitting you.
W.S: Should I be worried?
Me: Of course not.
W.S: I hope you're talking about your father.

And I hoped he wasn't traveling with Erin and that they had broken up for good. But a girl can dream, right?

Me: Hope is what keeps us going.
W.S: What keeps me going is that you'll stop going on blind dates. Or maybe we could pretend not to know each other if that's the kind of thing that turns you on. I can work with that. I'm open to experimenting. I want to know what you like.

Turns you on ... experimenting ... know what you like ... stop it!
I always had to be quick on my feet and fake self-confidence when texting with William. It was exciting but easier now that he wasn't sitting right beside me like when we rode back from the cottage last summer—although listening to his reactions from a front-row seat had been pretty fun too.

Me: Interesting. I could even pretend not to know what you do for a living and rekindle our bet.

He took a bit longer to reply, but he finally did.

W.S: I still can't get over that.

You know that awful feeling you get when you send a text, and you regret sending it a millisecond after you do? I felt that. I shouldn't have brought up the bet. That was one of the things that had angered him the most. It was a silly game, but it was *our* thing.

And it got ruined and then some.

Me: I wasn't happy about that either.

True. I daydreamed more times than I should've about how our date would've been because let's be honest ... I was going to lose. I wondered where he planned to take me, the things we would talk about, the kisses I would've allowed him to give me ... all gone. Nothing more than a daydream.

W.S: I'll think of some other way to trick you into a date with me, don't worry. Just don't google me before I get back to New York, ok?
Me: I thought you wanted me to google you.
W.S: I was furious. I said things I didn't mean that day. It's hard enough to pretend to be with Erin for the premieres. But I don't want you to see it. Once I'm back, I'll be done with the charade. I need you to trust me.

Trust—a struggle. I knew that refraining from googling the events was the most reasonable thing to do, but my curious nature would have difficulty resisting the temptation. And since hope was the night's theme ... I hoped William was telling the truth about Erin and that I could find the strength to stop worrying about it.

And Caleb ... Well, he didn't offer to walk me to my door when we arrived home.

Whatever.

CHAPTER 10

Cohen

October 29, 2009

I BARELY TALKED to William on the days he was away. I assumed he was busy working, and the time difference wasn't helpful either. He was promoting his new film in Europe, so he traveled to a different country every other day. I behaved myself and hadn't googled him, just as he asked me. That helped me not to think about him with Erin in that setting.

I still hadn't asked anyone to come with me to CJ's party, and I didn't have a costume. CJ had called to pressure me into inviting someone as soon as possible. He even offered to fix me up with someone, but that wasn't going to happen. Not again. I was in denial about going to the party. I don't know why.

William texted me today to let me know he would arrive in New York late at night. I still couldn't help but be skeptical about the things he said to me. Silent anxiety crept up on me like a night predator.

What was true is that I couldn't stop thinking about him. Maybe that's why I hadn't invited anyone to CJ's party. I was secretly hoping William would come with me. And I didn't know if that was even possible or if he would want to come. But I played around with the thought during class most of the day.

Our teacher dismissed us earlier than usual after handing in a project. It was still early. I decided to go for a run before training with Grant at 7:00 p.m.

Me: Caleb, I'm going out for a run. Can I meet you downstairs in ten?
Caleb: Of course, Miss Murphy. David and I will see you there.

Caleb kept calling me *Miss Murphy*, even when we were alone or when we texted privately. He couldn't get over the fact that my father saw us hugging and wanted to pretend like we weren't friends anymore. More like we never were or hadn't kissed more than a few times.

And I don't know about him, but that was kind of hard to forget.

On our way back from our run, I stopped at Gapstow Bridge, one of my favorite landmarks in Central Park. There are many beautiful spots here, but the stone's warmth and the climbing plants that envelop Gapstow Bridge captivated me.

"Caleb, I need to talk to you," I said with a commanding voice. He felt uncomfortable behaving as he used to around me. I tried changing how I directed myself to him too. It was either that or no communication whatsoever. If he sensed I was trying to be too friendly, he would back off and completely shut me out.

"Yes, Miss Murphy," he said in between subtle vaporous pants. It was a cold and foggy afternoon, and we all had stopped running abruptly, which made me feel out of breath too. I walked up toward the highest part of the bridge and waited for him. He quickly followed me and stood to my left with his annoying bodyguard stance.

"*This*—needs to stop, Caleb." I gestured from him to me and back. "We're friends. I know you're on duty right now, but that never stopped you before from being friendly with me. And now you're just—cold. Mean."

Caleb looked in every direction except mine as if he were evaluating the multiple potential *threats* around me.

Unnecessary.

"Caleb, look at me!" I didn't care about the few people staring as they walked by. His attitude was exasperating.

He peeked over his shoulders and took a few steps forward. He leaned in and whispered with his thick accent, "Miss Murphy, your father has made it perfectly clear about what his expectations are regarding my duties and responsibilities while on the job." He finally met my steady, unblinking gaze. "And off the job, too."

He was taking his *job* too seriously.

"What did you two talk about?" I wondered what my father had told him to make him act this way.

Caleb refused to answer my question. I explained how I'd cleared the air with my father concerning the hug—making it apparent that *I* had hugged him. Not the other way around.

"I reminded my father that we're friends and have been for a while now. He assured me he would talk to you after I mentioned how you felt uncomfortable by the situation. Did you get the opportunity to talk?"

Caleb took a deep breath while a couple of sweat droplets ran down his temples. Since he was unwilling to speak, I took my phone out and told him I would call my father for answers.

"Wait." He closed his eyes and rubbed his forehead. I tucked my phone back in my jacket pocket and waited for him to start talking. He placed both of his hands on the stone railing and let his head drop. "We did talk, and he wasn't happy," he began. "I know you tried explaining, but it wasn't enough. He told me he was disappointed and that he expected better from me. But I feel like shit now because he's right. I *should* know better than to get involved with my boss's daughter."

It was so disappointing to hear that my father had told me one thing and Caleb another. He was still treating me like a child, which made me feel like he didn't trust me to know how to make any right decisions for myself.

"So, you're saying we cannot be friends because my father says so?" I crossed my arms in front of me. "What are we, ten?"

Caleb couldn't avoid a short and wry chuckle from escaping him, but he quickly reigned in his emotions to where he wanted them—all to himself. "No, we can't. Not if I want to keep my job."

"You know you're ruining my favorite spot in the park, right?"

"I'm sorry, Miss Murphy. I intend to keep my job," he repeated. "And those are the conditions your father gave me. I need to keep my distance." Ironic. His job consisted of the very opposite of keeping his distance from me.

"Miss Murphy? We're *alone*, Caleb," I reminded him, looking around. "And you're going to keep calling me that?" That was some next-level bullshit.

My attempts to make him come around were useless. He had made up his mind about the situation.

"There's a reason why I never called you Red in front of anyone else who wasn't Aaron. I know your father. It was stupid of me to think he would ever be okay with us being together," he said with a scowl.

That was just mean.

"Well, I like it better when you're stupid." I walked away. "Let's go, Cohen. It's getting cold."

My muscles felt stiff. Resuming our run wasn't an option. I pulled my cell phone out and texted my father as we walked back home.

Me: I don't have many friends. Caleb was one of my closest ones. And not only did you take that friendship away from me, but you lied to me. You weren't supposed to make Caleb feel worse.

I sent my father the text as my throat threatened to close in on me. I had never been this angry with my father before. Not like this.

There was still time before my class with Grant started, but boy did I look forward to punching things around because I discovered I also had a temper. And not only that, but I was having difficulty hiding it.

My life before New York was so different—easygoing. Maybe I'd always been this way, but there hadn't been any significant events to trigger me into anger.

I was angry and disappointed not only with Caleb but more so with my father.

Why was he deceiving me like that? He didn't think I was capable of making my own choices. How could my friendship with Caleb harm me in any way? If anything, Caleb had saved me countless times of what I thought was a permanent feeling of dread. My father must've known that. He knew everything.

I needed Caleb to be Caleb.

But for now, he was going to be Cohen.

He needed to feel what I felt when he refused to stop calling me Miss Murphy. And maybe, that way, I would eventually make him come around. Or perhaps our friendship was destined to end. Permanently.

What was the use of him promising to stay if we couldn't even talk?

My mind kept going around in loops during Grant's class. He sensed I was distracted but kept training me as usual.

Tobias walked in while Grant removed my bandages. "Hey, Tob," I greeted him with a weary smile. It was odd that Tobias hadn't asked me if "everything was okay." I was thankful, though. Was I wearing a sign that said: *Don't mess with me?*

He countered his greeting with one of his big, bright, and sincere smiles instead and sat on the bench, waiting for Grant to be done with me. "Any plans for the weekend?" Tobias asked, resting his elbows on his knees, making small talk as I gathered my things.

"Um, yeah. I have this Halloween costume party tomorrow," I replied. "How about you?" I didn't want to sound disrespectful by not asking back, but all I wanted was to have a scorching shower to match my frustration and have some peace at home.

"Well, there's a charity gala tomorrow, and William wants me to go with him. It's one of those boring events where you need to dress up and say hi to a bunch of people you don't know." He chuckled.

It bummed me out that William was busy tomorrow. He hadn't texted me either. I didn't know at what time he'd be arriving. I foolishly thought I could find a way for him to come with me to CJ's party. I knew I could trick William into inviting himself and make it seem like it was his idea.

I guess I was stuck with *Cohen* and David as my plus twos.

"Oh, I know all about those events," I replied. My father had taken me to *plenty* of those types of functions in his past ambassador days—more than I would've liked. I didn't miss them. "But don't worry, I'm sure you can find yourselves some girls that would be willing enough to attend an afterparty at your apartment once you're done with the pleasantries."

Tobias laughed because that was probably what he had in mind.

"Tobias, let's go!" Grant shouted.

He rubbed his hands and stood up. "Have fun tomorrow."

"You too." *But not that much.*

I walked to my apartment, took a shower, and laid on my bed wearing my robe and a towel wrapped around my head. I couldn't even count to ten when my doorbell rang.

You've got to be kidding me!

I marched to the foyer, completely annoyed about having to stand up from my bed and screamed when I saw who it was.

CHAPTER 11

French Delivery

"BILLIE!" Sophie and Cecile yelled my name in unison and tackled me with a group hug.

"Oh, my God!" I couldn't believe my eyes. I felt immediately embarrassed by my outfit or lack of an appropriate one. I pulled the towel off my head because I looked ridiculous. Aaron and David rolled their luggage inside with a smile on their faces and excused themselves. Aaron knew how close we were, but it didn't take much to see how happy I was about the surprise visit.

I cried as we held each other.

"What's wrong?" Sophie asked with a pout.

"Nothing! I'm just so happy to see you. This is the best surprise ever! But how—why?" I didn't know how much I missed them until I saw them both standing in front of me.

"Your father thought you would appreciate us coming to see you," Cecile explained. "We're only staying until Sunday, though. It's an express visit. We have to get back to school. And ... Aaron said I should give you this."

A note.

Just a reminder that you have friends, kiddo.
James

My father was trying to make up for taking Caleb away from me. He didn't need me to send him an angry text to figure out I was probably not enjoying the situation. He obviously knew it. But even if I was still mad at him, he was undoubtedly on the right path to gaining my forgiveness. It was a grand gesture on his part.

"We're going to have so much fun!" Sophie screamed with excitement.

"Do you guys want to go out and have dinner?" I asked, brushing the silly tears away.

"That would be great," Cecile replied. "I thought we could go try some of that famous New York pizza everyone talks about."

"Perfect. Let me put some clothes on. This is your room if you want to get yourselves settled. I'll be right back."

We quickly got ready and left.

Cecile looked over her shoulder and said, "There's three of them now, huh?" as we walked to a nearby pizza place.

"They usually work in pairs," I whispered. "I guess my father wanted to make sure we're safe. He's out of town, and it must make him feel at ease to know we're well taken care of."

"Oh no, we won't be able to have a glass of wine!" Sophie complained, remembering we weren't twenty-one yet.

"I know, it sucks," I replied. "But don't worry. There's a party tomorrow, so you'll be able to have your glass of wine there. It's a couples costume party. CJ insists they're going to be strict about it at the door. We'll figure something out."

All the Caleb drama and the bummer of knowing William wouldn't come made me doubt if going was a good idea, but CJ would kill me if I didn't. Not going wasn't an option.

"We *have* to go," Sophie replied excitedly. "That sounds like so much fun. What are you planning to wear? We need to get costumes."

"I don't know yet. I thought we could buy or rent something tomorrow."

"So, what's been going on with you, Billie? Your father tells us he's been worried about you ever since you broke up with Thomas. I thought you were feeling confident in that decision. Is there something else going on, or do you just miss him?" Cecile asked, then took a bite of her pizza.

"No, no. It's *definitely* over with Thomas."

I hadn't mentioned anything about William or Caleb. I'd been secretive about the whole thing, even with them. The only information they had about William was that I had a stupidly handsome and annoying neighbor that was slowly growing in on me. But that was it. They didn't know *who* he was or anything else that had happened.

"Breaking up with Thomas was messy, literally." I explained how he kicked the artwork and pushed the flower vase the day I told him it was over for good.

"So, what are you not telling us?" Cecile narrowed her eyes. She knew me well.

"Do you remember I mentioned my neighbor before?"

"Sure, of course. William. What about him?" Cecile kept pressing.

I took a deep breath and came clean about everything. I told them about the cottage, the burnt cake, the kiss with Thomas, and how William saw us.

"Noooo!" Sophie exclaimed, biting her pizza.

"Yes," I replied with a quick and humorless grimace. "Thomas thought I was, and I quote 'into fucking celebrities now,' and so with that, he revealed William's profession, ruined our bet, and made William hate me." I sighed. Retelling the story was exhausting and hurtful.

"What is William's last name?" Sophie asked, dropping her pizza on the plate.

"Um, Sjöberg," I replied, biting the corner of my lower lip and looking down at my empty plate.

"What!" Sophie screamed. Cecile shushed her, and Sophie apologized with a whisper.

"How the hell didn't you know *who* he was?" Cecile asked, taking another bite of her pizza.

"I don't know. I'm a freak, I guess."

"You read too much. You need to get Netflix," Sophie said, nodding.

"No, she doesn't. I think it's cute you didn't recognize him. I bet he was going crazy about not having that power over you. You know, it must've been a breath of fresh air after all the girls he's dated."

"What do you mean?" I asked abruptly. Sophie glared at Cecile, who rarely had a filter. I saw girls coming in and out of the apartment building a few times during the summer, but I wanted to know what she meant. "What girls? Tell me what you know."

I knew he was a charmer. But I hadn't googled *him*—just that premiere where I saw him with Erin. And that had been enough googling for me.

"Well, it's only natural for a guy that looks like *that* to have an easy pick on who to date," Cecile voiced her opinion. "He's known for having dated many celebrities and models in the past years."

"So, he's a playboy?" I asked, wishing it was April 11, 2010, so I could order a glass of wine.

Thomas's words came flying back; "he's going to chew you up and spit you out." For all I knew, William was busy *chewing* on Erin. I just hoped he could *spit* her out for good. I wondered how many other Erin's had been there before. Shit.

"Who cares? I wouldn't," Sophie said, raising her hand and sipping on her coke.

"The problem is that he went back to his ex soon after all this happened. He's been telling me it's over, and I get the feeling he's, I don't know, interested in me? But I want to be sure things are *really* over with her and that he's not playing games with me just because he saw me kissing Caleb."

Oh, well, shit.

I took a bite on my first slice of pizza, hoping it would shut me up. It tasted like nothing.

"Excuse me, what?" Cecile asked in between coughs. I was afraid she would choke.

"Oh yeah, that too," I replied casually. "Caleb and I had a— situation. But it ended quickly after it began. We didn't want to ruin our friendship." I didn't want to get into any more details about my relationship with Caleb. It was still too complicated to explain.

"So, are you back to being friends?" Sophie asked.

"I don't know. I think that's why my father brought you here. He's trying to *cheer me up*"—I air-quoted—"because he saw me hugging Caleb last week outside of my apartment, and he wasn't thrilled. Now Caleb's freaked out on me, and he keeps calling me Miss Murphy. It's *so* annoying, and I don't know, I just feel like I lost him." I sighed and dared a quick peek toward the window, but he wasn't looking our way.

"I'm sure he'll come around. Give him time. You'll see. Caleb adores you," Cecile said. Was it that obvious? Because to me, it wasn't anymore. "I'm sorry, but I need to ask. Who's the best kisser?" Cecile's question made us laugh.

"Caleb's lips must be the most kissable ever, right? They're so … juicy." Sophie chuckled, looking over her shoulder in Caleb's direction.

"Sophie! He's standing right outside," I whispered. And taking into consideration my father's apprehension, I feared he had bugged my phone or purse. Or both. Or maybe *I* was bugged. But she urged me to answer. "Um, well, they both defended themselves nicely, I suppose." I lowered my brows and played around with my pizza. I couldn't help but browse through memories and replay said kisses in my mind. Mostly the ones with William.

"New York's suited you," Cecile added with a continuous approving nod. "And *we* are here to have fun and make the best of these few days we have together, okay?"

"I would like to add," I warned, looking at Sophie, "that not only does William live in the building, but his entire family does too. So it's highly probable we *might* run into any of them, and I want you to be cool. No sudden squeaking, or asking for photographs, autographs, or anything of the sort."

"Hey! What are you looking at me for?" Sophie complained.

"Sophie, come on," Cecile said, tilting her head. We all laughed because even Sophie knew that was true.

As we walked back home, I received a text from Lily.

Lily: Hey, Billie! Joel's not home right now. Wanna hang out?
Me: Hi! Sure. I'm a few blocks away. Two friends from Paris just got here a few hours ago. Do you mind if they join us?
Lily: Of course not! I'd love to meet them. Do you want to come up to my place?
Me: Sounds good. We'll be right there in a few minutes.

"That was Lily. Joel's girlfriend," I said, slipping my phone back inside my purse. "She's inviting us up to her apartment to hang out for a while. Do you feel up for it?"

"Yes!" Sophie replied instantly, almost breathlessly. Cecile shook her head at Sophie's overexcited reaction but agreed to go too.

Sophie stopped at a magazine kiosk on our way back and quickly grabbed one off the rack and stared at the cover.

"Do you want to get that?" I asked, and that's when I saw what Sophie was looking at: ***"WILLER: STRONGER THAN EVER!"***

Willer? They had their couple nickname and everything?

A paparazzi photograph of William and Erin holding hands

and walking down the street in what seemed like a European city accompanied the bold headline.

My blood dropped to my feet, and my breathing felt heavy—dense. Something resembling a heatstroke took over me. I couldn't stop staring at the magazine cover.

"Sophie, drop it. Let's go," Cecile ordered.

Caleb approached us to ask if everything was okay. *Now you're worried?*

"None of your business, *Cohen*," I replied, walking off with Sophie and Cecile on each arm.

William, you son of a bitch! He made me believe it was over—that he was finding it *hard* to stay away from me. All along, he was texting me with one hand while holding Erin's with the other.

I stormed to my apartment, and Caleb, not able to resist his busybody tendencies, followed us right up to my door.

"Miss Murphy, I—"

"That'll be all, Cohen," I cut him off and shut the door in his face.

We weren't friends with Cohen. Not anymore.

"Billie, do you want to talk about it?" Cecile whispered as she placed her bag on the foyer table. I nodded and walked to the living room. Sophie and I dropped our bags on the coffee table, and the three of us sat to talk.

I was fuming and couldn't recognize myself or understand why seeing those photographs affected me so much. And as much as I tried, I couldn't make myself snap out of it.

Breathe.

"I had my doubts, but still, deep down, a huge part of me was hopeful." I couldn't even cry. I was infuriated. "How could I have been that stupid? To think that someone like him would be interested in me?"

Cecile took a deep breath. They were both waiting for me to be done talking, but there wasn't much left to say. I was embarrassed and felt like the most pathetic human to ever set foot on the planet.

"Fuck him," Cecile muttered, squeezing my hand. "We're here for you."

"We should probably skip the party altogether."

"No." Cecile gripped my hand even harder. "We'll get our costumes tomorrow, and I'm sure you can ask three friends to come with us as a friendly group date, and we'll have the best time." She stared at me with an intoxicating determination. Sophie didn't seem to know what to say, but I could tell by the sad look on her face that she felt terrible about the situation.

"Okay, you're right," I replied, trying to convince myself that going to CJ's party was a good idea.

Sitting around to mope over William wasn't an option. I should've known better. And yes, I did have friends, and I was planning on having a great time with them.

I planned on texting Ren to invite him to the party. Maybe he could ask two more friends to come with us.

I took a deep breath and stood up.

"Come on, let's go. Lily's waiting for us."

My phone buzzed.

W.S: Hey, Guille. I'm at the airport.

Good for you. I tossed the phone back into my purse.

I would never believe a single word that came out of William's mouth ever again.

CHAPTER 12

Cheerio!

LILY OPENED THE DOOR and greeted me with a hug. "Lily, this is Sophie and Cecile. Sophie, Cecile, this is Lily." I introduced them, and after all the double cheek-kissing, we stepped into the apartment. I was doing my best to hide my emotions, but Lily quickly noticed something was off.

There was a bottle of red wine and four wine glasses on the coffee table waiting for us.

"Shiraz, anyone?" Lily offered.

"Yes, please," the three of us replied in unison. We laughed. We needed it. I needed a freaking glass of wine. Or two. We'd have to wait and see.

"For how long are you guys staying? Do you have any plans for the weekend?" Lily asked.

"We leave on Sunday," Sophie replied. I wished they could stay forever. Sunday was only three days away. I was already sad about them leaving, and they had just arrived a few hours ago.

"It's CJ's birthday tomorrow. We're going to his Halloween-themed party. But I have no idea what I'm going to wear yet or who I'm going to invite. We need three guys to get in."

Lily sprang up from her seat. "I have the perfect costume for you!" she cried excitedly and disappeared into her bedroom.

She came back holding a beautiful teal silk dress with a thigh-high slit and tiny rhinestones sewn on both the straps and the plunging v-neckline's hem. On her other hand, she held a short blonde wig with bangs.

"Elvira Hancock." She angled her head at the wig. "It will look *beautiful* on you. Besides, we're the same size."

I didn't know if I could pull that look off. I mean, that was some badass, revealing costume. Lily was taller than me, but the dress didn't seem very long. With the right pair of heels, it would work perfectly.

"Just try it on," she urged, walking toward the guest room. I followed her. She shut the door and said, "Okay, tell me what's wrong."

I pursed my lips and glanced at her from the corner of my eye as I undressed. "Lily, I don't know, it's—" I hesitated. I wanted so badly to tell her everything, but she was too close to William. I felt like she was his sister.

"You can trust me."

She removed the dress from the hanger and passed it to me.

"Okay." I sighed as I put the dress on. "It's about William."

"What did he do this time?" Lily asked, zipping me up.

"He's been telling me how he's ended things with Erin and that it's all for publicity. But Sophie just saw this stupid tabloid on a magazine stand with a photograph of Erin and William holding hands in Europe."

Lily's eyes went wide for a second. I sat on the bed and continued. "I'm so disappointed because I really like him, Lily. And I know I messed up kissing Thomas that day, but he didn't let me explain." I huffed air out with exasperation.

"Billy can be—a bit proud sometimes."

No shit.

"But it doesn't matter now because he's been lying to me this entire time."

"I know you're thinking the worst, but don't believe everything you read in tabloids. I'm not trying to defend him, but do you know how many times I've 'broken up' with Joel? I've lost count already. It's insane." Lily sat next to me.

"I get how words can be easily made up, but this was a paparazzi photograph, Lily. I saw it."

"Look, I know this sucks. And I wish I could tell you more, but I haven't talked to Billy. He's been super weird and hermetic about Erin. He's been away too, and he's not talking to Joel about her either. I don't know why that is, but he tends to shut off from the world sometimes, including us."

"I don't know why I even got excited about him. I should've known better."

"Well, he's insane. He would be the luckiest guy to have a girl like you as a girlfriend. And yeah, he's dated a shit ton of girls. I'm not going to lie to you. But I've never seen him like—*in love*, in love. And I thought I saw him genuinely excited about you during the summer."

Lily stood up and gave me a pair of heels to see if the length of the dress was okay. I tried them on and stood up to check. It was perfect.

"When we were at the cottage," Lily continued. "I thought I saw this—spark in his eyes. You two had some good fun that night, didn't you?"

I didn't want to remember that weekend at the cottage. Our conversation, the kissing, the flirting. I missed it. I saw that spark in William's eyes too, and I'm sure he saw a million more in mine. But a spark can extinguish as fast as it gets ignited.

"I guess we did." I wrinkled my lips to the side. It was useless to reminisce on any of that. "Please don't mention any of this to Joel."

"Of course not. You know I wouldn't." She placed her hands on my shoulders and led me out. "There's a floor-to-ceiling mirror in the foyer. You need to look at yourself and see what Billy's missing out on."

The dress was made for my body. It hugged me in all the right places. I was convinced Thomas would've asked me to change out of it.

"It looks great on you," Sophie said with a sunny smile.

"Mhm, it's a definite winner," Cecile agreed.

"You have to wear it." Lily insisted. "Besides, the wig is so much fun. Touch it. It's natural hair."

"Are you sure it's okay to borrow this?" I hesitated as I stared at my reflection in the mirror. The dress looked expensive, and I was afraid to ruin it.

"Of course, silly. I really don't mind. I've already used it twice."

I guess Lily had much more from where that dress came from. She told me how designers would give her lots of clothing, bags, shoes, etc., so I accepted Lily's offer and agreed to dress up as Elvira Hancock for the party.

We heard a key unlocking the door to Lily's apartment from the outside. And something tensed up inside me.

Joel walked in with a guy behind him, rolling a big suitcase each, and I relaxed once again because I didn't care to see William's face right now.

"Nate!" Lily shouted. "What on Earth are you doing here?" She ran to the door, kissed Joel, and hugged Nate.

"Nathan's moving back to New York. He'll be staying here until he finds an apartment," Joel said to Lily.

"Oh, my God! That's amazing! I don't know if I should be happy for you guys or worried about me. Please don't take my boyfriend away."

Nathan laughed. "I can't promise anything," he replied with a crisp British accent. "You know how clingy he is."

Joel shoved Nathan's shoulder with his and greeted me with a hug afterward.

"Nathan, Billie, Billie, Nathan."

"How do you do?" Nathan removed his jacket and grinned at me, looking down at my dress with his grayish-green eyes. He was wearing dark gray slacks and a neatly tucked-in white button-down shirt. His shoes looked pristine. He reminded me of my father, who always travels in style. The only thing that gave him away from the fact that he had just flown across the Atlantic was his brown, wavy hair that was a second away from looking unruly.

Hi.

"Nice to meet you, Nathan." I looked down at my dress and said, "I should probably go change."

"Nonsense, you look lovely."

The old Billie would've probably blushed right there on the spot. But no more blushing for anyone. Even if they look like— that. Like a real man. *How old is he?*

"Joel, this is Sophie and Cecile. They're Billie's friends from Paris. They're here for the weekend," Lily said. Both Joel and Nathan approached to greet them as I escaped to the guest room to change out of the dress.

Once back in my clothes, I opened the door, and Nathan was waiting right outside with his two suitcases. "Are we sharing the room?" he asked casually.

"Oh, no. I live downstairs in 9A. I was just trying on the dress for a costume party." I quickly stepped out of the room, holding the dress. Nathan rolled the suitcases inside and came back out.

There was a knock on the door, and Joel rushed to open it while I had a mini heart attack.

Tobias.

Please, no more brothers! I wouldn't be able to handle it if William arrived.

"Joel told me this son of a bitch had arrived," Tobias said. He walked up to Nathan, and they hugged each other with big pats on the back.

"Hey, Billie." He smiled. Sophie's eyes went big and round.

"Hey, Tob. This is Sophie and Cecile. They just arrived from Paris."

"Nice to meet you both." His gaze instantly darted toward Cecile.

Joel and Nathan took a seat in the living room with beers in their hands. Nathan rubbed his face. He looked exhausted.

Lily stared at me like a cobra and shifted her sight toward Nathan and back at me. She nodded once, and I shook my head twice. *Lily don't do it!*

"So, Billie, have you decided who to take to the party? You're three guys short." Lily dropped the bomb and walked to the kitchen to grab some snacks, she said.

"You didn't mention anything yesterday about needing dates for the party," Tobias said to me, his eyebrow moving up.

"Um, yeah. It's a silly requirement."

Nathan talked to Joel in Swedish but stopped to listen to our conversation.

"I thought we could get in the party with Aaron, Caleb, and David." I hadn't thought about that option before, but it could work. The person posted at the party's entrance could think they were disguised as bodyguards. I could probably make them wear sunglasses to complete their looks.

"Boring," Tobias interjected. "I'll go. You're two guys short now. But why don't you ask a couple of those guys you met from all the blind dates you've been going to recently?" He laughed as he took the free seat next to Cecile and picked at the snacks that Lily had just set on the table.

I glowered at him, but he just laughed even more. "Don't you have some boring event to go to with your brother?" But that wasn't a half-bad idea. I'd been thinking about asking Ren to come too. I could tell him it was a casual group date of sorts.

"I'm sure Billy will survive without me," Tobias replied. He was ditching William. Nice.

"Well, I'm free tomorrow," Nathan said casually, taking a sip of his beer. Lily, who stood behind him, stuck the tip of her tongue out at me. She got away with it.

But then I remembered … the background checks. Caleb would have to check Nathan out first. A hint of mortification brewed inside me, but I choked it immediately because I was done worrying about everything and everyone's opinion. If Nathan didn't want a background check, then whatever. Ren could bring another friend who wouldn't mind getting one.

"I'm going to need some ID." I laughed. At least I'd try to make it fun. Nathan stared at me. Curious.

"You're dead serious, aren't you?"

I stuck my hand out as a reply. He threw a curious-filled smile at me and stood up to take his wallet out of his pocket.

I snapped a picture of his ID from both sides and sent it to the security group chat.

1982. He's seven years and a few months older than me. I swallowed hard and gave Nathan his ID back. I excused myself and told him I would explain everything in a few minutes.

Me: I need Nathan Saunders approved for a date. It's for CJ's party. Tobias will be coming too, and I'm about to check with Ren if he's available. We won't be allowed inside the party without dates.

There I was asking Caleb if he could approve a date for me. That was the most insane dynamic ever! And probably my father's way of punishing him—*and* me.

Caleb: It's going to be tight, Miss Murphy.
Me: What do you mean?
Caleb: He's British. There's a different protocol for foreigners.
It could take a few days.
Me: What? The party's tomorrow. Ren has a Spanish ID, and
you cleared him in a few hours.
Caleb: We're being more thorough now. I'll get back to you.

I knew they had access to investigate anyone in minutes. But days? Perhaps Nathan's ID photograph wasn't stimulating for Caleb. He looked ... hot. Who looks like *that* in their ID? He did.

Everyone chit-chatted while I texted at the dining room table. I turned left and saw Nathan looking my way. He jerked his chin at me with a smile and turned his attention back to Joel.

Damn, okay. For a few seconds there, I forgot what I was doing sitting at the dining room table.

Ren. Yes, Ren.

Me: Hey Ren! What are you up to tomorrow night? A couple of
friends from Paris are here for the weekend, and we're going to
a costume party tomorrow. Do you want to join us? We could
meet at my apartment and leave together.
Ren: Hi, Billie! So glad you reached out to me. Sure thing.
Do I need to wear a costume?
Me: Mandatory.
Ren: I'll be there. Text me your address.

That was easy.

Tobias kept making small talk with Cecile, who sat there looking like the classical French beauty she is. She was still dating Paul and didn't seem excited about talking to Tobias. However, she was being friendly and reciprocating the conversation.

Sophie seemed starstruck while talking to Lily, but I knew she hoped she could be the one sitting next to Tobias.

I walked back to the living room and took a seat next to Nathan. In the old days, I would've sat on the other side of the living room, far from anyone who could make me nervous. But sitting next to Nathan was necessary. I needed to explain the background check situation to him.

"Hi." I smiled.

"Anything else you need from me?" he asked, reciprocating my gesture. "Passport? Bank statements? A letter of intent?" He laughed.

"Probably." I chuckled and took a deep breath. "Okay. So, you need to get approved by my guys. They'll run a quick check on you, and if you're cleared, you can come to the party."

"You're not joking, are you? I thought you were being cheeky."

"Sadly, no. Any—*surprises* they might bump into?" I asked jokingly.

"I'm squeaky clean. I'm a lawyer. I know how to cover my tracks."

I laughed with a tinge of nerves. The age difference startled me. He was about to turn twenty-eight on December 12. His neatly maintained stubble beard and rugged facial features sure made him look like a mature grown-up. But he was Joel's friend and a few months younger than him. No big deal.

I took my passport out and showed it to him because I needed to behave like a normal person. Caleb would've thrown a fit if he knew I allowed an *unauthorized stranger* to see my personal information, but Nathan needed to know my age. It was only fair. I'd let him find out for himself, of course.

"I'll have to take a picture of this too, Miss—" he said while he scanned through my information, "Murphy." He shot a picture of it and put his phone away as he stared at my passport photo. "You look so terribly young here."

Terribly.

"Um, yeah. I was seventeen when I renewed my passport." His eyes widened for a second when he heard the word *seventeen* as if it were a sin. I think the first word that probably came to his lawyer's mind was *illegal.* "But that was a few years ago," I said, reinforcing the fact that I was most definitely *not* seventeen anymore.

"Three exactly." He said it as if we were talking about days or weeks instead of years. He closed the passport with a frown and gave it back to me. "You don't look twenty."

"Oh, thanks. Do I look old to you?" I laughed.

"I thought you might be Lily's age, at least." *Thought or hoped?* "You're Zara's age," he said in barely a whisper, almost to himself.

"Who's Zara?"

"Baby sister."

Oh. He was shocked by my age, I could tell. I was also stunned by the almost eight-year difference, but who cares? My parents had a twelve year difference between them. Besides, I just met the guy. And who knew if Caleb would "approve." Since the decision now relied on him, I was probably not dating anyone for the rest of my life.

Sophie yawned, and that was my cue for us to leave. I'd forgotten they had just flown in from Europe and were likely exhausted.

"I think we should head back to the apartment," I said, standing up. "I need these two to rest for tomorrow."

"Oh, of course. I can imagine you must be tired," Lily quickly replied to them. "Make sure to text me a few pics of your final look tomorrow, okay?"

We all said our goodbyes and headed toward the elevator.

"Murphy!" Nathan shouted from the door. I turned around, and he was leaning against the door frame with his hands tucked inside his pockets. "Let me know if I should get a costume or not."

"You'll know when I know." I smiled and stepped inside the elevator.

"Fair 'nuff." He smiled back a sexy smile. "Cheerio!"

CHAPTER 13

Do Not Pass Go

October 30, 2009

I SKIPPED SCHOOL altogether because I wanted to spend the entire day with Sophie and Cecile. Plus, we needed to go shopping for our costumes. My training with Grant had to be canceled too.

Caleb, David, and I went for an early morning run since my friends were still sleeping. They needed to rest. And I sure needed a run. The whole William thing from last night still had my head spinning. I didn't wake up feeling sad about it, just angry and disappointed. Running always helped clear my head.

Caleb was extra weird and robotic before we left for our run. I asked him about Nathan's status, and he told me it was still in process. I was 99.999% sure that Nathan would be cleared, but Caleb wanted to keep me waiting until the last minute—his new way of having fun, I guess.

When I got back from my run, I poured myself a second cup of coffee and sat in my living room to check on my messages.

Tobias: Hey Billie! Why don't we meet at your place tonight before leaving? I'll bring a nice bottle of tequila.

It was barely nine in the morning, and Tobias was already

mentioning tequila. I couldn't help but roll my eyes at the screen with a smile. Meeting up before leaving seemed like a pretty good idea. That way, everyone would get a chance to meet Ren.

Me: Hey, Tob. Sure! How does 8 p.m. sound? P.S.
I'm scared about the tequila.
Tobias: Nate and I will take care of you, don't worry.
See you at 8.

Right. Well, we needed to wait for Caleb to feel like letting me know if Nathan could come, but sure.

I was about to set my phone back on the table when another message dropped in.

W.S: Morning, Guille. Did you check out early last night? I know it's Friday, so you better start canceling any blind dates you might have scheduled for today.

This guy. He thought I didn't answer because I was asleep when he texted me last night.

Nope.

I ignored you. Besides, didn't he have that charity gala event to go to? Why did he want me to cancel my plans for him if he wasn't even available? Scratch that. If he wasn't even *single.*

He warned me not to google him, which I didn't. We just happened to bump into that stupid tabloid. My mind battled against the possible scenarios. At first, I thought he asked me not to search his name online because of the fabricated stories going around about celebrities, and his name wasn't the exception on the headlines. But now I didn't know what to think. What if he was hiding something from me, and that was the perfect excuse to keep me in the dark?

Or maybe he wanted to see if things worked out well with me before he ended things with Erin for good. Unfortunately, there weren't many optimistic options to choose from.

It was the hardest thing to trust him! Because why would he choose me over Erin or any other beautiful celebrity, model, or girl he had at his disposal? I'd been stupid enough to believe that I was *that* special. And I didn't want to get hurt again because when he ghosted me a few months ago, it hurt more than I thought it would.

That wound was still healing.

Me: No blind dates for today. Just a good ol' regular date.
W.S: You don't even know Nathan. Seems blind enough for me.

That was fast, even for Tobias. I was sure he'd been the one to tell him. Or maybe Nathan told him himself. I didn't know how close they were. What I grasped from last night was that Nathan is Joel's friend, but I didn't really care. Of one thing I was sure: William didn't like the idea one bit.

Good.

Me: We did get to know each other last night. Don't worry.
W.S: Cancel. I'm taking you to the party.

That pissed me off. I wasn't going to take orders from him when I didn't even know the truth about where he stood with Erin. I wasn't going to take orders from him. Period. He was so used to having his way that it was automatic for him to demand things from others. His approach wasn't helping the situation.

Me: Stop telling me what to do.
W.S: You cannot go with him.

I ignored him, and that seemed to do the trick because he stopped texting me. So I took a shower and got ready. I hated to admit that my overall mood had been affected by my conversation with William, but I couldn't allow that to ruin my plans with my friends. We had our entire day mapped out. We wanted to go for brunch and costume shopping afterward.

By the time I came out of my room, Sophie and Cecile were already sitting in the living room, all dressed up and ready to go—staring at me.

"What's wrong?"

Sophie parted her mouth to speak but Cecile pulled her arm, and I obviously noticed.

"*What's wrong?*" I asked once again, my voice firm this time.

Cecile clicked her tongue and said, "Sophie googled William."

"And?" I took a couple of steps forward but stopped as if undecided about wanting to know or not.

Sophie flipped her phone to show me her screen. I narrowed my eyes and scurried their way. The article was from a week ago and the photos were taken in London. They showed different shots of Erin and William walking around, sitting in an ice cream shop, feeding each other ice cream and kissing. They weren't wearing the same clothes from the tabloid we saw. This was another outing.

The photo gallery was endless. I scrolled down hoping to get to the bottom of the page, but there was only more of the same. More kissing, more cuddling, more laughing. *William is still in a relationship with Erin.* There was absolutely no way for me to think otherwise now.

"Thanks." I shut my eyes as if someone had poured acid in them and handed Sophie her phone back.

"Billie, I'm sorry. I di—"

"It's okay." I smiled. "Thank you for telling me. It's best that I know the truth. Now let's go. We're running behind schedule."

They stood up from the couch and followed me, but as I opened the door for us to leave, William stepped out of the elevator. He dashed our way, rolling the sleeves of his soft-looking gray sweater up to his elbows, revealing his perfectly toned forearms, and giving off major alpha male vibes as if readying himself for a brawl.

With me.

Okay, so ignoring his last text wasn't as effective as I thought it was.

A tidal wave of his mouth-watering cologne moved in my direction, and I braced for impact. Or maybe he's the one who should've been doing that because I could feel the fire running through my veins and he might as well have been covered in fuel.

Not the safest combination out there.

Poor Sophie froze on-site and gaped for more than a few reasons when she realized it was him. Cecile grabbed her arm and pulled her back inside the apartment to give us the privacy it was so obvious we would need.

William looked, well … pissed. It was like looking at myself in the mirror. But his features softened up when he said, "At what time do I pick you up?" He aimed for a smile, but it wasn't the most genuine smile I've seen on his face.

I ran a hand over my forehead with exasperation as I watched him standing there—demanding shit because it was not his place to do that. I was not going to cancel on Nathan. He was an ice-cream-lick-from-Erin's-lips-caught-on-camera too late.

"Nathan's picking me up at eight."

William's jaw popped with a slow, controlled blink to go with it. I could tell he was having a hard time keeping it together.

"Joke's not funny anymore, Guille." But oh, was I enjoying watching him get all worked up about Nathan. "*I* am taking you to this party tonight." There he was, getting all territorial on me when there wasn't any land for him to claim. He looked even hotter when he was angry. It was maddening to watch.

"I'm afraid you won't clear the background check on time for tonight's party." I pretended to see the time on my watch. "Nathan's process is almost done, so logistically speaking, you can't come."

He smiled an angry smile to go with a short, sharp snort. "I'm sure your guys know what color my underwear is and what I had for breakfast this morning."

Yeah, that was probably accurate. William had been cleared since April when we moved back to New York. Everyone in the building was, for all I knew. But he needed to understand things didn't work that way with me. Not anymore. He shouldn't get to do whatever he wants with me, with Erin, or any other girl for that matter.

"Nathan's taking me to the party. *You* have a girlfriend. Please leave."

And go directly to hell. Do not pass GO. Do not collect $200.

I turned around and walked toward my door.

"I'm *done* with Erin." He snapped back with that husky and grave tone of his. He was about to lose it. *Join the club.* "She's not even in New York. She stayed in Europe." *How convenient.* I'd already lost it last night. It kind of felt like I would lose it for a second time any second now.

I turned around with a scowl and said, "It's in the goddamn news, William! Stop lying!"

Yup. I lost it. I lost it because a huge, and very stupid part of me believed him when he said it was over with Erin. I wanted to trust him, and for a second there I did, but it was too late. I was terrified of getting hurt again. I liked William too much, and I knew the downfall would be anything less than tragic if I allowed myself to believe him. It was best not to proceed.

As much as I tried, I couldn't find a logical explanation for the photographs that didn't include William lying or hiding something from me. If it had been just a story saying they were still together, I might've felt differently. But how do you talk yourself out of an image? Or a bunch of them.

I didn't want to be the naive girl who believes everything she's told. And I knew William could easily convince me with words. If they were *pretending* as William said, they didn't have to go around town holding hands and feeding each other ice cream. Showing up together for the premieres and press events was probably enough. And if things were still tricky with her and he was still trying to figure out his feelings, then I didn't want to be a part of it.

"You *googled* me?" William asked with a grimace as if *that* was the biggest sin a human could ever commit. Googling. "You weren't supposed to. You said you wouldn't." He ran a hand through his buttery golden hair as he always did and grabbed his neck. His movements were filled with frustration and very distracting, too. He needed to stay put. Or leave.

Yes, leave.

"*I* didn't google you. There was *no need*. The truth's out in every magazine kiosk in the city. You should walk around the streets of New York more often since you already seem to enjoy going for afternoon strolls so much."

"Tell me what you saw."

"Do you ever google yourself?"

"Of course not. Never."

"Out of sight, out of mind?" I snorted. Of course, he didn't. I wanted to believe he wouldn't have the nerve to be standing here, telling me these things, if he knew he'd been caught. Didn't he have a publicity team? A guy like him definitely should. And if he did, then it was time to hire new blood. "Perhaps you should do it from time to time. It might be easier for your stories to match if you did."

This conversation had gone for way longer than I intended it to last. He didn't deserve a single answer or explanation from me—

just silence like when he ignored me back in August. But it was impossible not to engage with him. With the situation.

"I don't know what you saw, but tabloids lie all the time. That's how they make money. It's all lies. Ask me anything."

"What is seen is not asked," I said with a bite. That's what William told *me* when he saw me kissing Thomas. I tried explaining, but instead, he said that. He never gave me the chance to explain. To talk things over with him. So why should I? It stung and burned then, and now I hoped it stung him.

"Touché." He snorted with a faint smile.

I crossed my arms loosely in front of my chest with an *anything else* expression on my face.

"You're impossible." He breathed with exasperation and walked away toward the elevator, saying, "And don't you dare waste any of those firsts of yours with Nathan, of all people." He stepped inside the elevator and shot a blood-boiling smirk at me. Finally, the doors snicked shut behind him. This was all a game to him.

Eight o'clock couldn't come any sooner. I was going to need that tequila.

CHAPTER 14

Background Checks

"I LOVE THIS ONE!" Sophie exclaimed, holding Cher's famous yellow plaid outfit from Clueless. The costume looked great on her, and it was easy to match with her long blonde hair. "I want to look cute tonight."

"Well, that looks *very* cute, Sophie. Go for it," I encouraged her. I was still fuming on the inside but trying my best to hide it. I wanted to enjoy my friends' company.

"I love the white knee socks. Those are sexy," Cecile added.

Sophie went back into the dressing room, looking enthusiastic about her costume of choice. Cecile kept browsing through the racks, undecided.

"See anything you like?" I asked her.

"Hmm, I don't know," she replied with a bored expression on her face.

"Are you okay?"

"Yeah, it's—Paul. He's been acting weird lately, and I'm getting sick of it." I knew a thing or two about that feeling. "We had the weirdest conversation right now through texts. But this weekend is not about me. We're here to have fun, and I'm planning to do just that. How about this?" She took a beautiful vintage twenties dress off the rack. It was black and had a silver fringe and details made of tiny beads and sequins.

"It's beautiful. You should try it on."

Sophie and I sat outside the dressing room, waiting for Cecile to come out. "I'm excited about tonight. Tobias is *so* hot." Sophie whispered.

Uh-oh.

I was almost sure Tobias liked Cecile, which was why I thought he wanted to come to the party. But who knew?

"How do I look?" Cecile twirled. The dress looked beautiful against her porcelain skin and tobacco brown hair.

"It looks great. It would go perfectly with a red lip," I suggested.

She rented out the dress and a few accessories to go with it—a hairpiece, earrings, and pearl bracelet. They found everything they needed for the party, so we walked around the city for about an hour, then returned to the apartment. We needed to start getting ready.

Tobias called me a few minutes after we arrived at my place.

"Hey, Tob, what's up?"

"G'day, Murph."

"Oh, hi, Nathan!"

"You've kept me waiting. So, what's the verdict? Am I good to go for tonight? Joel's lending me the white Scarface suit to match your costume. Just say the word, and I'll throw that thing on."

"Last time I asked, they still didn't have an answer. Let me check in with them again, okay? I'm *so* sorry for all of this."

"There's nothing to apologize about. What floor did you say you're on?"

"Ninth."

"On my way." He ended the call.

Shit. I was so embarrassed it was almost 5:00 p.m., and I still couldn't give him an answer. I could tell Nathan wanted to come, and I would lie if I said I didn't want him to. I was curious about him.

I called Caleb and asked him to come upstairs. He arrived before Nathan, just a couple of minutes after we hung up.

I opened the door, and he said, "You wanted to talk to me, Miss Murphy?"

"Yes. Is Nathan cleared yet? I need to give him an answer. It's five p.m."

"Yes ... and no."

"What do you mean?"

"He's clean. Too clean if you ask me." He lifted a brow and wet his lips. "But ... your father said no."

"What?" I was confused. I didn't understand why my father would refuse if his background check came out perfect. Wasn't that the only requirement?

"Look, I just hung up with him a few minutes ago. I was about to let you know when you called me." Caleb seemed genuine about it. "I'm sorry. It's not my call to make. I do want you to have fun." He glanced at the elevator. Nathan had just stepped out and was walking our way. He was in a full suit looking all—business. *Damn.*

"Hi, again," he said with a smile. "So, who's in charge?" He laughed.

I jerked my chin toward Caleb because my father was out of town, and Caleb did an awesome job representing him while he was away.

"Hey, mate. I'm Nathan."

Caleb introduced himself and shook Nathan's hand. But he already knew who Nathan was. He knew him better than I did at this point.

My phone buzzed—my father. I asked Caleb to fill Nathan in while I took the call. I didn't want him to leave. I wanted to apologize, but I needed my father to explain why he disapproved of Nathan.

"Hey, Dad … Yes, Caleb just told me … Why? He said everything was looking good … Dad, come on. Really?"

I took a few steps away from them. Nathan kept making small talk with Caleb. *Did I just see Caleb laughing?*

"Mom was twelve years younger than you. And we're just having fun. He's good friends with the Sjöbergs, and it's too late now to look for a date. I need to take someone, or else I won't get in the party."

His issue with Nathan was the age difference. Too old for me, he said. I kept arguing with my father when Nathan approached me. He lifted his index finger, asking to hear him out for a second.

I muted the call, and he extended his hand out to me. "Let me talk to him." *He's insane!* "Trust me. I'll take care of it."

My father is going to kill me.

I gave Nathan the phone because doing so was the only hope I had left. "Don't follow me," he warned. "It's best if you don't listen." He winked at me and took the call. "Mr. Murphy, this is Nathan Saunders …" He walked away, and that was the last thing I could hear.

I rushed back to Caleb and waited for Nathan to end the call with my father. "He's cool," Caleb said, placing his hands inside his pockets.

"He's—cool?" I placed my hand on Caleb's forehead. "You don't seem to have a fever. Or wait, maybe you're just dehydrated." He laughed. I laughed. It felt nice.

"I just want you to be happy," he said with a tight-lip smile.

"Me too." I smiled back and stared at him for a few seconds. "But I really need a date for the party, or CJ will kill me." I chuckled. "At this point, I don't care if it's Nathan or anyone else. I mean, I just met him yesterday. He seems nice, but I'm *done* dating for a while."

Caleb squinted at me as in, *I don't believe you.* I shoved his shoulder.

Nathan kept talking and gesturing in the distance. Smiling. Chuckling. Rubbing his cheek. Running a hand through his brown wavy hair. Smiling again. I was so curious about how that conversation was going.

"So—are you done being a robot?" I asked Caleb. "I like seeing you like this—smiling. Happy. But you're always mad at me now. It's exhausting."

"I know. I'm sorry about yesterday and these past few days. I was a jerk." He was. "I'm not—mad *at you.* You have to understand"— he rubbed his neck—"Your father put me in a challenging and awkward position. Just give me some time, Red." *There you go.* I felt lighter just by hearing him call me that. "Let's just keep it profesh around your father, okay?"

"Deal. I won't hug you ever again, okay?"

He laughed. "It doesn't have to be *ever.* But I think he's happier not knowing the details of our—friendship."

I smiled and heard Nathan's voice drawing near.

Nathan laughed and said, "*Of course, Mr. Murphy ... James, yes ... You can count on it ... I'll put your daughter back on the phone ... Cheers, have a good weekend.*"

Nathan handed my phone back to me.

"*Dad? ... Okay ... Okay. Of course, that sounds perfect ... Thank you so much ... I'll let them know ... Yes ... No, I know ... We'll talk tomorrow ... Thanks ... Love you too ... Bye.*"

I was in *shock.* Caleb offered me a small smile, probably assuming Nathan had convinced my father somehow. "We'll be downstairs, Miss Murphy. Let us know when you're ready to leave."

He nodded at Nathan and winked at me before he disappeared off to the emergency exit.

"What on *Earth* did you say to my father?" I asked Nathan immediately. I was more than impressed. "I think I might be requiring your legal services more often."

He laughed. "I ah—did my own *little research* on you. And hear this, my boss Oliver Chapman is a good friend of your father's. We talked a bit about that and agreed to grab a pint sometime next week when he arrives from D.C."

"You're kidding, right?" *These lawyers.* Apparently, he was a fabulous one.

"Of course not. Chapman & Payne has liaised on quite a few governmental projects between the United States and Great Britain. Your father was involved in such a venture a few years back," he explained, his voice all—*lawyerly.* "You must've been a poppet at the time. It was before his ambassador days, and as I said, he's close to Mr. Chapman."

"I meant the part with the beers—with *James.*" I chuckled. They were already going on a first-name basis. But I was impressed by the story—by him. And also, by how small he made the world seem.

"Oh, that. It'll practically be a business meeting. With beers." He grinned. "Would you be a lamb and give me his number?" That crisp accent was stirring up things inside me I had promised myself I wouldn't allow in a while. But somehow, I felt like a child beside him. He seemed like such a grown-up, and that made him feel so out of reach.

I gawked at him. "No one's ever asked for my father's number before mine."

There goes a first.

"That's because I already have your number, silly. Tobias gave it to me."

I crossed my arms loosely in front of me and puckered my lips to the side. I was still trying to decipher Nathan. But I can't deny I was curious about getting to know him better. "I should start figuring out how to make myself look like Michelle Pfeiffer," I told him. "See you at eight?"

"Looking forward to it, Murph," he said, walking away.

"Nathan!" I yelled. He looked over his shoulder and met my gaze. "Thanks." I smiled. I really meant it. I appreciated him having the guts to talk to my father and figuring a way to come with me to the party.

Nathan lifted the right corner of his mouth and said, "Pleasure." He turned around and left. Somehow, I didn't like the growing distance between us. And there I was, thinking I could take a break from dating for a while.

Well, crap.

CHAPTER 15

Sexy With A Side Of Trouble

I WENT BACK INSIDE my apartment and told Sophie and Cecile everything that happened with Nathan and Caleb. Cecile thought Nathan was one of the hottest guys she's ever seen. "He's so—manly. I don't know what's a good word to describe him. But he's *so* hot. William can suck it."

I replied with a nod, somewhat disagreeing on the inside. William had ruined me forever. It's as if I'd curated William in a create-your-perfect-man-machine of sorts. Too bad he had to be recalled afterward for its messed-up trustworthiness parameters.

But yeah, I obviously could understand what Cecile was saying about Nathan. I'm not freaking blind. I was just—annoyed. I needed to be alone for a while and just take a breather.

We kept mincing the topic, going over and over the same stuff, but it was getting late. And if nobody stopped us, we could go all night talking about everything and nothing.

Sophie and Cecile went to their room to get ready. I needed to take my time to figure out how to do my makeup properly since I never wore much. I googled images of Michelle Pfeiffer's makeup look in Scarface, and although it was a simple look, sometimes those are harder to achieve.

I went for a subtle smokey eye with a touch of golden eyeshadow on the inner eyelids. On the bottom, I used the same smoky taupe color as a liner. I applied lots of mascara and accentuated my cheekbones with a peachy blush. I tinted my lips with a rosy-terracotta shade topped off with clear gloss.

Sophie helped me secure the wig in place with a wig net I bought earlier at the costume place. I wore a pair of the many earrings that belonged to my mother to complete the look. The only thing missing was for me to spray some perfume and put the dress on.

Sophie was ready, and she looked super cute with her Cher outfit. Cecile looked extraordinary, and her blue eyes stood out wonderfully with the smokey shadow she applied to her eyelids.

The doorbell rang at eight sharp. My stomach felt immediately warm and overflowed with nerves as I opened the door.

Nathan wore Joel's Scarface white suit and the red shirt with the top three buttons undone. A chunky golden chain hung around his neck and rested on what seemed to be a *very* defined chest. *God, help me.*

"Hi! You guys look great!" My greeting came out a bit high-pitchy, but what are you gonna do? Tobias held the tequila bottle with a wicked smile. He wore a black suit, with a Superman logo t-shirt underneath his white button-down shirt, and topped it off with black-framed glasses. Sophie was going to flip. This was one handsome Clark Kent.

"Wow, Billie. You look—great," Tobias said, quickly eyeing me up and down. "The blonde hair suits you."

"Innit," Nathan said, kissing my cheek as they walked in. Really kissing it. It wasn't one of those air kisses. *Don't blush, don't blush, don't blush.*

I think I didn't.

"Um, thanks. So, Clark Kent?" I asked Tobias. Not that it wasn't obvious, but I needed to redirect my attention into something less distracting.

"Yeah, it was the easiest costume I could put together. I borrowed the glasses from Billy."

I'd never seen William wearing glasses. But then I thought about how there must be a ton of things I didn't know about him. I pressed a crooked smile on my face and gestured for them to follow me.

"You ladies all look great," Tobias said as he walked into the living room. Sophie and Cecile stood up to greet them both with double-cheek kisses.

"I'm kinda growing fond of these Parisian greetings," he said, looking at Cecile.

"I see you've come bearing gifts," she replied, eyeing the tequila bottle with a small smile.

"Yeah, I thought we could pregame before leaving for the party. We don't want to be dry when we get there." He threw an equally flirty and mischievous smile at Cecile.

"Wet is always better than dry," Cecile said with a raised brow. *Cecile!* That's what I meant when I said she didn't have a filter. But Tobias didn't seem to mind.

He laughed and high-fived Cecile with a grin. "My kind of girl." *Anyway ...*

"How do you want to drink this?" I asked Tobias, taking the bottle away from his hands.

"Shots?" he proposed.

"Um, sure." I widened my eyes with terror.

"Oh, come on!" Tobias gave me a side hug. "We'll take care of you, Billie. I told you. The three of you." He laughed as I walked hastily toward the kitchen to fetch the shot glasses. "Let's have some fun!"

"You've never done a tequila shot before?" Nathan asked behind me. He startled me. I didn't realize he'd followed me to the kitchen.

"You don't have to drink if you don't want to."

It was kind of Nathan to feel like protecting me from Tobias's peer pressure, but I *did* want to drink that tequila. I needed it. I was just afraid of Tobias's suggested presentation: shots.

"Well, I tried a few of those—aquavit thingies on Midsummer," I said, waving a limp hand while I searched for shot glasses through the upper cabinets. "But that's it. I've never had tequila before. I'm curious, though."

I turned around to face him, and he was leaning against the fridge with bunched-up brows.

"You do live here, right?" He teased. "You don't seem to know your way around the kitchen."

"Very funny." I smiled. "I almost burned my apartment into ashes a few months ago, so I try to stay as far away from the kitchen as possible."

"Were there actual flames?" He laughed.

It wasn't funny, but I couldn't help but laugh too. "Well, the flames didn't make it out of the oven, but yeah, there was mostly thick smoke everywhere," I replied, browsing around the cupboards.

Surprisingly, I finally found the shot glasses and placed them on the counter. I didn't think there would be any. Nathan grabbed four of them, and I took the other two.

"So, how did you put the fire out?" Nathan asked with genuine concern on his face as we walked back to the living room.

"I didn't. He did"—I jerked my chin at Tobias—"I passed out from the smoke inhalation and probably embarrassment, too." I chuckled. He didn't. But he did frown again.

"I'm glad you're okay," he said in a hushed voice. I was about to reply when Tobias complained about how we took too long to come back.

"Sorry, I couldn't find these things." Nathan and I placed the glasses on the coffee table. Tobias immediately grabbed the tequila bottle and opened it.

"I *love* tequila," Sophie said to Tobias, trying to get his attention. "Then you're *really* going to dig this one." He messily poured the tequila into the glass shots. "Billie, do you have any lime and salt? It's kind of important." He grinned.

"I do, actually. I'll be right back." I sliced a few limes, placed them in a small bowl, and brought another plate with salt.

The lame part of me was scared of drinking tequila because I had never tried it before. But the angry and bitter part encouraged me to drink it. I needed to forget about William, and the tequila smelled strong enough to perform such a task.

"Okay, let's do this." I extended my hand for him to give me one of the shots. Tobias explained how we had to lick the salt, drink the shot, and chew on the lemon. "Lick. Drink. Chew. Okay."

Nathan laughed. "Exactly. Lick, drink, chew. It's pretty straight-forward. I'll be right next to you if you forget any of the steps."

I lightly shoved his shoulder with a smile. *Damn it.*

We followed Tobias's instructions and downed the tequila shots in unison.

"Oh, my God—Tobias. I'm going to kill you!" I said in between coughs. He laughed. I clutched Nathan's arm and held on to it as a reaction to the burning sensation of my throat. It was more potent than the aquavit, and the shot was taller. "Was your shot filled with water?" I asked Nathan, who didn't grimace one bit and made it seem he'd just drank chocolate milk.

"I'm used to it. Are you okay?"

"Um, yeah. The lime helped a little."

The doorbell rang.

"I'll be right back," I said to Nathan, trying to smile, and rushed to open the door, feeling a shiver creeping up my spine. The tequila still stung at my throat.

"Hey, Ren!" He walked in dressed up as a Jedi Knight. "I love your costume!"

"Thanks, Billie," he said as I closed the door. "Wow, you look great."

"Thank you. I'm so glad you could make it."

As I introduced Ren to everyone, Tobias turned the TV on and searched for a music channel of his liking. Everyone hovered near the dining table.

I transferred the salt and the lime plates to the table and moved a couple of chairs away for easier access. With the music in the background and everyone standing up, it now felt like a mini party.

Cecile seemed distracted. I could tell she was making an effort to smile and keep up with the chit-chat. But she was probably still bothered by her issues with Paul.

"Let's have another," Sophie suggested.

"Okay." Cecile shrugged.

"Yes, ma'am," Tobias said, pouring the shots again. *Yes, ma'am.* Tequila didn't seem to work yet because that reminded me of William. *Keep the shots coming.*

We all downed another one, and Ren turned to me and made a remark about how good the tequila was. We switched to speaking Spanish for a bit. It was always fun to practice with him. But Nathan had stepped away from my side and was now talking to Tobias in Swedish. I could also hear Sophie and Cecile talking to each other in French.

I was worried Ren might've thought I asked *him* out on a date. I wanted him to know that he was free to roam and talk to my friends too. This was a group date. But he wouldn't leave my side, and I didn't mind talking to him. I always had a great time with Ren, but I also wanted to get to know Nathan better.

"Why don't we all switch to English?" I proposed. We all looked at each other, realizing that everyone had their own little chat going on in a different language, which sounds really fancy but not as fun.

Ren asked me one last question in Spanish before we regrouped: "*Tony Montana es tu date?*"[1]

"*¡No, para nada! Todos vamos en plan de amigos.*"[2]

"Hey! You're still speaking Spanish." Tobias complained.

"Sorry!" I switched to English and finished explaining things to Ren. "CJ wanted everyone to arrive with a plus one. That's why we asked the three of you to join us. And I thought it was a great opportunity for you to meet my friends too."

I hoped he didn't take it the wrong way. He looked chill about it.

"So, where's the party?" Tobias asked.

"It's in a loft in the West Village. A friend of CJ is an artist, and he uses it as a studio," I explained. "They were going to clear it out for the party."

Yup. I was starting to feel the alcohol kicking in. It'd been a while since I last had a drink, and tequila was proving its strength. The sensation was different from wine, though. It made me feel more upbeat and made me laugh more.

The guys seemed unaffected by the tequila. Sophie couldn't stop giggling, and even though Cecile kept a straight face, I could tell she was tipsy.

"I think we should get going," I proposed.

"One last shot before we go?" Tobias replied.

"Sure." Cecile held up her glass for Tobias to refill. He smiled at her and poured tequila into it.

"Me too," Sophie chirped.

"I'll have … half a shot," I said to Tobias, but Ren laughed as he grabbed his glass.

"Billie, there's no such thing as *half* a shot," Tobias said with a chuckle, filling it up to the top.

---

1 "Is Tony Montana your date?"
2 "No, not at all! We're all going as friends."

Nathan placed his hand on the small of my back and leaned in to grab the shot Tobias had just filled for me. "I'll take your half."

I looked over my shoulder, and his neck was *right there,* an inch away from my face. I looked up to meet his eyes and lightly pressed my lips. "Thanks." He smelled *delicious.*

Everyone else did their shot before us. I turned around to grab a lime because I couldn't do the shot without the lime, but there was only one left. And I knew I had no more left in the fridge.

"You can take it." I offered it to Nathan. He was a guest at my house.

"Tosh, you need it more than I do." He chuckled.

But I ignored him. I licked the salt, drank half of the shot, closed my eyes, and shook my head twice as I felt the burn on my throat again. I opened my eyes, and the lime was right in front of my lips. Nathan held it out for me. He nodded once, inviting me to chew it. I took a bite into it as he stared into my eyes.

That. Was. Hot.

Nathan drank the other half and clicked his tongue. He glanced at the empty shot in between his fingers and tossed the lime inside it, dropping the glass on the table.

This guy was killing me! He'd been subtle all night. But every little flirty thing he did had a raw edge to it. He had me wanting for more, wondering what he'd do next.

Focus. But how? The tequila was doing the exact opposite of that.

We were all ready to go, so I went to my bedroom, grabbed my golden clutch, my favorite green coat, and touched up my lipstick. We all left the apartment and headed downstairs.

"Are you—okay, Billie?" Tobias whispered as we stepped into the lobby.

"What do you mean?" I chuckled.

"I don't know. Do you usually drink like this?"

"All the time!" I messed up his hair and kept walking.

He grabbed my arm and said, "Take it easy, okay."

"You brought the tequila, remember? Besides, you said you'd take care of me."

"I know, but *he's* going to kill me if anything bad happens to you," Tobias kept whispering.

"Who's he?" I laughed again, faking dementia. I assumed Tobias meant William, but this wasn't a conversation I wanted to dive into with him. "Relax, Tob. You'll live."

Cecile grabbed my hand and pulled me away from Tobias. She was probably listening in on our conversation, and I was thankful she pulled me aside. I didn't want my night getting ruined by talking to Tobias about how his brother "worried" about me. Bullshit.

"Cohen!" I poked Caleb's back. He turned around to look at me, and his eyes widened. The blonde wig must've surprised him. "Can I have a cigarette, please?" I grinned. He didn't. His facial features rebooted to cyborg mode in record time.

My costume needed a cigarette as a prop. I wasn't planning on lighting it up, but he didn't need to know that.

Caleb's cyborg eyes scanned me, analyzing my costume as if he were my tailor looking for imperfections on the gown. I couldn't tell if he liked it or not. His eyes expressed one thing but his frown another.

But yeah, he was most definitely starting to malfunction, and I was glad to see him relaxing again around me because the robotic version of Caleb never laid an eye on me.

His hand reached into his coat pocket for the cigarette box I requested with his gaze fixed on mine like a hawk. He handed a single cigarette to me with hesitation. He noticed I was a little drunk. And *that* I could easily tell he didn't like.

"Ooh!" Sophie said, shooting in our direction. "I want one too!"

Caleb took another cigarette out and gave it to her, his expression denoting exasperation. Cecile extended her hand. "Do you have a lighter, Caleb?"

"I do, but I can't light you up in here. It's best to wait until you get to the party."

"Boring!" Sophie replied with a giggle.

"Hey mate, could I pinch a fag?" Nathan said behind me, greeting Caleb with a firm handshake. He looked quizzically at Nathan, and I burst out laughing.

"What?" Nathan chuckled.

"We said we were going to speak English." I teased.

He pinched my waist lightly and rephrased, looking at me, "Caleb, can I have a cigarette, please?"

I laughed again.

By context, I'd assumed that's what he wanted, but Caleb's puzzled face was priceless. He took out yet *another* cigarette and gave it to Nathan. He walked away immediately after that.

We all stepped out of the building and saw Big Mike (that's what the guys called him) standing beside a black town car. Our SUV was parked behind it, and David had the engine going.

"Hey, Mike," I greeted him. *God, he's scary.*

"Good evening, Miss Murphy."

Caleb's mouth twitched. I guess that was his newest version of a smile. He approached me again and said, "You're riding with Mike tonight. Both to and from the party. It's your father's orders. We'll take the rest of your friends in the SUV."

"What? Why?" I complained. "What if you or Aaron ride with Mike? I swear I'll let him drive me back home after the party. Come on, Caleb. I really want to be with my friends. They leave in a couple of days. We're having fun," I said with an exaggerated sad face.

Caleb scratched his face and said something to Aaron in Hebrew with a snippy tone. Aaron didn't seem happy either. "You're going to get us fired," he whispered and got in the front seat of the SUV. Aaron got in the car with Big Mike.

Yay!

Tobias and Cecile stepped into the last row of the SUV. Sophie and I sat in between Ren and Nathan. It was a group date, but we all knew who we were walking into the party with.

Sophie talked to Ren most of the way there, which I thought was perfect. Tobias kept making Cecile laugh, even though she was trying to act like she didn't care for him. Somehow the scene felt familiar.

We were so cramped up in the car, and it was inevitable for me and Nathan to find ourselves too close to one another the entire way there. He'd placed his cigarette behind his ear. "Do you smoke?" I asked him.

"Sometimes, when I drink. But not really."

I knew I asked Caleb for a cigarette, and Nathan probably thought I smoked because of it, but I was glad he wasn't a regular smoker.

Sophie then told me in French that she'd found Ren cute. Cecile agreed with Sophie as she joined in the conversation. Tobias went nuts.

"God, that is so sexy," he said, closing his eyes for a couple of seconds. "Is there anything hotter than a French girl?"

"Hey!" I complained. Tobias laughed at my discomfort. Ugh.

"American girls are my favorite," Nathan whispered to my ear.

Nope, nope, nope. Not blushing. I took a deep breath instead to drive the blood away from my face. He probably sensed that his remark made me nervous because he changed the subject.

"So, how many languages do you have up your sleeve?" He raised his brow with a teasing smile.

"Just French and Spanish." I bumped my shoulder against his. "My mother was Spanish. And I learned French when I lived in Paris," I explained. "I heard you speaking Swedish. Did you live in Sweden?" I could feel the subtle spin of the tequila swaying inside me, even more so inside the car.

"We moved to Sweden when I was about five or six years old for my father's work. I basically grew up there and went to school with the Sjöbergs. Joel and I became great friends. But I moved back to London for college. And then I got a job in New York, and Joel was already living here. I was then transferred back to London for a while, and now they sent me back here."

"So, you've worked in the same firm all this time?"

"Exactly. It's an English firm, but besides the London headquarters, there's the New York office and another in Delhi."

"And do you enjoy what you do?"

"I love it." He smiled, and I smiled back at him. He seemed really happy. This was a wholesome, mature, sexy, funny *man*.

Oh, was I in trouble ...

CHAPTER 16

CJ's Birthday Party Part 1

THERE WERE A COUPLE of guys at the door, making sure everyone coming in had a costume on, and if anyone arrived without one, they provided guests with eye masks.

"You're gonna need a mask to get in, boo," one of the guys said to Caleb. I had to bite the inside of my cheek really hard to prevent myself from laughing. Caleb protested but was left with no choice but to wear the black mask or leave. His bad mood was becoming apparent. "You too, big guy." Aaron received a mask, but he put it on his face without objection. He would probably toss it once inside.

The other guy posted at the entrance was taking care of David.

"I'm out of black masks, sugarplum. I hate to ruin your all-black, fierce ensemble, but I've got me some hot pink or neon green for you to choose from." David raised his brow at the guy, seemingly amused. "What's it gonna be?" David grabbed a hot pink mask, and we all finally stepped inside the party. Big Mike stayed behind and waited for us outside.

CJ greeted us dressed up as Hades from the Hercules animated movie. His costume was *amazing*. The pointy teeth, the crazy blue hair, and the makeup had all been professionally done.

I gave CJ a big, warm birthday hug, then introduced him to my friends. He pinched my arm when he saw Tobias. "Billie, what the hell?" he whispered without removing the prosthetic, fangy smile off his face. I hadn't told CJ about William, his revealed identity, or how the entire Sjöberg family lived in my building. He'd never run into any of them the few times he'd been to my place either.

"We'll talk later," I assured him.

"All right," CJ said with a smile. "I'll go see if David wants to be my Persephone."

I laughed, and Nathan placed a hand on my shoulder.

We moved further inside the gallery while CJ approached David, who beamed when he saw CJ's costume. Aaron and Caleb had their scary bodyguard faces on.

The party looked like a lot of fun. There was a bar installed at the very end, and a bunch of people were already dancing. We claimed a high table, and Nathan helped me out of my coat.

Nathan approached Caleb in the near distance and asked him for his lighter. He came back and lit up Sophie and Cecile's cigarettes. "Do you want me to light you up?"

"Um, sure."

Caleb took his lighter back, shot me a disapproving look, and joined Aaron and David, seeming utterly vexed.

"You look so badass," Tobias said to me. "Although I don't think that Bil—" he trailed off after I widened my eyes at him with a *cut-it-out* kind of look. Why was he insisting on mentioning William? Yes, William didn't like to see me smoking. I knew that. *Stop bringing him up!*

The five of us walked to the bar. Sophie and Cecile had a higher tolerance for alcohol than me, while Ren, Tobias, and Nathan were barely getting started.

"What are you having?" Nathan asked.

"Red wine?"

"I don't think that's a good idea," he replied. "You don't want to mix your poisons. You should stick to tequila. Perhaps a margie? Your friends ordered a couple."

"Sounds good."

Nathan ordered one for me and tequila with club soda for him. He took a sip of my margarita and said, "Mmm, scrummy." He licked his lips, clicked his tongue, and handed it over to me. My first margarita ever was delicious—another *first*.

Some guy pulled Cecile to the side to talk. Tobias didn't look too pleased. "I kinda like her," he said to Nathan and me.

"Well, she has a boyfriend back in Paris," I informed him.

"Who cares?" He laughed and I gaped at him. It was apparent that respecting other people's relationships didn't run in the family. "If *that* guy doesn't care that she has a boyfriend, then why should I? I would rather have it be me than him."

Cecile started dancing with the guy.

"So, what's her deal? Is she like you, Billie?" Tobias asked, staring intently at Cecile, sipping on his drink. I didn't understand his question.

"Like me, how?"

"Unaware of—*who* we are." *These Sjöbergs ...*

He wanted to know if Cecile wasn't giving him the attention he desperately desired because she didn't *know* he was a famous actor.

"Oh, no, she's the exact opposite of me," I replied nonchalantly, putting my cigarette out on a tray on our table.

"How so?"

"She knows who you are. She just doesn't care."

"You didn't know who these guys were?" Nathan asked, looking surprised. Almost like he could laugh. I shook my head twice. Fast. Sharp.

"She only recognized Lily from an event they both went to in Paris," Tobias replied.

"How did William's ego take it?" Nathan asked with a chuckle, bringing his cup to his lips, taking a sip. His movements were so elegant but still powerful.

Tobias snorted and said, "He definitely thought it was— interesting. A first for him, for sure."

Now I'm taking his firsts. Huh.

In our conversation at the cottage, he mentioned there were still a few firsts left in him if I wanted to claim them. At the time, it seemed like an interesting idea. *Not anymore.*

"I bet he did," Nathan replied, looking at me. "I'll have to take you to the movies sometime soon. Get you up to speed on your pop culture."

"I haven't been allowed to go for the last six years." I puckered my lips to the side.

"Nonsense, we'll have to speak to your father about this."

"I don't think he'll budge." I hoped he would. Going to the movies with Nathan sounded like something I'd like to try out sometime.

"I'll see what I can do." He winked. I was sure I'd be going to the movies in no time, having seen how persuasive Nathan could be.

Tobias downed what was left of his drink and dropped his cup on the table. "I'm going in." He walked away with determination in Cecile's direction. He was already tipsy by then.

Nathan yelled something to Tobias in Swedish and laughed. Tobias flipped him off as a reply without looking back at him, but that only made Nathan explode into laughter. He was obviously teasing him.

"What?" Nathan smiled as I kept staring at him.

"You sound nice in Swedish."

"Well, you sound pretty nice right now to me." He brushed my cheek with his finger.

I snorted and shot a small smile at him. I didn't want to like Nathan, but how could I not? He was the perfect mix of funny, sophisticated, and confident but easygoing.

"What?" he asked again with a flirty smile.

"I can't tell if your eyes are green or gray," I said, placing my hand on his cheek, staring into his eyes. Analyzing them. "There's a few yellowish lines that draw themselves out from around your pupil."

"They change depending on what I'm wearing." He placed his hand on top of mine and squeezed it. "I think we've got a similar eye color, but yours are more of an intense olive."

I dropped my hand off his face and he placed his around my waist.

"Can you say olive again?" He said it beautifully.

"Olive."

"I couldn't quite catch that. What?" I smiled.

"Olive." His face drew near me. "Do you like the sound of that?"

I nodded. His lips were about to meet mine, but I turned away, "Sorry, I—"

"It's okay. I can slow down." He took my empty cup from my hands and placed it on the cocktail table beside us. "So why aren't you allowed to go to the movies?" he asked instead, running a hand across his forehead.

"I don't know. Because it's dark and crowded?" I mused. "After my mother died, my father became like, *really* apprehensive about my safety." It probably wasn't the best idea to go that deep. I barely knew him, and we were at a Halloween party, but I don't know why my tongue ran loose around him. It had to be the tequila.

"Oh, Murph, I'm so sorry. I didn't know."

"Hey, it's okay." I smiled. The fact that I didn't feel like my chest was about to collapse when I mentioned my mother to Nathan was proof enough that talking to someone about it had been helpful. That someone being William that day on the rooftop. But I shoved down the memories of that night deep into my *Not Now* binder and said, "Could we talk about this some other time?"

"I'd love to." He poked my chin. "How about a dance?"

He pulled me into the area where other people were dancing before I could even say yes, not that I would refuse him.

Nathan twirled me and arched me backward. He then pulled me up and against him, stretched his arm, pushing me away, and pulled me back in. He repeated the combination a few times, disregarding the rhythm of the music altogether. He was making me laugh as I allowed him to lead me through his silly dance. It distracted me and helped to change the vibe from the previous conversation.

We slow-danced to a chill-out lounge tune afterward. All the twirling, combined with the tequila, made me feel a bit dizzy and out of breath.

"I wasn't expecting to find you," he said in my ear, giving me goosebumps all over.

"I wasn't either," I whispered back. I settled my cheek on his chest and kept swaying. My arms rested around his neck.

Being with Nathan felt so easy. Peaceful. Like a breath of fresh air. Sort of how I used to feel with William before I figured out he was a liar and a cheater. What a slap in the face that'd been.

The song ended, and Nathan gave me a quick peck on my cheek. "I've got to go to the loo," he said, his accent crisp and vivid.

"Me too. Let's go."

There was a line for the men's restroom, but the ladies' room was empty.

"My God, what a sausage fest!" Nathan said with a laugh as he stepped into the long queue. I walked away, laughing and shaking my head at his silliness.

I came back out, and he was still in line. There were only a few guys ahead of him. "I'll see you in a bit." I smiled. He reciprocated it with a nod.

Cecile was lighting up a cigarette, standing next to Tobias. "Do you want one? I snatched a few from Caleb. We'll have to get him a new box tomorrow," Cecile said. I was surprised there were still cigarettes coming out of that box.

"Sure, thanks."

Ren approached me and said, "Billie, can I talk to you?"

"Of course. What's up?" We took a few steps away from them. Sophie joined Tobias and Cecile.

"I don't really speak French, but I took a few classes back in high school, so I understand a few words," he started. "We're friends, right?"

He was trying to tell me he understood what Sophie said to me about finding him cute and probably wanted to double-check if I was okay with the situation. He was so sweet.

"Of course. We're friends, Ren, and Sophie's the best. I think it's great that you agreed to come with us today. And I'm glad you're having fun with her." I gripped his shoulder. He grinned, seemingly relieved as I was when he walked back to Sophie.

I spotted Nina in the distance, dressed up as Wonder Woman. She looked stunning and was talking to Caleb. Big whoop. No Juan Pablo on site. They were laughing and seemingly having fun. I guess that's why Caleb wasn't circling around me like a famished great white.

I thought he'd be uneasy about this being my first time out with Nathan, but when you're *that* entertained, I guess it's hard even to remember that you're working. Ugh.

CJ wouldn't leave David's side, either. They both laughed, talked, and flirted. Aaron stood a few steps beside them, looking out like he always did. And he didn't seem thrilled with the dynamic happening beside him. *Yeah, that makes two of us, buddy.*

Seeing Caleb with Nina always made me jealous. If he were talking to a random girl I didn't know, I probably wouldn't have minded as much. I think. I just didn't like seeing him flirting with my friends. That had always been an issue for me.

I didn't want him to end up with a friend and have to see them doing whatever people in relationships do in front of me through all of eternity. It was easier to pretend like all he did on his time off was sleep alone in his bed like a good boy—thus the need to avoid him ending up with a friend of mine.

For a second there, I stood by myself, waiting for Nathan to come out of the bathroom, and a guy wearing a black hoodie and a Guy Fawkes mask walked up to me. He looked over his shoulder and removed his mask.

"Thomas?"

CHAPTER 17

CJ's Birthday Party Part 2

"HI, BILLIE." Thomas leaned in and kissed my cheek in a painfully slow motion. "You look—beautiful." He took a deep breath, his eyes looking glazed as he analyzed my costume. Thomas strategically gave his back to my security detail, so they hadn't spotted him yet.

Caleb and David were too distracted to pay attention to what was happening around them. And the place was packed at this point.

Something about the look on Thomas's face made me feel uneasy. I couldn't tell if he was drunk or just plain miserable. Probably an unfortunate mixture of both. He kept his usually soft, curvy lips in a constant tight, harsh line.

"Since when do you smoke?" He took a step closer to me and leaned in to look into my eyes. "Are you drunk?"

I took a step back.

"Who came with you to the party?" He continued. "Did you bring a date?"

This isn't happening.

I didn't answer any of his questions. I didn't even want to talk to him. He stared at me, waiting for a reply that'd gone rogue. And just to make sure, I took a couple of extra steps back, but Thomas easily grasped my arm, making my cigarette fall to the floor.

The lights dimmed out, and a strobe light effect flooded the space. The music became louder as the DJ switched to deep house because apparently, he'd been hired to play the soundtrack of my interactions with Thomas.

"Why are you doing this to me?" he shouted over the music. "You know how much I love you! I can't sleep! I—" He pulled the hoodie off his head and dragged a rough, angry hand through his messy hair.

"Thomas, you're hurting me," I said with a calm but stern voice. His hand was still attached to my arm. The strobing lights made Thomas's features look harsh. Somber.

"I *need you* to come back to me." His grip around my arm got even tighter. "I promise I'll tell you everything. And once you know, you'll understand why I've been acting the way I have. I'm ready now." He was looking down into my eyes, his face too close to mine. "Please don't look at me like that. Like I'm this—insane person."

"You're *hurting* me!" I tried shoving him off, but he grabbed both of my arms and pulled me closer to him.

"Babe, just—please," he begged. "I swear everything will go back to the way it used to be in the beginning. Don't you miss me at all?"

"Get your *bleeding* hands off her," Nathan said with a growl. Thomas finally released me from his grasp. "Now sod off."

My arm was going to be bruised the next day. It hurt like hell.

"Who the fuck is *this?*" Thomas snarled back at me, demanding an answer.

I threaded my fingers in between Nathan's and squeezed his hand with a quick pulse, and said, "This is Nathan, my boyfriend."

"What?" He grimaced in Nathan's direction. His eyes narrowed as he scanned him up and down. Maybe if Thomas thought I was with someone else, he would back off for good and reconcile with the idea of us not getting back together.

Another guy stood next to Thomas and revealed his identity by removing a Guy Fawkes mask like the one Thomas wore over his head.

"Hey, ginger. Long time no see." And that's what a douchebag with a grin looks like.

I squeezed Nathan's hand again in an involuntary reaction to seeing Nicholas's annoying face. He placed his arm around my waist and said, "Let's go, love."

"Love?" Nicholas said before bursting into laughter. "Oh, Tommy! Brit-Brit here is snatching you good. I know you said she tastes all kinds of sweet, but no pussy's worth the—"

Boom.

Nathan plastered Nicholas's face on the floor before he could finish the sentence by grabbing his arm and twisting it in a swift move that made him fall to the ground.

Tobias ran up to us as soon as he saw what was happening and yelled something to Nathan in Swedish. Nathan ignored him. He was busy with the arm-twisting thingy.

"Tob, go get the guys!" I yelled. He turned around and ran off to get them.

It'd all been too fast that when Thomas realized what had happened, he immediately launched at Nathan. Nicholas groaned on the floor.

Nathan used Thomas's weight against him and easily shoved him to the side. Nicholas was back up on his feet when Thomas fell on the floor on all fours.

Thomas jumped up and thrust himself in Nathan's direction again but was quickly neutralized by Aaron and Caleb before he could reach him. Nicholas shoved Nathan's chest and threw a punch at him, but Nathan easily dodged it, cupped his hand and struck at Nicholas's nose in an upward motion. The entire party must've heard the *crack*. I looked away after hearing Nicholas scream with pain. That nose was *shattered*.

David immediately seized Nicholas, but he wriggled like a desperate fish out of water, blood trickling heavily from his nose. Behind them, a mountain of a man made his way to the fight scene. Big Mike.

He collected Nicholas, making him stop fidgeting in two seconds. "You broke my nose, you piece of shit!" he yelled at Nathan through bloody teeth. "I'll fucking sue you motherfucker!" He was deranged.

Nathan chuckled, and that just made Nicholas start swearing a combination of words I'd never even heard someone use before in a sentence.

"I'll be delighted!" Nathan replied, coloring every syllable. Nicholas spat blood in Nathan's direction as David and Big Mike pulled him away, but the blood didn't get anywhere near him.

Aaron and Caleb moved Thomas out, but he looked over his shoulder and said to Nathan, "You're dead—*mate*."

Nathan stood with his arms crossed at his chest, clearly unmoved by Thomas's threat, waiting for him to be taken out. Ren embraced Sophie, who was deeply startled by the fight. I held on to Cecile's arm, and Tobias stood next to us.

"Billie, are you okay?" Tobias asked me. His gaze trained on my arm, probably trying to find any damage.

"Just sore, but I'm fine, Tob."

He didn't seem convinced.

Once Thomas disappeared through the main entrance, Nathan joined us. "I'm so sorry!" I hugged him tight around his waist. "Are you okay?" He looked perfect—not a single hair out of place.

"My God, Murph. Your arm's blazing red where he gripped it." He took his phone out and snapped a picture of my arm.

"What are you doing?"

"Evidence of physical abuse, threats. Tobias told me he's your ex. Quite the nutter if you ask me. But he really cocked up. We can easily file for an order of protection against him. I'll be right back."

Order of what now?

"Nathan!"

He walked up to Aaron and Caleb, who had returned from kicking out Nicholas and Thomas, and chatted with them. David and Big Mike stayed outside, probably making sure they would actually leave. I hoped Thomas took Nicholas to the hospital.

"Billie, what the hell just happened?" CJ hugged me.

"It was Thomas," I replied. Nina had approached us too.

"He's *insane*," Nina said, hugging me. "He seemed so different when we met him. What did he want?"

"He's just—having trouble accepting it's over." I took a deep breath, and Nina squeezed her lips together. "Where's Juan Pablo?" I asked, trying to change the subject.

"We got into an ugly argument last night. We're not talking right now. I didn't feel like coming to the party with him."

"Oh, I'm so sorry to hear that. I hope you can sort things out."

"I'm sure we will," she said with a sad smile.

"I think I'm heading out, CJ. We had lots of fun tonight, but I just want to go home if that's okay."

"Of course. I'm so glad you came, and I'm so sorry about Thomas sneaking in. There's a list, but they must've—"

"There's no reason to apologize." I hugged him and Nina.

"David's got me all turned on and shit. You know, after seeing him in action," CJ whispered with a naughty smile. "I'd ask if I could borrow him for the rest of the night, but I know that *big guy* over there won't allow him to stay."

He meant Aaron, of course. I laughed because he was right. There was no way David could stay. Not after what happened.

"I could've helped him take the edge off, if you know what I mean." CJ winked at me and pulled Nina away, where they joined a group of friends who idled near us. I shook my head with a laugh.

CJ really liked David. It was more than evident.

I joined Sophie and Cecile and told them I wanted to leave but offered them to stay if they wanted to. Their night didn't have to be ruined just because mine was.

"Are you insane?" Sophie said, widening her eyes. "Definitely not. Let's go," She looked scared and agitated from having witnessed the fight. I was upset too, but mostly glad Thomas and Nicholas had left.

"We could go back to my place if you still want to hang out," I proposed. Ren and Sophie turned to look at each other, then nodded my way. Nathan heavily gestured in the distance while talking to Aaron and Caleb. He tapped Aaron's shoulder twice and turned around to make his way back to us.

"I'm in," Tobias said, holding Cecile's hand. She didn't seem bothered by it. She seemed drunk.

"We're heading back to the apartment," I said to Nathan. "I'm just—not in the mood for staying."

"I can imagine. Let's go."

We took our coats and walked out of the party.

Nathan and I stepped in the car with Big Mike as I promised I would. Everyone else rode back in the SUV.

I asked Big Mike to stop at a convenience store to get a new cigarette pack for Caleb. We had cleaned him out. Nathan volunteered to buy them.

"Seeing you fight these guys was impressive," I said to Nathan once he returned from the store. "Is it some type of martial art?"

"Ah, yes. Krav Maga. It's an Israeli military self-defense and fighting system."

"Wow. How did you get into it?" Caleb and I had talked about it. Both Aaron and Caleb were trained in Krav Maga. Caleb insisted on teaching me when we were in Paris. He offered to train me in secret, but we never found the perfect time and place to do so since it had to be done behind my father's back.

"Let's say I was a rebellious teen," Nathan said with a tight-lipped smile. "My parents signed me up when I was thirteen to help channel my—emotions." His eyes looked sad when he said that. "It served me well."

"Maybe I should sign up too," I said in a breath. Whatever helps channel emotions.

"Why?" He weaved his fingers with mine. I shook my head twice, slowly, trying to dismiss my remark. "Don't worry," he said. "We'll have plenty of time to talk."

"I'm sorry about what happened with Thomas. I didn't know he was going to show up to the party." I was embarrassed about it. I also wanted to know what he talked about with Aaron and Caleb after taking a picture of my arm. "You mentioned something about an order of protection? What's that?"

"Do you want me to take care of it? I can have someone at the office talk to your father's attorney and fix that for you. That way, Thomas won't be legally able to get near you or contact you in any way."

That sounded harsh. It would probably come with inevitable repercussions for Thomas. "I'd like to wait. I don't want that to affect him at school or something."

"He physically hurt you and threatened me ... 'your boyfriend.'" He grinned for a second. "There were eye-witnesses. We can file one against Nicholas, too, if you will. It's easy peasy."

For Nathan, all of this legal jargon was normal. But I didn't want to affect Thomas. He would probably get kicked out of the rowing team or worse. I knew he loved rowing crew, and I wasn't comfortable jumping into a legal conundrum. At least not yet.

Thomas was still hurting from the breakup. He just needed more time to accept it. Besides, I had three guys taking care of me 24/7. Maybe it was only a matter of reinforcing security for a while. I'd prefer to try that out first before affecting his life forever. I wanted to think Thomas wouldn't dare hurt me. Although, he kind of already had.

"Was that what you were talking about with Aaron and Caleb just now?"

"Yes. And they agreed with me." I understood now why Caleb thought Nathan "was cool." They were both equally exaggerated about these matters.

"Could you give it a few weeks or so? Let's see what happens. I don't think it will be necessary."

"Of course. It's your choice to make. Not mine." He smiled.

"I think he's part of the reasons I'm annoyed about—dating," I confessed.

Nathan squeezed my hand. "And what's the other part?"

Shit.

"Um. I don't know. I'm just disappointed in general," I said, looking away. I was telling the truth, but I wasn't being specific.

"It's a good thing then that we're only pretending to date. That way, we can go on a bunch of pretend dates, and I could give you a pretend snog or two."

"A snog?" I asked, turning to look at him. My gaze instinctively drifted to his lips.

He leaned in and whispered, "A kiss." His minty breath brushed against my lips. His hand wandered up along the exposed skin from the thigh-high slit of my dress. "But I think you figured that one out pretty quickly, didn't you?"

Big Mike harrumphed as he parked the car outside of my apartment building. Nathan and I straightened ourselves on our seats.

"I only have to report on things that happen. Not on those that don't happen," Big Mike said when he opened the door for us. *Got it.* I liked him already.

Aaron, David, and Caleb stood outside the apartment building, waiting for us to arrive. Nathan's phone buzzed with an incoming call. I walked up to Caleb and gave him the pack of menthols. "I'm sorry," I said with an exaggerated grin.

"That wasn't necessary, Miss Murphy," Caleb replied. He looked worried and—embarrassed? Why?

"Is everything okay?" I asked him.

"We weren't paying enough attention. Thomas approaching you and that bruise on your arm is on us."

"What? Of course not," I whispered. "It was dark and crowded. Don't worry about it. I'm fine, and you dealt with it perfectly, okay?" Caleb looked at me like there was nothing I could say to convince him otherwise.

Nathan came back, so our conversation came to a halt.

"Where's everybody?" I asked the guys.

"They didn't say, Miss Murphy," David replied. "They just went upstairs."

"It's Tobias," Nathan said. "Everyone's at Lily and Joel's."

Who's everyone? I needed clarification on that one.

Nathan thanked the guys once again, and we stepped inside the lobby. "Do you want to come up for a bit?" he asked as we waited for the elevator.

"I don't know. You must be tired after all the Mortal Kombat you pulled at the party." I laughed. I didn't want William to be there, but I was sure Sophie and Cecile would let me know if he was. Besides, he had that charity event Tobias told me about. Perhaps he hadn't returned yet.

"I'm not," he said, pressing the eleventh-floor button. "I swear I'm good. Are you okay?"

"Yes, of course. Let's go."

Lily opened the door for us and squealed with excitement. "Oh, my God! You both look *so* good! You never sent me the picture of you all dressed up," she said. "Come in, come in!" She looked tipsy, and her teeth were purple. I laughed. I was happy to see her.

"Aren't we a wee bit squiffy?" Nathan said to Lily. She bumped her shoulder against his.

"I'm not sure what that means," she replied. "But I'm sure I am." She turned around with a chuckle and floated off to the living room, where she sat next to Joel.

Sophie, Cecile, Ren, and Tobias sat with them. Sophie and Ren weren't drinking anymore, but Cecile had a glass of wine in her hand. Tobias had pulled out another bottle of tequila.

I excused myself to go to the bathroom and hung my coat on the foyer's coat rack beforehand. The wig was itchy and uncomfortable. It was time to take it off. My hair fell on my shoulders when I picked out the few pins attached to the wig net. I teased my hair with my fingers trying to untangle it and make it look better.

I stepped out of the bathroom and gave the wig back to Lily.

"Murph, you look exquisite," Nathan said in front of everybody.

I lost the battle. That was the first time I blushed for Nathan. The way he said it, like he *genuinely* meant it made my body thaw in Lily's living room.

I thanked him with a shy smile and detoured toward the kitchen with the excuse of grabbing a glass of water. He followed me.

"So, for how long are you staying here at Lily's?" I asked Nathan as I looked through the cupboards for a glass.

"Top left," he said. "Um—about a week or so. I found a flat today, but it's not ready yet." I pulled my bottom lip up with disappointment.

"What?" he asked. "Are you going to miss having me around the building?" He took the glass out of my hands and poured some water in it for me.

"Of course not," I said with a proud face, clearly joking.

"I won't be too far from here." He took a few steps in my direction and licked his lower lip. "You know, this is exactly how I met you. Green dress, auburn hair beside your face. I'll never forget it." He placed his hands on my shoulders and teased the straps of my dress with his fingertips. "It's unfair if you ask me. I'd just arrived from the airport. I was shattered." He grazed my arm, where my bruise was with the back of his fingers.

"Well, if that's what *shattered* looks like ..."

He bit his lower lip with a smile and grabbed my hand to pull me closer to him. I wet my lips and swallowed.

"Billie, what the heck happened at the party?" Lily asked, walking into the kitchen. "Did Thomas hurt you?" I'm sure Tobias was the one to tell her.

"Thomas showed up. But Nathan, he—took care of it."

"He was about to rip her arm off," Nathan tossed in.

"Thomas did *what?*" Lily looked shocked and then some. That probably got her sobered up.

"I'm fine. I swear."

"The sad-arsed prick got to her when I was in the loo," Nathan continued.

"And where were Aaron and Caleb and—"

"It's not their fault. Thomas and Nicholas wore these—masks when they walked into the party. The place was dark and packed. And I'm always asking them to back off. If anything, it's my fault."

"It's not," Nathan said firmly.

Lily offered a bag of frozen vegetables, and I accepted it. It felt great on my sore skin.

We joined everyone in the living room and chatted for a while, but my eyes felt heavier by the minute. I was exhausted.

Ren and Sophie kept talking and laughing. Cecile had her head reclined on the sofa's backrest, and Tobias sat sideways, leaning closer to her face. They were whispering and chuckling. Cecile's glassy eyes gave away her level of drunkenness, which wasn't of the worrying kind yet. She placed her hand on Tobias's face, and he got even closer to her. Damn. I looked away.

"I think I'm ready to go," I said to Nathan, yawning.

"Can I walk you?" he asked. I nodded.

Sophie and Cecile wanted to stay for a while longer. I told them I would send the key back with Nathan.

As we waited for the elevator, two girls stepped out of apartment 11A with big smiles on their faces. One had a fancy dress on. She wore her long, wavy, chocolate-brown hair down. The other one wore jeans and a sweater with her golden hair in a high ponytail. She looked cute with those rosy cheeks and freckles. Ugh.

William came out with messy hair, wearing cotton shorts and a hoodie. And as if it were any more possible, the remnants of tequila flowing through my body made William look even more handsome, alluring, hot—*unfaithful*.

So, he took the girl in the dress to the gala because Erin's away and then called up the other for a two-on-one action type of situation? *What in the actual fuck is happening? This guy is insane!*

"William!" Nathan exclaimed with a grin, shaking his hand with a clap. I took a deep breath and said hello to the two girls with a close-lipped smile.

William introduced the two girls to us. Alice was the brunette, and Luna was the blonde one with the cute freckles. They both shared looks after the introduction.

William placed his hands on Luna's shoulders. "How was your evening? Did you enjoy yourselves?" he asked, trying to seem casual with the small talk.

"We did," Nathan replied, throwing his arm around me.

William looked at me and redirected his gaze toward my bruised arm which at this point was already gaining a little color.

He bit the corner of his lower lip and flared his nostrils just a tad. But I noticed. He probably wanted to know what happened to my arm, but he didn't ask.

And since we were all clearly out of things to talk about, I grabbed Nathan's hand, making sure our fingers were intertwined in such a way that would make William cringe. But his acting skills were top-notch, as expected. He did a great job with his rendition of: *This is my I don't give a fuck face, have a good night.*

"See you around, mate," Nathan said as we stepped inside the elevator.

I needed to move out of the building. It was getting harder to watch William with other girls. Every time hurt more than the last. But watching him act like he cared one day and didn't the next was the worst part of all.

He probably didn't care.

CHAPTER 18

A Proper Snog

"DO YOU WANT TO COME IN?" I asked Nathan as I unlocked my apartment door. Our previous interaction with William still had me shook. I wanted to distract myself, and Nathan had proved to be a great distractor. I wasn't ready to say good night to him either.

"I'd love to." He smiled and walked in.

"Do you mind if I change first?"

"Just a little," he replied, taking one last look at my dress. I guess he was joking, but he didn't laugh. "I'll wait in the living room." He looked a bit serious now.

I changed out of my dress into leggings and an oversized hoodie. I pulled my hair back into a pony and joined him in the living room.

Nathan raised a brow when he saw me come back. I offered him water, but he declined. I poured myself a glass and sat next to him.

"Is *he* the other part of the reason?" Nathan asked, his face unreadable.

"Yes," I replied, looking into his eyes, both of us aware of who *he* was. "He is."

I couldn't lie to him. Enough lies had been spilled in the last months. I wanted a clean slate. Nathan needed to know because as much as I tried to deny it, I liked him. And I could tell he liked me too.

It was stupid to think he wouldn't eventually notice the weird interactions between William and me, especially with how he usually handled things.

"Was it that obvious?" I asked, feeling a crease taking shape in between my brows.

"Sort of," he quickly replied.

I bit my bottom lip and shook my head a couple of times, looking away from Nathan. I didn't want to cause any drama between them. They knew each other from way back. Nathan could choose any other girl in New York City, and being single was the convenient choice for me.

"You're close with the Sjöbergs. You have known them since you were a kid," I said, feeling sad about it. I wished they didn't know each other at all. "I had fun tonight, but I think it's best if we just—leave it at that."

"Joel's my friend, and William is Joel's brother. That's it. It's always been like that with him. We could never really get along," he said, searching for my hand. "Is there still something going on with him?"

"No, of course not. I-I—don't trust him. We had this"—I shook my head trying to push the images away—"twenty-four-hour summer fling where we kissed a few times, and that was that. He then got back together with Erin. And I thought they were still dating until a few minutes ago when I saw those two girls coming out of his apartment. Maybe he still is. With William, you never know, but you can count for there to be a few girls circling around him all the time, whether he's single or not." Bitterness gushed out of every word I uttered. "I'm sorry, I—I'm sure you weren't expecting any of this."

"The only thing I wasn't *expecting* was meeting you on day one," he said, drawing a line with his finger on the back of my hand. "I'm fresh off a three-year relationship, and to be honest, I thought I didn't want to jump into anything serious for a while too, but your hand feels kind of great in between mine."

Nathan's fingers found mine and melded into a single perfect fist.

"I agree." I squeezed his hand with a soft smile.

"We could take it slow. I know you're still dealing with your totally mental ex-boyfriend. Plus, that dodgy upstairs neighbor of yours isn't going anywhere." He grinned. "Perhaps I could do a thing or two to help out with everything. To help you sort things out."

I laughed. Nathan had this incredible sense of humor that helped me relax and stop taking things so seriously.

"We could start going on a pretend date or two if you will. See where it goes from there," he proposed. I nodded and smiled. "It was *your* idea, after all. The pretending part."

"Well, you didn't seem uncomfortable with the idea." I teased, dropping my head back on the sofa's backrest.

"I also need to teach you what a proper snog is." He licked his lips and came closer to my face, realizing I wanted to be taught. I'd always been quite the teacher's pet.

His lips were right there in front of mine. Eager and waiting. "Is it something like this?" I leaned in and pressed my lips into his for a short but gentle kiss.

"Exactly," he whispered, our lips still touching. "And something like this, too." He crushed his lips against mine as I caressed his soft stubble. His right hand traveled behind my neck while his other hand wandered up my thigh, higher and higher.

I grabbed his hand, and he groaned back in protest. He wanted to continue doing whatever it was he intended to do. Some other time, maybe. Not before being sure of what I wanted. But at that moment, I wanted him so badly.

I knew I needed to stop, so I convinced my lips to unlock from his.

"So that was snogging," he said, caressing my warm, flushed cheek with the back of his fingers. "Let me know if I wasn't thorough enough with my demonstration."

"I do lean toward forgetfulness." I brushed my fingers through his soft, brown waves, lightly combing them, familiarizing myself with him.

"Splendid," he said under his breath. His lips idled near mine.

"Aren't you going to test me on my newly acquired skill?" I asked. "I'm looking forward to acing this test."

"Oh, God, yes."

CHAPTER 19

Lovers For A Night

October 31, 2009

NATHAN LEFT AFTER "a proper snogging session" when he saw I couldn't keep my eyes open any longer from exhaustion. He took my apartment key with him and gave it to Sophie and Cecile so they could come back whenever they felt like it. All I wanted was to sleep.

I woke up a few minutes past 9:00 a.m. with a slight headache. I opened the door to the guest room just a tad and found Sophie sleeping alone in the bed. The living room and kitchen were also empty. Strange.

I poured myself a big cup of morning fuel and grabbed my cell phone to check my messages.

Tobias: Cecile's phone is dead. She's staying over.

That message came in at 3:47 a.m. Dammit. That was odd coming from Cecile. She was still Paul's girlfriend. It's one thing to go to a party and have fun in a group setting, but spending the night with Tobias? I just hoped she wasn't too drunk or hadn't made any decisions she would regret.

As I peered out the window, the day greeted me with a *go back to bed* vibe. It appeared to be chilly and gray. Running out in the cold wasn't an option for me today. I was exhausted from last night.

I finished my coffee and took a shower. I couldn't stop thinking about Nathan. He really had been a surprise I didn't see coming. The only thing that worried me was the three-year relationship he had just gotten out of. But taking things slowly as he suggested would help ease that worry. I didn't want to fall for another guy who didn't know what he wanted.

On the other hand, I couldn't brush off the frustration I felt with William. One second he's all worked up and demanding things from me, asking me to cancel on Nathan to come with me to the party, and the next he's stepping out of his apartment with two girls. Two!

And the way he walked out, with his hair all wild, the comfy clothes he probably threw on after whatever happened inside that bedroom was even more disappointing. I couldn't even imagine how something like that would work, not that I wanted to dwell much into that image.

A stubborn, and foolish, part of my mind wanted to think of an alternative scenario. Something to explain what those two girls coming out in the wee hours of the night, looking all plump and pretty, might've meant.

I couldn't come up with any options for the life of me other than: *threesome parade*. Ugh. I couldn't stomach it. It was so confusing because something inside me insisted that William wasn't that type of guy. He couldn't be. Not the William I've had the opportunity to know. But the evidence was right there in front of me, and that's what made it so grueling. It was driving me nuts.

It was best to drop the illusion, turn the page, and move on.

Mimi arrived to save the day and offered to cook breakfast for me. I accepted since Sophie was still sleeping, and I wanted her to rest.

Cecile worried me. I just wanted to know if she was okay, but

I was sure she and Tobias were asleep too. Mimi said she would prepare food for everyone. That way, they could eat later when they woke up.

Nathan: Morning, Murph.

Looking at Nathan's text made fluttering butterflies, and all these other tingling feelings materialize themselves in my stomach. How was it possible that I missed him already?

Me: Hey, you! What are you up to?
Nathan: Just woke up five minutes ago thinking about you.
Me: I was probably thinking about you too. Do you want to come down for breakfast? Mimi's cooking all sorts of yummy things.
Nathan: I don't know who Mimi is, but I sure want to eat whatever she's making.
Me: You do.
Nathan: I'll be there in a few minutes.

I helped set the table with the biggest smile on my face. Mimi kept curiously staring my way. She seemed happy to see me happy, even though she didn't know why that was.

I ran to my bedroom and splashed some perfume behind my ears and neck. I dabbed my lips with my favorite rosy lipstick, and then the doorbell rang. *Oh, my God!* The nerves were real.

"I've got it, Mimi, thanks," I said with a grin. She was about to open the door, but she turned on her heel and rushed back to the kitchen.

"Ah! You look lovely," Nathan said when I opened the door. He placed his hand on the small of my back and gave me a quick peck on the lips. I gawked at him for his forward yet *very* charming gesture.

"Why are you so surprised?" He laughed. "You weren't making that face last night."

"Well, last night, we were *pretending* to date."

"I was under the impression that we aren't done pretending." He frowned, amused.

"We certainly aren't." My hand searched for his. He was right. They did feel great together.

"Glad to hear it." He smiled and pulled me closer to him for a warm and cozy hug. "How's your arm?" he asked, his arms locked tightly around my shoulders.

"Turning purple mixed up with different yucky, greenish shades." I smiled and searched for his gaze. He didn't smile back.

"Hmm." His brows lowered with disgust on his face. "I really wanted to go find the blighter last night. If I only knew where that sorry-arsed prick lays his head at night."

The blight-what? I knew he was talking about Thomas, but hell, I needed to write all these words down and google them.

"I take it you're not a morning person," I replied, gently pulling away. His eyelids still looked heavy, and his voice was all grumpy and rough. I thought it was so endearing.

"You're not wrong about that. But I'm just troubled about the prick hurting you like that."

"I swear I'm fine, don't worry." I grabbed his hand and pulled him to the dining room. "You need food and coffee."

"Yes, please."

The table looked like a buffet. There was a lot to choose from: eggs, bacon, croissants, berry jam, sausage, fruit, yogurt, cottage cheese, and a big jug with coffee. Mimi went all in.

"Everything looks delicious," Nathan said, helping me to my seat.

We sat and ate, and once we were halfway done with our breakfast, Mimi approached the table. She wanted to see if we needed anything else. I took the opportunity to introduce them.

"Nathan, this is Mrs. Mullins, or Mimi, as we like to call her. Mimi, this is Nathan. He's staying with the Sjöbergs for a few days."

"Pleased to meet you, Mrs. Mullins." He stood up and held his hand out to her.

"Pleasure is ool mine. Please call me Mimi," she said with a warm smile and a firm handshake.

"Is that a Scottish accent?" Nathan asked her.

"Aye. It's rusty 'round the edges noo. Too many years ooh-way from home."

It wasn't as rusty as she thought it was. I invited her to sit with us for the remainder of our meal. She poured herself some coffee and kept chatting with us.

"Ye knoo, Billie's grandparents from her father's side were Scottish. They couldn't have been kinder than to hire me as I was just a wee lass, inexperienced, and nooly-rived in America. James, Billie's father," she said, looking at me, "hired me when they passed ooh-way."

"She's family," I said, smiling at her.

"I see where the red hair comes from now," Nathan said, placing a strand behind my ear. "It's lovely."

"Are ye Billie's boyfriend, dear?" she asked Nathan. "She can't seem to stop smiling ever since she stepped oot of her bedroom this morning."

"Mimi!" I laughed.

"I'm her *pretend* boyfriend." He laughed too, grabbing my free hand. "Imagine how big her smile will be when we start dating for real."

"How not? Why pretend, then?" Mimi asked, looking perplexed. "Sataboot?"

"Let me explain," I replied. I told Mimi what happened the night before. My father was going to find out anyway when he got the report. I told her Thomas and Nicholas showed up at the party and started a fight with Nathan after telling them he was my boyfriend.

Mimi seemed shocked when I pulled up my sleeve and showed her the ugly bruise Thomas left on my arm. "And what aboot Aaron and—"

"They stopped the fight in time and kicked Nicholas and Thomas out," I reassured her.

"Yer father willnae be pleased," Mimi said, sipping on her coffee. *I knoo.*

Sophie walked out of her room, looking pretty, wearing jeans and a brown sweater. Her hair was still damp from her shower. "*Bonjour,*" she said sweetly. We all said good morning back to her.

I offered her breakfast, and Mimi excused herself from the table, taking her cup with her. "Where's Cecile? I never heard her arrive," Sophie asked, pouring herself a cup of coffee.

"Um, she spent the night with Tobias," I said, looking at Nathan. "At least that's what he told me in a text."

"What?" Sophie grimaced and sipped on her coffee. "That is so unlike her. Have you tried texting or calling her?"

"Cecile's phone is out of battery. I guess we'll have to wait for her to come back."

Nathan and I sat with Sophie while she ate her breakfast. We kept talking about how screwed up Thomas's surprise visit was. Sophie seemed worried about it and agreed with Nathan about the order of protection. I explained why I didn't want to do it yet, but she didn't understand my reasons, or at least she didn't want to. It was best to change the subject.

"Did you have fun with Ren?" I asked Sophie with a big smile.

"Oh my God, yes! He's so cute, Billie! Such a nice, decent guy. Smart, funny …"

I was so glad they clicked.

"He's such a nice guy," I told her.

"He is. Guys like him are hard to find. Too bad we're leaving tomorrow. But he's going to Spain for Christmas break, and he might take a trip to Paris for New Year's Eve." She grinned.

"Sophie, that sounds amazing!"

There was a faint knock on the door, and I ran to see who it was.

Cecile was standing on the other side wearing her 20s dress from last night. Sobs escaped her as soon as she saw me. I immediately placed my arms around her.

I'm going to kill Tobias.

CHAPTER 20

Tug o' War

"HEY, IT'S OKAY." I pulled back slightly to see Cecile's face. "What happened?" I asked her, watching her soul thaw into tears. It broke my heart. Nathan walked to the foyer where we stood. He excused himself and told me he would call me later. He surely wanted to give us privacy so we could talk.

Cecile and I took the conversation to the guest room. Sophie followed us.

"I feel terrible. So guilty," Cecile said in between sobs. "I don't know *why* I did it. What am I going to do now?" She covered her face with her hands. "I have to tell Paul. He'll definitely want to end things after this."

"Did you—sleep with him or?" Sophie asked.

"Of course, I did! Look at him! He's just so—" She couldn't stop crying. "Ah! I *hate* him."

She was devastated.

"You did consent to it, right?" I mused. "I just want to make sure he didn't—"

"No, no, no. It wasn't like that." Cecile quickly cut me off. "I *was* drunk. But I remember everything. I remember how bad I wanted Tobias. But I was so mad at Paul about this stupid fight we had, and now I'm a cheater. I ruined everything!" Cecile threw herself into my arms again.

I saw red. I knew Cecile wasn't a victim. She slept with Tobias because that's what she thought she wanted. But those Sjöberg brothers were getting on my nerves, always taking what they want, when they want it, having no respect for other people's relationships, or thinking about the consequences.

I know Cecile did it because she felt like it. But I know how tempting William was when I was with Thomas and how he messed with my head—always meddling where he shouldn't because he just didn't care about anyone but himself.

And now Tobias was proving to be exactly like his brother.

I'm not so sure if Cecile would've slept with him if she was sober. That's what made me so angry. That Tobias might've taken advantage of the situation.

"I'll be right back," I said to them, gently unlocking my arms from around Cecile. I stormed out of the room without looking back. I needed to talk to Tobias. I considered him a friend, and I trusted him with one of my best friends ever. And she comes back drenched in tears? Not on my goddamned watch.

"Billie, *attendez!*" Cecile shouted. I left anyway. It had to be done.

I took the elevator to the eleventh floor, fully aware that I was headed to William's turf but not really caring.

After knocking a few times, Tobias opened the door with red-rimmed, heavy eyes, wearing nothing but black cotton shorts. *Jesus.*

"Get dressed," I said, looking away with a haphazard wave in his direction. "We need to talk." They were all *infuriating* with their abs and shit.

"Good morning to you too," he said in a low, rough voice. He looked destroyed. And that made me feel festive. I hope he had a terrible headache too. Tobias gestured for me to come in and disappeared into his room.

Thankfully, William was nowhere to be found. Probably busy masterminding his plans for tonight, wondering which and how many girls to bring in next, or whatever. The guy was greedy.

I waited for Tobias in the living room, too angry to realize sooner it was the first time I set foot in William's apartment. Everything was impeccable. It had a similar style and color palette as the cottage but a few more hints of color here and there. There was a beautiful, black grand piano that took almost half the living room space.

And these guys had even more books than I did. There was a loaded floor-to-ceiling bookcase, neatly organized by spine color. It made me want to stand up and figure out how else they'd been cataloged. It was hard to understand how they found the time to read since they were always busy womanizing and such.

I rolled my eyes at the bookcase because it was really nice, and Tobias walked out of his room, pulling a t-shirt over his head in a lazy motion.

"Why are you looking at me like you want to kill me or some shit like that?" He brushed his face with his hands, trying to dry it. His hair dripped with water here and there. Good thing he threw some water on his face. I needed him to be fully awake for this.

"Because I'm seriously considering it," I replied. "Cecile just walked back to my apartment in tears, Tob. She feels terrible about what happened last night." Tobias took a seat in front of me. "She has a boyfriend. I told you. Several times, actually. But you didn't care. I thought I could trust you, but you're just like William. Selfish to the core."

I wished William was here to listen. He might've found the conversation enlightening.

"Billie, I didn't do anything she didn't want to do too. You know me. You know I would never—"

"She was drunk, Tob. And come on, you know you're not that hard to look at, either."

Tobias smiled for a second, but he cleared his throat with a furrowed brow once he noticed how serious I was about the conversation. I wasn't here to blow up his ego. I was just laying the facts on the table. Tobias is *gorgeous*. Fact. And Cecile agrees. Another fact.

"What do you want me to say! I'm sorry, okay," he said in a snappy tone, rubbing his temples. "I didn't mean to hurt her. I like her, actually—a lot. And I wished she didn't have to leave. If it were up to me, I wouldn't leave it at a one-night stand. I'd still want her here with me right now. But she woke up and just—took off."

"You liked her yesterday. And today, you're going to like someone else—tomorrow, who knows." I huffed slowly. "I thought you were different." I couldn't help but look away.

"Look, I know she loves blackcurrant gelato. It's her favorite. She likes going to that place in Saint-Michel, where they make the ice cream look like a flower," Tobias began, standing up. The actor inside him took the lead.

I raised a brow, crossed my arms in front of me, and leaned back on the couch. I was getting a front-row seat to Tobias's monologue, and I was there for it.

He looked at me, and I nodded, gesturing with a haphazard hand for him to continue.

He paced back and forth along the space between the sofa and the coffee table. "I know she's studying Marketing and how she would love to work here in New York after graduation. I know she loves you very much"—he glanced at me—"because she couldn't stop talking about it." He smiled, his blue eyes looking straight into mine. Hell, they were just like William's.

I looked away again, heavily annoyed by that.

He took a seat and rested his elbows on his knees, leaning in, his hands in a single fist. "I *know* I like Cecile, and I know she's one of the most beautiful girls I've ever seen. It sucks that she's in a relationship with someone else and that she's feeling terrible about what happened last night because I don't. I'm glad I met her and that it happened."

"She does love going to Amorino," I said through my teeth. We often went for ice cream there. I had to take the deepest breath. This whole speech-monologue thingy Tobias had just thrown at me was kind of romantic. I didn't know what to think anymore.

"I didn't mean to hurt her. I swear," Tobias insisted. I stared at him, trying to make him suffer as he waited for my verdict. A few seconds stared back, waiting for my answer too. "So? You're not going to kill me, right?"

"Who's killing who?" William asked from behind me. He startled me. Like he always did. There he was, all ... male, smelling like autumn and citrus, wearing a green cap backward, black fitted joggers, and a white t-shirt, of course—torture in an image.

"Well, as long as Tobias's speech wasn't an acting exercise or a line taken out of some script, he'll live," I said, still looking at Tobias. "But *you* can take a number."

"What did I do?" William complained with a laugh. I glared at him from the corner of my eye.

"So that's it? She fucking hates me?" Tobias asked with a grimace. He seemed genuinely disappointed by the situation, bordering on bitter.

"Cecile feels terrible right now, okay. She doesn't *hate* you, but I don't think she wants to see you anytime soon." She did say I hate *him*, but I knew she didn't. I perfectly understood where she was coming from. It was anything but hate, but things get blurred up like that sometimes. It's a confusing, dangerous, thin line. Sometimes you have to look down at your feet to see exactly on which side of the line you're standing.

"Fuck," he muttered, brushing his messy, light brown hair back with his fingers. I guess he did like her a lot. My trust issues and my protective instincts were sparking up and getting in the way, but I had to give Tobias the benefit of the doubt.

"I'll go see how she's doing." I stood up. "We'll talk later."

"Please apologize for me, will ya?" Tobias said, his eyes sad but hopeful. "I'd do it myself, but I'm not sure that's a good idea right now."

I nodded.

"You could learn a thing or two from your brother," I said to William, poking his chest as I walked past him to see myself out. He followed me to the door. I could sense his towering presence behind me—all six-feet-four-inches of him.

I spotted the photograph he took of me during Midsummer with Emily Dickinson's quotes facing front hung on the wall right beside the door. *What?* I missed it when I arrived.

I quickly looked away and pulled the doorknob.

"I like reading it every day before I leave the apartment," William said, pushing the door shut. I turned around, and the corded muscles of his arm were on display beside me, his palm firmly placed against the door—an inconvenience.

"My number's up. Time for you to scold me next. What did I do this time?" No smile, no gestures.

Is he out of his mind? How did he not register the fact that I saw two girls coming out of his apartment last night? Two!

"I wouldn't know where to start with you. We could be here all day. So it's best if I don't go there." I turned around and went for the doorknob again.

"I want you to," he said in his usual deep voice. "And that doesn't sound like a half-bad idea. You here—all day. With me."

That freaking voice.

"Nathan's waiting for me." I looked at my watch. "We're probably going to the movies." A lie. I just wanted to hurt him, although I didn't even know if he cared or not. But it wouldn't do me any harm in trying. "It will be the first time I go in almost seven years. Can you believe that? I guess that surely counts as a first. What do you think?"

William ran his tongue over his teeth, and his face went red. He smiled an angry smile that had my name on it.

So, he does *care? Or is it just his ego?*

There was only one way to find out, and that was by poking him with a wooden stick.

"You know, yesterday I tried tequila for the first time. I also had my first margarita ever," I tossed in, looking up to meet his fierce and untamed blue eyes with a small smile. "It was so *scrummy*." I said scrummy in a British accent as a reference to Nathan just to piss him off. It worked.

"Guille"—his Adam's apple moving as he swallowed down the venom—"stop."

No.

He didn't get to say my name like that. Like he owned it or something.

"Nathan's also my first pretend boyfriend," I carried on. "I'm sure Tobias can tell you about it. It's a cute story."

"I know all about that. I know *everything*." He took a deep breath, staring at me like a hawk, refusing to budge. I leveled his gaze, not planning to look away. I could do this all day.

I was not backing down. Not until I left him burning in rage. The same I felt when I saw the photographs of him and Erin, when I found out he was a liar, and when I saw those two girls coming out of his apartment when he said he wanted to drop the event and take me to CJ's party a few hours before that.

"I thought Nathan could take me to the Metropolitan Opera. It would be my first time going there. I just saw that *L'Elisir d'Amore* premieres in mid-December. Now *that* would be a big, juicy first." I pretended to check my nails as I waited for a reply.

William had me cornered against the wall. I had no space to move, but I was sure he would let me go any second now.

"It's a special two-day function, and unfortunately for Nathan"—he almost spat his name—"it's sold out." I looked away, sullen. I really wanted to go. But wait. *Did he check for ticket availability? Why?*

"And I only pretended to date Erin for the premieres. It was a work thing, and I accepted because I was enraged! I saw you kissing Thomas a day after *we* kissed. A day after I opened up myself to you and told you how she had cheated on me. What did you want me to think? I was disappointed." He closed his eyes for a second and continued. "I've told you this *plenty* of times, but you don't seem to care or listen."

Care. Wow. *Look who's talking.*

"*You* could've listened to me, and you wouldn't have to *think ... things*," I told him. "You would've known the truth. But you're too proud to listen."

"I don't care about that kiss or the reason behind it. I don't. All I want is for you to believe me because I haven't lied to you. Ever."

"That's the part I've been struggling with," I said, out of space to take a step back. I couldn't think clearly when he was that close to me, but he didn't seem to care about the lack of space between us. "Sometimes words aren't enough. I don't trust you anymore. I did at first, but now ..." The conversation was useless. He was offering me more words. Words that I couldn't rely on. Words I could easily toss to the side.

"You need to stop this—*pretending to date Nathan* thing you've got going on because I've already stopped pretending to date Erin. It's bullshit."

And what about the pictures of him holding Erin's hand and kissing her a few days ago? But I wasn't going to get into that again. He knew I saw something in the tabloids. And he claimed not to know what it was.

But the photographs couldn't have been more explicit. And it's not like he was sleepwalking around Europe holding hands with her and licking ice cream off her mouth, unaware of his actions. What I didn't understand is why he thought he could keep lying to me about her. About that.

"*We* will stop pretending whenever we feel like it." I turned around, opened the door once again, and stormed out of his apartment. He didn't stop me this time.

"Did he kiss you?" he asked in barely a whisper as I waited for the elevator to take me away.

"No," I replied without turning around. William sighed with relief. "*I* kissed him."

I stepped into the elevator, and he darted behind me. I clicked the door close button (that doesn't work for shit) five times, hoping for a miracle. William stepped in with me, and the doors closed a wink later behind him.

He groaned. "You're just saying that because you're hurt. I know that much."

"No. I'm saying that because it's the truth. I'm not a liar like you are. *I* kissed him first. It's the first time I kiss a guy before they kiss me. I hope you're taking note of things to cross out from your firsts list. Soon I'll have no more left for you to claim."

William cursed under his breath. "You think I'm a liar because you don't want to listen to what I have to say. And when I do get the chance to say *anything*, you don't believe me. I'll just have to show you instead of telling you. And I know how to do that."

"You just don't get it, do you? You've shown enough, believe me," I replied, exasperation exuding out of every word I uttered.

I knocked on my apartment door since I left without a key. Sophie still had it. She opened the door for me, and her eyes went wide with surprise. She was starstruck.

"Hope you enjoyed the threesome yesterday," I said, taking a step inside my apartment. I looked over my shoulder and said, "Oh, and those photographs of you and Erin kissing in London are cute too." I couldn't shut up, couldn't I?

"I see now," he said with a surprised look on his face, almost amused. "Is that what you think that was? A threesome?"

"I know it was. Say hi to Erin for me. Perhaps we can go on a double date sometime when she's back from Europe. Or a triple date. God knows how many women you'd show up with."

He laughed—the cynic.

I shut the door in his face, doubting my assumptions about the so-called threesome. But I didn't care anymore to know what the truth was.

Well, maybe a little.

I hated that William had this powerful magnetic pull over me. But one thing I knew for sure—Nathan was starting to have an equally strong pull as well.

CHAPTER 21

You Can't Pretend Forever

November 28, 2009

THE DOORBELL RANG, but I was still on the phone with Cecile. We'd been talking for over an hour. She was still having a hard time dealing with her breakup with Paul. She told him everything as soon as she went back to Paris. But I applauded her for her honesty. She could've said nothing, and he would've probably never found out. But that's not Cecile.

Paul was deeply hurt, but she wouldn't have been able to deal with the guilt for long if she kept it to herself.

I opened the door and saw Nathan wearing his gym clothes and holding a single red rose. We were going out for a morning run to Central Park.

"I'll have to call you back," I said to Cecile with the biggest smile on my face.

"Hey, you." I extended my hand to him, pulled him inside, and shut the door behind him.

"I feel like I've known you for way longer than a few weeks," he said, dropping a small duffel bag on the floor. "It's like, I've known you forever, but I just hadn't seen you in a while, and then I found you again. Am I making any sense?"

"You are." I gave him a quick peck on the cheek, and he echoed my move. It had all happened so fast with Nathan. When I met him, I felt exactly the same—like I already knew him. I immediately trusted him and felt like I could talk to him about anything. I knew he would never judge me, and that made me feel safe around him.

"This is for you," he said, giving the rose to me. This was my first *no reason* rose. And I loved it more than all of Thomas's huge *forgive me* flower arrangements.

Nathan and I were still playing our game of pretending. He'd taken me out on a few dinner dates, we hung out with Lily and Joel a lot too, and he'd come over to my place a few times to watch a movie.

We actually watched one of Joel's films once. It was so surreal. I understood why Lily was so jealous now. All that kissing on screen— must be hard to stomach.

Nathan's job was demanding, but so was school. We both felt this energy drawing us together, and we didn't fight it. We gave in to it.

And he wasn't lying when he said he'd be nearby. His apartment was four blocks down on 3rd Avenue on a thirtieth-something floor. It had a fantastic view. He'd already given me a quick tour. His office was also nearby, right on Park, so it was convenient for him to live in Midtown East.

I brought the flower to my nose and smelled it. "Thank you. It's beautiful." I looked up into his eyes and smiled at him.

He grabbed my waist and pulled me near him. "I love that smile. And I love how you crease up when I say something stupid, which is more often than not. I love the smell of you," he said, drawing his nose closer to my neck and inhaling. He gently kissed it afterward. "You're the first thing on my mind when I wake up and the last before going to bed at night. I swear it."

Nathan brushed his lips against mine and said, "I don't want to pretend anymore." I could feel his fresh, sweet, minty breath merging with mine.

"Me neither," I said with a sigh. His fingers unzipped my running jacket and pulled it off my back.

"Thank God," he whispered.

Nathan kissed my neck, and I could already feel my body aching for him. His lips traveled from my neck to my jawline as he took a few slow steps until my back was pressed against the empty gallery wall.

Finally, his lips met mine, and for the first time, I felt him unleash himself upon me. That raw and intense energy I felt the day I met him had been reigned in for the past weeks, and now it was finally set free.

He gently pulled on my hair tie, releasing my hair from my ponytail, making it fall over my shoulders.

Shit. *Focus.*

"I love your hair," he whispered, "and I can't stop thinking about how bad I want you."

He pulled my long-sleeved running shirt in a swift move over my head. His right hand wandered up my thigh slowly, making me gasp. Higher and higher. This time I didn't stop him. I wanted him to keep going.

His fingers teased me for a second, but he carried me, wrapped my legs around his waist, and took me to my room as I held on tightly to his neck—our lips unwilling to break apart. He dropped me gently on my back and took his shirt off.

Damn.

I'd only imagined his body until now. He was perfect. He removed his shorts, and I could see how eager he was to be with me.

He thrust himself at me and kissed me like the world was going to end in three minutes.

"Do I need to use this, or are you—"

"On the pill, yes," I muttered in between subtle pants. "And are you—"

"Clean and healthy," he said with a smile, tossing the condom to the side. I trusted him blindly.

I was ready for him, but I wasn't prepared for what came next. He was something else. The way he looked at me. The way he touched me with both gentleness and despair.

"Are you okay?" he asked when I felt him for the first time. I nodded and managed to smile in return. I couldn't think anymore. Everything spun around us, but all I could focus on was him. My senses belonged to him. There weren't any other arms I'd rather have around my body than his.

"You're beautiful—exactly how I imagined you, and more," he whispered. Electric shockwaves rushed up through my spine in constant surges that clashed on my forehead, impairing my sight but enhancing my sense of touch.

He was going to drive me crazy.

And he did.

☾

Nathan and I skipped our run and went for brunch with Lily and Joel afterward to celebrate making our relationship official.

My security detail always took extra precautions on outings with them. Although we were invisible most of the time, there would be occasions when a paparazzi or two, sometimes more, would try to get too near and get a shot of Lily and Joel together.

Lily was ecstatic when we told her we were now officially dating. "I'm thrilled for you guys. You both deserve to be happy." She smiled and rested her head on Joel's shoulder.

Nathan cupped my chin. "I'm chuffed," he replied and laid a quick kiss on my lips.

"I hope that's a good thing," I said with a chuckle.

"He's *delighted,*" Joel said in a British accent. We all laughed.

Joel surely knew what all Nathan's British expressions meant by now. I still had to get familiarized with them. They were too many.

"I am," Nathan said, kissing me again.

"Get a room," Joel said with a laugh. Lily bumped Joel's shoulder with hers.

"We already did before coming here, actually," Nathan said casually.

"Nathan!" I widened my eyes at him. He grabbed the check and laughed when he saw the raw mortification on my face. Joel wanted to split the bill, but Nathan refused.

"Ha! I dig the *chuffed* Nate," Joel said, bumping his fist on the table. "Keep up the good work, Billie. I'd like the free meals to keep rolling out."

"Don't get too excited," Nathan replied with a lifted brow and a subtle laugh. "I'm not dating you."

"Are you trying to make me jealous?" Joel replied with a grin. "Because it's working."

"Ugh," Lily complained, sticking her tongue out, faking disgust. "You better get used to the bromance, Billie. It's deeply ingrained." They both laughed. They didn't deny it. "So, any word from outside?" Lily asked me. I pulled my phone out of my bag to check.

We couldn't see what was happening outside on the street from where we sat. The guys usually texted me to let me know if any paparazzi were waiting for Lily and Joel to step out. If there were, Nathan and I would leave first and get in the car. Joel and Lily would follow behind. That way, it was easier to get everyone safely back in the car.

"Coast is clear," I replied, tucking my phone back in my bag.

The four of us stood up and stepped out of the restaurant together.

"I have a fitting to get too. It's only a few blocks away," Lily said. "Joel's coming with me, so I guess we'll see you later?" Lily and Joel thanked Nathan for taking care of the check again. I hugged Lily, and a few screams coming from afar startled us.

A small group of teenage girls walking down the street were more than excited to see Joel. They begged him for selfies. Lily took a few steps away from them with an angry pout. David was already behind the wheel. Aaron and Caleb lingered close by, making sure the situation was under control.

Joel, a total sweetheart, agreed to the girls' request for a photograph. Lily, Nathan, and I watched as the girls took their selfies. They all thanked Joel, and one of them grabbed him by the shirt, got on her tiptoes, and kissed him on the lips. I cringed.

"Thank you, girls! Have a nice day!" Joel seemed flustered. He took a few steps back, shaking his head with a troubled expression on his face. Lily was *furious*. She turned around and stalked away. Nathan would laugh and tease Joel about it every single time. But not this time. It'd been too much for Lily.

"*Sötnos!*" Joel cried. But Lily kept walking. "You should see what it's like to go out with Billy. This is nothing." He apologized for having to leave like that and ran to catch up with Lily.

That was crazy.

I still couldn't hear William being mentioned without getting *the collywobbles*, as Nathan liked to say.

"Let's go." Nathan grabbed my shoulders and led me to the car.

"What's *sötnos*?" I asked, stepping into the car. I'd heard Joel call Lily that before, but I never asked about it.

"It's a term of endearment. Sort of like, sweetheart. It literally means sweet nose." He poked my nose, and his phone buzzed. He took the call and intertwined his fingers with mine. The call only lasted a few seconds.

"It was the office. I have to sit down for a brief meeting and sign some papers," he said with disappointment. "I'm sorry. I really wanted to spend the entire day with you."

"It's fine, don't worry. But it's Thanksgiving weekend. It's absurd they make you go to work today."

"They don't really care about that at the office." He laughed and promised not to take too long. We dropped him off there on our way back.

David parked the car outside my apartment building, and there was a cordoned-off area on the sidewalk beside the main entrance. I couldn't tell if the giant crane was hoisting or lowering a grand piano. A bunch of people curiously looked up to see the maneuver from afar.

I wonder ...

"Red, come on," Caleb said, motioning me to step inside the building. "I'll walk you up."

Caleb and I were back to being *us*. It was odd, but once Nathan came into the picture, I felt like he was more at ease. I couldn't understand why that was.

My father was delighted when he found out I was seeing Nathan. They actually did go for beers a few days after the Halloween Party. My father couldn't stop talking about how great Nathan was and vice versa. They had so much in common. They just clicked.

"You seem different today," Caleb said as the elevator went up to the ninth floor. "Happier." He was always hyper-aware of every little nuance regarding my state of mind.

"Um—Nathan and I are official now."

"Oh. Congratulations," he said with a tight-lipped smile. "I know he can make you happy." He frowned a bit but then smiled again as we stepped out of the elevator.

"Is it—still awkward for you? I know it is sometimes for me and—"

"No, hey. It's okay," he said, grabbing my arm to stop me. "Look, Red, we've always been friends. I know we tried, but it's just—I don't know, I didn't want to lose you."

"I didn't want to lose you either. And my father, he—it was so hard to deal with that. The thought of him finding out and—" I trailed off, afraid of my thoughts.

He searched for my gaze. "I promised you I'd stay. It seems like it wasn't—meant to be. And yes, it was hard to deal with your father's disapproval. But hey, I'd rather see you with Nathan than—*him*," he said, looking behind my shoulder and jerking his chin.

I turned around, and there were a ton of boxes outside apartment 9B. William was carrying a couple of them inside. Caleb didn't like him. But I still didn't know exactly why. With Thomas, it was evident—a trust issue. But I'd never talked about his opinion on William. It was useless now.

A few men pulled new furniture out of the service elevator, while others arranged everything inside.

Caleb groaned, raising a brow. "Seems to me like you have a new next-door neighbor." He shook his head. "Or is it—neighbors?" He tilted his head and narrowed his eyes.

Alice and Luna, the threesome girls, also carried boxes inside. *Are they all moving in together?* Maybe it was one of those polyamorous things they had going on. Not that I'm against it. To each their own. It's just that I don't really know how that works, but I know I'm not going to be very supportive if it involves William.

"We'll see," I replied, my train of thought darting out of the station in a timely manner. "Thanks, Caleb. I'll see you later."

Caleb left, and I sauntered toward my apartment. My curiosity was about to make my head explode. I couldn't stop staring at all the movement going on in front of me. I needed to know everything.

William dropped a box on the floor and walked in my direction. "I'm 9B. Nice to meet you," he said, dropping a kiss on each of my cheeks. I crossed my arms in front of me and shook my head a few times. William smiled at my reaction. "Alice, could you put those two boxes in my bedroom, please? They aren't heavy."

"Hi, Billie," she said with a sweet smile. "I'm Alice. We met the other day."

We did.

"Hi, Alice. Yes, of course, I remember." *How could I not?* I coaxed a smile in return. "Are you—moving in?"

She laughed. She wore a wine-colored Adidas tracksuit with her hair down.

"No, no, no. This is William's apartment. Now that Eric's moving in with Tobias, William's finally becoming a grown-up," she said with a chuckle. "He's ready to leave his roommate days behind." She stuck her tongue out at him, and he rolled his eyes at her. I still couldn't understand the dynamic before me.

Thing 2 stepped out of the apartment with a grin. "Hi, Billie!" Luna chirped. Her hair was in a high pony again. She looked so pretty wearing a baby-blue sweater, indigo-blue jeans, and white sneakers.

"This is my girlfriend, Luna. You met her the other day, too," Alice said, carrying another box inside.

Ohhh! So that's ... Not what I thought it was.

"Ah, yes! Hi Luna."

"Alice is my personal assistant, and Luna's just tagging along because she loves being around me so much." William teased her.

"For free." Luna snorted with a smile and walked away. "See you around, Billie." Luna moved another box inside, and Alice was now instructing the movers where to put some chairs.

William seemed to enjoy my reactions. I was so embarrassed about having accused him of the threesome. My face surely indicated my surprise because he stepped closer to me and whispered, "Threesomes aren't my thing. I don't like sharing."

I bit the inside of my lip, not knowing what else to say. I felt so stupid.

"Can you give me two seconds?" William asked. "Don't go anywhere."

He walked up to Alice and said something to her, but I couldn't hear a thing from where I stood. Alice rushed inside and came out with two white envelopes like the one he used to send the film rolls and the photograph a few months ago.

"Here you go," William said, giving them to me. They both said *Guillermina Murphy* on the outside and were numbered 1 and 2, respectively. *Deja vu.* "Since we're next-door neighbors now, there's no use for me to walk downstairs and put these in your mailbox."

I narrowed my eyes at him with curiosity. I wanted to rip the envelopes to pieces and reveal their contents as a child does on Christmas morning.

"It took me a while to find what's in envelope number one. Well, it took *Alice* a while," he said with a faint laugh. "But envelope number two is my personal favorite."

I kept staring at the envelopes, hoping I had x-ray vision.

"I thought you were moving out of the building when I saw the crane moving the piano." I kept feeling the envelopes in my hands, trying to guess what was inside them. Both of them felt flat and smooth.

"And how did that make you feel?" He tilted his head, expecting an answer, it seemed.

"Relieved."

He laughed a hearty laugh that got under my skin in a fraction of a second. But yeah, how could I blame him for laughing when I didn't believe it myself. "Sorry to disappoint you but, I would *never* abandon you like that," he said with a wink.

He turned around and walked toward the pile of boxes still waiting to be moved inside his apartment. "I told you I was going to show you the truth." He turned around and jerked his chin at the envelopes. "You're holding it in your hands. Let me know what you make of it."

CHAPTER 22

A Divergence

THE ENVELOPES WERE two beating Jumanji drums that wouldn't stop pounding, urging me to open them. I could hear the furniture being dragged on the floor beside my room—still unable to grasp the fact that William was going to sleep a wall away from my bed every single night.

Anyway.

Envelope number one included another smaller envelope inside that read, *I'm sorry,* and one of those tabloid magazines dated November 2008—a year ago. The cover showed a photograph of William and Erin on a red carpet event. The title of the picture read:

William & Erin's Secret Romance!

There was a red tab stuck to one page of the magazine. I opened it there to see half a page dedicated to the details of their relationship. I didn't feel like reading it. The article came with a paparazzi shot of William and Erin walking down the street holding hands and another one of them having ice cream—the *same* photographs I saw a few weeks ago on the magazine stand and Sophie's phone.

OhmyGodohmyGodohmyGod! Still in shock, I opened the letter.

Hej älskling,
I'm so sorry about everything. I should've listened to what you had to say after what happened with Thomas. My pride blinded me, and I admit that I was wrong. I know I don't deserve an opportunity to explain myself, but I can't live in a world where you think I'm a liar and a cheat. I know I have a past, and I can't change it, but I would never lie to you. Let me prove it to you. Please forgive me.
Forever yours,
W.S.
P.S. Can I have my green hair tie with the golden stars back?

A tear streamed down my cheek, falling on William's letter. I quickly brushed it off, swallowed down the rest, and shook the paper to dry it out. This letter I would never dare tear apart like the first one he sent me—forever mine. And yes, I still had that green hair tie. It was inside my nightstand drawer.

I took a deep breath and opened envelope number two. There was another tabloid magazine with the day's date: November 28, 2009. One of the few titles on the cover read:

WILLER: IT'S OVER!

There was a picture of William and Erin inside a broken heart just below the title.

Who designs this?

I opened the magazine on the tabbed page where they wrote about the breakup news. Now, *this* was the kind of journalism that piqued my interest. The brief article read:

Sources close to the couple confirm their relationship is officially over with no possibility of reconciliation for the near future.

The couple had called it quits last April after three months of making their relationship official but rekindled their romance in August of the present year. A source close to the couple confirms their breakup happened last month at the beginning of October. "They have nothing but the utmost respect for each other. William hopes nothing but the best for Erin," the source added. Powell's rep was unavailable for comment.

A small note read: *Had to work around the breakup dates to avoid a breach in contract with the film directives. We found out that Erin and her team were feeding the old paparazzi photos of us to the media.*

I closed the magazine and tossed it on my bedroom sofa. I threw myself on my bed and hugged my pillow in a fetal position. A considerable part of my heart broke into a million pieces. He really was too late. I'd just formalized things with Nathan, but it was my fault too. I'd also been too proud to listen, to allow him to explain, and most of all—to believe him. I only did when I saw the evidence which he managed to put together until today.

What am I going to do now?

I texted him.

Me: Hey. Can we talk?

A couple of minutes later, I heard him yell from across the wall, "Coming!" The sound was murky and muffled, sort of like talking into a piece of cloth, but I heard him alright.

He knocked twice on my door ten seconds later.

"Those are some paper-thin walls," I told him when I opened the door.

He laughed. "You heard me? You better behave then." He teased.

"Me?" My eyes went wide. "You're the one who should be worried about the wall's width."

"Oh yeah, with all the threesomes I've got going on, it's sure to get crazy in there. You probably will want to buy one of those white noise machines or get yourself a pair of earplugs. That is if you want to get some sleep at night."

"Very funny." I wrinkled my nose. I took a deep breath and said, "I read your letter."

"Can I—come in?" he asked with a raised brow. I was hesitant about letting him in, but we really needed to talk, and I didn't feel like doing it in the hall with random people coming in and out of his apartment. The last time he set foot in my apartment, everything went to shit five seconds later.

"Sure." I opened the door fully, and he stepped in, taking in the space as if it were his first time coming in. We stood in the foyer because I didn't want to make the conversation any more intimate than it had to be. "I saw the magazines too. I'm sorry. I should've believed you, and I didn't but—"

William took two steps in my direction and embraced me. I stopped talking. The usual mouthwatering smell of him surrounded me, and I didn't pull away from his arms. "I needed you to know," he said, resting his chin on the top of my head. "I think we were both hurt, and that's why we reacted the way we did. I just hope you can forgive me. For everything."

His embrace was warm and protective. And a whole bunch of other stuff too. Damn it. Allowing William to hold me like that felt all kinds of good and bad at the same time.

All I could see was Nathan's face in my mind, and a harrowing feeling of *I'm failing Nathan* took over me. I didn't want to feel that way.

Slowly but reluctantly, I broke away from William's embrace. "Thank you for putting this together for me. I'm still embarrassed about being so quick to judge. It was never my intention," I said. He kept trying to capture my wandering gaze.

"Can you stop pretending now?" he said softly, almost a plea. "I learned my lesson. Just thinking about Nathan with you has been driving me—" He closed his eyes for a second and looked away. "Please, just stop." His voice was low and grave again.

He didn't know. I thought maybe Joel had called him after brunch to let him know that Nathan and I were official now. But William was oblivious of that fact, and now I had to be the one to tell him. It was going to be so hard to do.

"We're not pretending anymore," I started. He smiled and took a step closer. I wish I didn't have to be the one to tell him. "We're now officially dating." The other part of my heart, still untouched, finally vaporized inside my chest when I said that to him. And the discouraged look in his eyes just broke me—broke my soul in half.

"No."

"I'm so sorry. I thought you were with Erin, and I just couldn't—"

"But it's all been cleared up now." William took yet another dangerous step in my direction and cupped my cheeks with both of his hands. "Look at me," he demanded. I couldn't. I knew I couldn't. "Look at me and tell me you feel nothing."

"William, please," I begged with my eyes closed. A betraying tear rolled down my face.

"Look at me."

I opened my eyes and peered into his hypnotizing blue eyes. "How can you deny *this*?" He waved a limp hand back and forth between us. "You need to tell me how you do it because I can't." He brushed his lower lip with his thumb. "Remember this?" I nodded. It was our sign.

"Now touch your lips or tell me you don't feel a thing, and I'll walk away. Right now."

He knew I'd always felt something for him. Since the day I met him, something inside me clicked—like a bell that couldn't stop ringing. And the only way to make it stop was having him near me. Listening to his voice. Looking at his face. Feeling his touch on my skin. Kissing me. But as my feelings for him grew, so did my doubt, my uncertainty, and my suspicion.

It's as if I couldn't believe I'd found someone so perfect for me. Then Nathan came along and gave me everything to ease away the bad feelings that clouded my mind. Feelings I shouldn't have felt but did because I was proud and stubborn, just as William.

"I'm sorry."

"Just say it, then." He insisted. His hands went back to holding my face.

"I can't. I thought you were with Erin, and Nathan came along, and—"

William spat words in Swedish under his breath. What did he want me to say! If I told him that I felt nothing, I would probably collapse on the spot, and I couldn't admit that my heart needed to be restarted every time I saw him either.

A piece of my heart belonged to Nathan now, too. I didn't want to end things with him. I'd mourned William already, and he was now rising from the dead, pulling a Notting Hill on me.

"I'll back off whenever you're willing to tell me that you feel nothing." He turned around and opened the door to leave.

"William!" I cried. He looked over his shoulder, still holding the doorknob. "Can't we at least—try—to be friends?"

He snorted. "Perhaps in another life, when you don't look like—that, and I don't feel this way." He turned around again but stood still, placing his forehead against the door.

"William."

"I laid myself bare for you. More than I ever—" He cut himself off sharply and said in barely a whisper, "Never." He stepped out and shut the door behind him.

How could I disagree with him? Friends?

In another life—a thousand years from now.
And even so … no. Never.

CHAPTER 23

Uni

Nathan: Stepping out of the office. Are you home?
Me: Yes. See you here?
Nathan: I'll be there in 15 minutes.

The *collywobbles* invaded my stomach, just thinking of Nathan stepping onto the ninth floor and watching William moving in right beside me.

I paced back and forth from the living room to the foyer and back, waiting for Nathan to arrive. I needed to feel his arms around me, and that way, I'd know everything was going to be okay.

Finally, he knocked.

"What the bloody hell is going on?" Nathan asked as soon as I opened the door. He was staring toward apartment 9B, watching everyone move stuff in. William talked to one of the movers at the far end of the hall.

"Um, why don't you come in?"

"William's moving in next door?"

"He is. Apparently, he's owned that apartment for a while. And now that Eric's moving in with Tobias, well, he kinda needed to move out," I explained. I wasn't sure if that version was authentic. "At least that's what I understood from what Alice told me."

"Who's Alice? His new girlfriend?" Nathan asked as we walked to the living room.

"No. Alice is William's personal assistant. Remember the two girls we saw outside his apartment after CJ's party? One of them was Alice. The other one, Luna, is Alice's girlfriend," I explained.

His eyebrows moved up and down. "I thought that was something totally different," he replied with a frown. At least I wasn't the only one. I was relieved when I found out Alice was just his assistant, while Nathan seemed disappointed that she was just that.

"Why don't you two get along? It's just weird that being Joel's best friend and so close in age with William that you wouldn't get along."

"I do like him. But I feel like he's always been jealous of my relationship with Joel. He's always had this—wall. And then Joel and William became famous, which is the oddest thing ever. And I never saw William much after that," he said, resting his head on my lap and placing my hand on his head. He loved it when I played around with his hair. He was so spoiled.

"Besides, you said it was just a quick fling. I don't see any issues with us all being civil. We're almost thirty years old, for God's sake."

The only problem was that William had made it clear he didn't want to be friends with me. Ever. And I assumed that included Nathan. I couldn't see a scenario where we all got along. It was never going to happen, and I don't think it had anything to do with age.

Nathan probably wanted reassurance that William living next to me wasn't going to be a problem or a threat to our relationship. It wasn't. I couldn't be. I didn't know if *quick fling* was the correct word to define my relationship with William. Heck, I didn't even know what it'd been or how to describe it myself. So, sure, quick fling, final answer.

But what was I to say? No, we cannot be civil?

"I don't care if William lives next door, upstairs, or wherever he wants to live. You're the one I want to be with, and today couldn't have been any more perfect," I said, twirling his hair around my fingers.

It was best to change the subject and not give it much importance. We all knew what we were doing.

"I'm so happy about *us*. I was hoping my boyfriend would take me out for dinner tonight. Just the two of us." Nathan sat up straight to face me. He placed his hand behind my neck and pulled me in for a kiss. This is what I needed—to refocus my attention on him and remind myself of how good we were together.

"I'd love to," he replied. I hugged him and rested my face on his chest, listening to the strong and steady beat of his heart, thinking about how much I cared for it and how I wanted to protect it. It was the least I could do when he was helping put mine back together.

☾

Nathan loved sushi. We went to his favorite spot on Bleecker St. He knew some employees who still worked there from a few years back. He was so excited to take me there, knowing I was a foodie and loved sushi as much as he did.

The restaurant looked like a traditional Japanese place. Very minimalistic. The walls were covered with wooden panels of the same natural color as the furniture. There were only a few tables and eight spots on the sushi bar, where we sat.

We had just ordered our drinks when two girls walked into the restaurant. They seemed to be around Nathan's age. He acknowledged them and turned to look at me, clearing his throat.

"Are you okay?" I asked.

He was about to reply when one girl squinted in our direction and said, "Nate?"

Nathan sprung from his seat and clutched one of my shoulders with his hand.

"Hi, Hannah, how are you doing?"

"I'm good, thanks. It's been a while," she said, readjusting her bag's strap on her shoulder. The other girl waved hello to Nathan from afar and took a seat at one of the tables.

"Hannah, this is my girlfriend, Billie," he said to her. "Billie, this is Hannah."

"Nice to meet you," Hannah said, eyes wide, brows closing up, no smile. She seemed startled. I could tell she was trying to act normal, but she couldn't hide her surprise.

Why?

"Say hi to Nikki for me," Nathan said, taking a seat.

"She's actually joining us for dinner in a few minutes," Hannah replied to him. I didn't know who Nikki was, but something told me I didn't want her to join them for dinner. "It was nice seeing you, Nate." Hannah nodded once my way and turned around to join her friend at their table.

"That was tense," I said to Nathan. "Who's Nikki?"

"Dominique. My ex. I haven't seen her in a while. Since we broke up, that is. Hannah is her best friend." He seemed uncomfortable while ordering a few things from the chef stationed behind the sushi bar.

"Do you want to leave?" I asked in barely a whisper. "She said your ex's going to join them for dinner." *Let's go!*

"No, of course not. This is *my* place. It's always been my place," he said as if trying to convince himself of that. But after three years of dating, it was probably Dominique's place too. "I've wanted to bring you here for a while now. I've already ordered." He met my gaze and smiled. I smiled back.

"Why don't we take the food to my apartment? We can come back some other time and sit right here on the bar again. This place is tiny. Don't you think it will be—awkward?" I kept whispering.

I felt like I wasn't going to be able to talk to Nathan freely about anything if we stayed. Their table was a few feet away from where we sat.

"What are the odds …" Nathan sighed. "Okay. Let's do that. But I'm going to order everything," he warned playfully. "We're going to walk out of here with a couple of bags each, at least."

He grabbed a menu, added a few more things to our order, and asked the waiter if he could make it to go.

I was so curious about his ex, their relationship, why they broke up, when … But that conversation had to wait until we were alone in my apartment. I could see from the corner of my eye how Dominique's friends kept looking our way. It was making me uncomfortable.

A while later, our order was ready. Thankfully, Dominique hadn't arrived yet.

"We're going to need a few more hands." I laughed. There were four bags and two containers with hot soups waiting for us to take away. "Let me ask Caleb to help us out." I texted Caleb to ask for his help and to let him know we were leaving. He rushed inside a few seconds later, coat flying through the tables.

We walked toward the exit and said goodbye to Hannah and her friend. They both stared at Caleb, of course.

I had just taken a step out of the restaurant and spotted two girls fast approaching our way. One of them was obviously Dominique because, of course, we had to bump into each other. And from the look on her face, it was apparent she knew all about Nathan and his *new girlfriend*. Hi.

Dominique marched in our direction, staring at Nathan. She was a woman on a mission.

I jumped in the car, fleeing the scene, and Caleb handed me the bags he was carrying. I placed them all on the floor. I didn't care to interact with her. At all.

"Nate," she said with a vacant smile. I could see and hear them talking. Caleb left the door open, probably thinking Nathan would get in the car any second now. That made two of us.

"Hi, Nikki."

"Could we—talk for a minute?" she asked, taking a quick look at me without making any eye contact. Nathan met my gaze, and I nodded, hoping he would keep it brief. A minute doesn't hurt anyone.

The other girl who arrived with Dominique said hi to Nathan and joined their friends inside the restaurant. Caleb took the bags off Nathan's hands and passed them to me.

Dominique took a few steps away from the SUV, looking for privacy. She seemed distraught. Caleb closed the door, making me lose the opportunity to hear anything. *Caleb!*

A minute turned into *fifteen* freaking minutes, and Nathan finally joined me in the car with a weird smile.

"I'm terribly sorry about that, Murph." He grabbed my hand and squeezed it. I nodded, displeased, because really? *Fifteen minutes* I had to wait in the car for him to talk it out with his ex? Hell no.

"You okay?" He asked, seemingly relieved to be back in the car with me, but I could still notice a tad of concern in his eyes. And I wasn't okay. I was pissed.

I pressed my lips and took a deep breath. "Are you really done with her?" I was not going to sugarcoat things for him. We were just starting out, and it was best to know right away where he stood with her. I didn't want to be the girl he dated, only to realize he loves his ex and ride off into the sunset with her.

"What? Of course I'm done," he said, grabbing my other hand too. "Murph, look at me." I met his gaze with reluctance. "I'm sorry I made you wait. I didn't mean for our conversation to stretch out as it did. She kept asking questions. I thought it was best to be done with that awkward conversation for good. Because I'm *done* with her, I swear it."

"Okay," I said in a whisper. I trusted Nathan. Not only did I know he wasn't lying about it, but I could sense it in how my stomach didn't go into knots or got attacked by hot tiny knives. I'd been accustomed to doubt. And to feel all these horrible things inside me *all the time* when Thomas explained himself about anything. As if my body could detect the bullshit and react to it. "And … are you okay?"

We'd made the conversation about me, but that didn't mean Nathan hadn't also gone through an uncomfortable situation just now. I wanted to make sure how he was feeling about it.

"I am now." He kissed my cheek, and I settled my head on his shoulder.

"I swore your ex was British. I had no idea she lived in New York."

"I met her a few months after I first started working here. When I was transferred back to London, we kept our relationship going. I still traveled to New York for work, so we saw each other fairly often. But it was practically a long-distance relationship for the most part," he explained. I didn't ask for any explanations about their relationship, but I appreciated him opening up to me about it. It was reassuring.

"Is that why you broke up? The long-distance?"

"Yes, and no. Long-distance is always hard, but the real reason we broke up is because she wanted to get married. I didn't," he said, taking a deep breath. It's as if he were reliving the stress of his relationship just by talking about it. "Nikki's a year older than me. We'd been dating for three years. She thought getting engaged was the next obvious thing to do."

Thinking about Nathan engaged to someone else made my blood sugar drop to the floor.

"When did you guys break up?"

"Mid-August."

Damn.

We parked outside of my apartment building, and Caleb helped us bring some takeout bags up to my place. There were still people moving furniture inside William's apartment. I could see Alice walking back and forth in the distance, but William was luckily nowhere to be found. I didn't need any more drama.

I quickly set the table while Nathan unpacked the food. I was still curious to know a few more things about his relationship with Dominique.

"Why didn't you want to get married? Don't get me wrong; I'm glad you didn't," I said with a nervous laugh. "I just wonder why."

"I don't know. I couldn't see it happening. I'm not particularly against marriage. It's hard to explain, but I was gutted every time I thought about it. I didn't want to do it just to make her happy. I wanted to feel happy too. And I clearly wasn't there with her."

I'd never thought about marriage. It's one of those things one assumes can or might happen eventually, but that's when it hit me that Nathan's previous relationship had been significant, and it scared me to think that we might be in different stages of our lives.

And let's not get into the whole having kids thing. Terrifying.

"Was she—upset? To see you with someone else?" I needed to know if she was going to be a problem for the relationship. Or if she would try to get in the way somehow.

"Disappointed," he replied, serving a bunch of food on my plate. "When we broke up, aside from telling her I wasn't ready for marriage. I said I needed to be alone for a while. That's what I thought I needed. She was *shocked* to see me with someone else so soon. She kept asking about your age too. I think she was rather cross by how young you are."

My brows lowered into a crease. I hoped Nathan was ready for a relationship after coming out of another one so recently. A serious one, to be exact. One thing is to think you're ready, and another is to *be* ready. I didn't want to get hurt. But he read my face in an instant. "The day I met you, I was honest with you. I told you how I wasn't expecting you." He dropped his chopsticks and cupped my cheek. "You've been the best surprise of my life." He stood up slightly from his chair and reached out to kiss my cheek.

I stared into his pale ashy-green eyes for a few seconds, then smiled with a tinge of shyness. I couldn't believe the guy sitting in front of me. He was perfect. And I needed to trust him and relax.

After my relationship with Thomas and the few hiccups I went through with William, I thought I'd have difficulty trusting someone new. But that wasn't the case with Nathan. Every word that came out of his mouth exuded honesty. I could feel it in my bones.

I smiled again and said, "This plate's crazy." There was a little of everything he ordered on my plate, which was a lot. Plus, the insanely good-looking miso soup.

Nathan explained what each thing was before I tried it. He loved that place. He kept moaning with pleasure every time he placed something in his mouth, saying over and over again how good the food was. It was very distracting, mind you. I even teased him about it.

"The uni was delicious," I agreed with him. I couldn't finish everything on my plate, but I tried it all.

"Glad you liked it. You know, uni is considered an aphrodisiac." He shot this naughty smile at me, and everything inside me melted.

"Is it now? I don't think I need any extra motivation." I laughed. "Seeing you eat your favorite sushi did the trick for me."

He got up and pushed his chair back, pulling me up from my seat.

"Did it, now?" He carried me in his arms and walked toward my bedroom. "Well, I had *loads* of uni, and I've found myself to be rather susceptible to its effects," he whispered in my ear. "I'm hoping you are too. I just have to make a quick check."

After he showed me how *susceptible* he was to uni, I was left with no choice but to add it to my top three favorite foods of all time.

CHAPTER 24

A Cream Sweater And
A Green Hoodie

December 3, 2009

IT WAS A FEW MINUTES past 4:00 p.m., and I had just arrived home from school with Nolan. We were going to work on our final projects together. We stepped out of the elevator and saw Eric sitting on the floor, leaning against William's door. His forehead rested on his knees.

"Eric?" I called, walking in his direction. "Is everything okay?"

"Hey, Billie," he replied, with a slight tremble of his lips. His eyes were glazed. I gave Nolan my camera bag and the keys to my apartment and told him I'd join him in a few minutes.

"What's wrong?" I sat on the floor beside Eric, who was already crying. I hugged him, and he hugged me back. "Please, tell me what's going on." I feared someone had died, and he wasn't telling me who.

"My parents are getting divorced," he said in between subtle pants. He was devastated. "That's why I moved in with Tobias."

So that's why William moved out? A foolish and vain part of me thought William wanted to be closer to me. But that wasn't the case.

The situation forced him to move out to make room for Eric. I was constantly misjudging William's actions.

"Oh, Eric. I'm so sorry to hear that." I broke away from the embrace and placed my hand on his back. "Did you just find out about it?"

"Apparently, I'm the last one to know. I didn't understand why I was moving in with Tobias. I don't mind it. I've been looking forward to it actually, but my mother didn't want me to move out until I turned eighteen. I'm turning sixteen next February. That's why I didn't get it."

"But why the need to move out? Can't you keep living with your mother?"

"She left." The meaning of those two words seemed to have done a lot of damage. "She went to Stockholm a few weeks ago. I don't know when she'll be back, and my father's working in L.A. all the time. They didn't want me to be living alone in their apartment. I just hung up with her. She explained everything," Eric said with a huff. "I'm so pissed at my brothers for not telling me before. Everyone keeps treating me like a fucking child. I'm so over it."

I took a deep breath because I could relate to that feeling. "So, are you waiting for William to arrive? Or why are you sitting here outside?"

"The four of us are supposed to meet here to talk about this. They should be here any minute now," he replied, his voice breaking again. My heart was crushed for him. I don't think anyone wants their parents to have issues and split up, but the younger you are when it happens, the harder it must be to understand.

I asked Eric if he wanted to wait in my apartment. I didn't like seeing him sitting alone on the floor when I knew he was feeling miserable. Eric came in and asked if he could use the bathroom.

William and Tobias stepped out of the elevator when I was about to close the door to my apartment. I hadn't talked to William since we agreed never to be friends in this life or any other.

I could hear doors being shut or the faint sound of his guitar, especially at night, so I knew he was officially living beside me, but we hadn't bumped into each other until now.

"Billie!" Tobias said, walking in my direction.

William approached my door wearing a light crew-neck cream sweater and jeans. He kissed both of my cheeks. *Really?* Tobias snorted with a faint chuckle as I stood there looking like an out-of-service robot, not knowing how to react to William's customary way of greeting me. His cologne almost made me fall on my ass, though. It was intoxicating, as expected.

I shook my head a few times in the hopes of snapping back to reality and said, "Eric's in the bathroom. He was pretty upset when I arrived a few minutes ago. He told me about your parents' divorce. I'm so sorry. I know how close you all are." William kept staring at the hoodie I was wearing—analyzing it.

"Yeah, it's pretty messed up," Tobias said. "I didn't see it coming."

Joel arrived too. He was walking our way when Eric stepped out of the bathroom and scowled at his brothers. His eyes were red-rimmed and irritated, and his pale skin was blotchy from all the crying.

"Hey, Billie." Joel hugged me. We had become close. Nathan and I saw him and Lily often. His face looked grim once he saw how unhappy Eric looked.

"I'll see you in the gym in a few hours," Tobias said to me.

"Oh, I canceled my class today," I replied. "I have a bunch of homework to get done."

William took one last look at my hoodie, pursed his lips slightly, and excused himself to unlock his apartment door. *What is his problem?*

I hugged Eric and said, "Everything's going to be okay. If you need anything, you know I'm always here for you." He forced back a smile. Joel turned to look at me and mouthed, "Thank you," as he grabbed Eric's shoulders and directed him to William's apartment.

☾

Nolan had left more than an hour ago when I heard a knock on my door. Nathan was caught up at work, so I knew it wasn't him. I looked through the peephole—William. He was still wearing the cream sweater that looked so disgustingly good on him.

"Hey, neighbor. Do you need a cup of sugar?" I joked when I opened the door.

Ugh. He didn't laugh, smile, or gesture. He probably had different varieties of fancy sugar from where to choose from.

He sniffed sharp and fast. Once. "Please take that off," he said, jerking his chin and looking at my Hammarby hoodie.

"Excuse me?"

"It doesn't fit you well." He frowned. "It's—too big."

"It's green. It's warm and cozy. I like it." I love green.

I didn't even know what Hammarby was before meeting Nathan. Yet I loved wearing it. It smelled like him. But William already knew it wasn't mine, and apparently, that's what was bothering him—me wearing Nathan's clothes.

I remember how *keen* he was about having me wear his white t-shirt when I spent the night at the cottage. He didn't mind it being too big for me then. He actually *liked* that, if I recall correctly.

"I'm not leaving until you take that off." He crossed his arms in front of him, and I believed him.

Nathan told me how they were all die-hard Hammarby fans. They'd gotten together to watch a few games, and William would never show up. It saddened me to think he refused to watch a soccer game with his brothers because Nathan was there. I couldn't help but feel like it was my fault.

"William, come on," I said with a chuckle. He was being immature. Although, I didn't know what feelings would boil inside me if he handed out pieces of clothing to some other girl.

Nothing. The answer to that should be nothing. I'd probably hate it in secret, of course. But that wasn't the point. He knew I was with Nathan. What did he expect?

"I'll stand here all night if I have to," he said, leaning against the doorframe with his arms still crossed in front of his chest and an ankle in front of the other—balking.

Making him respect my relationship with Nathan was going to be harder than I thought. But I couldn't have him stand there forever. I knew how stubborn he could be, and I knew I wasn't strong enough physically to push him away, either. When he wanted to act like a tree, he was a sequoia. Impossible to move.

Unfortunately, he wasn't drunk like when he tried to kiss me on Midsummer. He was easier to shove away that day.

I pulled the hoodie over my head and tossed it on the foyer table. I was wearing a white, long-sleeve t-shirt underneath.

"Anything else?" I asked.

William pulled the right corner of his mouth slightly upward, looking triumphant. "Are you taking requests? I do have a list, remember?"

"Not really," I replied, not able to hold in a smile.

"Wait." He took a few steps forward and took my scrunchie off my hair, making my hair fall on my back, tossing all these memories and feelings back at me like a cold, hard slap to the face.

"I love that scrunchie," I protested. I tried stealing it back from him, but he held it over his head. I wasn't going to make a fool out of myself and start jumping like a circus dog.

Keep it.

"You know I like your hair down." He offered me the most playful grin ever. "Wanna trade?" he asked, looking at Nathan's hoodie.

"Never!" I grabbed the hoodie and hugged it. I was afraid he would snatch it away too.

He shook his head and clicked his tongue a few times with disapproval. My eyes followed his hands as he placed my scrunchie on his wrist and turned around to leave. It was all so bittersweet.

"That's it? That's why you came knocking at my door? To have me take the hoodie off and steal my scrunchie?"

"Yes." He walked back and stood right where he did before—not a single step further than that. I hadn't invited him in. Nor did I plan to. He knew that much.

"At least tell me how Eric is doing."

"He's not okay." William's gaze turned to the floor with a furrowed brow. "He's angry and disappointed right now. It'll take time for him to make sense of it. It's normal, I guess."

"And how are you doing?"

"I've known about their issues for a while. Joel too. I kinda saw it coming. I'm close to my father. We talk a lot about these—sorts of things. Tobias and Eric were clueless."

"You still haven't answered my question." He wanted to act like he was okay, but I could tell the situation had moved him too. He was trying to be strong for his brothers, but it wasn't his burden to carry.

"I'm fine. Just disappointed. My mother couldn't cope with my father's profession, which is *my* profession, too. And a few other—stuff that I can't really talk about." He looked away. "It gets you thinking."

His father was always away from home for long periods of time, working. I'd only seen him twice since I moved to New York. That couldn't have been easy for his mother.

"I'm sure it will all turn out for the best," I said, my lips going into a tight smile.

William nodded once, but he seemed uncomfortable with the

conversation. Talking about his feelings like that wasn't his forte. He struggled with that. "So ... Thank you for talking to Eric. Have a good night, Guille."

He took five ridiculous steps away from where he stood and arrived at his door. "Don't you dare put that hoodie back on," he said with a smirk. "I'll get you a new one. Your *first* Hammarby hoodie. I'll make sure it's green and cozy." He winked and quickly brushed his lower lip before disappearing into his apartment while a betraying voice inside my head suggested I touch my lower lip just as he did. I ignored that voice, of course. Instead, I threw Nathan's hoodie back on.

Ah! *I hate William Sjöberg*!

But I hated even more how that wasn't even close to being true.

CHAPTER 25

A Green Box

December 11, 2009

WE WERE GOING to celebrate Nathan's birthday by going to dinner with Lily and Joel. I was on my way to have his present professionally wrapped. I'm sure I'd make a mess of it if I tried doing it myself. I was so excited about Nathan's gift. I knew he would love it.

"I'll help you carry it," Caleb said, stepping out of the car. The trunk opened up, and I smiled when I saw it again. It was a 20" by 20" portrait of myself. I usually printed these 40" by 40", but I didn't want to come off too strong and territorial by giving him a *massive* portrait of myself. I wanted it to be discreet without being too small either.

Caleb grabbed it and followed me inside the shop. He carefully placed it on the counter, and a store clerk wearing a light blue apron approached us quickly afterward. Gary.

"Wow! Nice shot," Gary said. "Do you want this wrapped or just a big bow on it?"

"Um, both?" I wanted Nathan to unwrap it without knowing what it was. Gary suggested wrapping it in brown paper with a navy-blue bow made of silk-like ribbon.

"It's gonna take me about fifteen minutes. There's a waiting area on the mezzanine, or feel free to take a look around. I won't take long."

Caleb followed me as I walked around the place, looking at different papers, ribbons, and bows. It was a lovely shop.

"Who took that photograph of you? Am I getting one too for my birthday?" Caleb laughed. "I know exactly where to hang it."

I nudged his arm with my shoulder playfully and said, "Nope. I already bought your birthday present." His birthday wasn't until March, but when I saw it, I bought it.

He looked surprised, but I don't know why when he knew how much I cared about him.

"And I shot my own portrait using a tripod. Nolan insisted on taking it for me, but I thought it would be more special if I did it myself. I had to go back and forth a few times until I got the lighting right."

"I don't think it's fair that you have a portrait of me, and I don't have yours," Caleb said, drumming his fingers against a glass counter, acting as if he were outraged about it.

That was true.

I did have Caleb's portrait, the one I took at school in Paris. And it was a beautiful one. Looking at it made me sigh every time. He looked so handsome. I had a 4" by 6" printed out and stored it inside my Paris memorabilia box, where I kept many other photographs.

"Well, life isn't always fair," I replied with a chuckle. "But nice try." I looked in Gary's direction, and he hadn't even started wrapping the portrait. I suggested going upstairs to the mezzanine to wait for Gary to be done.

I sat on one of the sofas, and Caleb stood behind me with his bodyguard stance. I looked up at him and said, "Can't you sit for a minute?"

"When have I ever sat with you, Miss Murphy?" he asked playfully. He was in a fabulous mood. He'd been in a great mood for a while, and I was here for it.

"I can remember a few times. At the *Bassin Octagonal*? Remember? Our last day in Paris."

"I was making an exception," he replied. "It was your birthday."

"And that other time after school when I'd had a terrible day. It was your first week on the job. You sat with me and talked before we left."

"Oh, yeah. That's right." His gaze drifted away into thought. "I sure as hell remember that day. You were crying. I couldn't allow that. Not on my watch."

"I know." I smiled. He'd been so gentle with me that day. It was our first conversation. For a second there, we stared at each other, remembering, I guess. But I looked away first and said, "Oh, come on, sit. It's just for a few minutes." I tapped the seat beside me twice. "Although you might want to check the old lady by the ribbons. Looks shady."

He laughed but took a quick look at the poor lady before sitting next to me. *Geez.*

Caleb remembered a story about one of the chefs carrying a big cake for an event and how he fell on his butt, ruining the cake, of course. He recreated the chef's gestures, and I couldn't stop laughing. "Karma's a bitch," I said in between laughs. "You're so mean."

My phone buzzed.

"Hey, you," I said with a chuckle. Caleb made that chef's face again, and I guffawed.

"What's so funny?" Nathan asked with a weak laugh. I stood up and walked away from Caleb so I could concentrate on the call. He also jumped up from his seat.

"I'm sorry. Caleb's making me laugh. Ready for tonight?" I was excited to celebrate his birthday and even more excited to give him his gift.

"That's what I wanted to talk to you about. Where are you, by the way?" He sounded gloomy.

"Just running a few errands. What is it you wanted to tell me?"

"I'm stuck at the office. There's a bloody inconvenience we need to get fixed right away, and I cannot leave until it's dealt with. I won't be able to make it on time for that early dinner with Lily and Joel. I've already let them know. But I'll see you for sure as soon as I'm out. I don't care how late it is. I want to be with you at midnight."

"You promise? I want to be the first to say happy birthday to you."

"I swear I'll do my best to leave as soon as possible. I'm so sorry, Murph." He was upset about it, I could tell.

"Don't worry. I'll wait for you, okay?"

"I know it's been a crazy week, but that's how it is every year right before Christmas." He sighed. He was so stressed out about work. "I can't stop thinking about you. I miss you."

Between finals and his crazy schedule, we hadn't seen much of each other that week. All I wanted was to feel his arms around me and his lips melting on mine.

"I miss you too."

"I know it's my birthday tomorrow, but I have a surprise for you. I know you're going to love it."

"What is it?" That's the worst thing you can do to me. The intense curiosity was already eating me up from the inside.

"Well, that's why it's a surprise. You'll see. I really need to go, but I'll see you later, okay?"

"Okay, sounds good."

☾

"Miss Murphy, a package arrived for you," Aaron said when we came back from the shop. Caleb carried Nathan's wrapped gift, and Aaron held a large dark green box in his hands. "We'll help you take everything upstairs."

Caleb laid Nathan's gift on the chair by the foyer. That way, it'd be the first thing Nathan saw when he came in. Aaron placed the green box on the foyer table.

The box itself was lovely. I carried it to my room and opened it. There was a beautiful evening gown and two silver envelopes inside. I took the dress out and extended it on my bed. It was a black, strapless, velvet dress. The straight-across neckline had a thick white stripe of velvet fabric. The hem of the dress had thin white piping all around. The tag on the dress read *Enzio de Luca*. No wonder why it looked so expensive.

I opened one of the silver envelopes, and there was a single ticket for *L'Elisir d'Amore*.

Oh, my God, Nathan! It was such an unexpected gift. William told me the two dates were sold out. I was so impressed by Nathan's resourcefulness. He knew how badly I wanted to go.

The Metropolitan Opera
L'Elisir d'Amore
December 11, 2009. Friday Evening 8:00 p.m.
Parterre Box 26 Row 1 Seat 1

The second silver envelope had a small, printed note inside.

I know how much you love L'Elisir d'Amore, and I would love nothing else but to be the one to take you to the Metropolitan Opera for the first time. I'm a bit caught up at work, but I'll meet you there and promise to arrive before it starts. That dress is going to look spectacular on you. I cannot wait to see you wearing it. I chose it myself.

—Quanto è bella, quanto è cara!
Più la vedo e più mi piace ...

My jaw ached from my incapacity to keep myself from smiling. The last two lines were part of an aria where Nemorino sings about Adina:

She is so beautiful; she is so sweet!
The more I see her, the more I like her ...

Nathan knew me well.

☾

The dress fitted me perfectly. I was convinced Nathan had asked Lily for help with my size. The fabric was delicious, so soft and supple, making it a very comfortable dress to wear. I wore my hair up in a sleek, low chignon, and my lips couldn't have been any other color than red.

The occasion justified for me to take my mother's teardrop-shaped pendant diamond earrings out of the safe. They completed the look beautifully. I'd never worn them before.

Aaron, Caleb, and David were going to drive me to the Opera. Since a lot of people were expected to attend, they wanted to keep security tighter that evening. And I didn't mind. I was so happy and excited about going with Nathan that Big Mike could come too if he wanted to.

I stepped out of the car right in front of Lincoln Square and was impressed by the extraordinary architecture.

Aaron and Caleb escorted me inside while David stayed in the car. *Just in case*, Aaron said.

More people arrived, all wearing tuxes and beautiful evening gowns. I couldn't wait to see Nathan all dressed up too. He was going to look so handsome.

Box twenty-six.

Aaron inspected it before I went inside. It was empty. I was the first one to arrive. The view from our box was incredible. I took a seat and decided to text Nathan since it was almost 8:00 p.m.

Me: Hey, you! Are you on your way?

The lights went out, and the orchestra began playing the overture. I just hoped Nathan had been able to get off work. I didn't want to sit there alone. He was hopefully on his way to meet me.

The door opened behind me, and I saw a silhouette stepping inside and walking my way.

"Hej, älskling," William whispered, taking a seat beside me. He kissed my cheeks slowly. "You look breathtaking. I knew that dress would fit you perfectly."

William, you son of a ...

My phone buzzed in my hand.

Nathan: Murph, I'm on a conference call. Can't pick up. I'll call you later.

Fuck.

CHAPTER 26

Quanto è Bella, Quanto è Ingenua

WHAT'S A STRONGER WORD for furious? Enraged? Yes. I could feel the rage and the indignation snaking through my veins, filling every cell inside my body. Boiling me up. I should've known better. Nathan's suggestion of a surprise made me assume he was the one who sent the green box.

Falling into William's trap made me feel so stupid and naive.

I looked down at the beautiful dress, took a deep breath, and stood up to leave. William held my hand and said, "Stay."

"No." I walked toward the door, but he gently held my arm before I could grab the doorknob.

"You're here. It's already started. You look beautiful, by the way." He smiled and kept scanning me from head to toe, analyzing the dress *he'd* chosen for me. Not Nathan.

"Nathan's going to be pissed. *I'm* pissed. Why would you do this?"

I hadn't had the opportunity to mention how ridiculously handsome William looked. In-freaking-sane. That tux ... That smell ... That face.

Lock me up in a tower and toss away the key. I didn't deserve to come out in years. I was too stupid to live in the real world.

"Because you love this opera, and it's your first time coming here. That's why I did it." The orchestra playing in the background made the situation feel more dramatic than it already was. "I'm sure Nathan would want you to stay. He should know how much you wanted to see it. Come on, let's take a seat," he insisted.

I pinched the bridge of my nose and shook my head with disbelief. I didn't want to leave! But I felt deceived. No. I *was* deceived.

"I thought you didn't want to be friends with me." I met his gaze.

He laughed and said, "You just don't get it, do you? I'm being *friendly*. That's different."

Caleb opened the door. "Is everything okay, Miss Murphy?" he asked with a death-stare that had William's name on it.

I'm not okay! I don't know what to do. "Um, yes. I—" I broke off.

"Do you want to leave, Miss Murphy?" Caleb's stare was fixed on me. He knew what was going on. I could see it in his eyes. Both William and Caleb refused to take their eyes off me—waiting for my response. *Yes or no? Staying or leaving?*

The orchestra carried on with "*Quanto è Bella*."

"Fuck," I said in barely a breath, mostly to myself—feeling defeated. I looked at the floor and brushed my forehead while I kept thinking about what to do. I took a few steps forward and saw Rolando Villazón coming onto the stage. *Fuck, indeed.* I couldn't leave now. Nope.

"She's staying," William replied, placing his hands on my shoulders, guiding me to our seats. "Thank you, Caleb."

"Miss Murphy." Caleb insisted on my confirmation.

I was so ashamed of myself for wanting to stay, but that was one of my favorite arias being sung by Rolando *freaking* Villazón. I looked over my shoulder and dispatched a quick nod in Caleb's direction, refusing to make eye contact with him. I quickly turned away to take my seat because I didn't want to see his reaction as he judged my decision.

"Why don't you enjoy yourself today and go back to pretending to hate me tomorrow?" William whispered in my ear when he took a seat beside me. "You know, in the same way you keep pretending to like Nathan more than you like me."

"Stop," I whispered back. If he planned on taunting me like that for the next three hours, I wouldn't be able to power through the entire thing. *Three hours.* Next to William. I swallowed hard at the thought.

I took a deep breath and tried disconnecting myself from the situation and direct my focus on the performance. But I kept thinking about how *Una Furtiva Lagrima* wouldn't come up until the last twenty minutes of the second act. And not seeing Rolando Villazón performing it would be a tragedy. I needed to talk to Nathan and let him know where I was and that I planned to stay.

I texted him once *Quanto è Bella* was over.

Me: I know you're busy. I'm so sorry to keep bothering you. But something happened. I need to tell you something.

Half an hour went by, and no reply from Nathan. William behaved and seemed to be enjoying the opera. He kept up with the translation screen and laughed a few times with Dulcamara's aria, where he launches into the longest and shadiest list of his potion's miraculous effects. Finally, luring Nemorino into buying it to hopefully make Adina fall in love with him.

I kept glancing at my phone's screen, but still, no reply from Nathan.

And just like that, ninety minutes went by like nothing, and the curtains came down for the intermission.

"Do you want to get something to drink?" William asked casually.

I accepted. My throat was dry, and I needed to stretch my legs.

We stepped out of the box, and William guided me through the corridors. Aaron and Caleb followed close behind.

"Hey, you're walking too fast for me," I complained. I was wearing heels and wanted to look around the place. It was beautiful. "It's best if we don't stop," he replied, keeping his head down. I guess he didn't want to be recognized. I remembered what Joel told us about how crazy it could get with William.

A few people stared at us, and I even saw a young woman pointing at William as we walked past a bar. I wondered why we weren't stopping there since we were going to get something to drink.

We made our way to the Grand Tier level of the house and walked up to a door just off the stairs.

Patron Lounge.

We stepped inside. Only a few people mingled around the place.

The private lounge was divided into two interconnected, elegant, and classically decorated rooms. One had plum-colored walls with beige colored sofas and a bar made of solid wood. The other space had gray-colored walls with gray and plum-colored sofas. There were huge windows with beautiful views of the city.

"Are you a Patron?" I asked William.

A server approached us and offered champagne. William grabbed two glasses. "As of recently, yes," he replied, offering one to me. "Skål." He bumped his glass against mine and took a long sip of his champagne.

"I didn't know you were a donor." I sipped on my champagne too, wondering if I would get arrested for underage drinking. That would've topped off my night nicely.

"Since the event was sold out, I had to make a big donation."

I couldn't believe what I was hearing. *He did that just to bring me here?*

I'd barely given my glass a few sips when another server walked by with more champagne and switched William's empty glass for a fresh one.

"Thirsty?" I asked with a smile.

"Parched." He echoed my smile. "I had a stressful day."

"Why? Work-related, or?"

"Not really," he replied, downing half his champagne in a single gulp.

Hmm. William was always too vague for my too-curious mind.

I looked down at my dress and said, "It's a beautiful dress. You said you chose it yourself?"

"Of course, I did. I was presented with a few options, but I was torn between this one and a sexy blue gown, but it had a deep V neckline"—he poked my belly a couple of inches above my navel— "up to here. And damn, I was tempted to see you wearing it. Perhaps some other time."

There wasn't going to be another time. I'd learned my lesson. I was making a cross-referenced list of William's tricks.

He raised a brow and licked his lips before taking another sip of his champagne. "It was fun choosing something for you to wear."

"William Sjöberg. You have a passion for fashion, don't you?" I smiled, and he rolled his eyes at me.

It was evident. William was always immaculate, clean, perfectly dressed for the occasion. And even his white t-shirts weren't just any kind of cotton. They were soft but sturdy. I know because I wore one and remember how it slipped on my skin like butter.

"How did you know my dress size, by the way? Did you ask Lily?" It fit me like a glove. And it was soft, soft, soft.

"Lily?" he asked with a grimace, almost spitting her name. Like *how dare I* ask that question. "You forget, I've held you in my arms before. When we kissed in the pool, I acquired a *precise* notion about your—size." His mouth twitched into a wicked little smile.

My eyes went wide.

I bit my lower lip and looked away, trying to push back the memories of the pool-kissing scenario. He took another step closer. *Stopstopstop.* But I did nothing to stop him. My mind had poached all my energy and paralyzed the rest of my bodily functions. "You have something in your hair," he said with a frown. "May I?" "Um, s-sure." My eyes followed the movements of his hand.

He pulled on the two pearl-encrusted hairpins that held my updo, and my hair fell over my shoulders.

"William!" I closed my eyes and exhaled slowly. I held my hand out, and he placed the hairpins on it. "Thank you." I tucked them inside my clutch.

"You insist on putting your hair up." He smiled like he was enjoying my reaction. Like he planned on doing it every single time he could and didn't give a shit about it.

My phone buzzed. It was Nathan. I shook my head at William and walked away to take the call. A few people immediately approached William and talked to him. A woman even pulled her phone out for a selfie. William was smiling, but I could tell it was forced. Not the real smiles I'd seen on his face more than a few times by now.

"Murph, I'm sorry I didn't call you back sooner. I'm finally out. I'm on my way to your flat. So what is it you wanted to tell me? Is everything okay?" A slab of steel fell upon me. He sounded exhausted, and I needed to start explaining.

William stared at me from afar with this *look* on his face. The very same I remember when we kissed at the pool. And his bedroom. And the car. *Look away! Please?*

I cleared my throat and chugged down what was left of my champagne. "Um, so you know how you mentioned something about a surprise?" I was finding it hard to explain—hard to spill it out. I was embarrassed, too, about what happened.

"Yes, love. I'll show you what it is as soon as I arrive."

"Well, there was some sort of a mix-up, I'm afraid." I turned to look at William, and he was still staring my way, even as people talked to him. He knew I was talking to Nathan, but his face told me he couldn't care less about it.

"When I arrived home today from my errands, Aaron gave me a box with a dress, a letter, and a ticket for today's Opera at the Met." I sighed. "I thought it was all from you. I thought it was *your* surprise."

"William?" he asked. But I guess he already knew the answer to that question.

"Yes. I'm so, so sorry. I tried calling you as soon as William arrived in your stead, but you were busy, and then Rolando Villazón started singing, and I couldn't find it in me to leave. But I swear if you want me to, I'll do it right now. It's killing me that you're not here with me."

"William's lost the plot," Nathan said in almost a growl. I wasn't sure what he meant by that, but by context, I got that he was annoyed and thought that William was probably insane.

"I'm sorry. I'll leave okay. I shouldn't have stayed. I—"

"No. You're already dressed up and halfway through that thing. William tricked you into it. You should stay. I know perfectly well how he is. I'll deal with him later."

"I don't feel comfortable staying, knowing how upset you are about this. I don't want to cause any trouble. Believe me. I'm angry too about how it all happened. But I'm just trying to enjoy the opportunity of being here."

"Have you heard your favorite song? The one you told me about?" He sighed.

"No. It doesn't come until the end of act two."

"Then, more reason for you to stay until the end. I'll be at Joel's. Meet me there when you get back."

"I promise to be there before midnight. I still want to be the first one to give you a big birthday hug. I'll make it up to you, I promise."

"Hmm. What exactly did you have in mind?" he asked with a naughty tone over the phone. I laughed, mostly because I was relieved to hear him shifting away from anger.

"*Lots* of things. You'll just have to wait and see."

"Can't wait for you to come back. I have more than a few things in mind too."

William cocked his head toward the exit and tapped his watch twice.

"The intermission is almost over. I'll see you later, okay?"

"Of course. Enjoy, love."

William and I rushed back to the box, and just before we went inside, Caleb asked for a word. William stepped inside while I talked to him.

"Are you sure everything's okay?" Caleb asked. I bet he couldn't understand why I'd chosen to stay with William.

"Yes, of course. There was a slight misunderstanding, but everything's okay."

"Slight?" he asked with raised brows.

"Caleb, come on. Not you too. I'm already dealing with William and Nathan. I can't do this right now. I swear I'm fine," I replied with a tinge of exasperation. Caleb's fabulous mood streak had gone down the drain in an instant. I'd been trying to keep it together, but I couldn't deal with him too. I was out of random-access memory space for the time being, but I didn't want to make him feel bad about worrying about me either.

"I'm sorry," I said with a sigh. "It's been a weird night. I know you're just looking out for me."

"No need to apologize," he replied, opening the door for me. "Go ahead. It's already started."

When I joined William, I saw him silencing a call from Nathan.

Just thinking about Nathan calling William made me feel anxious. But I had to allow Nathan to do whatever he needed to do to feel at ease. I trusted him.

Knowing I would eventually listen to *Una Furtiva Lagrima* kept me going during the second act. After speaking to Nathan on the phone, I was ready to leave. But he told me to stay, and I knew he was genuine about it.

☾

The opera was finally over. When we walked out of the box, William asked me if I wanted to meet Rolando Villazón. "I'm sorry, what?" I was in shock. Of course I wanted to meet him!

William pulled out a couple of backstage passes with our names on them. "So, what do you say?" he asked, looking at his watch. I pulled my cell phone out of my clutch—11:15 p.m. I needed to get back. He knew it was Nathan's birthday at midnight. He knew everything. He was tempting me.

"I'm sorry. I don't want to be late for—"

"Nathan." He snorted and shook his head twice. "Look at us finishing each other's sentences," he said sarcastically, probably irritated I was choosing Nathan over him.

As angry as I was with William for tricking me into coming, I wanted to thank him. It was a grand gesture on his part. The dress, the donation to get the tickets, the notes. He knew how much I loved notes and letters.

"Thank you. For all of this," I said, looking down at my dress. "This is the closest I'll get to go to a concert, I guess. You didn't have to."

"I *had* to." We were walking down the stairs, and I could feel people's gazes directed at us like programmed missiles. He leaned in and whispered, "A little bird told me Nathan was bringing you here tomorrow. But that's a big first I couldn't allow him to take away from us."

Nooooo!

"William—h-how could you," I whispered back with a glower. I could feel my lips shaking and twitching with rage. I shook my head at him, disappointed, and walked out and away into the cold night. Aaron and Caleb walked close behind me.

I peeked over my shoulder and saw William trying to follow me, but a horde of photographers and, I don't know—*fans*—surrounded him once they noticed *William Sjöberg* attended the event. Aaron and Caleb immediately responded by directing me hastily toward the SUV that David had waiting for us in the distance.

I took one last look at William, and he was staring at me, watching me leave. He brushed his lower lip with his thumb and looked away to smile that synthetic smile he used for the cameras.

William definitely lost the plot.

CHAPTER 27

Even The Score

IT WAS 11:37 P.M., and I arrived just in time for Nathan's birthday. I knocked on Lily and Joel's apartment, and Nathan opened the door. "That bastard has good taste. I need to give him that," he said, eyeing me up and down. His expression was made up of a mix of anger, annoyance, and hunger.

"He's still a bastard," I replied, throwing myself into his arms. Nathan's lips immediately sought mine. We kissed as if we hadn't kissed in years. We were both looking forward to tonight—to seeing each other. I missed him, and I knew he missed me too.

"He can give you all the dresses he wants, but I'll always be the one to take them off you," he whispered into my ear. My skin reacted to his breath, and tiny sparks of electricity curled all around me.

"How about right now?" I asked, biting into his lower lip.

Nathan shouted something to Joel in Swedish and closed the door behind him. "Now sounds perfect." He grabbed my hand and guided me toward the elevator.

I unlocked my apartment and saw Nathan's gift in the foyer. "Your gift," I said with a smile. "Do you want to open it now or?"

"Or. Definitely or," he replied, unzipping my dress. "I can't stop thinking about the *lots of things* you said you had in mind to make it up to me." The dress fell to the floor, and he knelt to kiss my stomach, gently kissing his way up, making me gasp. "You're exquisite."

He stood behind me and kissed my neck and my shoulders as he guided me toward my bedroom.

I laid in my bed, and Nathan removed his suit. Piece by piece. His eyes were deeply fixed on mine as I waited for him to join me.

He laid beside me and whispered, "I love you," placing a soft kiss on my lips. It was the first time he told me he loved me. My chest swelled with both joy and excitement. My heart said yes.

"I love you too," I said in between a slow and delicious kiss.

"We're not having sex tonight," Nathan said, kissing my shoulders.

"Why?" I complained. "Are you upset with me? I swear I—"

"Shh." He placed a finger over my lips, and I took a playful bite on it. A low groan escaped his throat. "Tonight, I'm going to make love to you."

☾

"Happy birthday," I whispered in Nathan's ear. It was already past midnight. We were both still lying together in bed, refusing to let go of one another. I combed the soft waves of his hair with my fingers and said, "Is that a gray hair I see?" His hair was a rich, medium-brown color. Not a single gray hair on his head yet.

He laughed. "Very funny, young lady." Nathan tickled me as a punishment for teasing him.

"Nathan!" I'm extremely ticklish. "Stop!"

"You'll be twenty-eight one day, too," he said, finally releasing me from the torture.

"Yeah, in eight years. I have my entire life ahead of me." I laughed again.

"Aren't you cheeky?" Nathan tickled me again.

"Truce!" I shouted in between roars of laughter. He stopped, and I took a deep breath, a chuckle still escaping me here and there. "How about—pizza?" I suggested.

"Splendid," Nathan replied in his lovely accent.

"I'll text the guys and see if they can get it for us," I replied. "I'm starving."

"Are you sure? We can have it delivered too."

"Their shift doesn't end until you leave." I grabbed my phone from the nightstand.

"Oh. I thought I could spend the night." He kissed my cheek. "I'm nowhere near done with you." I could feel my face getting warm. I turned to look at him, and my heart fluttered. He looked so handsome, and we were having fun. I didn't want him to leave either.

"We could tell them you're staying over at Joel's. They won't believe us, of course," I said with an exaggerated grin. "But at least the report won't say you stayed over."

Aaron replied immediately to my text, indicating they would gladly bring the pizza to us.

"Pizza is on its way." I stood up and walked to the bathroom. I turned on the shower, and a few seconds later, Nathan joined me.

"Our first shower together," he said, placing his hands on my waist and a kiss on my shoulder.

"Were you taking me to the opera tomorrow? Today that is."

"Yes, I was. Mr. Chapman called in a favor and got us a couple of boxed seats," he replied, grabbing the shampoo bottle. "How do you know I was taking you?"

"William told me. He found out about it, somehow. I'm sure Tobias told him. He's proven to be a snitch in the past," I said with a sad laugh.

"It doesn't matter now. We're not going. I'm returning the

tickets. I'm sure someone else at the office would love to attend." His tone was getting serious again. He stepped into the stream of water and rinsed the shampoo off his hair.

"We could go. I'd love for you to take me. I don't mind going again," I said, combing his hair with my fingers.

"It's okay, really. William ruined the surprise." Nathan grabbed the loofah, added shower gel, and lathered my skin with it. "You already saw it, which was what I wanted—for you to see it again. We can do anything else. I truly can't be arsed by that prick."

Shit.

Nathan added more shower gel to the loofah and lathered himself.

"I'm sorry. I feel like it's my fault too. I should've called you first, but you were busy working, and I never imagined it would be him."

"Please, don't apologize. You did nothing wrong."

The doorbell rang.

"It must be the pizza."

"I'll get it." He kissed my lips, jumped out of the shower, and quickly dried himself off. He grabbed a pair of cotton sweatpants he kept at my place. He liked changing out of his suit when he came straight from work.

Nathan walked out of my bedroom without a shirt on, and I thought I would die from the mortification. I just prayed Caleb wasn't the one who brought the pizza. Wet hair, sweatpants, no shirt. Too obvious.

I stepped out of the shower too and changed into black leggings and Nathan's green Hammarby hoodie. It was the comfiest ever and one of my favorite pieces of clothing in my closet.

There was a conversation going on in the distance. Nathan was speaking in Swedish. No—*yelling* in Swedish.

I ran to see what was happening, my hair dripping wet. Aaron stood just outside the door. Nathan held the pizza box and argued with William, who apparently had just arrived home. He stood only a few steps away from Nathan.

"What's going on?" They stopped talking and turned to look at me. William's eyes were blazing with anger. I didn't know if his glare burned for having to watch a just showered and shirtless Nathan beside me, for the dress he gave me lying messily on the floor, or for the freaking hoodie I was wearing. Probably an explosive mixture of all of the above.

"Thank you, Aaron." I took the pizza out of Nathan's hands. "Good night, William." But Aaron and William didn't leave.

I turned to look at Nathan and nodded. I didn't want our night to be ruined. It was his birthday, for God's sake. I didn't want him to spend it arguing with William. It wasn't worth it.

But I wasn't convincing enough.

Nathan's nostrils flared for a second before he grabbed the dress from the floor. He threw it at William and said, "It's a beautiful dress." William caught it midair with a bored expression on his face. "It fit her *perfectly*."

"Nathan, the pizza is getting cold. Come on."

He was provoking William unnecessarily. They both stared at each other like a couple of king cobras about to get into a brawl. All I wanted was for Nathan to shut the damn door so we could continue to celebrate his birthday at peace.

I settled the pizza box on the foyer table and pulled Nathan's arm, trying to get him to snap out of his trance.

"It was *so* easy to take off, too," Nathan threw in. "Thanks, mate." Aaron clicked on his earpiece, and that's when I knew I needed to take a few steps back.

William took a couple of slow steps in Nathan's direction, but Aaron placed his hand on his chest and politely, but firmly, invited him to walk away. He turned to look at me, running his tongue over his teeth, and disappeared off to his apartment before I could even realize he was gone.

I took a deep breath and exhaled slowly out through my mouth. Aaron excused himself after I thanked him once again. I was so embarrassed he had to listen to the drama, including that bit about how easily Nathan had taken the dress off *me*.

"Are you okay?" I asked Nathan, finally closing the door.

"Never better." He smiled. "He cannot have you, and it *kills him*. So I just had to remind him of that fact. But now we're even."

I was glad they didn't get into a physical altercation. Remembering how easily Nathan broke Nicholas's nose made me shudder. And just by looking at William's size, I was sure he could do a fair amount of damage too. I didn't want to see William or Nathan getting hurt.

"Do you want to open your gift?" I asked him, trying to change the vibe. It was best to pick up where we left off and pretend as if nothing had happened. He agreed and unwrapped it.

"Oh, God! I absolutely *love* it," he said, looking at it. "You look so beautiful. Thank you, Murph."

I gave him a big hug and a quick peck on the lips. "I'm glad you liked it. I shot it myself."

"Really? It's perfect."

We ate our pizza with a bottle of wine and talked for hours. It had been the longest day, and my eyelids felt heavy, but I wanted to keep talking to Nathan.

His phone buzzed. It was a few minutes past two in the morning.

"It's the London office. I need to take this," he said, rubbing his face. His work was insanely demanding. I wondered how many calls he took while he slept every night.

"I'll be in my bedroom." I stood up and kissed his hair. I brushed my teeth with big plans of waiting for Nathan to be done with his call, although I didn't think I was capable of keeping myself awake any longer.

I was about to turn off my phone when I saw a text notification from William on my screen.

W.S: My offer stands. I'll back off whenever you're willing to tell me you feel nothing.
Me: I feel lots of things. Anger, exasperation, disappointment, and frustration, to name a few. It was one thing to trick me into going, but ruining Nathan's surprise for me? That was a low blow.
W.S: You'll always have the freedom to choose with me. Say the word, and I'll stop.
Me: Back off.
W.S: That's not how it works.
Me: What do you want from me?
W.S: Tell me you feel nothing. That's the cue.
Me: I feel nothing.
W.S: That's the spirit. The only problem is I don't believe you. But I appreciate the effort.

Tiny daggers came at my chest this time—a million of them. William had to fade away with time, and then I'd be able to say I felt nothing and actually feel *nothing*. I hated how he could see right through me. There was no way to cloak myself from him.

Me: I feel nothing.

Perhaps if I wrote it a few times, it'd come true.
And I swear I heard a laugh across the wall.

W.S: You can always try again some other time because I'm not getting much "nothing" vibes over here. Sweet dreams, älskling.

Oh my God! He had this tailor-made magic formula of how to

flawlessly get under my skin until it hit the bone. I was tempted to throw my phone against the wall. Instead, I took a deep breath and turned it off.

Once my head was comfortably resting on my pillow, the sound of William's piano became audible. The sound was soft and distant, but I could hear it.

It was the first time I ever heard him play. He wasn't playing fluidly. It's as if he were learning a new song, but I couldn't tell which one it was. The notes were lovely, and even though he was playing around with them, the sound lulled me into an ironically deep and peaceful sleep.

CHAPTER 28

Holiday Interlude

December 22, 2009

MY DOORBELL RANG. I heard it loud and clear, but my body wouldn't respond. My eyes felt heavy, and I fell asleep again—a dream.

My phone buzzed on my nightstand. *William?*

"Mmm," I groaned, still half-asleep, eyes shut.

"Guille. I need you to wake up," he urged. "Can you open the door? I'm in a hurry."

"Mhm." I hung up the phone and closed my eyes again because *it's definitely a dream.*

My phone vibrated in my hand, startling me. I answered it again.

"Guille. Door. This is not a dream."

"Okay, okay," I replied with a raspy voice. "Give me two seconds."

5:14 a.m. *You've got to be kidding me.* I sat on the bed with my eyes closed for an undetermined amount of time until my cell phone vibrated again.

W.S: I left something outside your door.

It was still dark outside. I dragged myself out of bed and went to see what it was. There was a green box like the one he used to send me the dress and opera tickets sitting right outside my door, but this one had a red ribbon made into a bow.

William was stepping into the elevator wearing jeans and a black coat over a gray sweater. He was rolling his luggage behind him when he heard me come out. He caught the elevator door with his suitcase and said with a chuckle, "Good morning, älskling." I ran my fingers through my hair, trying to placate the bedhead. "You look cute. You don't need to do that." He grinned. I'm sure I looked anything but cute in my fleece pajamas.

And you look ... way too good. He always did. That was *the* most annoying trait of his.

The trail of scent he left when he walked away from my door was knocking my drowsiness away.

"You have something on your lips," he said, frowning.

Still half-asleep, I brushed my lips with my thumb and figured out quickly after that it was just one of his tricks. I shook my head, and William laughed as he disappeared into the elevator.

"See you in March!" he shouted from afar.

"*March?*" I asked in a pitchy tone, watching how the elevator doors snicked shut behind him. I knew the Sjöbergs were leaving to spend Christmas in Sweden. They would meet their mother there. I'd even said goodbye to Joel and Tobias the day before. Eric left sooner when school was out.

My stomach felt hollow. I'd been falling asleep every night listening to him playing the piano. He was making progress learning that song he kept practicing. I was secretly going to miss that.

But it wasn't a half-bad idea for him to leave for a while. After the opera stunt, some critical distance wouldn't hurt anyone. Maybe once he came back, we could all get along.

I took the box to my bedroom and immediately pulled on the

silky red ribbon to untie it. I took the lid off, and it's as if William were standing right here with me. The scent of his cologne invaded my room in two seconds.

Damn it. I scowled at the box.

A green Hammarby hoodie. It was *not* my size. It was even larger than Nathan's. William had essentially dipped the hoodie in a tub of his cologne, impregnating it with the usual smell of him. He undoubtedly did that on purpose.

Everything William sent always came with a note. He didn't disappoint this time either. And unlike the opera letter, this one was handwritten like the others. I could recognize his writing now. That's why he typed the last one. It would've given him away in a heartbeat.

Guille,
I'm sure this hoodie is comfier and would look way better on you. Since I couldn't get anyone to send me a new one from Sweden, I decided to give you mine. Don't worry. I'll buy one for myself in the next few days. Merry Christmas.
W.S.

He couldn't get anyone to send him one. Who's going to believe that? He just wanted me to have his hoodie. A hoodie I would never be able to use.

I folded the hoodie and placed it back in the box where it belonged. And now my room smelled like William. Even gone, he found a way to keep making himself present.

I climbed back to my bed and shut my eyes. No piano. Pure silence.

Until March, then. It was for the best.

CHAPTER 29

Happy Christmas

December 22, 2009

I KNOCKED ON NATHAN'S DOOR, and he opened it with a grin. "Hey, you." He lifted me from the floor with a hug and kissed me. My portrait was hanging on the wall to the left.

Nathan was leaving later that day, too. At midnight. He was going to London for the holidays, but he planned on coming back on the twenty-ninth. He wanted to spend New Year's Eve with me.

"I miss you already. I don't want you to leave."

"I should probably steal you away," he said, putting me down.

"Now *that's* a way to get on my father's bad side." I joked.

"I'd love to spend the holidays with you. But my sisters will murder me if I don't go. Olly too. Everyone's dying to meet you. Olly keeps asking my sister about you. They've shown him pictures of us together." He smiled.

"That is so sweet! I can't wait to meet Olly. Are you a good uncle?"

We walked to his bedroom. Nathan needed to start packing and wanted moral support. He hated packing. Who doesn't?

I couldn't believe he was an uncle. That was such a grownup thing to be.

"I am the best," he said with a short laugh. "As long as he doesn't go *poo-poo* because then I'm the worst uncle ever."

I laughed but bit the inside of my cheek afterward as my mind drifted into thought. Nathan has three sisters: Evie, Charlotte, and Zara. Evie's two years older than Nathan and Ollie's mother. Charlotte is four years younger than Nathan, and Zara's my age.

"What's wrong?"

"Nothing. It just hit me that I'll never be an aunt." I'd never given much thought to that until Nathan talked to me about Ollie and how much he loves and cares for him.

"Of course, you will. My sister's kids will be your nephews and nieces," he said casually, throwing a few pairs of socks into his suitcase. Too casually. "I mean eventually—someday when we get married."

Married.

I thought Nathan didn't want to get married. Well, he didn't want to get married to Dominique. But still. Wow.

His remark surprised me. A part of me even felt excited about the idea. But another part freaked out on me big time. We've only been dating for almost two months if you count the pretending part, which Nathan liked considering.

He enjoyed thinking we started dating the day after we met, which kind of happened that way. It was pretty amazing. Everything happened so fast with Nathan. Everything was *still* happening so fast. I just hoped I could keep up with him.

Nathan was so determined. He knew what he wanted, and he never edited himself in speaking his mind about things. I loved that. It was a new relaxing way of getting to know someone. Nathan had always been honest and transparent with me. I never had to fish the answers out of him.

He kept folding and packing while I thought about what a suitable response to his previous comment might be.

"I'd do it all with you," he said. "Wedding, kids. But not before a big fat ring, of course."

Ring. Wedding. Kids. I knew he didn't mean right away, but I was about to hyperventilate. It made me so happy to hear him say all those things. How could it not? He drove me crazy and made me feel like the most wanted girl in the world—all the time. But still, overwhelming.

I smiled. "I thought you didn't want to get married." I don't think that was what he wanted to hear as a reply, but that's the best I could come up with, and I was curious to listen to what he had to say about that. What had changed his mind?

"I know. Me neither." He stood up and sat next to me on the bed. "I just feel like I want to do everything with you. I want to be the one to make you happy. Always." He gently laid me back on the bed and kissed me. "Don't worry, love. It's not something that's going to happen tomorrow. There's no rush. Besides, you're still studying," he said, playing around with my hair with his fingers. "I'm sorry if you were taken aback by my—enthusiasm."

I'm sure the look on my face gave me away.

"No, no. It's not like that. It's just that I'd never talked about these things with anybody. It does make me happy to know you feel that way, though."

"We'll have to go to London sometime next year," he said, giving me one last peck on the lips before going back to packing. "My family's going to *love* you." I rolled on my belly, rested my elbows on the bed, and held my chin with my hands.

Just thinking about the idea of going to London stressed me out. A normal person would buy a ticket and go—end of story. But I had three guys following me around and an extremely apprehensive father. I didn't know how I'd be able to pull that off. I was sure Nathan could talk my father into it somehow. I hoped.

"It's easy for you to say when you became besties with my father before we even started dating," I said with a nervous laugh. "I have your three sisters, your parents, and Olly to impress."

Nathan laughed. "I *swear* they'll love you, just like I love you."

"I love you too."

Being a single child, and with my mother gone, I appreciated Nathan having a big family. I was glad that they were all so close because I knew how taxing Thomas's issues at home were for our relationship. He suffered because of it, and in a way, that was what triggered his insecurities.

Nathan's phone buzzed, and he took the call in front of me.

"Zara! … Packing, dear. How's everything? … Yes, she's right here with me."

Nathan shot a big smile my way and mouthed, "It's Zara," and carried on with the call. Yeah, I could tell it was her. It was endearing to see him so excited to talk to her.

"Right … What do you mean? Have you talked to Mum about it? … Christ! Not again with this nonsense … Can't you do one of those Skype things instead?"

Nathan pinched the bridge of his nose and shut his eyes for a second. He seemed annoyed.

"Exactly, I don't *understand, and I don't know if I ever will … I'll be in London for just a few days, and I also haven't seen you in a while … Yeah, yeah, yeah … Thanks for letting me know, and let's hope your flight gets on time for dinner or Mum will be throwing a wobbly … Oh, yes … What? Do you need money? … Because you're a starving actress, that's why!"*

Nathan laughed.

"Ah! I'm bloody joking ... Innit ... Right well, I best be off ... Luv you too ... Bye ... Buh-bye ... Right, cheers."

My God, I needed to know all about that call. My wide eyes must've communicated that to Nathan because he laughed and told me all about it right away.

"Zara, she—wants to stay a few days in Stockholm. Apparently, William called her and asked her to stay for a few days." *What?* He opened a drawer and took more clothes out. "They're close, Zara and William, always have been," Nathan said with a deep crease between his eyes.

So William called her? Asked her to stay? I knew Zara lived in Stockholm. She stayed there when her parents moved back to London. She was born there. Her entire life was in Sweden. Friends, everything.

"She's always loved hanging out with the Sjöbergs. She *admires* them— wants to be an actress too. But I"—he took a sharp breath through his nose—"I don't get it."

I couldn't help but feel jealous. I wanted to know more about Zara's relationship with William. About her. What she was like. Everything.

It was the first time I ever heard of them being so close. But I couldn't ask. I was afraid to sound too obvious, but the curiosity was going to eat me away, one brain cell at a time.

Well, maybe I could sneak in a question. I couldn't neglect my mental health like that. "But like, have they ever—dated or?"

"Oh, no." Nathan smiled a nervous smile. "No, no, no. No, definitely *not*. He wouldn't be alive if he touched her. He knows she's off-limits. They're just ... I don't know—best friends? I don't get why she's so fixated with him, especially. I thought you might've known about this." Nope. Nada. "But she's *well aware* that nothing can happen between them or else."

Well … okay. Wow. Best friends? Weirdly, William never mentioned her, not even once.

Ughhh! More secrets kept popping up every time. I would never be done discovering William. At least they were both cautioned about not trying to move their relationship past the friend zone. But William never knew what the word *rules* and *limits* meant. I was sure that was probably the reason that relationship might've been even more appealing to him. Who knows?

There was a knock on the door, and Nathan stood up to open it. I could hear him talking to Caleb in the distance. He walked back with a manila folder.

"Is everything okay?" I stood up from the bed. It always made me nervous whenever they came up to talk to me about anything. It made me feel like something terrible had happened.

"You need to sign these," he said, looking at the paperwork inside the folder. I sighed with relief. My shoulders loosened up. "Do you want me to check it out for you? I do charge by the hour, but I'm sure we can think of something."

I walked up to him and placed my arms around his neck. "How about this?" I stood on my tiptoes and kissed him slowly. Deeply. "How much time does this buy for me?"

"Probably just a few minutes. I need *at least* half an hour to read through the entire thing. Wouldn't want there to be any loopholes."

"Name your fee then," I whispered to his lips.

"I know *exactly* how you can pay me." He guided me to his bed. "I usually require one-hundred percent upfront payment for my services."

☾

I fell asleep after making love with Nathan. I was still tired after William woke me up early in the morning. Even though I tried to shut my eyes after he left, I didn't get much sleep afterward.

When I woke up from my power nap, I saw Nathan sitting on the edge of the bed, reading through the paperwork without a shirt on. That was one *sexy lawyer*.

"Hey, you," I said, stretching my arms over my head, my body still under the covers. "So, what's that all about?"

"It's a two-year contract renewal for your security detail. Since you're turning twenty-one in a few months, you're now obligated to sign these contracts. It's pretty standard," Nathan replied with his Britishly crisp accent and a businesslike lawyerly tone.

"Pretty standard? So, I overpaid for your services?" I teased.

"I'm afraid so." He laughed and sat next to me. "You need to sign here, here—and here." He gave me the pen, and I signed those contracts away. "Nice doing business with you." He winked and placed the paperwork back in the folder.

Nathan opened his nightstand drawer and pulled out an envelope. "Christmas present."

I opened it, and there was a handwritten note inside.

Valid for acrylic print with my portrait. You get to choose the size. Happy Christmas, love.

"Thank you!" I gave him a quick kiss. "Your portrait will look amazing on my empty gallery wall." I needed to hang something there. The empty wall reminded me of Thomas. It's as if I could still see his portrait on the wall. And what better way to replace that feeling than having Nathan's face there instead?

"I loved your portrait so much I thought you might want to have mine too. You would have to take my picture, of course, but I'll have it printed out for you."

That right there was the actual gift—having him sit for the portrait. I was going to enjoy shooting him so much. I usually always carried a camera with me everywhere we went. I had snapped more than a few candid shots of Nathan. But not a portrait like the ones I loved shooting. I was excited about it.

I stood up and got dressed.

"Let's do it next week when you come back from London," I suggested. "And this is for you." I grabbed an envelope out of my purse and handed it to him.

He opened it and took two tickets out.

"No, no, no. No *fucking* way!" Nathan shouted when he saw what it was. "Are these for real?" He carried me. My feet left the floor, and I locked my legs around his waist as he kissed me.

"Of course they are," I replied as he dropped me back on my feet and tossed the envelope on the bed. He then placed his hands firmly around my waist. "I'm sure this counts as Joel's Christmas present too. You'll probably want to take him because I'm obviously *not* allowed to go," I said, caressing his neatly kept stubble with my fingers.

"I love you." He kissed me over and over again. "This is the best gift ever."

"Hey! I thought my portrait was the best gift ever." I joked. "I love you too."

He laughed. "You know how utterly *obsessed* I am with The Who. I need to let Joel know we're going to the Super Bowl." He took his phone out of his pocket and sent the text.

"I hope Lily doesn't get mad at me for sending you two to Miami alone for the weekend," I said, taking a seat on the bed.

"Of course not. She knows we want to go. And we'll behave, of course." He grinned.

I knew they would. He didn't even have to tell me.

"William, the bastard, has four tickets, and Joel insisted on me using the fourth since Eric's not going. But there's no way *in hell* I'd take anything from him. I mean, I'm sure we're all going to hang out in Miami, and I can't be arsed by that, but I wanted to have my own ticket. And since I'd just asked my boss for help to take you to the opera, it just felt too soon to ask him about the Super Bowl."

I still felt awful about the surprise being ruined.

After the opera *mix-up* drama, I could totally understand Nathan's posture. William had crossed a line, and Nathan's pride would never allow him to accept anything from William. Even if that meant he had to miss seeing his favorite band performing live at the Super Bowl.

They both had powerful personalities. And every day that went by, I understood more and more why they could never get along. They were two very alpha males.

"How did you get the tickets?" Nathan asked, throwing a few more things into his suitcase.

"Was it your father?"

I nodded. "Consider it a gift from him as well."

"I'll have to call him and thank him for this later today."

"I'm happy you're happy." I smiled. He stared at me for a few seconds without saying a word. "Is everything okay?"

Nathan kissed my hair and said, "Everything's *perfect*."

CHAPTER 30

Circle Of Mistrust

February 5, 2010

IT WAS THE COLDEST DAY EVER. I'd just arrived from school and changed into my gym clothes. I refused to go for a run. I was freezing and tired, but I made myself go.

I stepped out of my apartment, and Caleb was stationed outside my door.

"Hey! What's up?" I asked with a smile.

"I'll walk you to the gym."

Weird.

Once inside the apartment building, I was usually free to roam around by myself as long as I texted them about my whereabouts.

"Is everything okay?"

"Of course." He tried smiling, but it wasn't genuine.

"Caleb."

"You know how your father gets these—*waves* of apprehension when he travels. He wants us to tighten security for a few days. That's all. Everything's okay, Red."

It all sounded like a bunch of *bollocks* to me.

I loved it when Nathan used that word and how he said it. He was leaving the next day to Miami for the Super Bowl. I was excited for him, although I knew I was going to miss him.

We did see each other almost every day, but it was usually for a little while. Our real quality time was during the weekends—they were sacred. And even so, there would be times when he had to show up at the office on a Saturday, which was super annoying.

It was odd to think that Nathan and William were going to have to coexist in Miami. But things had been quiet and calm with William gone. Empty, almost. I could feel the void emanating from his vacant apartment—a peaceful torture.

My relationship with Nathan was going great because of that, too. I thought I could learn to get used to William not being around.

Caleb walked me to the gym and stood right outside the glass door with his bodyguard stance firmly in place.

I quickly realized I wasn't in the mood for running, so I switched to a brisk walk instead. "Caleb!" He immediately came inside and stood next to my treadmill.

"Yes, Miss Murphy?" He smiled, raising an eyebrow.

"I'm bored," I said with a chuckle, "and I forgot my cell phone."

"I can ask Aaron to go get it," he said, bringing his finger up to his earpiece.

"No, it's okay. I thought we could just—chat. It's been a while since we had time to talk. Or is the gym a threat big enough for you to get distracted?"

"We can talk." He leaned in against the treadmill's handrail.

"Okay. Entertain me then."

I missed Caleb. He was one of my best friends, but he behaved differently now that I was with Nathan. With Thomas, Caleb felt like he needed to keep close tabs on me. With good reason. I'd been too blind to see Thomas for who he was.

I guess he felt I was in good hands with Nathan. That's why he distanced himself from me more than usual. I wasn't a fan of that.

We talked about school, his family, and how they were all doing. And, of course, Paris. We always talked about Paris. It was our happy place. The stories were the same every time, but oh, how we loved going over them again and again.

We walked out of the gym, and the floor was wet as it had just been mopped. Caleb walked ahead of me, trying to summon the elevator, but he slipped and fell on his ass, just like the story about the poor chef in Paris he loved making fun of.

He cursed in Hebrew and jumped up to his feet in a second. I burst out laughing, and he couldn't help but laugh too. "Karma," I sang, laughing again.

"Shit." He shook his head with a grin, clicking on the elevator's up button.

"Oh, Caleb, come on. No one saw you but me." I tried not to laugh.

"And that's one too many. I'm sure you'll make me remember this forever."

"Absolutely."

The elevator doors opened up, and we stepped out on the ninth floor, still laughing.

Nathan was standing outside my apartment door with a frown. But he smiled a tight-lip smile when he saw us. Caleb immediately composed himself. I sighed, still trying to catch my breath from the laughter.

"Hey, you," I said as Nathan hugged me and gave me a quick kiss on the lips. "I'm all sweaty!" I tried pulling away, but he didn't care. Caleb was still *very much* standing behind us. It would forever be uncomfortable to flaunt hugs and kisses in front of Caleb after having done that with him too.

"I was worried sick," he said with an anxious tone. "You weren't answering your phone." He turned to look at Caleb and scanned him from head to toe.

"I'm sorry. I left my phone in the apartment. Do you want to come in?"

"Actually … Caleb, could I have a quick word?" Caleb nodded.

"Hey, what's wrong?" I asked in barely a whisper. Maybe he didn't like me being friends with Caleb. I didn't want Nathan to scare him away as my father did before.

"Why don't you go take a shower, and I'll meet you inside in a few minutes?" He smiled, but I could see something was off. And I didn't enjoy being dismissed like that by him either. I hate being told what to do.

"Okay. I'll see you inside." I closed the door and huffed my way to the shower, hoping Nathan would return soon so he could tell me what the heck he talked about with Caleb.

I stepped out of the shower and wrapped a towel around my body as I dried off my hair and combed it.

Nathan knocked on my bathroom door, which was already open. He stared at me with raw hunger in his eyes. "I'm going to need you to put some clothes on," he said—another order.

I bit my lower lip, trying to prevent myself from replying something of the same caliber. I was starting to lose my temper with all that ordering around.

My body was still damp. I unwrapped the towel to dry myself completely, but Nathan was still standing there in front of me.

"Fuck," he uttered with exasperation. He turned around and sat on my bedroom's couch, running his fingers through his hair. *What is his problem?*

I joined him a few minutes later, *fully clothed*, as he requested, and sat next to him. "Can you please tell me what's going on? I've never seen you like this before. What did you talk about with Caleb? We're friends, and we were just laughing and—"

"I know that, Murph. But that's not why I pulled him aside."

The doorbell rang. Nathan rushed to the door, but I followed him. He was up to something, and I was going to find out exactly what that was.

Caleb and Aaron stood behind a guy in a fancy suit. "Hey Gabe, this is my girlfriend, Billie. Why don't you come in?"

"Nice to meet you, Billie." He was holding a binder.

What the hell is happening!

Nathan guided Gabe toward the dining room, and I took a seat beside Nathan as Gabe pulled out a stack of papers. He placed them in front of Nathan and handed him a pen.

"Thank you for putting this together on such short notice," Nathan said, signing the documents. "Do you have the dossier?"

"It's all in here." Gabe tapped a sealed letter-sized envelope. Nathan grabbed my hand and squeezed it. He knew that not only was I clueless, but that I was getting nervous.

"I'll submit the paperwork right away. I'll text you once it's done," Gabe said, standing up. "Pleasure meeting you, Billie." He shook my hand and walked himself out of the apartment.

"Nathan, *what's going on?*"

"I just signed an order of protection against Thomas," he said, licking his lower lip. He knew I would react to it. He was waiting for the blow.

"What?" I said in a high-pitched tone. "I told you I wasn't comfortable doing that. Why wouldn't you talk to me about it first?" I stood up from my seat.

"I'll have to call Joel. I don't think I can go to Miami tomorrow." He was rambling to himself instead of answering my questions.

"Nathan."

He stood up and sighed. "Thomas just showed up at my office. He's got his knickers in a twist about the order of protection we filed against him on your behalf. The firm's security team took care of it, but things are getting out of hand with this lad."

"Took care of it—how?"

"They made sure he left. No one was harmed."

"I'm lost here, Nathan. I haven't seen or talked to Thomas since

CJ's party, so why file an order of protection against him on *my* behalf?"

"Well, I have. I've been dealing with Thomas ever since that night. We didn't want to tell you anything so you wouldn't worry. But we thought it was best to file the order of protection to see if we could get him to back off, but now that he's showed up at work … I can't allow that. So that's why I just signed off on one against him for myself."

"*We* thought? Who's *we*?"

"Your father and me." Nathan kept anxiously running his fingers through his hair.

"I see now why you two get along so well. All this time …" I bit my lip and looked away. *This isn't happening.* I took a deep breath and faced him. "All your *liquid lunches* and pints after work. You've been plotting this behind my back, haven't you? Deciding what's *best for me.*" I stormed off into my bedroom.

I was furious at Nathan, at my father, at Caleb because he surely had been in on it too. That's why he'd been acting smooth as silk around Nathan. He approved of Nathan's decisions regarding Thomas, and I knew how much Caleb hated Thomas. I felt betrayed by *everyone.* They were supposed to be my circle of trust.

And once again, I was the naive little girl that needed to be kept in the dark so she could live her life thinking everything was unicorns and rainbows. Why would they want that kind of life for me? I was so incredibly disappointed.

"Murph, let's talk. Don't walk away," he said, following me.

"Can't you see this is exactly the kind of thing that bothers me the most? You lied to me! Those contracts Caleb brought up the day you left for England … I was signing the order of protection, wasn't I?" Caleb was definitely in on it. He'd brought up the paperwork knowing what it was.

"Yes, but you need to understand we couldn't risk having you say no again. It *had* to be done. And we didn't want you to worry about it, either." Nathan ran a rough hand down his face and tried coming near me, but I took a couple of steps back. "We were just trying to protect you."

"Don't!" Tears rolled down my face, and I could see Nathan wasn't enjoying seeing me cry. But I needed physical space. "I expected this from my father, but not from you. You're *exactly* like him. Maybe that's why I feel so—so drawn to you. You remind me of him. You think alike. But you can't do this to me, Nathan. Hide things from me to 'protect me.'

"It's been almost seven years since my mother died, and no one tells me shit about *why* she was murdered. Do you think I don't know *they* know? She was an ambassador's wife, for fuck's sake! They must've figured everything out within the hour.

"And I have learned to live with that. With the secrets my father keeps for *my own good*. But not you too. I won't have it."

Nathan frowned and took a sharp breath through his nose. "Please forgive me, Murph. I know I should've told you. But this is how your father wanted things to be handled. And you're right. We should've told you everything. It's your right to know." I closed my eyes and looked away. The situation was so frustrating.

"I can't leave you after seeing how out of control Thomas is. I want to be here to protect you."

"I have three guys for that. Twenty-four-seven. And I never thought I would have to say this to you too, but I don't need a fourth bodyguard. I need you to be my boyfriend. I need you to take my side. Always. Not my father's side. I know how convincing he is. He's a diplomat!" I laughed a sad, sad laugh.

"That's what he does for a living. And I know he loves me, and everything he does is out of fear of losing me too, but I'm *choking* here knowing you're going down that same path. And worst of all, behind my back.

"When we moved back to New York, I thought things were going to be different. That security would decrease with time. But that hasn't been the case. It keeps getting tighter, and I hate knowing you're somehow—encouraging my father."

Nathan took another step forward, but I took two steps back.

"Please forgive me, love. I'll stay, and I'll tell you everything that's been happening, and I won't leave anything out."

"That would've been great *before* you decided to lie to me and make me sign the order of protection without my consent. If you thought it was *that* important, I would've listened to you and agreed to sign it myself. We could've decided on it together."

I climbed up on my bed and sat crossed legged, hugging one of my pillows. Tears kept streaming down my face. I was deeply hurt. I trusted Nathan blindly, and I never in a million years thought he would do this to me.

"You should go to Miami. I can take care of myself."

"Well, too bad because I'm not going."

"I *don't* want you to stay," I said, staring into his eyes. It stung to utter those words, but I was furious. I needed to be alone with my anger. "Just go."

"Murph, please don't do this."

"I'll see you on Monday. Or do I need to ask Aaron and Caleb to walk you out? I've done it before. I can be the girl with the bodyguards if that's the kind of thing that gets you off."

Nathan's expression switched from sad and worried to plain angry. He kept gnawing at his lower lip but wouldn't stop staring directly at me. I wasn't enjoying this one bit.

I didn't want to have to say those things, but he hit me where it hurt the most—my sense of freedom. I knew I wasn't free, but at least I hoped he could be the one to help me feel less trapped, not guide me inside the cage with the excuse of doing it for my own good.

Nathan launched at me, and his mouth met mine for a second, two seconds, three, four, five, ten … I stopped counting. I could stay there forever. He wanted to kiss and makeup, but I needed space. "No," I said, pulling away from him, panting. He was sitting on the bed beside me, his chest heaving.

"I can't leave if you're upset."

"Yes, you can." I extended my arm and clicked on one of the four panic buttons installed in my apartment. I'd obviously never used them before. They seemed too much for my taste. I was sure I would never use them, but they gave my father peace of mind.

Aaron, Caleb, and David got the first notification on their phones if I pushed a button. If unattended, it would go directly to the DSS. But I knew they were standing outside my apartment, and they would shut down the beacon immediately.

A few beats later, Aaron and Caleb dashed into my bedroom. Nathan jumped up from the bed, and so did I. "Miss Murphy," Caleb said, eyeing Nathan and me from head to toe, sizing up the situation, trying to figure out if I was hurt. I was. Not that he would be able to see it with his eyes. Or maybe he could. He saw everything.

"Could you please"—I cleared my throat—"escort Nathan out of my apartment?" My voice was calm, melodic even.

"Murph, don't do this." Nathan extended his hand out to me, but I didn't take it. I knew we would be able to talk it through. I knew I would forgive him. But I needed time and space, and his approach to solving this was different than mine.

"This is what it feels like when people decide for you," I replied.

Nathan saw himself out right after I said that, as I expected he would. I was not trying to make a scene. But I did want him to know what it's like to have someone overpower you. And I'm sure he didn't like it one bit.

The second Nathan walked away, I fell apart. Aaron followed

Nathan out, and Caleb stood there looking at me, at how I cried my heart out.

"I want to be alone." I laid on my bed and gave my back to Caleb, holding on to my pillow as if it were going to save me from my sorrows somehow.

"Red, you need to understand. Thomas is out of control. He's been stalking Nathan, threatening him. We've spotted him a couple of times at Parsons, too. This is serious."

They still couldn't understand that the order of protection itself was not the issue. The real problem was how they all snuck around my back, plotted the whole thing, lied to me, and made me sign it without my consent. I would've obviously signed it if I knew all of that.

And these are supposed to be the three people I trust the most in the world? That was the most heartbreaking part of all. But they couldn't see it.

I clicked on the panic button again, and Caleb immediately turned it off with his phone.

"That's for you. Please see yourself out."

Caleb snorted with disbelief and quickly left afterward.

I closed my eyes and held my breath for a few seconds. I wanted complete silence. And in that silence, I swear I heard William's piano.

CHAPTER 31

The Walls Have Ears

February 6, 2010

I TOSSED AND TURNED all night, unable to sleep for more than a few hours. Before I knew it, dawn was breaking, and Nathan was leaving for Miami. He had an early flight and was meeting Joel and the others later that day.

I started crying again and refused to leave my bed, still wearing the same clothes from last night.

Isn't one supposed to wake up feeling better after you've slept it off? I guess the problem was I didn't get to the sleeping part.

I wanted to call Nathan and ask him to stay. To come back to me. But I'd dismissed him pretty badly. He must've been feeling hurt because of it too. It was best if we both gave each other some breathing space.

It was going to be a long weekend.

My cell phone buzzed. It had to be him.

W.S: I can hear you crying.

What?

Me: No, you don't. It's not March.
W.S: I'm here, but I'm not back yet.

I didn't know what to reply, so I closed my eyes, knowing I would lay in bed all day, doing everything except sleeping. Was he really in his apartment? Perhaps William found out somehow about the fight, and that was his way of asking if I was okay.

A knock. It came from the wall next to William's bedroom. The piano wasn't a figment of my imagination, after all. I stared at the wall but did nothing.

Two knocks. *Ugh*!

I stood up and knocked back, placing my forehead on the wall afterward. I shouldn't have done that. I know better than to play along to William's games. Slowly, I sat on the floor and rested the back of my head against the wall. I needed a few seconds before I could stand up again.

W.S: Door.
Me: Not you too.
W.S: Me too, what?
Me: Ordering me around.
W.S: I like it best when you're the one giving the orders.

My doorbell rang.

W.S: Better?
Me: I hate that doorbell. Knock.
W.S: Are you trying to turn me on?

He knocked on my door. I took a deep breath, knowing it was a bad idea, but I was crumbling. And whatever compass William used to identify the moments when I needed someone the most worked like a charm. He showed up every single time, even when he was supposed to be a million miles away.

Me: I need a minute.

I combed my hair because I wasn't going to pretend like I didn't care about how I looked in front of him. I washed my face with cold water, but there wasn't much I could do to hide the red rims bordering my eyes, giving me away.

"Hey," I said, persuading myself to smile, an afflicted smile for sure. "Aren't you supposed to be … I don't even know where you've been, but—there?"

"Ireland."

"Ireland." I nodded once. He wasn't as far as I thought he was. It felt as though.

"I flew back yesterday to go to the Super Bowl. Tobias and I will fly to Miami in a few hours." He stared at me, but I didn't know what else to say. I couldn't stop thinking about how I wouldn't be able to see Nathan in the next couple of days while trying not to drown in this ocean of feelings.

A single tear threatened to ruin my recently washed face. But I swallowed it back and felt the trail of it burning my throat.

"Nathan?" He raised a brow.

"On his way to Miami." I took a slow and deep breath in.

"That's not what I meant to ask," he said with a tad of exasperation.

I shrugged.

William looked over my shoulder and saw Nathan's portrait hanging behind me. He licked his lower lip with a frown but said … *nada*. That was new. I thought he was going to ask me to take it down. Which I wouldn't.

"What happened?" he asked with a demanding tone.

"Nada."

"Nothing." He snorted with a sarcastic smile. "So, besides the fact that he's an idiot who left you here to cry alone, is he ordering you around?"

"No, he's not. I mean—he messed up, but we're going to be okay. I just needed some space. I messed up too. I got a little—quick-tempered right there in the end."

"No! You? Quick-tempered?" He made a *psh* sound afterward just to get on my nerves.

"Shut up," I said with a smile that felt like torture as I looked up into his eyes.

"I'm impressed he's not the one complaining about being bossed around. He might enjoy it. I know I do."

"I don't boss Nathan around."

"So, just me, then?" William leaned sideways against the doorframe, hands inside his pants pockets, foot crossed in front of the other. "Huh. I can't say I don't like that even better."

William was used to being pleased by everyone. No one ever said no to him. That must've been so convenient for him—boring too. But I didn't know *that* William. The one everyone wanted to satisfy so badly. To me, he was just—him.

And he definitely liked the game he thought we were playing. Was I playing along? I could tell by the way he was looking at me that he probably thought I was. That was my cue to go back inside.

"Don't you have a plane to catch?" I asked, trying to get the conversation to fade to black.

"Plane leaves whenever I feel like leaving. And I don't feel like leaving just yet." He smirked.

Of course. Why would he fly commercial?

The way he kept looking at me made me nervous—the kind of good nervous that made me feel bad. Guilty. "Just go," I said with an awkward laugh.

"Yes, ma'am." He tapped his forehead with two fingers and turned around to leave.

"That was easy!" I said to his back.

He looked over his shoulder. "I'm at your will," he said with a wink, walking to his apartment. "But I do know one thing. I wouldn't have left for Miami if I were him. Sadly, he doesn't know you like I do."

His brilliant blue gaze traveled from my eyes to my lips as he unlocked his apartment. "One has to know when to disobey such orders, as exciting as they can be."

He disappeared into his apartment and shut the door behind him.

Why didn't he brush his lip?

CHAPTER 32

Super Bowl

February 7, 2010

LILY AND I WERE GOING to watch the Super Bowl together. We didn't care about the game, but we wanted to watch the half-time show, and Lily swore the commercials were the best part of all. Plus, it was a great excuse to hang out just the two of us. Fashion Week started next weekend, and she would be working and traveling like crazy.

Lily: Your place or mine?
Me: Yours?

I needed to get out. I hadn't left my apartment since Friday. And I tried smiling as much as I could for Mimi. I didn't want her to worry or start asking questions. Ultimately, she reported back to my father, and I didn't feel like talking to him. Not yet. I wanted things to be okay with Nathan first.

Lily waited for me with two bottles of wine and a bunch of snacks. *Now that's what I'm talking about.*

"I have a surprise for you," she said, disappearing into her room. She came back holding a large yellow Louis Vuitton paper bag. "Here. It's all yours."

"Lily, you just gave me that black Celine bag last month," I replied as Lily placed the bag on my lap.

"I already have this bag in another color. Please, take it. Don't you want to see it?" She moved her eyebrows up and down while biting on her lower lip.

I wanted to see it, of course, so I opened it. It was a bucket-shaped bag with the Louis Vuitton monogram metallic canvas in a green shade. It was beautiful.

"Let me see," she said, taking a small note out of a personalized envelope. "Monogram Eden Neo."

I kept looking at the bag as if I were an inspector.

"If you don't want it, I guess I can give it away to someone—"

"No!" I laughed. Lily laughed too.

"That's what I thought."

"And you're sure it's okay?"

Lily rolled her eyes and poured wine into the two wineglasses.

"A toast," she said, giving one to me. "For your new badass purse that's not even in stores yet." We clicked our glasses and sipped on our wine.

"Thank you, Lily. It's a beautiful bag."

"And all yours."

I took a deep breath and sipped on my wine again. My mind drifted away, but I forced myself to stop thinking about my fight with Nathan. I wondered how he was. He hadn't called me once since he left.

Lily and I talked for a while, ordered pizza, and finally, the half-time show was about to begin. The backstage crew was setting up the stage, and the camera pin-pointed celebrities who were attending the Super Bowl in the meanwhile.

"Oh, my God! It's William and Tobias!" Lily shouted. They were inside a suite box, looking out. There were two other guys with them I didn't recognize. I couldn't help but think Joel and Nathan could've been there instead, but they weren't because of me. I hated feeling like I was the reason for splitting them up for the event.

A bar appeared at the bottom of the screen with the names of the four of them. Lily told me the two other guys were actors too. Friends with the Sjöbergs.

When they realized they were being projected into the big screens around the stadium, William brushed his lower lip and made a *yes, ma'am* gesture afterward.

OH, MY GOD!

William and Tobias yelled something holding their fists up and chugged down their beers. They all laughed afterward, and the camera switched to the next celebrity they spotted. They seemed to be having a lot of fun.

My reaction consisted of thrusting my warm face against one of the throw pillows. No. My hot face. I was surely red *and then some* when Lily forced me to stop doing that.

She laughed. "What just happened? Look at your face!"

"What? Nothing," I said, pouring myself more wine. Oh, yeah, I needed wine. More wine, please.

"William?" she dared ask.

"Uh-uh," I hummed, sipping on my wine, saying *no* with my index finger.

The lights went off in the stadium, and the half-time show started. How could I not think of Nathan? He was about to see his favorite band performing live, and I couldn't even text him and be excited about it with him. My mood switched from giddy to sad in one second. I was a mess.

"What's wrong?" Lily insisted, setting her glass on the coffee table.

"The show's started," I replied, staring at my wineglass. I didn't have any tears left to cry.

"I'd rather know if you're okay. I don't really care about The

Who. Sue me."

I chuckled. I wanted to see it because it was important for Nathan. "Can we wait until the performance is over? We'll have the entire second boring half to talk. I'll tell you everything." I needed to talk to someone and let it all out. And by all, I meant *all*.

Seven minutes into The Who's performance, I got a call from Nathan.

When I took the call, I could hear the concert roaring behind him and a bunch of people singing and screaming. He sang—or better said, *shouted* the song being performed by The Who over the phone.

"I love you, Murph!" He ended the call, and I smiled. He was most likely drunk, but I was glad he called me to let me know he was enjoying the show and thinking of me.

"Was that Nate?" Lily asked. I nodded with a small, crooked smile. She immediately noticed something was wrong.

The half-time show ended, and Lily immediately shut the TV off. "Okay, we're done pretending to care about the Super Bowl. Tell me everything."

I laughed but sobered up in a second. "William or Nathan?"

"Both! But Nate first. Are you guys fighting?" Lily had a genuinely worried face. She loved Nathan too. How could she not? Nathan's the best.

"Nathan tricked me into signing a restraining order against Thomas on my behalf. He planned it all with my father, and Caleb helped too. He told me the documents were a contract renewal of my security detail, so I signed them off without even looking at them. I trusted his word."

"What? But why wouldn't they talk to you about it? Why hide it from you?" I could see she didn't agree with how they handled it either.

"I didn't know this until two days ago, but Thomas has been threatening Nathan ever since we saw him at CJ's party. And last

Friday, he even went looking for Nathan at his office. I don't know all the details because we were arguing about the whole: *making me sign things without my consent* thing.

"Nathan's excuse was that they didn't want me to worry. But that's how my father operates. He keeps things from me to protect me, and now he's grooming Nathan into doing the same. That's what hurt me the most."

"I'm so sorry. The Thomas situation is pretty crazy. I guess the restraining order isn't such a bad idea, right?"

"It's *not* a bad idea. And I would've agreed to it immediately. I don't want Thomas to hurt Nathan. Not that I thought he would, but now I don't know what to expect from him." I bit the inside of my cheek, trying to keep the tears away. It seemed like I wasn't done crying. "They don't trust me to have common sense. It's ridiculous."

Lily sat next to me and hugged me. "It's okay. I'm sure Nate didn't mean any harm with this. It could've been your father, the one who wanted things to be handled this way."

"He did mention something of the sort," I said, brushing a few tears away. "But I still feel awful about how I reacted. I dismissed him in the worst possible way. He wanted to stay. He tried to talk to me about it, and I pushed him away. But I was furious! I needed space and—"

"Hey, don't be too hard on yourself. I'm sure you'll figure things out once he gets back from Miami," she said, picking up her phone from the coffee table. "Do you want me to call Joel and ask him how Nathan's been doing?"

I nodded, almost desperately. Nathan seemed to be having a good time when he called me, but I didn't mind listening to Joel's opinion on the matter.

But Joel didn't pick up. There was still a while to go before the game ended. They were probably drinking and having fun. I huffed and took another sip of my wine.

A couple of minutes later, Joel returned the call, and Lily quickly took it.

"Hey! … Yeah, of course … Are you guys having fun? … What do you mean?"

Lily's face went grim, and I got anxious.

"Is he okay? … Please call me back once you're in the hotel … Love you, too."

"What's going on?" I asked reactively.

"Um—Nate had a little too much to drink, and Joel's taking him back to the hotel. He said he's fine, just well—drunk."

"Shit, this is all my fault," I said, crouching on the sofa.

"It *definitely* isn't your fault. Nate's old enough to know what he's doing. I guess he was having a hard time too, and that's how he tried to forget about it." Lily dropped her phone back on the table. "He'll be okay, don't worry. Joel will call me in a few minutes."

Twenty minutes later, Lily's phone rang again.

"Nate wants to talk to you," Lily whispered. "They're back at the hotel." I snatched the phone away from her hands and took the call.

"Hey, you."

"A-a-a-alriiiiight," he said with a chuckle. "Murph, Imissye."

"I—miss you too," I said, thinking how he probably wouldn't remember our conversation the next day. I hoped he remembered the half-time show, though. "How are you feeling? Are you okay?"

"I—know I dropped a clanger," he said lazily, "but I luv-ye."

"I love you too. I'll see you tomorrow. Try to get some sleep." He babbled something I couldn't understand. He sounded gone. "Nathan?"

"Billie?" It was Joel now. Nathan couldn't even put two words together anymore. I was so worried.

"Joel, is he okay? He doesn't sound good. Maybe he needs to go to the hospital and—"

"No, no, no. Don't worry. I've got this. I don't think I've seen Nate this wasted since high school, but he'll be okay, I swear. It ain't his first rodeo. He just needs to sleep it off." Joel sounded confident about the situation, which reassured me Nathan was going to be okay. "Um—I have to go." Joel yelled something to Nathan in Swedish and hung up the phone.

Shit.

"He's going to be okay, Billie. Don't worry. Joel will make sure of it," she said, pouring herself more wine with a slight frown. The situation had stressed her too, but I could tell she was trying to seem put together for my sake. "Why don't you tell me what's up with Billy?"

Damn it. I hoped she would forget about it. But it's Lily. Of course, she wouldn't forget. "It's um—really nothing, just—"

"Is he bothering you again?" she interrupted. "You can tell me."

"No." I didn't even know what to tell her or how to even start talking about it. I just had to face the music. "Do you think it's possible to have feelings for two people at the same time?"

Lily's eyes went wide. "I do ... think it's possible. Why? Do you have feelings for Billy?"

"I don't know. I don't want to, but—it's been well—I don't know," I stammered and covered my face afterward. "What William did just now on TV ... it was for me. I mean, it's a sign he uses with me. Unless he's doing that with a bunch of other girls, which wouldn't surprise me but—"

"The lip-brushing thing he did?"

"Yes. And the *yes, ma'am* gesture."

"What does it all mean?" she asked with a smile. She seemed

strangely excited about the conversation. I thought she was going to tell me to ignore him or something of the sort. She didn't.

"You know this song from Dave Matthews Band, Crash Into Me?" I asked. Lily nodded quickly, rushing me to continue. "It's one of my favorite songs ever. And you know this part of the lyrics that says, *touch your lips?*" Lily nodded again. "Well, when we were at the cottage, he played the song with his guitar and stopped when he sang that part, insisting I touch my lips." I smiled at the memory. "So then, we started using it as our little sign."

Lily's eyes turned into hearts. *Stop!* She wasn't being helpful! She encouraged me to continue as she swooned.

"He's been teasing me for months now. Every time he sees me, he brushes his lower lip, just like he did right now. He wants to see me do it, too. But I never do, of course.

"And the day Nathan and I made our relationship official, William sent me two magazines where he showed me how the paparazzi photos of him and Erin were actually old photographs." I sighed. "You were right, Lily, about it all being fake. The other magazine had a small article talking about William and Erin's breakup."

I covered my face again with my elbows resting on my thighs for a second. "He was upset when I told him I was now officially dating Nathan. I was upset, too, of course. But I had already grown fond of Nathan—we were close. I felt like my heart was getting ripped in half."

Lily kept gnawing at her lips.

"And, the *yes, ma'am* thing? What does it mean?" She wanted to know everything.

"He keeps insisting on how I'm always bossy around him. Which he—likes? I don't know, I hadn't seen him since before Christmas, and now that I saw him yesterday, I just—he always stirs things up inside me, and I don't want to feel or understand whatever *that* is, but I do, and then I feel guilty for feeling it."

"Did you bump into him, or … ?"

"He heard me crying. You know how our bedrooms are next to each other … He just wanted to make sure I was okay."

"Ah, yes. Billy told us how the previous owner had apartments 9A and 9B configured as a single huge apartment. The person who bought it afterward divided it into two again and sold them separately years later. I guess the walls that separate your bedrooms must be drywall."

"I'm sure they are because I can hear him playing the piano and his guitar." *Every single night when he's around.*

"Do you think he can listen to you and Nathan having sex?" Lily bit her lower lip with a *cheeky* smile.

"Lily!" I shouted with embarrassment. I'd never given any thought to that, but now that she mentioned it, I was mortified.

"Well, if he can hear you cry … I mean, aren't the sounds kind of similar?" She laughed.

I threw one of the small throw pillows at her, but she kept laughing. "I'm not having sex *ever again* with Nathan at my apartment," I said with a nervous chuckle.

"Of course you are. I'm just kidding. Billy's never around anyway. I don't think he's ever heard a thing," she said, trying to make me feel better, but now I couldn't stop thinking about it.

"And don't get me wrong. Nathan and I are doing great together. I know we're going to be fine after the argument we had on Friday. And when William's away, Nathan really makes me forget about him, but when I see him …" I shook my head and shuddered, but it was almost undetectable. "I'm sure the feeling will fade away with time." I hoped.

"I mean, sure …" Lily said with hesitation.

"Lily! You're not helping!" I laughed out of pure nerves because the conversation wasn't funny.

"I'm sorry! It's just … I don't know. I care so much about Billy and Nathan. I really don't know what to say. It's a tough situation. I guess what happened with Billy is you two never could explore things. He might feel the same, and that's why you both can't seem to get over that fact. You know what I mean? Like you haven't been able to get each other out of your systems.

"Maybe once Billy finds someone else who makes him happy, he'll stop doing these things that only confuse you," she said. "That would probably be the best thing for everyone. I know how much you love Nathan."

William finding someone else who makes him happy.

I swallowed the huge lump in my throat. Nathan made me happy, so I should've wanted to wish the same for William.

But I guess I'm not as well-intentioned as I thought.

CHAPTER 33

A Multiverse Of Jealousy
Part 1

February 8, 2010

NATHAN MISSED his early morning flight. He slept in. The airport in Miami was swarming with people who had flown in for the Super Bowl. There weren't any available flights for him to take instead, and he needed to get back to work as soon as possible.

Joel convinced him to fly back with them. Nathan had to set his pride aside and return to New York on the same plane as William. It was either that or stay another day in Miami. That wasn't an option. He told me he had an early morning meeting on Tuesday he couldn't miss.

Nathan texted me to let me know they had arrived in New York and that he would drop by my apartment before going back to work. He wanted to see me. And I did too. We still needed to talk about what happened, but I was in a much better headspace to do that.

Aaron and David drove me back from school. I hadn't seen Caleb since Friday, and although I was still a little angry, a tad sad, and a whole lot disappointed about what happened, I also wanted to talk to him and try to put everything behind us.

My phone buzzed. It was CJ. "Heeeey, Billie! Nina and I need your help."

"Hey! Of course, what's up?"

"Our landlord is kicking us out of our apartment. Her daughter is going to use it from now on. We already found another one we liked, but it'll be ready by the eighth of March. Do you think Nina and I could stay with you for a few weeks?"

"Of course! But you would be sharing a room. Is that okay?"

"Ugh, you're a doll. And we don't mind. You're a lifesaver," CJ replied.

"Hey, Billie! Thank you so much for taking us in!" Nina shouted over the phone. "I'll make sure CJ behaves, don't worry."

I laughed. "Absolutely. No problem at all. So when do you need to be out of your current apartment?"

"February fifteen. We would be staying with you for three weeks. Are you *sure* it's okay?" CJ asked. "I know I'm a lot to take in." He laughed.

"You are." I joked with a laugh. "But I'd love to have you here with me. I'll have everything ready for you by then." It was going to be an interesting three weeks.

CJ thanked me a million more times before ending the call. At least Nina was still dating Juan Pablo. I'd hate to see her flirting with Caleb.

As I waited for Nathan to arrive, anxiety slithered up my spine. I didn't know how he was feeling about the argument. What I knew for sure was that he was going to arrive with a terrible hangover.

I rushed to the front door after hearing a knock. But it wasn't Nathan.

"Hey, Red," Caleb said with a deep crease in between his brows. He wasn't wearing his suit and tie, but jeans and a military green hoodie that made his eyes shine beautifully. He was off duty for the rest of the day. "I know you're angry, and you probably don't want to talk to me, but please hear me out."

I nodded and stepped outside, closing the door behind me.

"I don't want to make up any excuses, and I will only speak for myself. I just wanted to tell you that I know I messed up. I shouldn't have lied to you about the documents or plotted anything behind your back. I know how much you hate that, and I will do my best to avoid situations like those from happening again in the future."

"Thank you. I appreciate you saying that. And in all honesty, I'm not so angry anymore. I'm mostly sad about what happened. You know how I light up like a match but cool down just as fast."

Caleb snorted and smiled after I said that. He knew me.

"And ultimately, I know you were just following orders from my father and that you genuinely worry about me," I said, lifting the corners of my lips into a brief but genuine smile. I was still furious with my father. He was the one who orchestrated everything and pressured Nathan into doing things his way. "I'm sorry about the whole panic button thing. It's good to know they work, though, right?"

"I never thought you would ever need to use them, let alone to kick *me* out." He laughed.

That reminded me how I did that to Nathan, but worse. I needed to apologize. But fretting about it wasn't helpful. I needed to distract myself.

"I don't think I've ever seen you wearing jeans before," I said to him. It was the truth. It was always either a suit and tie or gym clothes. I always enjoyed talking to Caleb when he looked like him.

"Even I feel weird," he said, looking down at his outfit with a big smile. "But I had some errands to run earlier today, and since I had the rest of the day off, I decided to wear my clothes before they rot in the closet."

"How's your ass doing?" I asked, unable to hold back from laughing. "Still sore?"

He smiled and tried not to laugh, but it'd been too funny seeing him fall. "You're never going to drop that, are you?"

"Nope."

Caleb grabbed my hands and pulled me closer to him. He used his right foot to make me lose my balance. Half a second later, I fell on my butt on the floor, but Caleb controlled the entire movement to avoid having me bump in a way that would hurt me. I couldn't stop laughing.

Caleb squatted in front of me and grinned. "Gottcha."

The elevator doors opened. Nathan and William walked out, each rolling a small suitcase behind them. A wave of nervousness swam through my veins. It was so weird seeing the two of them together.

Nathan said goodbye to Joel and Tobias, who were inside the elevator. He looked drained.

William wore sunglasses, a cap, and a long face to go with his evident hangover. I was still sitting on the floor. Caleb offered his hands and pulled me up, glaring in William's direction. Caleb disliked him too much.

"I'll be downstairs if you need anything," Caleb said and turned around to leave. He shook Nathan's hand when he passed beside him and nodded at William. Once. Fast. Sharp.

William clicked his tongue and addressed Caleb, "Mixing business with pleasure?" *William*! He tapped his sunglasses down just slightly with a smirk.

Caleb ignored him, which I guess hadn't been easy for him, and marched away through the stairs.

Yes. Caleb was off duty, but still, he wasn't going to get into an argument with William over absolutely nothing. Especially not in front of Nathan, who already seemed puzzled about William's remark.

Nathan wasn't aware of something happening between Caleb

and me in the past. Since it hadn't ever been a topic, I never told him. Why would I bring it up out of the blue? Besides, Caleb and I were in a good place with our friendship, and he was more than respectful of my relationship with Nathan.

But William *had* seen us kissing on the rooftop, and I knew for a fact that he hadn't been thrilled about it. I remember his face perfectly well. They couldn't stand each other.

"Are you okay?" Nathan asked with a raspy voice. He kissed my cheek, and I could see William opening the door to his apartment, looking my way, smirk gone from his face. *That's right.*

A second later, he shut the door behind him. Nathan looked so serious with that firmly placed frown in between his eyes.

"I'm okay. Let's go inside," I said, opening the door. "How are you feeling?"

Nathan dropped his things in the foyer and hugged me. "Like shit." He kissed my hair. "My head is about to explode."

"Do you want some medicine or something to drink? Coffee?"

"Coffee would be splendid, thank you."

I was setting up the machine to make the coffee when Nathan walked into the kitchen and placed his chin on my shoulder and his arms around my waist. "I'm so sorry, love." He kissed my neck. "About everything." His nose grazed my jaw, and I could feel my skin reacting to him. I'd missed him so much.

"I'm so sorry too." I turned around to face him. "I shouldn't have made you leave the way I did. I—"

"It's okay. I fucked up." He kissed me with an underlying sense of urgency. "I promise never to hide anything from you again. I swear. I want you to keep trusting me as you have until now. I won't let you down again." His hands traveled up my back inside my sweater. He wanted to pull it over my head, but I stopped him. "What's wrong?" he whispered in my ear.

Nothing was *wrong*, but I couldn't stop thinking about what

Lily told me. William was in his apartment, and now I feared he could listen to us having sex.

"I don't know. Are you feeling okay? I'm afraid you'll collapse," I whispered back with a gentle chuckle.

"I'll collapse if I don't have you *right now*."

I thought I could lead him to the living room instead of my bedroom, but then Mimi and Caleb had keys to my apartment. Mimi had left for the day, and Caleb would never barge in unannounced, but just knowing I wasn't the only one with keys made me feel uneasy. And he would probably find it odd if I led him to the guest room.

I felt safe and comfortable in my bedroom. But William had to live right beside me, and now I felt like my sex life with Nathan was going to be ruined. Hopefully, William would leave for Ireland again soon. And I wouldn't have to worry about such matters until March.

I needed to get out of my head.

The smell of freshly brewed coffee invaded the kitchen. Nathan pulled my sweater over my head and unhooked my bra. There was no turning back now. I would collapse right there with him if I made him stop.

C

"You were awfully quiet today," Nathan said, kissing my cheek softly. "Is everything okay? That is so—unlike you." He poked my chin with his finger, offering a subdued smile.

He noticed.

"Was I?" *Shit.* I thought I could be *more reserved* in my reactions, which had required a lot of concentration. But it wasn't going to be a sustainable practice. At least not an enjoyable one.

"Perhaps there's something else I can do?" he said, his hand wandering up my thigh. "You know how I love listening to how you enjoy yourself with me."

"I swear everything's okay," I said with a gasp. Nathan's fingers were already doing their thing.

"Sure? You don't seem sure to me," he said with a lazy smile.

"I—I'm sure." I closed my eyes and bit my lower lip.

"Why were you holding back on me?" he asked as he carried on. "I don't want you to. I love it when you don't."

"I'm not," I said in between heavy breaths. I opened my eyes and locked my gaze with his.

"Yes, you did. You are doing it right now. Are you still angry at me?" His eyes were trained on my face, analyzing every little reaction, word, breath, and noise coming out from me. "Tell me what to do, and I'll do it. I'll do anything for you."

"No, I'm not—it's not—" I couldn't hold back on him anymore. It became an impossible effort to overcome.

"No, you're not angry? Or no, you're not holding back?"

"Both!"

"Is it because of him?" Nathan asked. All I could think of saying was *no*. I didn't know who he meant by *him*, and my mind couldn't process his question for me to come up with an elaborate answer. Not while he was touching me like that. My mind was elsewhere. Nowhere.

"No!" I said a few times under my breath.

"I see the way he looks at you, and I don't like it. Not one bit," he said, kissing my neck. "You're mine."

"Yes!" I gasped.

"Mine."

"Yours," I said in Nathan's ear, holding tight to his neck. I took a deep breath, and found it inevitable to censor the volume of my reactions when I found my release, feeling sparks moving up my spine, turning into crashing stars at my forehead that relaxed my body once again. Nathan's proud expression on his face let me know he was *now* satisfied with my feedback.

As we both laid in bed, waiting for me to catch my breath again, all I could hear was William playing the piano. I closed my eyes for a second, then asked Nathan in between soft pants, "Who's *him?*"

"Caleb, of course."

"Caleb?" I shook my head slowly. I was expecting a completely different answer from him. "But we're just friends. He likes you. He never likes anyone."

"It's okay." He swept a loose strand of hair away from my face. "But I see it in his eyes. You're not just a friend to him. And I don't mind, as long as he doesn't try anything with you."

I was about to say *he would never try anything with me*. But he had. However, it was before I even met Nathan. So maybe I *could* say it, meaning from this point forth.

No. I couldn't do it. I couldn't pretend nothing had happened. I wanted honesty and full disclosure from Nathan, and that meant I had to start with myself. At least with the things he wanted to know or asked about directly.

I sat on the bed, fully convinced to tell him all that had happened with Caleb.

"That is very distracting," Nathan said, looking at me up and down a few times. I smiled and covered myself up with the comforter. "I just said it was distracting, not that I wanted you to cover yourself up."

He laughed, and I pushed his head back on the pillow. But I kept myself covered because I needed his full attention.

"Okay—um. Something *did* happen with Caleb," I said, meeting his gaze. I saw how panic flooded Nathan's wide eyes. "No, wait. It was before I met you, and it didn't last long. We were doomed from the start. He never felt comfortable enough around me, and he feared my father's reaction if he found out. It was too complicated.

Too risky. We didn't want to gamble with our friendship."

"I see," he said with a frown. I was impressed by his reaction. He wasn't happy about it, I could tell. But he was mature about it, something I wasn't used to before. Thomas would've set the building on fire. "So why did William say that to him about—the mixing business with pleasure? Does William know something happened with Caleb?"

"He saw us kissing once when he was still with Erin. Tobias saw us too." I felt a weight falling off my shoulders. A weight I didn't know was there. It felt good to know I didn't have to hide that part from Nathan and that he was, in a way, taking it so well.

"Okay, I get it now. William just wanted to piss me off," Nathan said, feeling like he was gaining awareness on the matter. I shrugged. I wasn't sure if *that* was the reason why William said that to Caleb. But it could've probably been the second reason why. Nevertheless, knowing why William did what he did and said what he said was a tricky business. And I didn't plan on dwelling on it at the moment.

"Well, I'm not giving him the pleasure," he added. "Are you sure you're comfortable being friends with Caleb?"

"Yes. Yes, of course. He's been there for me—a true friend. When my mother died, I feel like it was mostly thanks to him that I came back to life. He made me happy when I was in a bad place. Everything was lifeless. Dull.

"And he hasn't expressed anything about wanting to be with me or anything of the sort ever since I met you. We understood we're better off as friends. My father disapproved, and we feared our friendship would end up damaged because of it. Caleb knows that. He wouldn't risk it, and honestly, I wouldn't either."

"I thought all of this happened behind your father's back."

"It did. My father never knew about it. Caleb and I had already decided to go back to being friends. But a simple hug was all it took for my father to go ballistic on Caleb. My father made it clear to him that if he tried something with me, he would lose his job." *And Caleb promised to stay.* "And as I said, Caleb wouldn't risk it."

Nathan sighed. Was it relief? Hopefully.

His phone buzzed on my nightstand. He read the incoming text and said, "I'm sorry, Murph. They need me at the office. Is it okay if—"

"Sure, sure." I smiled. "Don't worry about it."

Nathan took a quick shower and changed into a full suit. He looked so incredibly handsome. "You don't look like a guy who drunk dialed his girlfriend yesterday while singing along to his favorite band." I laughed as we walked to the front door.

"Bloody hell." He seemed embarrassed about it. And by the look on his face, I could tell he was trying to shove those memories to the back of his mind.

"I just hope you remember watching the concert," I said as he opened the door to leave.

He laughed. "I do, actually. I feel like my body disconnected the second they were done with the show." He held me tight in his arms. "I'll call you later. I love you."

"I love you too," I said, looking up into his eyes.

Nathan left. I walked to my room and threw myself face-first onto my bed, hugging my pillows.

A few minutes later, there was a knock on my wall. *William.* It's as if I knew he was going to do it. I didn't know if he heard us or not. I still kept wishing he didn't. But I knew I had to stop being paranoid, or I could end up going nuts about nothing.

He knocked again, heavier this time, probably trying to get a response from me. Only this time, I didn't knock back. It was time for me to let him go.

For good.

CHAPTER 34

A Multiverse Of Jealousy
Part 2

March 5, 2009

NINA AND CJ had been staying with me for over two weeks now. It was their last weekend in my apartment. The dynamic was comfortable and fun. They were both studying business at NYU and had a varied school schedule. Sometimes they would be gone in the mornings, other times in the afternoon, but we tried having dinner together almost every night.

CJ loved the kitchen. He always had a new recipe he wanted to cook for us. Some of his dishes were better than others, but overall, he did considerably well most of the time.

There were a few nights, especially on the weekends, where Nina didn't come back to sleep. She would stay over with Juan Pablo. CJ told me they were having issues with their relationship, but Nina hadn't opened up to me about them.

Oddly enough, Nina and Caleb hadn't been flirting with each other. They would say hi, maybe ask how they were doing, and that was that.

Nina and CJ knew the Sjöbergs were my neighbors. But they weren't aware William lived right next door. Since he was still away and I didn't know what day he was coming back, I thought it was best not to say anything, mostly to respect William's privacy.

We were going to eat a special chilly recipe CJ wanted to cook tonight. Juan Pablo was coming over for dinner, and his presence always made me nervous. Something about him didn't click for me, but I couldn't identify what it was. And it always made me feel a little guilty for judging him without any real reason. But isn't our gut supposed to be the best compass? I know mine shrunk whenever I saw his dark eyes directed at me.

Luckily, Nathan was going to join us too. As always, his presence gave me peace and comfort.

C

Grant was pulling my gloves off when Tobias walked into the gym. "Hey, Tob!"

"Billie!" he said with a huge smile. "Sup, Grant?" He walked up to the mirror and combed his hair with his fingers.

He was always smiling, but this was a different kind of smile— an excited smile. "What's going on?" I asked.

"I'm just excited," he quickly replied, as if he were waiting for me to ask. So I did. I asked him why. "A film I worked on a year and a half ago is finally premiering here in New York in a couple of weeks."

"Oh my God, Tob! I'm so happy for you. What kind of film is it?"

"It's an action film with a lot of guns and stunts," he said with a laugh as Grant bandaged his hands.

"And do you have the leading role?"

"Why do you think I'm so excited? It's my first film as a lead actor." He honestly couldn't stop smiling.

"Wow! I'm so proud of you. Good luck with the premiere. You'll have to tell me all about it," I said, walking toward the exit.

"Wait, you have to come. You and Nathan, of course."

"Oh, of course. I'd love to! Besides, I haven't seen a film on the big screen since I was fourteen, so I guess I'm going to be more excited than you about going," I said with a subtle laugh.

"Then you *definitely* have to come. I'll fill you in with all the deets in the next few days."

"Sounds good."

I said goodbye to Grant and Tobias and walked back to my apartment. I stepped out on the ninth floor while answering a text from Nathan. He wrote to tell me he would get out of the office early today.

Yay!

A delicious and familiar scent caught my attention. I looked up from my phone's screen and saw William standing outside his apartment door, which was wide open. And he wasn't alone. He was talking to Nina. Laughing, too. I could feel my blood heating up into a boil.

Breathe.

"Billie! Why *on Earth* didn't you tell me *William Sjöberg* was our next-door neighbor?" she said, leaning her back on the wall beside William. Too close. Wow. Okay. She was getting herself comfortable on that spot, wasn't she? But wait … *our neighbor?*

Smile.

"Well, that's because he's never around," I said, walking toward my apartment. I wasn't planning on making small talk with the two of them. *Uh-uh.*

William snorted. "I'm around," he said with his usual and infuriating smirk. "I'm actually going to be around for a while now. I'm taking a well-deserved vacation."

"Oh, I'm sure you deserve it. You must work like crazy," Nina said, placing her hand on William's arm. His white t-shirt revealed his slightly golden skin and corded muscles.

Freaking Viking … Why couldn't he wear a sweater or a bunch of layers like a normal person? It was thirty-six degrees outside!

But no. No. No. He was wearing a white t-shirt just like the one he made me wear last summer. He must've had a ton of them. That was his official uniform, and I wasn't going to complain, but it left his arms exposed for Nina to fondle them in the hallway.

"Oh, wow! You play the piano?" Nina asked, peering inside his apartment.

I rolled my eyes on the inside and remembered all of a sudden I had lungs and pulled some air into them *slowly* to avoid passing out from exasperation.

"I do. Do you want to come in for a drink?" William asked her. *WHAT!* "Perhaps I can play something for you."

Why am I still standing here?

My limbs were paralyzed.

I bit the corner of my bottom lip so hard I could feel the coppery taste of the tiny drop of blood that leaked out of my broken skin and made contact with my tongue.

She has to say no. She has a boyfriend! She keeps forgetting—

"Sure! I'd love to!" Nina accepted with an overexcited grin. "Do you know how to play Für Elise?"

He turned to look at me and replied to her, "It's your lucky day."

Nina disappeared into William's apartment and shouted from the inside, "I'll see you in a bit, Billie!"

William shut the door behind him, and I stormed away into my apartment. He hadn't even been back for more than a few hours, and he had already found a new and efficient way to torture me.

How would I forget about him when he did things like these? I'm sure he was just taunting me. *But what if he actually liked her?*

I promised myself I would be happy for him if he found someone he liked. I had to. Maybe that someone was Nina.

Please don't let it be Nina!

Happy was not a feeling I could relate to at the moment. I was enraged. Utterly infuriated.

CJ shouted from the kitchen, "Nina! Is that you?"

Nina, Nina, Nina.

"No! It's Billie! I'm going to take a shower!"

"Where is she? She was supposed to help me out with the salad!"

Sadly, *salad* was the last thing on Nina's mind right now.

"Who knows! I think you should call her!" *Pull her out of William's apartment, too, while you're at it.*

Please?

I was going to start hyperventilating any minute now.

Breeeeeathe.

I jumped in the shower and counted to ten, but that never actually works, does it? I never even got to five. I tried to think happy thoughts instead, but they all included different ways of dragging Nina out of William's apartment.

Ugh!

Why was it always her? I never told her anything about what happened with William. She wasn't trying to hurt me or anything like that. But she was the meanest flirt machine ever!

And William ... I didn't even want to think about him. But all I could see was that look on his face before he disappeared off into his apartment—with *her.*

I rinsed my hair while various thoughts invaded my mind: *What are they doing? What are they talking about? Is he making her laugh? Is he playing the piano for her? Is she touching him?*

I stepped out of the shower feeling defeated. My stomach felt weird. Hollow.

Wait.

I ran to the toilet and threw up nothing but bile.

What is wrong with me?

I sat on the floor with my towel tightly tucked around my body.

I rested my head back on the wall and closed my eyes for a few seconds.

Okay. I needed to get up. Nathan was going to be here any minute now. I brushed my teeth twice, mouthwash and all, and quickly blow-dried my hair just to make it stop dripping. I changed into jeans and a comfy navy-blue sweater.

Once I walked into my bedroom, I heard William's piano. He was playing Tiny fucking Dancer for her. What an excellent way to ruin a perfect song.

A knock on my bedroom door.

"Hey, you!"

Oh, I was so glad to see Nathan. I needed to hug him. He was going to make me feel better. He quickly placed his arms around me. "You smell delicious," he whispered in my ear. "So fresh and clean."

I closed my eyes and huffed air out of my mouth. I felt so bad. It was a mixture of anger, a tad of sadness, and a lot of guilt. Guilt because Nathan was standing right in front of me, and I'd just thrown up because William had invited Nina in. It was the worst feeling ever.

But I was honestly the happiest to see Nathan. All I wanted was for him to hold me. He always made me feel like everything was going to be okay.

"Murph, what's wrong?"

"Just stress and an upset stomach. But I'm fine. I'm better now that you're here."

"Come here," he said, pulling me into his arms again. He kissed my hair several times. "It's okay. Do you want me to stay over tonight?" I pressed my lips together and nodded. "Let's get you something to eat."

Nathan grabbed my hand and led me out into the dining room. "It's okay. I'm here now."

I grabbed his face and kissed him. He was the sweetest. I wondered why I even bothered getting upset at all because of William.

We sat in the living room, waiting for Juan Pablo to arrive and for Nina to return from William's apartment.

"Ooh, I love your sweater," CJ said, placing a small bowl with olives on the coffee table. I loved how he felt at home in my apartment. It was nice to have other people around too. It felt more … homey.

It was a bittersweet feeling, but thankfully, they were leaving in a few days. I had a great time with both of them, but I wasn't interested in having Nina and William parading themselves in front of me.

Nina waltzed back into the apartment with a big, proud grin.

"This girl over here," Nina said, pointing at me, "has been keeping a secret. Did you know William Sjöberg lives *right* beside us?"

Again with the *us*.

"What!" CJ shouted. "Billie! What the hell?"

"I'll go get us something to drink," Nathan whispered. I'm sure he wasn't too keen on listening to Nina fangirling over William.

"Well, he's never around. I didn't think you would be interested."

"Oh, we're interested," CJ said, taking a seat on the sofa.

"He's *sooooo* hot. And *pfft*, those arms … are they for real?" Nina whispered. "He's also an *amazing* piano player. Ugh. Too perfect." She threw an olive into her mouth and sat beside me.

At that point, I felt nothing. All the bad feelings had literally gone down the drain and left a void in my stomach.

Juan Pablo knocked on the door, and Nina rushed to open it. He walked in with a big smile that never ceased to creep me out. His dark eyes focused on me. *Okay, here we go.*

Nathan gave me a glass of wine, and I immediately took a sip.

"You have a dark aura around you, Billie," he groaned, brushing the space around my shoulders with his hand.

Hello to you too.

Is he fixing my aura? I'd heard Nina talk about it before. I wasn't closed off to the idea of asking him if he could do it. Perhaps he could brush William away too while he was at it—if such a thing could be accomplished, of course. I'm sure that's where all the darkness came from.

Nathan shook Juan Pablo's hand with a poker face. They already knew each other, but he had never gotten holistic on us before. Nathan thought I was exaggerating when I told him about Juan Pablo and the things he did and mostly ... said. I'm sure he didn't believe I was exaggerating now.

We sat for dinner, and I barely touched my food. My stomach was still doing the upsetting thing for me since I had to put a smile on my face when deep down, all I wanted was to curl up into a ball in my bed and have Nathan hug me all night long. The wine didn't agree with me either.

We had all just finished clearing the table when Juan Pablo's phone rang. He sat in the living room and took the call there. Nathan and I sat with him while Nina helped CJ out with dessert.

Juan Pablo spoke in Spanish while I laid my head on Nathan's lap. He stroked my hair while we both waited in comfortable silence.

I didn't want to pry into Juan Pablo's conversation, but he was sitting right next to us. I inevitably heard everything he was saying. And it was not good. I was sure he didn't know I speak Spanish, or he wouldn't have said the things he did.

Damn it.

I looked up into Nathan's eyes, widening mine just a bit, and squeezed his hand. He jerked his chin up with a frown, wondering what was wrong.

I couldn't stop listening to Juan Pablo, and all I could think of was how he didn't deserve Nina. She was such a pretty, fun, and smart girl. And from what I heard, Juan Pablo was most likely cheating on her.

I pressed my thumb and index finger together, asking Nathan to wait, and pulled my hand up to his cheek. I was so thankful to have him.

Nina and CJ came back with ice cream bowls on steroids. They had all these crazy toppings on them. I didn't even know where all of that came from.

Juan Pablo immediately ended the call, and I excused myself for a bit. I grabbed Nathan's hand and asked him to come with me.

"What's going on?" Nathan asked as I shut my bedroom door.

"I think Juan Pablo's cheating on Nina. I just heard him talking on the phone. He kept saying *mi amor,* which means my love. And he was telling whoever was on the other side of the call that he was sorry, that he was having dinner with his girlfriend, that he would try to sneak out later tonight, that he missed her too. He even said *I love you* before ending the call. Do you think that could be anything other than cheating? Maybe a family member, or … ?"

"That sounds a bit dodgy. But still, we can't be sure of who he was talking to. You can't tell Nina if you're not sure," he said. "What are you planning to do?"

"I don't know, but I feel like I can't do *nothing* about it. Maybe I can talk to him? I don't want to meddle, but I would hate it if a friend of mine knew you were cheating and didn't tell me anything, you know what I mean?"

"I would never cheat on you," he said, kissing me slowly. I loved his slow kisses.

"I know. I wouldn't either." That made my stomach churn. I wasn't cheating on Nathan, nor would I dare or want to do it, but I couldn't control my feelings, and I felt so bad for caring about seeing William flirting around with Nina. *Is that cheating?*

I really hoped it wasn't because I didn't want to care.

"Let's go back outside. I'll see if I can find a window to talk to him."

"How about we stay here, instead?" he said, kissing me again.

"I can stay here all weekend if you want me to," I replied with a laugh. "But let me see if I can talk to him. If not, we'll elope."

"I have a few friends in the courthouse who could help with that." He smiled. Every time he could, he snuck in a marriage joke. And I didn't mind them, but my neck did. It felt stiff.

"Not that kind of eloping," I replied, biting into his lower lip. "More like running away from everyone and locking ourselves up in my bedroom kind of eloping."

"I'm not against that either."

"Come on, let's go before you convince me to stay." I grabbed his hand and pulled him out of my bedroom. They had finished their ice cream when we joined them in the living room.

"We didn't know if you two lovebirds were coming back," CJ said to us. "Your ice cream is in the fridge."

I went for Nathan's bowl and gave it to him. I left mine in the fridge. I wasn't in an ice cream kind of mood at the moment.

"Juan Pablo, could I talk to you for a second?" I asked him. Everyone turned to look at me—even Nathan. I don't think he was expecting me to take the bull by the horns. But the sooner I talked to Juan Pablo, the sooner I'd get to *elope* with Nathan. I craved some alone time with him.

"Sure." He stood up, and I guided him out to the hall. "What's up, Billie?" He asked, brushing his hand around the space above my head and my shoulders again. "Do you mind?"

"Umm, no?" My eyes followed his hands.

"That,"—he pointed his finger over my shoulders from side to side—"can be easily fixed."

I looked over my shoulders again with a puzzled expression on my face, trying to find the so-called damage he was mentioning. But my efforts were to no avail. I couldn't see shit. But I did feel a crushing heaviness around me because of what happened earlier with Nina and William.

"Make sure you tell me later. Um—I need to tell you something. It's important." I was convinced his psychic abilities didn't cover that much ground because his face was genuinely shocked when I said, "I speak Spanish."

"Oh," he said, a small smile drawing on his face. "So, you heard my conversation on the phone, and now you're curious about my intentions with Nina?"

I nodded. At least he was quick-witted. "I don't want to meddle in your affairs. I'm not even sure of what any of that was, but Nina's my friend, and I care about her. I don't want her to get hurt."

Juan Pablo sighed.

"Look, I have a way more open mind for such matters than Nina does. That's where we've struggled. She's recently become aware of—a few of my kindred spirit relationships in the past." *A few? What is wrong with this guy?*

"But you know what? I really love Nina. She's not only a kindred spirit but a twin flame."

Twin-what? So was Nina his *main* kindred spirit? I didn't know what he meant by those terms, but it sure as hell sounded like a holistic excuse to mess around with other girls while dating Nina.

"Well, I don't know if that's fair to her when she doesn't necessarily agree with you. Does she know you tell other girls that you love them?"

"Not exactly. But that's because she's not evolved yet into the realm of universal and unconditional love. She doesn't understand that love can be felt and emanated in such ways. Monogamy and commitment aren't mutually exclusive."

Wow.

Nina wasn't evolved enough for Juan Pablo to let her know that he's constantly cheating on her? *What a sack of bollocks.*

"Well, I don't feel comfortable having heard your conversation over the phone. I didn't choose to do it. And you can call me unevolved, but I don't understand those concepts, and for what you're telling me, neither does Nina.

"I think it's best if you could talk to her and let her know about it because I feel obligated as a friend to inform her. And I'm sure she would appreciate it even more if it came directly from you. I know I would if I were in her position."

"Of course," he said with a nod. I could hear movement behind William's door. He walked out, all dressed up—impeccable as always and smelling like heaven.

"Hey, man! Nice to meet you. I'm Juan Pablo," he said with a grin. "You're William Sjöberg, right?"

William coaxed a smile back and shook Juan Pablo's hand. "Yes, I am. Nice to meet you, Juan Pablo."

"Juan Pablo is Nina's boyfriend," I pitched in. I thought he might find my remark to be an interesting and educational one.

"Oh, I see," he said, raising his left brow. But that dreaded frown of his appeared in between his blue eyes afterward. "I'm running late. Have a good evening. Nice to meet you, Juan Pablo."

My hands were shaking, so I crossed my arms in front of me to keep it from showing. William clicked on the elevator button and kept looking my way.

Juan Pablo gave his back to William and looked at my shoulders and that immediate space above my head again as he did when we first stepped out to talk.

"Interesting," he said, brushing his chin.

"What's interesting?" I asked, too quickly to sound relaxed.

William disappeared into the elevator and didn't brush his lower lip like he always did. I guess he was trying to *brush me away* instead, as I should've been doing too.

"I was just thinking about how interesting it is that the cause or the reason for our ailments can sometimes also be the cure. You know? Like antivenom."

Interesting analogy. But Juan Pablo was diving too deep into a conversation I was finding hard to follow.

"It's funny how you claim not to understand the concepts of love I just mentioned before when I could see how both of your auras are intertwined from crown to base," he said, lifting the right corners of his lips into a lopsided smile.

He can see what?

"I—you'll need to explain that to me. Who's intertwined?" I asked quizzically.

"I just saw William's aura." Juan Pablo jerked his head toward the elevator. "I can see your energy in his electromagnetic field. And in yours, I see his. Would you say he's a kindred spirit? Or is the connection deeper than that?" Juan Pablo asked with a subtle frown. He seemed entertained.

"Um, I don't—he's my neighbor. My—my aura should be fully charged with Nathan's energy. You're probably mixing them up."

This entire conversation was backfiring on me.

"Nathan's there too. Don't worry," he said, placing his hand on my shoulder. It made me feel extremely uncomfortable. "You're basically getting an aura reading right now. This one's on me." He winked.

There isn't going to be another one.

"I'm going to end this conversation because I can tell you're uncomfortable." Juan Pablo closed his eyes for a second. "Mhm. You're not ready for any more information at the moment. But there's just this one piece of information I'm being allowed to share with you. May I?"

I nodded because what the heck. The conversation was already weird enough as it was. I was curious about what he wanted to say.

"Don't be too hard on yourself."

"What do you mean?"

"It means you need to think about that," he said, walking up to the door. "I'll talk to Nina today right before I leave. I promise."

"Thank you."

"And don't forget, Billie," he said with a laugh. "The heart wants what it wants."

CHAPTER 35

Not Yet

March 15, 2010

Lily: Hey! Are you home? Can you come up to my apartment really quickly?
Me: Sure! I'll be right there.
Lily: See yourself in. Door's open.

Tobias's movie premiere was next Thursday. I was so happy and excited for him. It was also going to be my first time going to the movies in almost seven years. I was thrilled about doing that with Nathan. It was an unconventional date, but still, we were going to dress up and sit down to see a film in a movie theater. We were looking forward to it.

I walked into Lily's apartment, and there were three racks of dresses, two elegantly dressed guys in all-black suits, and a woman with short, curly, grayish hair and translucent acetate glasses talking to Lily. One of the guys went through the clothes while the other one sat with his leg crossed, taking notes on a small pad.

Joel sat in the living room and drank a beer as he watched a deferred transmission of a Hammarby soccer match as if all of that wasn't happening right beside him.

"Billie! You're here!" Lily shouted from afar. I walked toward them and said hi to Joel on my way there. "This is Ilaria, Marcus, and Elijah."

"Hi! Nice to meet you." I shook their hands as Marcus eyed me from head to toe.

"Can you remove your jacket, please?" Marcus said to me. "Eli ... yes." Elijah handed Marcus a measuring tape. I glanced at Lily, wondering what was happening.

"Ilaria is our stylist, and Marcus and Elijah work for Enzio de Luca. They're here to dress us for the premiere."

"Us?" I asked as Marcus took my bust, waist, and hips measurements.

"She's basically a Lily but somewhat shorter from what I can tell. And a bit more—" Marcus squeezed his butt. "But same hip-width, so it doesn't change things much. We'll raise the hem once Ilaria chooses the shoes." Elijah kept taking notes on his pad.

"Nathan is going to flip when he sees you on Thursday," Lily said, going through one of the racks. "Ah! I'm so excited!"

"Lily, I don't think it's necessary. I mean, I have a couple of dresses. I was planning to wear one of those, and—"

"Nonononono. You're arriving with us. Sitting with us. And leaving with us. People are going to take your picture, believe me."

Pictures. I swallowed hard.

I was so excited about sitting in the theater to watch a movie that I hadn't given much thought to the event's logistics. I thought Nathan and I could probably sneak in while they walked the red carpet.

"You're practically family. They're happy to dress you. Right, Marcus?"

"Elated," he said, shuffling through the rack with dark-colored outfits. I don't know if he sounded as *elated* as he said he was.

Most of the looks had moons on them—crescent moons. They were literally stuck on the clothes. Later that day, I googled the collection. And in fact, Enzio de Luca had inspired himself on the moon when designing it. Wow.

"Ilaria, what do you think?" Marcus pulled out a navy-blue strapless gown with thin, black horizontal lines throughout the shiny fabric. The dress looked simple and elegant. Beautiful. This was one of the dresses that had no moon on it. I guess the moon reference was the shiny fabric itself. "Number twenty-six of the Spring twenty-ten collection," Marcus shouted. Elijah kept taking notes.

"It can look *spettacolare* with the red hair," Ilaria said. "Billie, come." She moved her fingers back and forth. I was afraid to go near her. She had such a strong personality.

"We also have the beige—" Marcus said, pulling another dress.

"No beige," Ilaria cut him off. "I want beige for Lily. What else?"

Elijah took the navy dress to the guest room and hung it on an empty rack for me to try on while Marcus kept looking for another option.

"Wait!" Marcus said before Ilaria shut the door to the guest room. "Look fourteen. You know how Enzio loved these pantsuit looks. He might want these to be photographed on the red carpet."

It was a blush-pink pantsuit with straight, angular shoulder pads. The pants were slightly flared on the bottom. The jacket had a big, shiny, silver moon on the front instead of a button. The silhouette was feminine and sophisticated. I *loved* it.

"I remember this look. It's the one Frida wore on the runway. I love it!" Lily said with excitement. "What do you think, Ilaria?"

"Let's see it on her," Ilaria replied. Elijah rushed to the guest room and hung the outfit on the rack next to the dark blue dress.

"Who's Frida?" I asked as Lily pulled me to the guest room.

"Gustavsson. She's a friend of ours—a model. Swedish, too."

Lily closed the door to the guest room, and Ilaria asked me to undress. I put on the pants. They fitted me well, but they were way too long. I almost tripped on them.

"No bra," Ilaria ordered.

I gave my back to them and took it off. Ilaria helped me with the jacket, and I quickly closed it before turning around. I was a little embarrassed to have them see my breasts.

"She's not a model, *vero?*" Ilaria asked Lily.

"No, she's not," she replied.

"I can tell. Too shy." Ilaria used the sparkling silver moon to clip the jacket close. The deep V neckline had a shiny fabric trim of the same blush-pink color. "You might be wearing this. I like it," Ilaria said. "Marcus!" She opened the door and walked away, looking for him.

I hadn't even seen myself in the mirror.

"You look stunning," Lily said. "Want to take a look?"

I tiptoed to the big mirror in the foyer. I didn't want to trip on my pants.

Oh. My. God. The outfit was amazing.

Someone whistled behind me, and when I looked around, I saw William darting my way. He was coming back from the kitchen holding a beer. He approached me and kissed my cheeks. I was a second away from pushing him away.

I hadn't seen much of William after I saw him flirting with Nina. And he had been remarkably annoying that day. So let's say I wasn't too excited to see him.

"Is that for the premiere?" he asked, scanning me. "I like it." He glimpsed at the crescent moon on my jacket and raised his brows. I turned to look at Lily, and she was staring back. Her eyes slightly widened.

William brushed the moon with his index finger and whispered, "Now I like it even better. Besides, it's the same color you wore last year for Midsummer. It reminds me of our first kiss."

"We didn't kiss. I pushed you away. But you keep forgetting."

Not that I would have if I weren't dating Thomas at the time.

At least Marcus, Elijah, and Ilaria were busy picking something for Lily and not listening to our conversation.

"Our lips met, didn't they?" William winked at me and turned around. *They did.* And now I had to shove away the memories of the other times that happened "Ilaria. She's wearing this, right? I like it. Make sure she wears her hair down." William took a seat next to Joel to watch the game and sipped on his beer.

Excuse me? If I wore this, it would be because *I* liked it. Not because he did or commanded me to wear it.

"She might. But I want to see the strapless dress on her, too," Ilaria said to him.

Okay. I guess Ilaria had the final word on what I was going to wear.

"She already wore that black strapless dress you guys sent me in December," William replied, watching the soccer match and throwing a snack into his mouth. He screamed something in Swedish at the screen. "It's best to change it up."

"Oh, *you* wore the black and white velvet dress?" Marcus asked with a grin. "How did it fit you, girl? William wouldn't let me come for a fitting."

Now he seemed elated.

"Like a glove," I said with a frown, walking back to stand beside Lily. That reminded me of what William said about why he could guess my measurements.

"Ah! You are a couple?" Ilaria asked with her sharp Italian accent. Marcus and Elijah turned my way at the same time.

I parted my mouth to answer, but before I could say "no," William had responded, "Not yet," and laughed.

"No," I finally answered right after him.

"Billy," Lily said as a warning, giving him *a look.*

Joel then said something to William in Swedish, but he kept laughing and said, "I don't give a fuck." I wondered what it was he didn't give a fuck about—probably his behavior.

"Hmm. She will wear that," Ilaria said, pointing at me. "Marcus the hem—pull it up before she falls on face." Ilaria chose a pair of heels, and Elijah helped me put them on. "Carolina and Frankie will come for hair and makeup Thursday morning. I'll meet you both here to dress you afterward."

"I have to go to school in the morning. But I can do my hair and makeup," I suggested.

Ilaria laughed. "You'll skip class, yes?"

Ilaria was the kind of woman to whom you couldn't say no. "I'll see what I can do," I said instead, feeling stupid about my reply. I knew I was most probably skipping class.

Marcus presented a dress option for Lily. It was long and of a beautiful light champagne color. The neckline was straight with an asymmetrical one-shoulder design. The top part of the dress shined from the beautiful champagne-colored sequins.

Her look had no moon, only the shiny sequins to represent it. It was stunning. "Frida wore this too. Look thirty-four, Eli," Marcus dictated.

Ilaria, Lily, and I walked inside the guest room, and I changed out of my suit as Lily tried the dress on.

"*Ecco!*" Ilaria said when she zipped up Lily's dress.

"You look beautiful, Lily," I said with a smile.

"This needs adjustment," Ilaria said, pulling on the fabric along the waist. Poor Lily huffed after Ilaria almost broke her ribs. I couldn't help but laugh.

"Lily, I need to go. But thank you—for all of this. Thank you, Ilaria." I hugged Lily and walked out of the room.

"Thursday, ten a.m., yes?" Ilaria reminded me with a tone that sounded more like a warning.

"Of course." I smiled. Yeah, I was skipping school.

I thanked Marcus and Elijah on my way out and said goodbye

to William and Joel. I was about to close the door, but William pulled the doorknob from the inside and followed me out.

"Why don't you ditch Nathan and let me tick two firsts off my list?"

"Two?" I asked.

"Your first premiere, of many more to come. And your first time at the movies in a while." He smiled.

"You're delusional. Nina might be available. She's single now," I said, summoning the elevator. I was playing with fire. What if he did find that interesting?

"Is she?" he asked, scratching his cheek with an annoyed face. "You want me to *call* Nina and invite her to the premiere—as my date?"

"I mean, if you want to, of course. Why not?"

William followed me inside the elevator and replied right after taking a sip of his beer, "She's not my type." He kept trying to meet my gaze, but I stared at the doors.

"Didn't seem like she wasn't your type the other day. Don't you like pretty girls?" I stepped out of the elevator and walked toward my apartment with haste.

"Oh, I know what I like," he said to my back. "And I know you were furious about what happened with Nina the other day. You can't deny it. I saw it in your eyes. You still are."

"Psh. Of course not," I said, unlocking my apartment. I didn't want to turn to look at him.

"Well, now you know how I feel every single day when you disappear off to your apartment with Nathan behind you."

My hand was shaking on the doorknob. I knew he had invited Nina in to taunt me. And it worked. But I was never going to admit it. I didn't even want to admit it to myself!

What was I to say to that?

I looked over my shoulder and finally met his gaze, my hand

still holding the doorknob. My breathing got heavier. We both stood there for a few seconds, looking straight into each other's eyes in silence.

"Well," William said, taking a step back and snapping out of the trance we were under. "I'll see you on Thursday." He forced a one-second smile at me, turned around, and took the stairs to head back to Joel's, for sure.

It was probably best if I didn't go to the premiere.

CHAPTER 36

Cut It

March 18, 2010

I TRIED CANCELING my attendance to the premiere, but Tobias showed up at my apartment to complain about it when Lily told him. I wanted to enjoy my movie date with Nathan, but I didn't want William to make things weird for me. Tobias insisted, so I finally agreed to go. As long as I was with Nathan, I knew everything would be okay.

I skipped school because Ilaria was a scary, scary person. I asked Nolan to hand in an assignment on my behalf and let me know if there was anything important I needed to know. I didn't want to miss class. Spring break was next week, anyway, but I was helpless.

It was also Caleb's birthday today, so I texted him right away.

Me: Happy Birthday! They're making me go to this hair and makeup appointment for the premiere. I know you have the morning off, but I was hoping to give you a birthday hug and your present before heading out to the event, okay?
Caleb: Thank you, Red. Of course! Let me know once you're done.

I poured myself a cup of coffee in an insulated mug and went up to Lily's. There were a couple of director-style chairs with a folding table in front of them filled with all kinds of makeup and hair products. I slightly grimaced at the sight of that. I just wanted to look natural, and I'd never had anyone do my makeup before.

Lily dragged herself out of her room, looking exhausted. She had just taken a bath. Her hair was dripping. "Hey Billie," she said with a raspy voice. "This is Carolina and Frankie. They are the absolute best in what they do. I cannot live without them." They both smiled and shook my hand.

Lily and I sat on our chairs. "Caro, could you do Billie's makeup first? I'm a mess." She yawned. "I need something for this." She pointed a limp finger at her eyes.

"Hmm. You went out last night, right?" Carolina asked with a disapproving look. "Lemme put these eye patches on you while Frankie does your hair, m'kay girl?"

"I know I'm sorry, mama. It was a friend's birthday party, and one thing led to another," Lily explained as Carolina placed the golden-colored patches under her eyes. "Ugh. And Joel's still sleeping. I hate that he'll get ready in five minutes and will probably look better than me."

"Not under my watch, baby girl. I'll make sure of it," Carolina replied. "But you should learn from your friend. She's looking fresh."

"Yeah, well, I'm probably not as fun as Lily, that's why," I said with a chuckle, which was true. The night before, I went to bed early because Nathan got caught up at work, and we didn't see each other.

"That's *not* true," Lily replied quickly after. "You should see her after she's had a few glasses of wine." She laughed, and I shook my head with a smile.

"Who said wine?" Frankie joked, drying the excess humidity from Lily's hair with a towel. She wore thin, black acetate glasses and had her beautiful blonde-silverish hair up in an effortless chignon. Her lips were painted in a bright shade of red. She looked so cool.

And come on, it was ten a.m., and she was suggesting wine? I liked her already.

"I won't be able to see anything with alcohol for a few days," Lily said to her.

"No, no, no. You're doing it wrong. You need to *connect* it," Frankie replied to Lily. "If you keep yourself *a little* drunk, then you don't let the hangover hit you, see?" Carolina burst out laughing as she applied moisturizer to my skin. Lily laughed too. They obviously knew Frankie well, and I bet she was a total entertainer, always making them laugh, for sure.

I immediately tensed up, wondering what Carolina would do with my face, but I didn't have the guts to ask. And something told me I wouldn't have a say in what I wanted. And I didn't want much, actually. The less, the better.

She applied primer on my eyelids and asked me to keep my eyes shut for a while. *Damn it!* I took one last sip of my coffee and hoped for the best.

After a few minutes, I was allowed to open my eyes. I could see Carolina dabbing her brushes away, but I couldn't see what colors she was using.

"You need to relax, m'kay, mama? You're tensing up," Carolina said with a warm smile. She had long, sleek, black hair and her skin was a shade of light brown. She was so maternal in her way of talking and moving. She made you feel safe and taken care of in an instant. I liked her immediately.

"See? She's tense, Lily. For God's sake, just get the wine out already," Frankie said with a serious face. That's what made her funny, that she wasn't trying too hard to crack a joke.

We all laughed.

Lily's hair was looking great. Frankie gave her a sleek, pulled-back pony and used a few hair extensions to make it appear longer. I knew we couldn't have the same hairdo, but I would've loved that look on myself. It looked so pretty and elegant.

Carolina handed me a mirror when she was done with my makeup. I was in shock.

"Oh, my God. It's as if I weren't wearing any makeup. I love it!"

"Thank you!" She laughed. "That's the biggest compliment ever. I'm glad you liked it. This is what Ilaria asked for, and I think you look gorgeous, mama." Carolina made me close my eyes for a few seconds and splashed some makeup-setting spray on my face. "This will make your makeup last for a week."

"You look beautiful," Lily said, stepping down from her chair.

"Your hair looks amazing. I love sleek updos a lot," I said, switching chairs so Frankie could do my hair, hoping she would take a hint.

"Well, too bad because you're wearing your hair down," Frankie said with a laugh. "Ilaria's orders." *More like William's orders.* Evidently, Ilaria liked pleasing William, which wasn't surprising. "I was thinking of straight hair, parted in the middle, and we could pull the front part behind your ears to make it look sleek, and that way your hair won't cover your jacket, which Ilaria wants to avoid."

"What if you cut it?" I asked Frankie. She widened her eyes with a smile. If that wasn't an excited face …

"Are you sure? I could call Ilaria and see what she thinks. But I'm always eager for a makeover."

"Billie, but your hair," Lily said, touching it.

I wanted to send a message to William by doing this. He didn't call the shots here. I did. I would wear my hair down, but cutting it would undoubtedly make a statement.

"Maybe something around—here," I said, touching my shoulder. "And I agree with you. Straight and sleek. I'm sure Ilaria would approve. I would still be wearing my hair down as requested."

"Fuck it. Let's do it," Frankie said, placing her cutting tools out on the table.

"I can't believe you're doing this," Lily said, touching my hair for the last time.

My hair was *so* long, a few inches below my breasts. And that's the way I'd had it all my life. Long, straight, boring. It was time for a change.

I took a deep breath and rubbed my hands together. "Okay, do your thing before I change my mind."

"I'm going to braid you up first. Would you like to donate it?" Frankie asked. "You would make someone extremely happy with this beautiful hair."

"Of course! I'd love to."

Frankie braided my hair, and without warning, she chopped it off. Lily screamed, and I laughed at her reaction. "Frankie's not cutting your hair. You're aware of that, right?" I told Lily, still laughing.

"I'm shook. Billie, you're a new woman. You know what Coco Chanel said about a woman who cuts her hair, right?"

"What did she say?"

"That she's about to change her life."

"Oh." I didn't know if I was in a *change my life* kind of mood, but it sure was liberating.

Frankie kept cutting my hair, giving it shape and making it look great. "You've made my day. You have no idea," she said, giving it the final touches. "Ready for the big reveal?"

I nodded.

Frankie placed the mirror in front of me, and I couldn't believe it. It looked great. I looked so different. Good different. "I love it, Frankie. Thank you so much." In the end, she parted my hair to the side. It looked silky and smooth.

It was noon when we were finally done. I was getting hungry, so I went back to my apartment to eat something while Ilaria arrived. She wanted us to be ready at 3:00 p.m. so we could leave at 4:00 p.m. So there was still plenty of time before we left.

Me: I'm headed down to my apartment. Meet you there?
Caleb: I'll be right up.

I kept thinking about Nathan and what his reaction would be to my short hair. I knew he loved my long hair. I just hoped he liked it.

Caleb knocked, and I rushed to the door.

"Happy birthday!" I gave him a big, warm hug.

"Your hair! You cut it," he said, observing it.

"I—did. What do you think?"

"It's—wow. I mean, you look so different. I like it. It's going to take some time to get used to this new look for sure. But you look beautiful," he said, his mouth slightly curving into a small smile.

"Thank you. This is for you." I gave him a small box with a red bow. "Go ahead, open it."

Caleb took a Statue of Liberty keychain out of the small box and read the note inside: "*We'll always have Paris, but New York isn't half bad either.*" He grinned. "Thank you."

It was a simple gift but full of meaning. I loved the Eiffel Tower keychain he gave me last year, and I thought I'd reciprocate the gesture.

"I really appreciate this. I—thank you," he said again. "I'll keep it forever."

I planned to keep my Eiffel Tower keychain forever too.

I smiled at him and said, "I wanted to give you your present, but I guess I'll see you later?" I hugged him again and went back inside to have something to eat. Mimi had the table ready for me.

I was almost done eating when Nathan texted me.

Nathan: I'm about to call you from an unknown number.
Please pick it up.
Me: Of course.

"Hey, you! What's up?"

"Hey, Murph. Can you hear me all right?" A deep *zoom* noise in the background clouded his voice a bit, but I could hear him.

"Yes, I do. Where are you?"

"I'm in a meeting in Mr. Chapman's airplane. We just took off. We're on our way to London," he said with a genuinely disappointed tone. "I'm so sorry, love. I obviously won't be able to make it to Tobias's premiere. I know how excited you were about going. I was too."

"Oh, no! Couldn't you have the meeting before he left? I really wanted you to come with me."

"I know. I'm so terribly sorry, love. But Mr. Chapman had to go back to London, and we needed to talk about a situation going on with a client, so that's why he brought us with him. Aiden and I will fly back on the next available flight once we get there."

"Okay, I'll um—talk to Tobias and tell him I won't go. I don't want to go without you."

"Nonsense. You're going. Besides, don't you already have your outfit? You're probably getting ready, right?"

"Well, yeah. Lily and I had our hair and makeup done already."

"I'm sure you look lovely," he whispered.

"I had a surprise for you. But now you'll have to wait until you get back," I said, trying to tease him about leaving.

"What surprise? You can't do this to me. Come on."

"I don't know if you're going to be happy about it, but … I cut my hair."

"You did? How much? Like a couple of inches or?"

"Right above my shoulders. I even donated it."

"What! Oh, God, I can't wait to see you. You know how much I love your hair, but I'm sure you'll look just as beautiful. Perhaps you can send me a picky?"

"Of course!"

"I need to go, Murph. Please text me once you get back and tell me all about the premiere, all right?"

"Of course. I love you. I'll talk to you later."

"Love you too."

I took a selfie and sent it to Nathan. I was so nervous to see what his reaction would be. I looked so different.

Nathan: You look smashing, love! I can't wait to kiss my new short-haired girlfriend.
Me: I'm glad you liked it. I love you.
Nathan: I love you too.

☾

Ilaria cried out when she saw my hair. I held my breath when she stepped forward to touch it. "Ah! *Fantastico!*"

Phew. She loved it.

"Let's get you two dressed. Where's Joel? I want him in his suit now. I still need to decide about that tie."

"He's taking a shower," Lily replied to her. "He woke up a few minutes ago. I hate him." Lily yawned. She was exhausted, but it didn't seem like it. She looked great.

Ilaria used double stick tape for my jacket because I insisted on how the neckline was too deep, and I was afraid of having a wardrobe malfunction. I don't have large breasts, but I still didn't want one popping out of my jacket.

I was getting nervous. Not having Nathan coming with me made me feel uneasy. "Do you want anything to drink? You look jumpy," Lily said.

"I don't know. Are you having something?" I asked, dabbing my lips with the lipstick I borrowed from Carolina.

"I seriously can't drink, but I can get you a glass of wine."

Ilaria was helping Joel with his jacket. I was about to sit down, and Ilaria screamed, "No! No, sitting! You will get the clothes wrinkled."

I didn't know exactly how we were supposed to ride to the event, if not sitting down.

Lily brought the wine, and Ilaria almost fainted. "You two want to give me a heart attack. No wine. No sitting." I guess she was right. I was wearing light colors. What if I spilled a drop? I didn't want to imagine the wrath.

Joel was finally ready, and the four of us walked downstairs. A doorman I'd never seen before opened the door for us with a cheery smile. Senad was inside the small cubicle beside the entrance talking on the phone. We said goodbye to Ilaria, and she left in a car that was waiting for her.

There were two more black cars parked in front of our SUV. The two drivers were talking to Aaron, Caleb, and David.

Caleb turned to look at me and raised his brows. "How's the birthday boy doing?" I asked with a smile. Lily and Joel congratulated him afterward.

"Do you think I could ride with you?" I asked Lily. "I'm so nervous about arriving there alone. I don't even know what to do once I get there or where to go."

"Of course. We'll ride in the first car. Billy and Tobias will go in the second one." William and Tobias hadn't come down yet. "Shoot, I forgot my phone. I'll be right back. You can wait for us in the car." Lily rushed back inside the building.

"Hey guys," I said, walking up to Aaron, Caleb, and David. "Is it okay if I ride with Lily and Joel? Nathan's not coming. He's flying to London right now. And I don't want to arrive at the event all by myself."

"Of course, Miss Murphy," Aaron replied. "No problem. We'll follow you."

I walked up to Lily and Joel's car, and Caleb opened the door for me. "You look great, by the way," he said with a wink. "We'll see you there."

"Thank you." I smiled, and he left the door open for Lily and Joel to come in once Lily returned. A driver sat behind the wheel.

"Good afternoon, miss. My name is Cooper. I'll be driving you today." I recognized him. I'd seen him a few times before.

I was about to reply when William sat next to me, shut the door, and said, "Cooper, go. *Now.*"

CHAPTER 37

The Premiere

"WILLIAM! What the hell are you doing?" I shouted. Cooper sped off as instructed, and I quickly buckled my seat belt. I looked over my shoulder and saw Aaron, Caleb, and David jumping into the SUV.

William seemed to have stepped into a comedy show because he wouldn't stop laughing.

"This isn't funny," I said to him, frustration spewing out of every syllable. "Cooper, *slow* down. Let them catch up with us."

Cooper was young and reckless. He grinned, seemingly excited about the car chase. I just hoped he was equally focused on the road ahead of him.

William's laugh faded out. He scanned my face, my lips, my hair, my clothes and unbuckled my seat belt. "You'll get your clothes wrinkled. We're only a few blocks away." He was right. I was more scared of Ilaria than I was of crashing without a seat belt on.

His gaze was still fixed on me. "I'm flattered," he said, tucking my hair behind my ear, grazing my cheek as he pulled his hand back.

"Why?" I asked, my eyes wide and impatient for a reply.

"It's endearing," he began to say, "that you'd do something like that just to piss me off." He waved a haphazard hand toward my hair, then looked at his knees with a smile. "You know I loved your long hair." He clicked his tongue. "But how can I be bothered by it when the reason you did it is so obvious."

"I donated my hair. That's why I did it."

He laughed and brought his hand to my hair, touching it again. "I wouldn't mess with my hair if I were you," I said, slightly flinching away. I didn't need William touching me right now. Or ever. "Ilaria might materialize herself and scold you for it."

"It's cute. I like your hair either way." He rested his hands on his knees.

Stop staring at me! I was nervous enough as it was.

"Whoa." I tried grabbing the handlebar when Cooper made a sharp right turn, but I missed it. I slid over to William's side. My hand ended up on his thigh, and his hands conveniently on my waist. "Sorry." I frowned and bolted to my seat after gaining back my balance. "And don't you dare laugh." William was amused and then some.

"Relax"—he brushed the flaps of his jacket—"it's not a big deal. You act like we haven't touched each other before."

Cooper cleared his throat and straightened in his seat. I shook my head, mostly to myself for being so stupid and getting caught up in this type of situation again, where I exist merely for William's entertainment.

I looked over my shoulder and saw our SUV trapped behind a car that got stuck at a red light.

"Cooper, *please* slow down." His erratic style of driving was getting on my nerves. But he only answered to William, and he didn't care about my security detail getting trapped in traffic, of course.

"I know how you wished they didn't have to follow you around. Besides, we're almost there." William took a small aluminum box of cinnamon Altoids out of his inner coat pocket. "And—there they are," he said, looking out through the back window.

I turned around again, and the SUV had now caught up with us. David was behind the wheel, and the SUV's license plate was almost touching our car. They were that close.

Cooper couldn't wipe the grin off his face. He seemed to be utterly enjoying the car chase. "Altoid?" William offered with an air of nonchalance. "It always helps soothe the nerves."

So that's the secret to his delicious cinnamon breath?

"Thanks," I said, putting my hand out. *If it helps soothe the nerves.*

"Anyway ... I'm so glad you decided to ditch Nathan," he said, throwing a couple of mints on his tongue.

I took a deep breath and laughed. There was no use in explaining myself to him. He knew I didn't ditch Nathan, of course. It's not like Tobias didn't inform him about what happened.

"You're in much better hands now," he said, placing the Altoids back in his pocket.

"Well, that depends," I replied. "Do you think you can help me bypass the red carpet and go straight to the theater? I'm sure you know your way through these things."

"I do know all the shortcuts," he said, looking out the window.

"I'm not kidding. I'm nervous." The sweet and spicy taste of cinnamon invaded my tongue. It *was* kind of soothing. But it also reminded me of other things I didn't want to remember.

"You'll be fine as long as you're with me."

Shit. I honestly wished Nathan was with me instead.

The car stopped, and hundreds of people were on the other side of the street standing behind metal security railings. Caleb and Aaron jumped from the SUV and stood outside the door on William's side of the car. I was shaking.

"I don't think I can get out of the car. This is insane. I'm going back to the apartment. You go," I said, trying to buckle my seat belt.

William grabbed the seat belt and pushed it out of my way.

"We're hindering the flow of vehicles. We need to step out of the car. Come on. It's going to be okay," he said with a nod, his tone almost melodic.

I saw Caleb bending over just outside the door. He was surely trying to see if I was okay.

Okay, I can do this.

Aaron and Caleb were going to be with me the entire time. And I planned to ask Lily if I could sit next to her in the theater. Everything was going to be okay.

William stepped out of the car, and the screams were deafening. "Ready?" He offered his hand to me, and I took it.

"Are you okay, Miss Murphy?" Caleb asked, scowling at William next, who didn't even notice because he was busy waving hello to the fans that stood on the other side of the street with his fake-ass smile. Ugh. I liked his real smile better, as annoying as it could be.

"Ah, yes. Just nervous," I replied to Caleb. "William's going to help me go straight to the theater."

Caleb frowned, looking suspicious of William. Or maybe I was projecting myself on him.

William stood behind me and placed his hand on the small of my back. "Come on. Let's go inside that tent."

I was relieved to see Lily, Joel, and Tobias stepping out of their car.

We were only a few steps away from the tent, but the blinding lights from the photographers' cameras didn't stop for one second as we made our way there.

"I told you, you're safe with me," William said with a comforting smile.

Aaron and Caleb followed us to the tent. William said hi to some of the people around us. Some were elegantly dressed, while others wore all-black clothing and earpieces just like Aaron and Caleb.

"Billie!" Lily was walking our way. "I'm so sorry," she said, lowering her voice, looking at William. "I'll take it from here." She grabbed my hand, and William didn't look pleased. But I finally felt like I could breathe again—sort of.

"William said he was taking me through a shortcut that goes straight to the theater." As soon as I was done speaking, I knew there was no shortcut because Lily's face told me so.

"I mean, there is a way, but it's through the left side of the entrance. There are a lot of people who come to premieres and don't walk the red carpet. But we can't access it now. The photographers are blocking the way.

"Besides, Ilaria will flip if you aren't photographed in your outfit. I told her you would be arriving with us. I'm afraid we'll have to walk the carpet. But I'll do it with you, okay? And if you feel like it's too much, just keep walking until you get to the next tent. The carpet's not very long in this theater."

Joel and William were talking in Swedish behind us. I couldn't understand shit. Tobias was busy greeting people—or being greeted, that is. He looked great.

"Right this way," said one of the women in black to us as she held the tent's curtain open. Lily was still gripping my hand.

Aaron walked out of the tent and straight to the next one without looking back. Caleb stood close behind me.

Lily was right. The carpet wasn't very long. I could do this.

The woman in black clicked on her earpiece and said *okay* a bunch of times and then, "Off you go." Lily pulled me out, and William and Joel followed behind. Caleb stood just outside the tent, watching us walk the carpet.

A million flashing lights shot our way. It was blinding, uncomfortable, and surreal. Lily whispered in my ear, "You look great," and shot a comforting smile my way. I really missed Nathan.

The photographers kept yelling over and over, and all at once:

"*Lily! You look great!*"

"*William, over here, please!*"

"*Joel! Joel! Joel!*"

Joel and William were photographed together and separately too. Joel walked over to us, and the photographers took a few shots of the three of us. I then took a few steps away to allow Lily and Joel to be photographed together without me. I was ready to walk away, but someone yelled, "Billie!"

It was Tobias, sporting a grin from ear to ear. He looked so incredibly handsome. It was his big night; one could easily tell. The photographers went nuts when he stepped out, shouting his name, throwing crazy compliments at him.

And now they knew my name.

CHAPTER 38

Red Carpet

"I'M SO GLAD you showed up," Tobias said in my ear. He hugged me. "You look great."

"You don't look too bad yourself." He wore a bold, burnt orange, vintage-style suit that he obviously pulled off wonderfully. That face goes with anything.

"*Tobias, over here!*"

"*Billie! A shot together!*"

We turned to face the photographers. "Are you okay?" He asked, looking at the camera with a smile, his hand softly gripping my waist.

"Ah—yeah." I tried smiling too, but I was sure it came off stiff and awkward. It was weird hearing random people shouting my name. I was no one. A complete stranger. "But I think it's best if I meet you guys inside, okay?"

"*Is she your girlfriend?*"

"*Tobias! Please! Over here!*"

"*Who are you wearing?*"

Oh, God.

"Family friend!" Tobias shouted back to the photographers and reporters with a smile. However, they didn't seem satisfied with his reply because they kept yelling follow-up questions.

"You're sitting beside me. Nathan's orders, okay?" Tobias whispered. I nodded, making my best attempt to smile naturally, and took a few steps away from him. I could see Aaron standing just outside the next tent—the finish line. I needed to get myself there *now*.

Someone grabbed my hand and tugged me back, making me turn around. William placed his hand around my waist and pulled me toward him. He dropped a kiss on my cheek, and easily three hundred flashes captured the moment. *This is* not *going to photograph well ... shhhhit.*

And I wasn't going to make a scene in front of the press, so I smiled and said in barely a whisper, "William, you need to let go of me."

He pulled me closer to him. "I can't allow them to believe you're here with Tobias. That will only complicate things later. I know what I'm doing."

"Later? No one thinks I'm here with Tobias. Now let me go," I said, echoing William's big, synthetic smile. "Right now." I was two seconds away from pushing him. But he softly released my hand and waist. I took a deep breath and stared into his analytic eyes, letting him know how infuriated I was about his behavior.

How was I to explain the photographs to Nathan? I was already mortified about it.

"I'll see you inside," he replied. *I hate that freaking fake smile.* William approached a woman with a microphone and chirped, "Hey, Marissa! Nice to see you again."

Fans kept yelling William's name from across the street. He waved at them intermittently as he answered the reporter's questions. "No, no, no! We arrived together, but we're just friends," I heard him say with a studied laugh. That was the last thing I heard before I disappeared off to meet Aaron at the end of the red carpet. Caleb magically appeared beside me.

I'm going to be locked up in my apartment for life.

I didn't even know how my father agreed to let me come in the first place. This seemed much more elaborate than just going to the movies. I never understood his judgment. And those photographs with William were a complete disaster.

My father was probably making up for all the *lying to protect me* he'd done in the past. I wasn't talking to him much, not after how he handled the Thomas situation. But he knew how much I cared about Tobias, so I guess that's why he allowed me to come to the premiere.

Aaron and Caleb escorted me inside the theater, where I waited for everyone else to arrive. My phone buzzed non-stop as a bunch of incoming text messages flooded my screen all at once.

What. Is. Happening?

CJ, Nolan, and other friends from school were texting me images from the red carpet. They knew I was attending the event— *the power of the internet.* Heather even sent me a video of her TV, showing William's interview with the reporter, where I'm seen walking away in the background.

Some of the photographs they sent me reminded me of the ones I saw of William and Erin. We were looking at each other while William smiled down at me. It looked like such a romantic photograph, when in fact I was complaining about the situation. It gets you thinking about how most of the things we see on the internet can be fake.

I kept shaking my head at my phone's screen, unwilling to accept that those photographs were all over the web.

"What's wrong?" Caleb asked, standing in front of me, looking at how my hands gripped my phone. I handed the phone to him and showed him the photographs.

"Nathan's going to be pissed," I said, brushing my forehead, feeling like I could break into a cold sweat in any second.

"Yeah, I saw that. But I guess you would've hated it even more if I removed you from the carpet," he said and laughed a weak laugh. "I'm sure everything's going to be okay, Red." He handed back the phone with a slightly furrowed brow, looking away.

"Yeah, because you seem so convinced about it."

Caleb smiled a weird kind of smile bordering on sad. "You still like him, don't you?"

"What do you mean?" I asked with a pitchy tone. "I'm actually demanding him to let go of me in those shots." I pointed at my phone's screen with wide eyes. He turned to look at me but said nothing. "So, what? You're saying I-I—what? Enjoy William's little games?"

"No. I didn't say that," he replied softly. "I'm just saying it's strange that you both look happy in the pictures. It seems—real. But that doesn't mean shit, does it?"

"No. It doesn't." I lowered my voice and said, "William's an actor. He knows exactly how to pose—how to make things look a certain way. I saw how he did *just that* with Erin."

"My point is … I don't think he needs to act. And I can see how you light up when you look at him. And it"—he looked up, smiled, and bit his lower lip—"it's frustrating. I don't know why, but it hurts to watch. It always has."

"What? Caleb? What do you—"

"I shouldn't have said anything. Your friends are coming." He turned around and joined Aaron, who stood a few feet behind me.

Caleb's remarks threw me off guard. I didn't even know what to make of everything he said. I thought we were in a good place. He seemed okay with Nathan, my actual boyfriend, but why did he trip like that over William?

I didn't have the energy to get into that, so I shoved it right there next to the pile of other shit I didn't have time to deal with at the moment.

Lily, Joel, and Tobias walked into the theater as more people made their way inside too. I tucked my phone back in my clutch and felt an arm sliding around my shoulders.

"Altoid?"

I looked up, and William shook the small aluminum box twice. "No, thanks."

He leaned in and whispered in my ear, "First red carpet. First premiere. And once we watch the movie side by side, I'll tick that other first off my list too."

When he said that, something ignited inside me. I realized I was a hobby, a sport he liked to play—a mission to accomplish. I didn't understand the reason behind his obsession with my firsts anymore, and I was sure he didn't either.

Maybe it was how he said it, or perhaps it was the bottled-up anger I tried to keep from erupting regarding how he manipulated me into having those photographs taken by the press. But I was most definitely *fed up* with it.

And now, how was I going to face Nathan?

"This is all a game to you, isn't it?" I said, removing his hand off my shoulder, not caring about doing it gently. "I've *had it* with that 'firsts' list of yours. And it's not like you're getting much done. At least not anything of great significance."

He seemed like he was trying hard not to break into laughter but composed himself somehow and said, "You're this—*breathtaking* mixture of sexy and cute when you're angry. And the most adorable part of it all is that you're not even aware of it."

I shook my head, looking at the floor. He wasn't even listening to what I had to say. He couldn't take me seriously. Words never moved him.

But actions speak louder than words and all that crap. So I turned around, trying to walk away from him, but he blocked my way, of course. His towering presence had it easy for the five-feet seven inches of me.

"Get *out* of my face."

"You need to keep the dirty talk in check, Guille. If you expect me to leave, that is."

"Hey, Billie. Is everything okay?" Tobias asked, placing his hand on my shoulder. Four people I didn't know stared our way. Tobias was probably talking to them, and they were waiting for him to return. He was busy. It was his night to shine, not his night to be dealing with my drama.

"We're fine," William said, sniffing once and looking away. "We're just talking."

"I think it's best if I leave Tob. I'm sorry."

"What? You can't. I promised Nathan I'd make you feel comfortable tonight. I want you to stay. Come." He pulled me toward the three guys and the woman he was speaking to before and introduced me as a member of his family. He was the sweetest.

I didn't want to leave. I wanted to be there for him. I knew how important this night was for Tobias. But I couldn't stand to see William's face anymore.

A small group of people William seemed to know immediately approached him, and that was that. Joel and Lily were laughing with Eric and two other guys. They were having fun as I'm sure I'd be too if Nathan would've come with me. Nathalie, their mother, stood there with them, and although she was smiling, I could see that she seemed sad. It broke my heart.

People kept approaching Tobias and congratulating him for the film. He even introduced me to a few of his cast members.

We all made our way inside the screening room, and I sat next to him as promised. Another girl, around Tobias's age, sat to my left. Behind us sat Lily, Joel, William, Eric, and Nathalie. She smiled sweetly at me when we made eye contact.

"Is your father coming?" I asked Tobias. I hadn't seen him since we arrived.

"No, he's in L.A., working," he said, looking at the screen. I could tell he was disappointed. And it wasn't challenging for me to relate to that feeling. I knew firsthand what it felt like not having your father show up for you.

I knew my father had many responsibilities as an ambassador, but he did miss more than a few important events of mine growing up. I just hoped Nathan wasn't going down that same road—always putting work first.

The director took the microphone and said a few words before the film started. Joel and William kept tapping Tobias's shoulders with big smiles on their faces.

His father didn't show up, but we were all here for him.

Thank God I stayed.

CHAPTER 39

BFF

TOBIAS'S FILM was *amazing*, and he was great in it. There was a lot of action as promised. He looked so happy when it ended. Tobias hadn't seen any of it until today. It was so surreal to see him on the big screen. That reminded me of the many films William had been in and how I hadn't watched a single one. I'd lie if I said I wasn't curious.

There was an after-party right after the film was over, and I wasn't allowed to skip it, of course. I mostly hung out with Lily, Joel, and Eric. But I snuck out an hour after we arrived. It seemed to me like they would be there for a while, and I just wanted to go home and see if I could speak to Nathan. It all had been too much for me.

At least, I'd gotten my message across with William because he hadn't tried talking to me after we left the theater. I didn't see much of him at the after-party either.

We got home, and Caleb offered to walk me back to my apartment. "Are you okay?" I asked as soon as we were alone. I was worried about how our last conversation ended.

"Yeah, I shouldn't have said anything." He smiled as he summoned the elevator, but I didn't buy it. I couldn't stop thinking about what he said earlier, what he implied.

"I just want us to be okay," I said softly. He met my gaze with a sincere smile.

"We'll *always* be okay. No matter what." He grasped my shoulders and led me inside the elevator. I wanted to feel relieved when he said that, but I still didn't.

I learned that part of my overall well-being depended on *us* being okay.

"Then why do I still feel this—weird vibe between us?" I asked as he clicked the ninth-floor button.

He took a deep breath in and let it out with a defeated sigh. "You look at him the way you looked at me when we lived in Paris"—there was a long pause—"times ten," he added. "That's all."

That's all? He just threw *that* in my face and went all Miranda Priestly on me. What was I supposed to reply?

"Caleb, what are you talking about?" He kept looking at the doors, but I finally caught his attention and locked my gaze with his. "Why do you keep bringing William up? And why does he bother you that much and not Nathan? I'm with *Nathan*."

"Yes, you're with Nathan. And I know you love him, but the way you—look at William ..."

The doors opened up on the ninth floor, and we stepped out of the elevator but stood there, right beside it.

Caleb continued to say, "And when I met you—" He laughed a sad, nostalgic laugh. "Shit ... you *liked* me right away, didn't you?" My eyes widened with a thick brew of emotional terror and absolute shock. Realizing I was nothing but water and glass. So obviously transparent to him. I parted my mouth to say something, but he lifted a lazy hand and said, "Don't answer that."

"Caleb—"

"It's all good, I swear. I'm just trying to make a point."

"Which is?"

"You have feelings for William. Strong ones." He crossed his arms loosely at his chest and stared down at me—a hushed challenge. "And I don't think it's unilateral."

I shook my head because why was he doing this to me? Saying those things and coming from him … a civil war erupted inside my head, demanding answers and resolutions.

"I-I—don't."

"This is why I always had an issue with William and why I figured out quickly after we decided to give *us* a shot that it was never going to work out. But you didn't want to see it. You still don't. Your mind was elsewhere, and again, it was written all over your face. It *still* is.

"I saw the pain in your eyes when William's ex stepped on the rooftop that day. When you realized he was back with her, and you saw William holding her hand—refusing to acknowledge you. And I—I kissed you with everything I had, wishing I could've taken that pain away from you, but I knew I couldn't. You pulled away from me because of him.

"And I'm sure of this because I know your face better than I do my own. I've been studying it for years. The slight shifts in between your eyebrows, that imperceptible twitch in your mouth, how you widen your eyes for a second, how you inhale, exhale, and how depending on the speed and breadth of it means one thing and then another … I see it all. I could make a language with your face.

"And I didn't want to accept it then either. I didn't want to be the one to tell you, but I see how torn you are right now. It's as if I can almost feel it for you. And I'm learning to live with it because I can't"—he laughed again, almost silently—"*won't* stay away from you. So I'd just rather make you see it in the hopes of helping you gain some clarity."

I never agreed more or understood Caleb as much as when he said he *wouldn't* stay away from me because I couldn't stay away from him either. And he knew it. I simply wanted him in my life. Always. No matter what. There would forever be an unwavering and bespoke space in my heart created just for him.

"Besides, I made a promise, didn't I? I can't leave until you kick me to the curb." He laughed. Softly. As if trying to guard himself behind the humor. "But that doesn't mean it doesn't *hurt* to see the truth sometimes. Just as I know you wouldn't be jumping up and down with excitement if the roles were reversed somehow."

He was right. I would struggle to see him with someone, the mere thought of it was prickly and thorn-ridden, and I would accept it, of course. And I would be filled with genuine happiness to see *him* happy. But I realized how he had withstood so much when I'm sure I wouldn't have been able to handle a dab of what he had since we arrived in New York.

Caleb represented the most complex relationship I had in my life, saturated and intertwined with multiple thin, delicate lines throughout. There wasn't a guidebook for it, and we had navigated—blindfolded—on the expanse of it through the years. And now, it's as if something finally clicked. Made sense.

"I'm sorry, Red. I'm always trying my best, and I'm good, I swear. You're my best friend, and that's enough for me because that means I can have you forever."

My heart!

That was a lot.

He'd unloaded a truck full of truth and honesty right on top of me. I was trying to remember how to move my body to get out of the rubble, but the words came out automatically, "Of course. You *are* my best friend, Caleb." The realization of it hit me hard in the face. We already knew it. But hearing it out loud woke me up. It filled me with joy.

"Come here."

I walked the short distance between us and hugged him. He lifted me until my feet were no longer touching the ground. "Happy birthday," I whispered. "I want you to be happy ... always."

"I'm the happiest."

It was one of those days where hugging Caleb was allowed and not frowned upon, not even if my father saw me. He wasn't going to forbid me from congratulating him even if he disapproved of the way I'd chosen to do it.

"We're good?" I asked for verbal validation, just to make sure.

"Better than ever." He lowered me back on my feet, and I sighed with relief. He laughed at my reaction.

"You should go out and celebrate or something. I'm staying in for the rest of the night." I didn't want him to spend his birthday working. There was still time for him to go out and have some fun—clear his mind.

"I don't know. I might be getting old, but—I'm tired. I wouldn't mind staying in and getting some rest either," he replied, brushing his forehead. "Today was stressful, if I'm being honest. Your father insisted on how everything had to be perfect tonight. No surprises."

"I know. It was stressful for me too. But here I am. Perfectly safe and in one piece," I said, opening my arms and looking down at myself. "Thanks to you guys."

A door shut gently in the distance. I turned to see William, still in his full suit, sauntering toward my door. He leaned against it and shot a two-finger wave at me, placed his hands inside his pockets, and crossed one foot in front of the other. I imagined he wanted to talk.

Caleb suppressed a smile and lifted a brow. "Let me know if you need anything," he said, looking at William one last time. "We'll be—"

"Downstairs," I finished the sentence with a laugh. He laughed back and turned around to leave. "Caleb!" He looked over his shoulder, holding the emergency exit door handle. "And just for the record … you're wrong."

He knew what I meant by that. And I wanted so badly for him to be wrong about my heart being so painfully torn in half.

Caleb smiled one of his cocky smiles and said, "Red, I'm always right."

CHAPTER 40

To Hear, To See, To Smell, To Taste, To Feel

THIS NIGHT WAS like a four-dimensional video game, one where I kept jumping over hurdles, avoiding obstacles, wanting to quit a few times, looking for a lifeline. It'd just been one thing after the other.

I'd come out emotionally worn but triumphant after finishing *Caleb's level* just now, but William was waiting outside my door for the final boss fight. And from experience, I knew it was probably going to be set to expert mode.

"Hey," William said, standing up straight. "I beat you here."

I hadn't seen him leave the afterparty. "Well, that's because Cooper thinks he's Fittipaldi," I replied, walking up to him. He was blocking my door but stepped aside when I reached him.

"Can I talk to you?" William asked as I unlocked the door and opened it just a tad.

I held the doorknob for a few seconds before replying, "Sure," and turned around to face him.

"You're not a game I like to play. I do care," he said, looking down into my eyes. "I'm sorry about today. I know the red carpet was probably too much for you. But I'm used to that sort of thing, and I shouldn't have forced you into it like I did. It kinda seemed like a good idea at the moment—to have you there standing next to me."

How was I to remember I was furious when he kept saying distracting things to me?

Fo-cus.

"And the fact that Nathan's going to be hurt by those photographs? I've seen them. My friends are going crazy over them. Wondering. Speculating. I don't even want to know what my father will say either."

"Well, forgive me if I don't give a fuck about Nathan. Because I don't."

I shook my head, unable to believe what I was hearing.

"Why do you even bother? Since the day we met, you've been getting in the way of my relationships. And then I broke up with Thomas, which I thought you wanted, and you—pushed me away and ran back to *Erin* because you couldn't listen to me?

"You like pursuing me when I'm not available for you. So now you're trying to, I don't know, sabotage my relationship with Nathan, only so you can run away after I'm single and it's no longer exciting for you? What the hell do you want from me, William?"

"Nathan's the one getting in the way of *our* relationship," he snapped back with a tense jaw. "*We* happened first. And I've told you more than a few times already. I thought you wanted to get back together with Thomas."

I parted my mouth to speak, but he lifted his hand and closed his eyes for a second, his way of asking me to give him a chance to talk. So I shut my mouth and let him carry on.

"We had this—perfect night at the cottage, and then you got into that cake mishap, and I was so fucking worried all day at work that I couldn't even say my lines, but I got my shit together to get off the set, to rush back to you.

"And then I step into your bedroom, and Thomas is all over you and shit," he said, almost infuriated, but he took a deep breath and leveled his tone. "I was *hurt*. My stupid ego was hurt, and I was embarrassed and all that emotional crap because I didn't want us to be a one-night thing. I allowed myself, for *once*, to believe"—he ran a hand through his soft golden hair, down the back of his neck with frustration—"that you might be … it.

"And I tried moving on because I'd never felt so helpless. But I failed. I keep failing because I *know* you want this as much as I do. And I can't stop thinking about how fucking perfect all my nights would be with you in them."

He stopped himself for a second, allowing the information he'd thrown in my face to sink in. But he kept going even when I wasn't sure if I was ready for him to do so. It didn't seem to me like I had any other option but to keep listening.

"The overpowering feeling of having you in my house, in my bedroom, in my bed. And to be able to actually talk to someone—to *you*. To kiss *you* … that was perfect," he said, his voice getting softer. "But, don't you want more?" He took a step closer to me, trying to make a point. "Don't you *need* more? Because I know I do, and I feel like we deserve to give *us* a chance."

A *solid* point.

The heat radiating off his body and the raw honesty exuding from his words were almost palpable. And then he took another step too close—too damn *close*.

"I told you I would back off whenever you told me to do so, and you still haven't been able to tell me to do it—with honesty," he said. "I can see the way you look at me. And you're not exactly telling me to fuck off." He chuckled. "Even if sometimes you might feel like telling me something in that line. Like today. I know I deserved it."

I was trapped in the tide, trying to come out for air only to have a wave of thoughts, one after the other crashing above me and forcing me back down. But I somehow found letters to make words to put into a sentence.

"I-I love Nathan—we're happy." I looked up at his face with a frown.

He actually laughed and said, "You'd make a terrible actress." He mocked me as my vision went red. "All this time you've been together, not *once* have you ever thought about me? Or missed me when I've been gone? Because I sure do miss *the hell* out of you when I'm away. And I refuse to accept that it's a one-sided feeling. It can't be," he insisted, his impossibly blue eyes now brewing up a concoction of pain and irritation—anger even.

Was he expecting me to answer those questions? It was best to assume they were rhetoric.

"You've never opened that box with my hoodie just to smell it? I'm sure you still have it."

I had—more than a few times. I was *addicted* to his cologne.

"William, please, don't do this."

"I already know the answer to those questions because they're the same as mine. That's why I'm not going to insist you to answer them. I'm that sure," he said, cupping my cheek for a couple of heartbeats. He then dropped his warm, almost flaming hand from my face and took half a step back.

"And I know I've been obsessed with your firsts even since I met you. I desperately wanted to be your first *everything*. You were a breath of fresh air. You saw *me*. And it was almost—intoxicating.

"And I saw *you* too because you allowed me to. You opened up to me a couple of times about your mother. And I was so goddamn happy you'd chosen *me* to talk about it. You made me feel special—truly seen.

"I held you in my arms that night, and I really didn't want to let go. You trusted me … even then." William grabbed my hand and pulled me closer to him, his breath colliding against my face.

"I don't care about your firsts anymore," he said, almost happy—a realization. "All I care about *now* is to be the last. And I'll wait as long as you need until I get to be not only the one to claim your heart entirely but to be the last one to do it."

William let out a charged breath through his mouth.

"I know I'm at least halfway there. And that's the reason why I don't give two fucks about *Nathan*," he so colorfully added. "The moment I start to care about him, I'll lose you. So I'd rather be the bad guy."

William's hypnotic eyes stared back at me, and I knew I had to look away for my own good. But I couldn't. I never could. Not once our gazes had locked in the way they were right now.

"I know you'll do this on your own again. Sooner than you think," he muttered, brushing my lower lip with his thumb—my breath colliding against it. "*I see you.*"

I closed my eyes for an instant, remembering how I wrote that to him when I desperately tried to explain the kiss he saw with Thomas. When I wanted him to know how much I cared about him. But he shut me out by telling me what an *awful* person he was and how that would throw me off if I only knew.

I see you.

I saw him. Even then, I saw the real him and how great he was. He wanted to hide from me, but he couldn't. And still, he pushed me away, set me aside, and it hurt like hell and back. But I could tell how sorry he was about what happened. And it only made things more difficult.

William's breathing got deeper, and it made me open my eyes.

There had always been intense electricity between us. And I'd been trying to hide it all this time—to deny it. But I sucked at it when we were alone. I couldn't hide from him either.

Caleb's words came flashing back to me, and I kept hoping he was wrong—he *had* to be.

But he wasn't.

And at that moment, I knew that someone would get badly hurt for all of this. And I knew I wouldn't get out of it unscathed.

I held on to his wrist while he brushed my lip and pulled his hand down. Not because I wanted him to stop doing it, but because it was the right thing to do.

"I want ... to kiss you," he whispered, his face coming dangerously closer to mine. "I miss your lips. How they feel, how they taste. I've *never* felt the way I did when I kissed you last summer. I'm about to go *insane*."

I couldn't stop imagining Nathan kissing or having this conversation with someone else. *I'd* go insane. The thought of that happening made my stomach feel hot and hollow. But so did thinking about William doing so with someone else!

"I'm sorry." I tried to look away again, unsuccessfully. He frowned, and I wanted to know everything he was thinking because I cared about his mind and his heart and his thoughts, although I could tell he was mostly frustrated.

What was I to do?

I wanted to uncrease his brow with my fingers, to pull the corners of his mouth upward, to see him happy! Because he deserved to be. And it killed me to admit that I was so torn.

A huge part of me wanted to be responsible for that happiness— but how? And what about Nathan? *I love him*!

It was in moments like these when William ripped his heart out and threw it at my feet that made me feel most protective about it. It wasn't the first time he'd done it ... but never like this. And I wished I could pick up his heart and give it back to him, but that wasn't enough for him. He wanted me to keep it and rip mine out too and offer it back—to have us carry each other's hearts.

I sighed.

We could never coincide. And I'm *not* a cheater. I would've never done that to Nathan, but it was hard trying not to want to kiss him. The pull between us and the need to have him take that last step closer to me became overwhelming.

But my mind was still there—online and aware. And although it was physically impossible for me to cave in, the thought alone made me feel like shit.

William looked away and swore under his breath. He took in a sharp breath and said, "Stop lying to yourself." He waited a few seconds for a reply that never found its way out through the maze of my throat.

He turned around brusquely and stormed toward his door when he realized I was completely out of words. At least of those he wanted to hear.

William grabbed the door handle and stared at his door, moving a hand behind his neck, careful not to turn to look at me anymore.

He was done. I could feel it.

"And just in case you were wondering," he said, his gaze still fixed on his door, "yes, I can hear you." He cleared his throat and opened the door. "I can hear you moaning for him every other day. As soft and distant as the sound may be. And the shower is never cold enough to calm me the fuck down—to not want to fight the wall.

"So, I either leave when I can or play the piano, just to stop—listening. And I only get true peace when I travel—when I'm away." He looked up at the ceiling and laughed. "Paradoxical and ironic as fuck."

Shhhhit ... I knew it. I knew he could hear us.

William glared at my shocked face one last time and said, "At least today I'll get some decent sleep in my own bed for a change." He dashed inside his apartment and sealed the door behind him with the loudest blow.

My legs were now two wobbly sticks, unable to carry my weight.

And my heart was a puddle on the floor. I reached within to hold on to whatever strength and dignity left inside me and forced myself to walk back to my apartment.

If I could listen to his piano, his guitar, his doors shutting close … it was only obvious. But I didn't want to believe it.

How was I to face him ever again? And Nathan … Oh, God, Nathan. I needed to see him, to talk to him. He always could make things feel right. He knew how to make me feel at ease. So I planned to call him as soon as I walked inside my apartment, even though he was probably sleeping.

My shoes flew away as I pulled them off my feet. I grabbed my phone, threw my purse on the foyer table, and walked into my bedroom.

I screamed at the top of my lungs when I saw *him* sitting on my couch, wishing I could unplug the console and throw the controller out the window.

Game over. The ultimate boss fight was about to begin.

CHAPTER 41

Then Why Are You Still Breathing?

"HEY, BABE," Thomas said, looking over his shoulder. "I was getting turned on by all that heavy breathing out there."

"Oh, my God, Thomas. You scared me to death."

"Phone, please." He held out his hand and swiveled his fingers, looking at my phone in my hand.

I handed it in and said, "What are you doing here? How did—"

Two knocks on my wall cut me off.

Did William hear me scream? I hoped so because Thomas's purplish circles under his eyes made them look so cold and hollow. And they were freaking the hell out of me.

"Aren't you guys cute?" Thomas said, looking at the wall, sarcasm gushing out of every word. "Knock back."

"What?"

"You screamed. He heard you. Knock back, so he knows you're okay." He offered me the creepiest smile ever and leaned in to rest his elbows on his knees.

I took a few careful steps toward the wall and knocked twice. The panic button was only a few feet away from where I stood, but Thomas was an arm's reach away.

"You're not supposed to be here," I reminded him, taking a step sideways toward my nightstand. There was a document-sized envelope sitting beside him on the couch. It was the first time I felt frightened by his presence. Thomas looked tired—unhappy. "You can go to jail for this." He was in direct violation of the order of protection. But he already knew that.

"They've all been feeding you lies. All I've ever wanted was to talk to you. I know I'm risking everything being here, but I can't have you thinking I'm a monster. If you knew the truth, I know you would forgive me for everything. I *know* you'd understand."

Thomas placed my phone and a set of keys on top of the envelope. I recognized the keychain—a Scottish flag.

They were Mimi's.

Thomas wore one of those long-sleeved, button-down fishing shirts with jeans. It was black and oversized. I'd never seen him wearing that kind of shirt before.

As I evaluated my situation and the alternatives I had to either get out of here or ask for help, William started playing the song I loved on the piano. The one he usually played. That meant he couldn't hear anything happening in my bedroom anymore.

I quickly realized there was nothing much I could do but make a run for the panic button. It was now or never. So I dashed toward my nightstand, but Thomas gripped my arm tightly and tossed me on my bed like a rag doll. He pinned me down, clutching my wrists beside my head.

"Where's Mimi? What did you do to her?" I demanded, wriggling under his weight, but he had me pinned down good.

"I didn't want things to end this way. All I want is to talk to you. But I can't let you press that button," he said with a calm voice, which was even more disturbing. "Remember, I was here when they installed them. All four of them." He sighed. "Let me explain. I know you'll feel differently afterward."

"*Where* is she," I insisted, trying to move my arms with no success. I wouldn't be able to handle it if anything happened to Mimi because of me.

"She'll be asleep till Sunday, probably. That depends on the dose Nicholas decided to use on her."

I kept twisting under Thomas's grasp without much success in getting him off me as I said through my teeth, "I swear if anything happens to her—"

Thomas released one of my hands and slapped my face. Hard. I could feel my skin burning where he struck me. "That's for cheating on me," he said, holding my hand back down after I tried shoving him away. "I heard your conversation with William just now. All of it. I *knew* you two had something going on behind my back."

"I *never* cheated on you. I swear." Involuntary tears streamed down my face. "I *loved* you! You were the one who pushed me away. You lied to me and kept things from me. You hurt me! Many times. Just like you're doing right now."

He sighed. "I'm willing to forgive you for it. But I need you to stay calm, okay?" He stared into my eyes, nodding, but tightened his grip on me. "Can I trust you, babe?"

I pressed my lips tightly and whimpered. My wrists were about to pop. I could feel my bones grinding against each other. It was best to stop trying to fight him off.

"I'm sorry," he whispered, his eyes still trained on my face as if analyzing my every gesture. "I don't want to hurt you. I just need to talk to you. That's all I've ever been trying to do.

"I didn't have proof. That's why I couldn't tell you when we were together. But I do now. It's all inside that envelope. We can make him pay for what he did—together. I just need you to calm down and promise me you won't do anything stupid, okay? Let me explain."

"Okay—yes. *Yes*. Let's talk, but you need to let go of me. You're hurting me," I said softly and trying to smile, hoping to sound convincing. But his grip remained the same. Firm. Crushing. "You need to let me go. M-my wrists." I didn't know who *him* was. But my first guess went to his father. He was the reason for all of Thomas's traumas.

He stared at me, probably trying to decipher my level of honesty. "Thomas, please," I begged in between pants, as the slow and painful grating of my wrist bones threatened to become cracks in seconds.

Thomas softened his grip on me, careful not to let go of me completely. He seemed undecided, as if he were fighting against an impulse to doubt me.

I slowly bent my knees behind him. *I can do this.* Nathan had taught me three basic Krav Maga self-defense techniques. We used to practice this one a lot when we were in bed, which was very often.

But Nathan *never* held me as tight as Thomas was doing right now. Even as Thomas softened his hold, it was still painful.

He *had* to soften his grip on me some more for me to try the maneuver. I only had one shot at it. One shot, and if I missed, I wouldn't be able to gain back his trust.

"Thomas, hey. Let's talk, okay?" I actually smiled. "You're going to have to let go of me at some point. Please, babe, come on."

Thomas's eyes were filled with pain. And hope. He believed me, I could see it in his eyes, and I felt like I could throw up any second now. I was disgusted by him but mostly terrified of those eyes and how they changed so much from the last time I saw him.

"Babe, I miss you," he said, finally releasing me.

Ow! I swallowed back the pain and nodded with a smile.

He cupped my face and brought his face closer to mine. "I'm sorry. I didn't mean to hurt you. You need to understand. I—please forgive me."

Thomas kissed my cheek, and I closed my eyes, making sure I didn't shut them too hard to seem disturbed. He kissed my forehead, my nose, and finally … my lips. They smelled and tasted like alcohol. He didn't seem drunk, but he had something to drink *for sure*.

"God, I missed you." He kept going, placing kisses all over my face. I opened my eyes, but I couldn't take it anymore. I couldn't put up with this any longer. *Him* on top of me—kissing me. He held my wrists again. Shit. He wasn't hurting me, but I guess he wanted to have control over me, just in case. "I can't live without you, babe," he said with despair, almost a prayer.

I took a deep breath and said, "Then why are you still breathing?" I extended my left hand to the side and thrusted my hips upward to flip him. He was now on his back, and I landed on my knees. I immediately punched him in the groin with my free hand, just like Nathan taught me.

He cursed, cupping his crotch with one hand, but he crushed my right wrist when I tried to slip away from him.

I heard a *crack*, and I screamed. I screamed *so* loud that I hoped Aaron and Caleb could hear all the way to the second floor.

William's piano stopped playing abruptly.

He heard me! Yes! Yes, yes, yes!

"Williaaaam!" I yelled to the top of my lungs and poked Thomas's eyes with my hand positioned as a claw—another simple move Nathan taught me. That way, your fingers won't snap in half from the impact. And it worked, too, because he released me, and I feared my right hand was going to fall off my arm.

I ran toward the foyer, clicked on the panic button located underneath the table, and ran to the door. I unlocked the two deadbolts, but Thomas grabbed me from behind before I could snap the simple spring lock open on the door handle.

William started banging my door a heartbeat later. "Guille!" he roared with a grave voice. "Guille, open up!"

"Tell him to go away," Thomas whispered in my ear, dragging me farther away from the door.

"William!" I screamed again in between sobs as he frantically pulled on the doorknob.

Thomas immobilized me by tightly running his arm across my chest. He pulled a gun out of somewhere with his free hand and pointed it toward the door.

No. No, this isn't happening.

"Tell him to go away, or I'll start shooting."

I tried speaking, but the words were choking me. Thomas was a coward. He wouldn't actually shoot. He was a scared little boy holding out a gun to make a point.

William knocked the doorknob out after a few loud blows. I don't know how he did it, but he broke it and pushed the door wide open. Thomas was pointing his gun at him. William's eyes widened with terror at the scene before him. He looked at me and back at Thomas.

"Stay the fuck put," Thomas warned. William's nostrils flared as he scowled at Thomas. "If I can't have her, neither can you."

Thomas pulled the trigger without a second thought but missed. William launched at us, but Thomas took another shot, and he didn't miss this time. He got him. William held the left side of his stomach and looked back at his bloody hand with wide eyes before falling to his knees.

"William!" I shrieked, battling to release myself from Thomas's firm grasp. William placed his right hand on the floor and let his head hang. It was driving me crazy to see him helpless, wounded—because of me.

Thomas put the gun to my head next. And when I looked up, Aaron and Caleb were now pointing their weapons at him taking slow, steady steps in our direction.

My sobs were now flooding the apartment, and I felt like I couldn't breathe. William was now lying on the floor on his left side. A pool of blood flowing underneath him. His eyelids fluttered.

"Thomas, please!" I begged. "He needs help! He'll die if—"

"Take a step back! *Both of you*!" Thomas shouted. I could feel the gun shaking against my skin. I'm sure he was nervous, and that was even worse.

"Lower your gun, Mr. Hill, and nobody will get hurt," Aaron warned with a firm, grave voice. "More agents are on their way. This will end badly for you if you do not comply."

"Comply?" Thomas shouted and pressed his gun harder against my temple, making me whimper. "I was kicked out of crew, suspended twice from Princeton, and you poisoned her against me! She can't even look at me! I've lost *everything*!"

"I'm sorry," I said a few times in between pants. Aaron and Caleb's faces were cold, sharp, focused. They both took another careful step forward, flanking us.

I shut my eyes, and the last thing I saw was William on the ground with his eyes fully closed. *Is he still breathing?* I couldn't stop thinking about Nathan and how I wished I could've said goodbye. I didn't say goodbye.

A wrong kind of look, or a sound out of place, and Thomas could've easily pulled the trigger on me—out of pure nerves.

I had to get my shit together, but as much as I tried pulling air in, I really couldn't.

"Breathe for me," Caleb said to me.

"Don't—talk to her," Thomas said through his teeth.

"William's going to be okay. Everything's going to be okay, Red. I got you," Caleb continued, ignoring Thomas altogether. We locked eyes, and he nodded slowly.

"Let's agree to disagree," Thomas muttered. I felt his gun leaving my head, and three shots were fired.

CHAPTER 42

Panic

I FELL ON MY KNEES, and the only one standing up was Aaron. He was already making a call and checking on William when I came out of my daze. Thomas was lying on the floor beside me—a bullet hole in his forehead and another in his chest. I recoiled away from him and saw Caleb on his knees, holding his left shoulder with his right hand, staring into nothing.

"Caleb!" I got up and knelt in front of him, cupping his cheek with my good hand.

"Hey, it's okay," he said faintly. "I'll be okay. It's just my shoulder." His mouth twitched into a smile, but his ragged breathing was more than evident, and I didn't like it one bit.

And all I wanted to do was scream, scream, scream, but I couldn't. I didn't even know where to focus my attention. Caleb was shot. William was shot *and* passed out on the floor, Thomas was dead, and then my legs were missing, my arms dissolved, and my heart was one big splat on the floor. *Wake up!*

"He's alive, but his pulse is weak," Aaron said, checking William's vitals. "The ambulance is on its way." Aaron tried to reassure me. But all I wanted was to wake up from this nightmare. "They're both going to be okay, Miss Murphy."

David and five DSS agents arrived on the scene. Aaron

instructed them to carry William and Caleb down to the lobby. I was frozen on the floor, looking at all the blood on me and around me. I couldn't stand up—because again—paralyzed, and the pain in my right wrist had become unbearable.

Aaron instructed two of the agents to stay and wait for the police to arrive as he lifted me from the floor to carry me down to the lobby.

By the time we moved out of the building, paramedics were already carting William away on a wheeled stretcher into the ambulance. "Let me ride with him!" I cried out with desperation, trying to free myself from Aaron. But the paramedics closed the doors, and the ambulance vanished into the night.

William!

I begged Aaron to put me down, and my knees threatened to buckle on me when he did. "Where's the other ambulance? Caleb needs an ambulance too," I urged. Caleb was sitting on the sidewalk, leaning against the building, hissing as David applied pressure to his wound, trying to stop the bleeding.

I heard the sound of a siren approaching. *Thank God!*

Caleb was rushed inside the ambulance, and Aaron helped me step inside with him. I wasn't going to ask for anyone's permission this time. Aaron, David and the other three agents followed us on the SUV.

I immediately grabbed Caleb's cold hand and squeezed it as one of the paramedics placed an oxygen mask on his face. The other one kept to his wound.

The paramedics talked amongst themselves as the ambulance flew to the hospital. But I couldn't hear them. My entire attention was focused on Caleb. On how his lips were turning white, and his breathing was getting shallow.

I couldn't deal with this, knowing William was wounded too. Wondering if he was still breathing—still alive. It was all because of me. It was my fault they were hurt.

"Red," he said in a breath. "I—" His eyes blinked erratically.

"Caleb, stay with me," I said sternly. "What's happening?" I looked at the paramedics for answers.

"He's losing blood. The bullet must've somehow punctured the apex of the—"

No. I stopped listening. I was in denial. Not that I would understand much of whatever medical terms they were throwing at me. "Caleb." I squeezed his hand. "Caleb, listen to me. You're going to be okay."

"I-I'm—sorry, Red."

"No, there's nothing to be sorry about. I need you to stay with me, okay? You promised, remember?"

Caleb closed his eyes as the hospital staff opened the ambulance doors from the outside and took Caleb away into the emergency room. I lost my balance and almost tripped when getting off the ambulance. I tried running behind them, but Aaron was already waiting for me. He placed his arms around my waist and stopped me.

"You won't be allowed inside," he said, embracing me. "They'll take care of them. They're in good hands now. We need to get your wrist fixed, too."

"He closed his eyes, Aaron!" I tried slowing my breath, but I couldn't.

Breathebreathebreathe.

"He's going to be okay," Aaron reassured me, his deep blue eyes staring into mine.

In the middle of all the chaos, I'd forgotten about Mimi. "Thomas said that Nicholas drugged Mimi to get the keys—they took her keys. You have to—"

"We'll send someone over immediately," Aaron said, tightening his embrace around me. He nodded at the agent beside him, who immediately took his phone out and made a call. David was arguing with the hospital staff in the distance about God knows what. Probably about wanting to park right outside the emergency room.

Please, not again, not again. The scene was familiar. Shots had been fired. People were wounded. Aaron was hugging me—telling me that everything was going to be okay when it wasn't.

Please!

My chest collapsed, and I don't know if I was crying or merely suffering. I pulled away from Aaron. "I need to know if they're going to be okay."

Ow! The pain in my wrist was clouding my thoughts to the point that it bent me over. I placed my left hand over my knee and pulled my right hand closer to my chest. "I can't. Aaron, I can't brea—"

Aaron carried me again and rushed inside the hospital. He explained to one of the doctors that my right wrist was probably broken as I gasped for air. He kept talking to the doctor and answering his questions, but I stopped listening as my consciousness faded far, far away until I inevitably passed out in Aaron's arms.

CHAPTER 43

Waiting

March 19, 2010

THERE WAS AN IV connected to my left hand when I lifted it seconds after opening my eyes. A serum bag dripped a clear solution into my veins. I was wearing a hospital gown, and my right hand had been placed into a cast.

My father stood up reactively from the chair beside me. He had a few buttons of his shirt undone, and his jacket was neatly placed on the chair's backrest. His auburn hair was slightly disheveled. I could hear Aaron and David whispering outside the curtain. I was still in the emergency room.

"Kiddo!" He leaned in and hugged me tightly. His eyes were glazed and red-rimmed. I tried sitting up straight, but my head was like a bowling ball resting on the tip of a toothpick.

"Oh, thank God, you're okay," he said with an air of relief. "You're okay." He stroked my hair a few times while muttering, "I can't lose you too."

"William? Is he okay?" I asked with a panic-filled voice. "What about Caleb?"

"They're both in surgery. The doctors won't tell us anything yet."

"Has anyone reached out to his family?"

"They're all here, and his father's flying back from L.A. as we speak."

This can't be happening.

"And Mimi? Is she okay?"

"Mimi was found lying on the floor in her apartment, but they quickly brought her here too. The doctors are closely monitoring her vitals, but she's okay. She'll be okay," he said as if trying to convince himself of that. "Nicholas gave her a strong sedative, and it knocked her out."

"And Nicholas? Does anyone know where he is?" I hoped they found him quickly. He was insane. From the moment I met him, I knew he wasn't right in the head. He constantly poisoned Thomas's mind and egged him on when that wasn't the type of *help* Thomas needed.

"They'll find him," he said matter-of-factly. "The school and his parents have been notified about what happened, too, just in case he shows up at school or his parents' house in D.C. You never know."

My father asked a nurse to bring me some water.

The outfit I wore to the premiere was folded on a stainless steel table beside us. I didn't know if I got to keep it or if I had to give it back. Hopefully not because it was sprayed with blood here and there. The sight of it made me shudder and reminded me of Thomas lying lifeless on the floor beside me. I could feel my breathing getting heavy and uneven again.

"Are you okay, kiddo?" My father asked, analyzing me. The nurse came back with my glass of water, and I took a few sips. I wasn't. Not even close. But I nodded. It was an easier response. How was I to put my thoughts into words when I couldn't even grasp them? It was too much to process.

"Has anyone talked to Nathan?" I asked instead.

"I woke him up. He was supposed to fly back on a ten-thirty a.m. flight, but I talked to Oliver Chapman, and they're flying Nathan, and his co-worker Aiden back right now on his plane since a couple of people from the London office needed to fly to New

York, too. They were notified about leaving earlier. Their flight must've left half an hour ago."

"At what time will Nathan arrive then?" I asked. I needed him so badly. He must've been worried sick, and my phone was back at the apartment.

"Ten, Ten-thirty in the morning. I'll send someone to pick him up and bring him over immediately," he said reassuringly. "But you need to rest."

Rest.

The only way I would be able to rest is if they gave *me* a sedative. I couldn't stop thinking about William and Caleb. Hoping they'd make it okay out of surgery. They had to.

"Does your hand hurt?" my father asked. "Your wrist is broken. You'll have to wear the cast for eight weeks."

"It hurts less right now. I'm sure there's something in that to help with the pain," I said, jerking my chin at the serum bag. "What time is it, by the way?"

"It's ah"—he glanced at his watch—"two-thirty a.m. You were asleep for a couple of hours. They gave you a mild sedative." *Of course, they did.* He held my left hand and kissed my knuckles. "You had a panic attack."

I know.

It kind of felt like I could have another one if I didn't keep my mind distracted. But the remnants of the sedative were surely flowing through my veins, keeping me somewhat calm because all I wanted was to see William and Caleb again, and I wouldn't be able to fully relax on my own until I knew they were okay.

"Mr. Murphy?" Aaron said from outside the curtains. "May I come in?" My father opened the curtain for him. He carried inside a small bag and my phone. "Agent Robbins wants to talk to you."

"Stay with her," my father said to Aaron, standing up. "I'll be right back, kiddo." He kissed my forehead and left.

"We brought a change of clothes for you and other personal items you might need," Aaron said, dropping the bag on the table. "I'm glad you're okay, Miss Murphy," he whispered. "They're going to be okay too."

He knew how important they both were for me.

For a second, I swore I could smell William's cologne. And Aaron wasn't wearing any. I was already hallucinating.

"Thank you—for everything," I told him. He tightened his mouth and nodded. I couldn't comprehend that Thomas was dead. I had to bite my lips to prevent myself from crying again.

I couldn't understand how things escalated in such a way that Thomas had to end up dead and William and Caleb with bullet wounds because of him. Because of *me*.

Unfathomable. Unacceptable.

My mind drifted toward my mother as I tried to imagine what she went through. I could still hear the screams of terror of the people at school that day. I closed my eyes for a second and inhaled deeply through my nose, trying to distance myself from my thoughts.

"We opened Thomas's envelope," Aaron said suddenly, taking a seat, his brow creasing. "That's what Robbins wanted to talk to your father about. He's briefing him. There's a couple of detectives here too. They've wanted to talk to you, but your father's been asking them to back off until you feel better."

I didn't feel like talking to detectives. But I knew I would have to, eventually.

"And can you tell me what was inside that envelope?" I asked, attempting to sit up straight again.

He leaned in and took one last look at the curtain before continuing. "Senator Hill killed Joshua, Thomas's brother. All the evidence is inside that envelope. The surveillance tape clearly shows his father pushing Joshua down the stairs. I haven't seen it, but that's what I've been informed," Aaron explained. "Thomas's mother was standing behind Senator Hill when he did it. She had to see how her husband murdered her son."

"No!" I covered my mouth and looked away. I was in shock. It must've been so hard for Thomas to go through that—knowing his father had murdered his brother because he couldn't respect his sexuality. "He's a monster! He ruined Thomas's life. And his poor mother—" I couldn't hold the tears in any longer.

Aaron took a deep breath and continued. "There are a few recordings of Thomas's parents arguing about it on the phone where the conversation exhibits Senator Hill admitting to the crime," he added. "He *will* be apprehended for this. Let's hope things proceed accordingly."

My head fell back on the pillows. I was still feeling lightheaded, and I *hated* being stuck to this bed. I wanted to see William's family too. "Could you ask anyone out there if I'll be discharged anytime soon?"

Aaron looked at me with a disapproving look on his face. "I think you should rest. They're both still in surgery and might be in there for a while."

"Can I at least see Lily or William's brothers?"

"Your father doesn't want anyone coming into this area right now. I'm sorry, Miss Murphy. It's a direct order. And I really think it's best if you could find a way to get some sleep."

Impossible.

A nurse came in and asked how I was doing while injecting a syringe into my serum bag. She smiled at Aaron and me before leaving. I sunk my head deeper into the pillows and immediately felt relaxed again. A cloudy haze appeared before my eyes.

Shit, another sedative ... and it felt so good.

CHAPTER 44

No

I WOKE UP a few hours later in the emergency room. I was still wearing the hospital gown. My arm was still in a cast, and I *still* didn't know anything about William or Caleb.

This is not a drill.

Aaron was gone. A female agent sat on the chair next to me in his stead. Her skin was a golden shade of brown, and she wore her caramel-colored hair in a loose bun.

Behind the curtain, I could place two silhouettes. I couldn't tell who they were, and I didn't recognize their hushed voices either.

My phone indicated it was 5:37 a.m. There had to be news about William or Caleb by now.

"Hi, Billie. I'm Agent Johnson," she said in a sweet voice. "How are you feeling?"

"Hi. Nice to meet you," I replied, trying to sit up. Agent Johnson helped me up. "I'm okay, but I need to pee."

She smiled with a chuckle. "I can help you with that. Are you okay to walk?"

I nodded. "Do you have any information on William or Caleb?"

"I don't, but I'm sure we can ask someone. Let's take you to the bathroom first." She opened the curtain, and the two agents posted outside of my cubicle nodded at me. I nodded back. "Aaron and

David will be back soon," she said as we stepped out. "Your father asked them to—freshen up." Aaron's clothes were stained with blood, too. "Your father left word that he will also return shortly." Agent Johnson escorted me to the nearest restroom. When we got back, I sat on the edge of the bed. I didn't want to lie down anymore. I was ready to move on to what was next, even though my head felt heavy. I *needed* to know if William and Caleb were okay. Enough sleeping.

"How's my favorite patient doing?" Dr. Lindström said, walking in. I felt relieved when I saw him smiling. That meant William had to be okay.

"I'm doing fine and feeling ready to leave this bed," I replied with a modest smile. "Any news on William?"

"Yes. He's in the recovery room. His surgery went well," Dr. Lindström said, clutching my shoulder for a couple of seconds. "The bullet hit in his descending colon. It took the surgeons a few hours to fix the damage. They were done with the procedure a bit past four a.m."

"When can I see him?" I asked with a frown, already expecting a negative as an answer.

"Once he's back in his room," he said with a pursed smile, looking at his watch. "In about thirty minutes or so."

Yes!

"And when will I be discharged?"

"You're good to go. I've had someone take care of the paperwork. I can take you to see William's family if that's what you want."

"That would be great. Thank you," I said with a hopeful smile. "And Caleb? He's part of my security detail. He was shot too. They told me he was in surgery. Do you have any information?"

"I—wasn't aware there was an injured agent. I've only been monitoring William's progress, but I can check that for you."

Dr. Lindström called a nurse to help take my IV out of my

left wrist and excused himself. The nurse offered to help me change afterward.

Agent Johnson placed the bag with my things on the bed and unzipped it. William's scent spiraled out and filled the cubicle in seconds.

What the?

That was William's green Hammarby hoodie. Not Nathan's.

"Wha—why did they bring this hoodie?" I asked, confused.

"I brought it," Agent Johnson replied with wide eyes. "I'm sorry, is it not the right one? David said I should bring you underwear, leggings, tennis shoes, and a green Hammarby hoodie. It took me a while to find it. It was inside a green box in the bottom drawer."

I wore Nathan's hoodie so much that David might've thought I'd appreciate the gesture of bringing it over. But Mimi hadn't returned my clean clothes, and Nathan's hoodie was included in such laundry.

Agent Johnson was a go-getter, wasn't she? She'd found it in my not-so-secret hiding spot.

Damn it.

"No, it's okay. Don't worry," I replied with a smile, feeling a little panicky on the inside. "But I might need to change before ten a.m. It's—a long story."

"I'll send someone over and grab something else for you," she said matter-of-factly. "Anything in particular?"

"Any other hoodie from the closet is perfectly fine." I felt embarrassed about sending someone to my apartment again, but I couldn't wear this when Nathan arrived. It made me feel even worse to have to keep it a secret from him. But I didn't want to get rid of William's hoodie either.

I'm the worst.

"I'll take care of it," Agent Johnson replied as the nurse helped me into the hoodie. It was *huge*! I asked the nurse to help me roll up the sleeves to my elbows because they completely covered my hands if I left them untouched.

I finally left the cubicle smelling like William. Dr. Lindström waited nearby for me to come out. He took me to see William's family in a private waiting room.

"Billie!" Lily cried and ran in my direction when Dr. Lindström opened the door for me. We hugged each other tightly. "I'm so glad you're okay. How's your wrist? We were told it was fractured."

"It doesn't hurt much right now," I said to her. "They gave me meds for it during the night."

"We wanted to see you, but they wouldn't let us through," she whispered, looking at the two agents behind me. She wore jeans and a sweater, but her ponytail from last night was still intact. She had washed her face, and her eyes looked puffy. She'd been crying, for sure.

"I know. But my father's feeling extremely uneasy about the situation. He didn't want anyone coming to see me."

Lily explained how Eric had taken William's mother back to her apartment to rest for a while. She was deeply disturbed, and she was getting anxious sitting in the waiting room.

Dr. Lindström gave her one of his happy pills after telling her that William's surgery was a success, so she went to sleep while he was still in the recovery room because she hadn't slept all night.

Joel and Tobias stood up and hugged me too. They both looked weary and gloomy. Probably hungover too. Unlike Lily, they were both still wearing their formal attires from the night before, but they had taken their jackets and ties off.

"I'm so sorry," I said, crying. "I feel like it's all my fault."

Joel hugged me again and said, "There's nothing to be sorry about. This is *not* your fault, and he's going to be okay." Joel sniffed my neck and pulled back with a frown. "Why do you smell like Billy?"

I broke away from Joel's embrace, and Tobias said with a laugh, "I'm curious too. It's as if he were standing here. It threw me off a bit."

I'd already gotten used to the scent that I forgot I smelled like him.

"William gave me this hoodie back in December," I said, crying and laughing at the same time. "They brought it by mistake, thinking it was Nathan's. Someone's bringing something else over for me to change. Plus, it's huge."

Lily's eyes turned into hearts like the last time we talked about William on the night of the Super Bowl.

Suddenly, I felt lightheaded again and took a seat on one of the sofas. I needed to eat or drink something. Agent Johnson immediately approached me and asked if I needed anything as she pulled one of her toffee-colored curls away from her face.

"Coffee would be great. And—cookies?"

She nodded, and I thanked her afterward with a smile.

I needed to ask her what her name was. I was avoiding calling her by her last name. It felt weird.

Lily sat next to me, and my phone buzzed. It was an unknown number.

"Murph? Murph, can you hear me?"

"Hey, you," I said with a trembling voice. "Yes, I do. Can't wait for you to get here." I exhaled air slowly through my mouth, making my cheeks blow up. *Calm down.* The full weight of everything that happened was beginning to crash against me.

"Oh, God. How are you feeling? I'm about to go mad any second now," Nathan said, his voice infused with concern.

"I'm—fine."

"I'm so anxious to see you. Your father told me everything. I'm so sorry, love. I can't stop thinking about how I should've never left. I should've—"

"Nathan, this is—no. Don't say that, please. There was no way we could've known what Thomas was planning all this time."

Nathan took a few seconds to reply. I could hear him breathing on top of the airplane's loud thrumming in the background.

"How's your wrist? Your father told me it's broken."

"Yes, um. It's in a cast." I was having a hard time talking to him on the phone. I just wanted to see him so badly. "I'm just still … I don't know. It's all so surreal. I can't believe Thomas is dead, and William and Caleb—"

"Don't worry, love. I think it's best if we talk about everything once I get there. I just wanted to hear your voice. Everything's going to be okay. I'll make sure of it, okay? I promise."

"I really need you here," I said with a gasp that broke my voice.

"I want nothing more than to be there for you, too. I'll arrive in a few hours," he said with that soothing voice of his that I adored. "I love you."

"I love you too."

I ended the call, tucked my phone back in the hoodie's pocket, and huffed air out of my mouth. Lily gave me a side hug, and I let my head rest on her shoulder. We sat like that without talking for a while.

No one had anything else to say. I'm sure we were all thinking the same thing: *When* the hell *can we see William?*

Agent Johnson brought coffee and cookies for everyone.

She was a keeper.

We made small talk as we drank our coffee and ate our cookies. We mostly talked about Tobias's premiere and how good the film was. No one asked me a thing about what happened last night. I don't know if they'd already been informed or if they thought it was all too fresh to ask. But I was thankful. Talking about nothing was exactly what I needed.

Dr. Lindström came inside the waiting room, and I jumped up to my feet, placing my coffee cup on the side table. My father walked closed behind him. Their faces looked sullen. Dr. Lindström dropped his gaze to the floor, and my father looked at me shaking his head.

Oh God, no. No, no, no. Something happened to William.

CHAPTER 45

Heartstruck at Dawn

EVERYONE SPRANG reactively from their seats. "What's wrong?" Joel and I asked at the same time.

"Oh, kiddo." My father approached me and placed his arms around me. "Caleb, he—" he trailed off, unable to say the words. "I'm so sorry, sweetheart."

"No!" I yelled, pulling away from him. "He what? Caleb, what?"

"He didn't make it through the surgery," he managed to say. "He's gone."

"But he—no! I-it was just his shoulder! H-he was sitting on the curbside when the ambulance arrived. And he was losing blood, but—but that was it. No!" My sobs ran loose as my mind kept attempting to process the devastation. "He promised!" I screamed in between pants, trying to walk out of the waiting room, trying to leave, to go somewhere. Anywhere! But my father held me tightly. "I want to see him! You don't understand! H-he *promised* to stay."

Lily wept behind me.

This isn't happening.

I brought my hands to my face and rubbed my eyes roughly. Maybe *I* was dead and had gone straight to hell. I probably deserved it. But unfortunately, that wasn't the case. And Caleb had to pay for my stupid mistakes.

I took a few steps back and dropped on the couch with an empty gaze as I stared into nothing.

"I'm so sorry." My father held my hands and squatted on the floor in front of me. "You *will* be able to see him, but not right now."

"This is all my fault," I whispered to myself, my voice shaking. My father stood up and sat next to me.

Caleb *died* because of me.

William was *shot* because of me.

I never listened to Caleb. He didn't trust Thomas, and I never cared to listen—to trust his gut. All of this *was* my fault. All he ever cared about was my well-being. And I got him killed because I was too stubborn to believe him.

"It's not, kiddo," my father said softly, hugging me again.

Everything went dark around me—gray. Lifeless. All I could hear was that voice inside my head telling me, "*Well, it kind of is.*"

Caleb saved me when my mother died. I was paralyzed, and he helped me feel like myself again when I thought I couldn't. But without him, the numbness enveloped me once more, but now *he* was missing.

What the heck am I going to do now?

"He was my best friend—he—" I rested my elbow on my knee and shielded my eyes with my hand. My lungs tightened on me again.

Breathe. I could feel my lungs being squashed again by this invisible wrath brought to you by panic, grief, and unbounded denial.

I couldn't. I really, really couldn't.

My father stroked my back, but it wasn't helpful. It wasn't enough. Nothing would *ever* be enough.

Breathe, breathe, breathe.

Dr. Lindström walked back inside the private waiting room. I didn't even notice him leaving before. "Take this," he said, offering me a small paper cup with a pill and a glass of water.

There was no need to ask what it was to know that I wanted to push that pill down into my system. I was sure it would help me forget. For a while, at least. I'd rather deal with the pain later.

I angled the cup on my tongue, swallowed the pill with water, and dropped the glass on the table. All I needed was to disconnect myself from reality. I wasn't strong enough to deal with this. The cut was deep. Intolerable. Unbearable.

He's not dead. He can't be.

No.

I shut my eyes, my feet fidgeting on the floor as I waited for the pill to numb me out. To borrow the pain and hopefully forget to return it to me.

"Would you like to see William?" Dr. Lindström offered.

"Yes," I replied too quickly. Too desperate. I rose from my seat, and so did my father. Caleb was gone, but I couldn't lose William too. I needed to see for myself that he was okay, that he would get through this.

"He's in his room, but he's still asleep," Dr. Lindström said. "And he might be for a while. I can only have one of you come inside for now." He looked at William's brothers as if waiting for their opinion on the matter.

I glanced over my shoulder at Lily, Joel, and Tobias and implored with my eyes. *Let me be the first to go inside.* Joel replied with a simple nod.

"Are you sure you're okay to go?" my father asked. "You just took the medication. Perhaps we should take you home and rest for a while. We can come back later. William's very well taken care of. He's going to be okay."

I'd already heard that last night, and now Caleb was dead.

"No. I need to see him. Please," I begged. *Please don't take me home.* I didn't even want to set foot in my apartment.

"Okay," he replied with a hint of a smile. I hugged him. *Thank you.* "I'll be around taking care of everything for Caleb. Johnson and Robbins will be with you until Aaron and David come back, yes?" I nodded as involuntary tears rolled down my cheeks. My mind couldn't comprehend what was happening anymore, but my heart knew everything, and it was weeping.

I followed Dr. Lindström to William's room. Johnson and Robbins waited outside when I stepped in. There was an area to the left with a large three-seater sofa, a comfy-looking armchair, and a white marble coffee table. Dr. Lindström slid open a wooden door, and there he was. Sleeping beside a huge window at the far end of the room that overlooked the city.

There were three doors to my right that led to God knows where. William's hospital bed was bigger than usual—wider, longer. It's as if I had stepped into a hotel suite. It was impressive. I didn't even know these kinds of rooms existed.

Dr. Lindström showed me where an emergency button was behind the bed, just in case, and suggested I stayed for a little while because I would soon get sleepy. He told me to call him if I needed anything and excused himself to leave.

I carefully pulled a chair next to William's bed and sat there, looking at him. He looked so pale—gray. He wasn't shining brightly as he always did, and it killed me.

His hand felt cold when I took it.

It was still somewhat dark outside, but an early morning waxing crescent moon was drawn up in the sky.

That moon.

I shut my eyes for a second and squeezed William's hand. My heart ached as my mind went back to Caleb. He couldn't be dead. It couldn't be true.

Wake up! I screamed inside my head—at me, at William.

And then my eyelids felt heavy. I couldn't make myself open

them. An intense feeling of lassitude invaded me at once. This wasn't the same pill Dr. Lindström gave me a few months ago. This was stronger. It's as if my energy was being drained from me.

I settled my cheek on William's bed and allowed myself to fade away.

Seconds or minutes later, I wouldn't know how many, I felt a slight tug on my hand that made me pull myself back into awareness. I straightened on my seat to see William's face. His eyelids were shuttered, almost closed.

He licked his dry lips and whispered with a low, raspy voice, "I love the smell of me on you."

"Hey," I replied softly. I stood up from the chair and sat on the bed beside him. He groaned as my weight made him shift slightly. "I'm sorry." I got up again and released his hand to avoid hurting him, but he complained.

"Sit. Hand," he muttered, tapping the bed. I gently sat again and held his hand as instructed. He brushed his fingers against my cast. "How's your wrist?"

"Shut up," I replied, crying with a smile. He smiled back with a groan. He wasn't supposed to be asking me how *I* was doing. He'd been shot and had just come out of surgery because of me. My broken wrist was nothing compared to that. Not even close.

"Do you need anything?" I asked. "Does anything hurt? Should I call the nurse? Water? You need water."

"No. I've got everything I need right here with me," he said, squeezing my hand again.

Oh, William.

"I'm sorry," I whispered. He still seemed to have trouble opening his eyes completely. "I'm so sorry." I wanted to be strong for him, but I couldn't. Tears streamed down my cheeks as I squeezed his hand even harder, afraid he would somehow slip away from me.

"Stop. It's not—" He cut himself off and shook his head twice. "I'd do *anything* for you."

My heart!

I took in a sharp breath through my nose and tried wiping the tears away, but I was helpless against the blatant realizations—every single one of them.

"Thomas, is he ... ?" William asked, opening his eyes completely and looking at me.

"Dead," I said almost silently with a nod.

He sighed and asked, "Aaron and Caleb?"

My lips trembled, and I shook my head. Sobs escaped my mouth, and I said, "Caleb."

"Shit." William closed his eyes for a few seconds and bit his lower lip. "I'm so sorry, älskling." He huffed air out through his mouth, shaking his head slowly. "I know how much you cared about him." He seemed shocked. Upset. And I couldn't stop crying.

"I thought I lost you too," I said, letting my forehead rest on his chest with a sob. The idea of losing him ignited a war inside me. The unwarranted fear against the relief of it not happening canceled out the equation, but it was overwhelming—mind-altering.

"Never," he said, stroking my hair. I laid there for a few seconds, making sure he was really there with me, making sure he was real. That I was awake.

I sat up straight and took a tissue from his nightstand to wipe my face.

"Come here," he whispered. I leaned in again and got closer to his face. He gently brushed my lower lip with his thumb and said, "I see you." I closed my eyes, feeling the delight of his skin meeting mine. It felt like a million years had gone by since I last saw him.

My soul urged me to touch my lips, to unleash myself and allow him to see me doing it again. But my mind warned me against it, and my foolish heart kept going back to Nathan—loving him.

But what was this feeling that enraptured my entire being whenever William touched me, whenever I *saw* him or heard his voice … if not love, too?

I opened my eyes and touched his lower lip instead. I couldn't find the courage to touch mine yet—to let him *know*. "I see you," I whispered back as I locked my gaze with his and stroked his lower lip with my thumb.

At that moment, I understood that by touching his lip, I acknowledged his feelings for me. They were so clear to me now. I saw him, and he saw me, even if I wasn't ready to accept my feelings for him—if I didn't know how.

"Look," I whispered, jerking my chin at the window. "It's your moon. It always reminds me of you."

William turned to look at the early morning sky and smiled with a gentle snort. "*Our* moon." I smiled back—*our moon*.

Dawn was breaking, and the first golden rays of sunshine filled the room and painted the horizon in different hues of orange, blush-pink, and creamy yellow.

William asked me to lay beside him, so I immediately kicked off my shoes and carefully crawled in the bed. I rested my face on his chest and inhaled the insane familiarity of his scent emanating off my hoodie, enveloping us.

Finally, my eyelids lost the battle and gave in as I allowed myself to wane into an inescapable slumber, hoping it would somehow heal my heartstruck injuries.

END OF BOOK TWO

NOTE FROM THE AUTHOR

WARNING: The following **Note from the Author** contains spoilers about the ending of this book. Refrain from reading beyond this point if you haven't finished reading or if you don't mind having the ending spoiled.

I'm so sorry about that. I suffered deeply when I realized Caleb's fate. When I first drafted *Heartstruck at Dawn*, there was an alternate ending where Caleb made it out fine from the shooting. And I let the manuscript breathe for a few days to see how it felt, and I quickly realized it did not feel good. I was only fooling myself because I knew that I was in denial. It's almost as if I could hear Caleb telling me, "*You know it needs to be done. Don't worry about me. I'll be fine.*" And I cried to the point of soaking my keyboard as I rewrote the real ending.

As a writer, you grow attached to your characters, and the feelings are very real. But I promise you that this is not a pointless death or one to create drama. Everything will make sense once you read Book 3: *Awestruck at Dusk*. You can email or DM me if you need to talk about this. I'm always open and eager to discuss anything with my readers.

And as you might have read in *Moonstruck at Midnight*, the book was dedicated to one of my best friends who died when I was twenty years old, Billie's age. Also, you can see Mariel's date of birth is March 18, and so is Caleb's. Tying up their birthdays was symbolic for me. Mariel died because a guy who had been drinking crashed the car she was in, resulting in her death. Inevitably, writing this series has been very therapeutic for me. It's been fourteen years since she left, but the feelings are still there if I tap into them. So please remember: Don't drink and drive and thank you for reading *Heartstruck at Dawn*. I promise to mend your hearts and make it up to you with *Awestruck at Dusk*.

Much love,

A.xx

AKNOWLEDGMENTS

Here we go again. I *really* have to thank everyone who has picked up the books in the series. Every single one of you counts, and I know there are millions of great books out there and that we will only get to read a fraction of those great books in our lifetime, so thank you for including *Heartstruck at Dawn* and giving the series a chance.

To Germán, my husband: I'm so grateful for you and for the endless support and understanding you've given me throughout this process. Thank you for cheering me up and giving me the strength to carry on. And most of all, for believing in my dreams!

Marianna Andrade: You've done it again. Thank you for all those intense and honest conversations we had on the phone when I didn't know what to do next and how you helped me tap into new ideas and adventures for Billie. I can't say it enough: THANK YOU!

Sulamit Elizondo: Thank you for the amazing cover art. I love our brainstorming ideas and how well we connect to give Billie life on the canvas. I'm so excited to see what else you have in store for the next two books.

My brilliant Reedsy team: David Provolo, Kristen O'Connell, Denis Caron. You've played such a big part in all things marketing and design. Thank you for being part of the Moonstruck Series.

Jennifer Herrington: Working with you has been the greatest experience ever. Whenever I get a manuscript back from you, my face lights up as I review your in-document comments, notes, etc. It's just so much fun! My husband keeps teasing me about what a nerd I am because of it. I've learned so much in the process and couldn't be happier. Thank you for believing in Billie's story and helping me to make it the best it can be.

To the Krav-Maga (and other deadly martial arts) masters: Caleb Tonche and Gal Frishwaser. Thank you so much for taking the time to revise the different fight-scene and risk scenarios in the story and making them air-tight and perfect. Caleb, thank you for showing me how to free myself from a person's grasp if being pinned to the floor. Ha! My entire body ached just from recreating that scene a few times. It was so much fun, though. I was in shock when I met you, and you told me your name was Caleb. Mind blown!

Dr. Luis Fernando Arana: I just wanted to let everyone know that not only is he a great surgeon, but he's also my father-in-law and fellow writer. Thank you for sitting down with me and going through the options for William and Caleb's wounds during the shooting scene and your patience while I jotted down all the medical terms and notes. It's always so much fun talking to you about writing and medicine.

Karen Cantú: My favorite boss lady lawyer. Thank you so much for your legal advice regarding the situations that happened throughout the book. You are simply the best, and I love you so, so much!

To the Bookstagram community: You've been beyond amazing and have shown me more support than I've ever thought I would receive. I've also made a lot of new friends, you know who you are, and it's always amazing to be able to share a passion for words with other human beings that are equally excited as you. It really is the greatest online community ever! I'll be forever grateful.

To my son, Germán: Thank you for putting up with me and my writing. For your patience. I love how you've learned all the characters' names! I love you!

To my family: For supporting me and cheering me on through this adventure.

To my friends who keep encouraging me, you know who you are. Your support means the world to me. I love you guys!

And to everyone who's ever liked, shared, reposted, commented on a post, story, reel, etc., on social media. THANK YOU! Every gesture counts, and I know who's been supporting me from the start. I'll never forget it! Being an indie writer is no joke. It's so much hard work, and sometimes you can feel alone in the process even when people are cheering you on. Sometimes it's hard not to feel like you have that *traditional backup*, but the freedom to call the shots is amazing and rewarding.

Thank you for reading!

If you enjoyed *Heartstruck at Dawn*, please consider leaving a review on Goodreads and Amazon. Reviews are of the utmost importance for authors since they help other readers decide whether to pick up your book or not. Thank you!

Link for Goodreads: https://cutt.ly/Goodreads_HAD

Link for Amazon: https://cutt.ly/Amazon_HAD

Coming soon on the Moonstruck Series:

Book Three: *Awestruck at Dusk* comes out on January 6th, 2022
Don't forget to pre-order it now!
https://cutt.ly/Amazon_AAD or scan the code:

Do you want to read the first two chapters of *Awestruck at Dusk*?
Visit: https://cutt.ly/AwestruckatDusk or scan the code:

ABOUT THE AUTHOR

Alejandra lives in Mérida, Yucatán, México with her husband and son. She's a music lover, a geek at heart, and a fan of all things romance, Christopher Nolan, Star Wars, LOTR, GOT, et cetera. You can find her on social media on Facebook & Instagram as long as her 30-minute social media app limit hasn't elapsed.

CPSIA information can be obtained
at www.ICGtesting.com
Printed in the USA
LVHW100536010422
714871LV00002B/88

9 786072 928794